How to Bang a Billionaire

Praise for Alexis Hall and His Novels

"Simply the best writer I've come across in years."

—*New York Times* bestselling author Laura Kinsale

"A complex, poignant look at modern love, loneliness and sexual identity."

—*Washington Post* on *For Real*

"Hall blends pleasure and pain, both erotic and emotional, to create an engrossing romance with sharpness hidden in the sweetly traditional power-exchange relationship."

—*Publishers Weekly*, starred review, on *For Real*

"Heartbreaking, hopeful, gorgeous."

—*New York Times* bestselling author Stephanie Tyler/SE Jakes on *Glitterland*

"[A] vibrantly dark world…Readers will delight in this series."

—*Foreword Reviews* on *Shadows & Dreams*

"Utterly charming."

—*Publishers Weekly*, starred review, on *Looking for Group*

"[A] deeply real consideration of the ways people choose to pursue their passions." —*Kirkus Reviews* on *Looking for Group*

How to Bang a Billionaire

ALEXIS HALL

FOREVER YOURS

New York Boston

Forever Yours
Hachette Book Group
1290 Avenue of the Americas
New York, NY 10104
forever-romance.com
twitter.com/foreverromance

First ebook and print on demand edition: April 2017

Forever Yours is an imprint of Grand Central Publishing.
The Forever Yours name and logo are trademarks of Hachette Book Group, Inc.

ISBN 978-1-4555-7134-5 (ebook edition)
ISBN 978-1-4555-7132-1 (print on demand edition)

To CMC, you are the fucking best.

Acknowledgments

Thanks, as ever, to my partner, my agent, and my dear friend Kat: You're all amazing and I couldn't do this without any of you. And thanks, as ever, to all the readers who inexplicably stick with me. And finally, a huge, huge thank you to my editor, Madeleine, who I suspect didn't quite know what she was getting herself into. I'm so grateful for all your help and patience.

Sweet are the uses of adversity.
—*As You Like It*, William Shakespeare

How to Bang a Billionaire

PROLOGUE

The crop strikes me with a snap like breaking ice. The pain that follows is sharp and cold, but I don't cry out. I know I will, eventually, that I'll sob, gasp, scream perhaps, but I make him break me every time. He needs to see what he does to me. He needs to see what it costs to love him.

At last it's over.

I can feel him behind me, his heat and his hoarse breath. He'll be tender now as he takes me, though it's not my pleasure that brings the flush to his skin and the fire to his eyes. It's my pain.

This is the ugly truth of what he needs: someone to suffer for him.

He rolls me over. The sheets are rough against my burning skin. Another hurt I will bear and forgive.

I hear the soft slap of the crop as it falls. He looks desolate and savage, the sweat on him as bright as tears.

"I can't," he whispers. "I can't do this anymore."

He's said this before. But it always brings us back to this room.

And to this. Me on my knees. Or in chains. The marks of his shame and torment on my back.

I go to him and draw him into my arms. He resists for only a moment, then surrenders, pressing his damp face against my neck. I hold him as he shudders and weeps and shatters.

"Nathaniel." He lifts his head. His eyes are as cold as the moon. As empty. "I mean it. I can't keep hurting you."

"Then don't."

"It's not that simple. This is what I need."

"No." I press my hand over his frantically beating heart. "I believe you're better than this. Stronger than this. You don't have to be what he made you."

"I am what he made me. I don't deserve you. And I can't make you happy."

"But I love you."

"You shouldn't." His voice breaks. "Nobody should."

He leaves me in that terrible room, the room where I first understood what he would do to me and what had been done to him. Though he turns away now, though he denies me and rejects me and flees from me, I know he'll come back to me.

I am not the only man who has touched him but I'm the only one who truly knows him. The only one who loves him. The only one who ever could.

He's mine. My beloved. My monster. My broken prince.

He'll come back to me. And I will save him from himself.

CHAPTER 1

"Hello! I'm Arden St. Ives, calling from St. Sebastian's Colle—"

Click.

"Hello! I'm Arden St. Ives, calling from St. Sebastian's Colle—"

Click.

"Hello! I'm Arden St. Ives, calling from St. Sebastian's Colle—"

Click.

Oh dear. It was going to be a really, *really* long night.

I was supposed to be doing this college fund-raiser thing where undergraduates called up wealthy alumni and connected deeply with them in a way that got them all nostalgic and wallet-opening or bank-transferring. To be honest, I wasn't exactly an ideal candidate for the role. Given that I got all squirmy borrowing 60 pence for a can of Coke Zero from the vending machine, I had no fucking clue how I was going to work "and how would you feel about endowing a Chair of Philosophy in perpetuity" into a casual conversation with a complete stranger.

My best friend Nik was actually the one who'd signed up, but he'd come down with laryngitis. Which meant the telethon team ended up having to use me instead. I knew as soon as they gave me what was supposed to be two days of training in ten minutes that it was going to be awful. And a quick glance around the only slightly dank basement confirmed my worst fears: the rest of the volunteers were all engaged in life-enriching, college-benefiting conversations with opera singers, human rights lawyers, and boutique cheesemakers. Whereas I'd eaten my body weight in free doughnuts and been hung up on more times than an insurance salesman with underdeveloped people skills.

I dialed the next number. They'd told me you could hear the smile in someone's voice, so I made sure I was grinning as if I'd swallowed a coat hanger.

"HelloImArdenSt.IvescallingfromSt.Sebastian'sCollegepleasedonthanguponme."

Silence.

Then, "How did you get this number?"

"God, I don't know. It was just on the list. I'm helping with the..." My mind blanked out. Something about that implacable, cut-glass voice. "...telethon thingy."

"The telethon...thingy?"

"The St. Sebastian's College annual telethon. Um, you went here, right?"

"Isn't that why I'm on your list?"

"Oh yeah." I decided to pretend my utter incompetence was funny. "Good point. But there was a letter. You should have got a letter."

"I don't have time to read letters."

"Well, no wonder you miss stuff."

A laugh, quiet and almost shy, ghosted down the phone to me, and I felt it like fingers against my spine. "I assume that if the message is important, the sender will find a more efficient way to deliver it."

"Efficiency isn't always better, though."

"Under what circumstances is being effective at achieving what you set out to achieve less good than the alternative?"

I'd had tutorials like this. Blurting out some half-baked idea, which was swiftly revealed to be the most abject nonsense. So I did what I always do—the general refuge of the comfortable upper second—and promptly reframed. "Only if what you want to achieve is communicating something as simply, directly, and immediately as possible. Like, if you were on fire, a letter would be a really bad way of telling you."

"Also a flammable one." God, his voice. From the moment I'd heard it, I'd thought it was pretty sexy, in a chilly, upper-class way, but amusement-softened, it was as rich as honey. Irresistible.

I grinned foolishly at the receiver. "But if I wanted to say something with more nuance, something personal like I'm sorry or, thank you, or…or y'know…I love you, then maybe a letter would mean more than a text message or a Post-it note."

"I had no idea the Master of St. Sebastian's felt quite this strongly about me." A neat little pause. You had to appreciate a man with timing. "Do you think it's too late?"

"I'm not sure. Maybe if you chased after her in the pouring rain."

"She's not entirely my type."

"It's that purple houndstooth jacket, right?"

"I'm afraid it's a deal breaker."

I snuck another peek at the room, in case I was doing it wrong and everybody could tell, but nobody was paying any attention to me. I huddled a little closer to the phone and confessed, "I've actually only met her once. In my first year. She asked me what I was going to do when I grew up."

"And what are you going to do when you grow up?"

"Gosh, I don't know. Grow up, I guess?"

He was silent a moment. "I think that would be a shame."

"If I grew up?"

"If you changed."

I made a sort of hiccoughing noise. Surprise and bubbly pleasure. "You don't know me."

"No," he agreed. "But I've enjoyed talking to you and I'm sure others will too."

That sounded perilously close to goodbye and I panicked. Maybe it was just because I would have to start the cycle of doom all over again but I genuinely didn't want him to go. "To be honest, you're the only person who hasn't hung up on me halfway through my opening line."

There was another moment of silence. I might have been imagining it but it felt a little charged. "You asked me not to."

"I was honestly pretty desperate."

"Well, it seemed to work."

"I guess you took pity on me."

"I wouldn't call it pity."

I nearly asked him what he *would* call it, but I didn't quite have the balls. I'd been told to telebond, after all, not teleflirt. I wondered what he looked like. What he was doing right now as he was talking to me. Probably he was sixty-five and tending a bonsai tree, but his voice made me imagine wingback chairs and whisky. A riding crop with a silver tip laid idly across a knee... Okay, maybe that was too far. Or just far enough.

I shivered and suddenly realized how, well, *silent* silence was when the only thing connecting you was an electrical signal. I didn't know this man, and he didn't know me, and if I didn't say something soon, it was going to get super fucking uncomfortable. "So... um..." I fumbled with the cheat sheet of helpful icebreakers. "When was the last time you were here?"

"Ah." A chill syllable, as devastating as a dial tone. "I was wondering when we'd get to this part."

"Um, what part?"

"The part where we exchange charming stories about life at St. Sebastian's and then you ask me for money."

I actually yelped. I'd been sufficiently distracted by the awkward (and occasionally not awkward) conversation part of the arrangement that I'd managed to totally forget about the whole fund-raising thing.

He laughed and it wasn't like the other time. It was cold and harsh, and very, very resistible. "What else does it say on your list?"

"Pardon?"

"Your list. What else does it say about me?"

I hadn't expected the call to last more than five seconds, so I hadn't bothered to read anything beyond the number I was dialing. I looked now. "It says you're Caspian Leander Hart and you graduated in 2010 with a first in politics, philosophy, and economics. Oh my God, you were a PPEist."

"Someone has to be."

"And apparently you're the CEO of a multinational banking and financial services holding company. I don't know what much of that means."

"You can look it up on the Internet. Anything more?"

I stared at the next line. "It says you're a lovely person, and very kind to animals."

"Arden."

It showed how screwed up my priorities were right then that, for a moment, all I could think was, *He remembered my name.* I imagined his lips shaping it: *Arden, Arden, Arden.* "Uh, what?"

"What does it really say?"

My name, and the touch of sternness, raised all the hairs on my arms. "It says you're the third richest man in the UK with a net worth in the region of twelve billion quid."

I waited. No idea what *for*. I'd done as he'd commanded, but he wasn't exactly going to shower me in praise and cookies for it. I expected he would hang up but he didn't and so we were stuck here, fresh silence deepening between us into this well of infinite nothingness.

"Um..." I skimmed desperately over the cheat sheet. "It says here that I should ask you if you're enjoying it. But I don't know what the *it* is. Oh, right. The answer to the previous question. How are you enjoying being the third richest man in the UK?"

"I'm finding it quite enjoyable."

"You recommend insane wealth as a potential future for other St. Seb's graduates?"

And then…then he laughed again, the laugh I liked. And I could breathe. "I do. What's your next question?"

I checked. "Do you get the *Arrow*?"

"Since I don't know what that is, it seems safe to assume I don't."

"It's the Book of Making You Feel Bad About Yourself. You know, the St. Seb's magazine? It's full of stories about people who are living amazing lives and achieving amazing things while you're sitting around in your pants playing Tsum Tsum." I paused. "I guess you don't do that, what with being a billionaire and everything."

"I don't, no."

"And you don't have time for the post, so the whole thing's a bust really."

I must have sounded a bit woebegone because he said, "There isn't an e-copy you could sign me up for?" with the same kind of embarrassed gentleness you might show a three-legged kitten if you weren't all that keen on cats.

"I don't know. It just turns up in my pidgeon hole. It's this glossy thing and the cover story is always St. Sebastian's Graduate Now King of Everything Ever."

Another soft laugh. "In which case, I shall strongly resist being put on the mailing list."

"Oh my God," I wailed. "I'm epically bad at this. I've stirred you from apathy to active antipathy. Do you not like St. Sebastian's?"

"I haven't thought about it since I left."

"You don't have any good memories?"

"It's not that. It's simply that I prefer to focus my energy on the present."

"And you never look back?" I tried again. "Never miss anybody or feel thankful?"

"The past is merely a string of things that have already happened.""

I knew I was a dweller by nature, reliving every moment of embarrassment, every harsh word, every little loss, but I wasn't sure his way was the answer either. "That sounds alienating. Living out of time."

"I would rather control my future than concern myself something I can't change."

Something in the way he said it made the back of my neck prickle. "You can't control everything."

"On the contrary, with enough wealth, power, and conviction, one can control anything. Anyone."

Aaaand that really wasn't helping with my inappropriate telefeelz. I tried to laugh it off, but it came out way too shaky to be convincing. "You sound like… There's this line in *Ulysses* where someone describes history as a nightmare from which he's trying to awake."

"I'm already awake. And I haven't read *Ulysses*."

"You want to know a secret? Me neither."

"But you can quote from it." He seemed to have warmed

up again. Maybe he was even smiling. And I thought, *What would a man like this look like when he smiled?*

"That's what an English degree from Oxford teaches you. How to be convincing about a bunch of shit you actually know nothing about." And there I went. Fucking up again. "But I bet PPE was useful to you, right, and has shaped your career and helped you become the incredibly successful person you are today?"

"Oxford—as a brand—still carries a certain value when effectively leveraged."

I sat back in my chair, tucking a knee beneath me. I felt oddly sad suddenly. Not exactly for us but because of us. I'd basically squandered the last three years being disorganized and lazy and preoccupied with getting laid, and he'd just used the words *brand* and *leveraged* in cold blood. "But a world-class education…that's a gift, isn't it? It could make a real difference to someone. I mean, someone who was, y'know, better than we are."

He was quiet for what felt like far too long. "I think," he said at last, "when you claimed to be bad at this, you were either lying or sorely underestimating yourself."

"I wouldn't lie to you, Mr. Hart." It was hard to tell because we were on the phone but I thought I heard him draw in a sharp breath. Something I said? Or his name, which felt intimate somehow, in my mouth? Even though the formal address should have maintained a sense of distance, rather than the reverse. "It was just a thing I thought."

"That I should make a donation to my old college? Rather a convenient notion to cross your mind at a fund-raising telethon, don't you think?"

"Well, yes...I mean no...I mean. Fuck. All I meant was...I couldn't think of anything more powerful, or more important, than being able change the course of a life. To be able to give someone who truly deserved it an opportunity that money or circumstance or social inequality would otherwise deny them." That was when the magnitude of what I was suggesting finally sank in. I squeaked. "Or...or you could just buy a plant for the JCR. That would be cool too."

I was relieved to hear him laugh again. "You are a very dangerous young man."

"I'm really not." And I wasn't sure whether it had been intended as a compliment anyway.

"I'm going to say goodbye now and think about what you've said."

This was all moving a little fast for me. I wasn't even entirely sure what had happened. "God. Are you sure? You don't have to."

"No, I do. Charming though this conversation has been, I'm a very busy man and I never make financial decisions without considering them thoroughly first."

"I meant...you don't have to...give any money. Or anything."

"Courage, Arden. Never flinch before you seal the deal."

"But I wasn't trying to...to deal with you."

"Perhaps that's why you succeeded. I had forgotten how potent sincerity can be."

Maybe I should have been celebrating but I felt terrible. As if I'd accidentally perpetrated an epic deception on a billionaire alumnus. And then I suddenly remembered there was a formal dinner and I was supposed to invite anybody who seemed donatey. "You should come visit," I blurted out.

"Pardon?"

"Before you decide anything. You could come to the dinner at the end of the week. I mean, it's free food." Oh, what was I saying? "Though I guess that probably isn't much of a motivation for you. But can...do you think...would you..."

He cut over my flailing. "Put me down as a maybe."

A click. And the line went dead.

CHAPTER 2

My shift ended at nine, the next group of eager volunteers filing in to reach out to alumni in different time zones. While I hadn't spoken to any more billionaires, I'd actually done okay. Somehow, my conversation with Caspian Hart had given me more confidence in what I was doing and my ability to do it. He'd said I was doing a good job, after all. And, coming from him, that had to mean something. Unless he was being sarcastic.

Oh shit. What if he was?

In any case, I'd even started to enjoy myself once I got into the swing of things. Nearly everyone had memories to share or stories to tell, and as I made my way back to my room across the moonlit quad, I found myself wondering what my story was.

I'd done so well at school that I'd come to university expecting a cross between *Brideshead Revisited* and an English version of *The Secret History*, and fully prepared to be a genius.

Except Oxford wasn't like that at all. And neither was I.

And here I was, two and a half years later, finals looming and…

Fuuuck.

I climbed the stairs and pushed open the door to my room. Well, rooms technically—set of rooms—the ultimate Oxford status symbol. I'd come bottom of the ballot, which meant I should have been living in a dustbin round the back of college, but Nik had come near the top, and since he needed someone to share with, that had hiked me up.

He was huddled on the sofa under a duvet, looking tragic.

"Feeling better?" I asked.

"Blah."

"I'm sorry." It was hard to know how to sympathize with someone who sounded like Emperor Palpatine. "But, hey, you can do an awesome impression of Emperor Palpatine."

That seemed to perk him up.

"Go on. Say *Now witness the firepower of this fully armed and operational battle station*."

"*Now witness the firepower of this fully armed and operational battle station,*" he rasped.

I gave him a thumbs-up and went into my bedroom to slip into something less socially acceptable, emerging a few seconds later in my boxers and an I'M FABULOUS AND I KNOW IT My Little Pony T-shirt.

We'd been roommates long enough to have established our chairs—though, unfortunately, mine was currently a make-do revision station, consisting of my laptop, a pile of books, and a half-drunk bottle of £1.99 Tesco's own brand booze. Which you could tell was the good stuff because it was just called *wine* and had a screw cap.

Mooching over, I grabbed the nearest book and curled up, waiting for knowledge to miraculously osmote from page to brain. Because that was totally how it worked.

Nik stirred in his duvet cocoon. "How's it going?"

"Terrible."

"What have you got to worry about? It's English lit."

He wasn't actually being mean. My course had a reputation for being easy—probably deservedly, since the earliest lectures started at eleven and, while they weren't presented as optional, hardly anyone went to them anyway.

"Yes, but how am I supposed to revise every book written in English from 650 to the present day. That's"—my voice went a bit shrill—"not reasonable."

"Can't you prioritize the important ones or something?"

"Do I look like Harold Bloom?"

"I'd be able to tell you if I knew who that was."

I could have explained *The Western Canon*, but nobody deserved that. And Nik, whose full name was Niklaus Johannsson-Carrington, was my best and oldest friend. We'd been on the same staircase in my first year and stuck together ever since, despite having nothing in common (except maybe the time he'd been drunk enough to let me wank him off).

He was reading Materials, whatever that meant, and constantly getting internships at MIT. He was also captain of the first VIII (which I thought was a rowing thing), played football for the men's seconds, and had recently returned from Uganda, where he'd been part of a team that was repairing a health center. All of which made him the perfect person to do fund-raising telethons... except for the temporarily-sounding-like-Emperor-Palpatine thing. That would have probably been pretty off-putting.

"In Stephen Fry's autobiography—" I began.

"Which one? The man's written more autobiographies than you've written essays."

I mimed being stabbed through the heart. "Impugned! But he said he did well at Cambridge by memorizing a set of first-quality essays and then shoehorning them into whatever question happened to be on the paper."

Nik nodded. "Sounds like a good plan."

"With one minor drawback."

"What?"

"I haven't written any first-quality essays." They were mostly seconds and upper seconds, and one returned to sender because it was about *Finnegans Wake*, and I'd written it stoned at half four in the morning when the book had taken on this terrible clarity and I'd been briefly convinced that maybe I was brilliant after all.

"You can still memorize what you've got."

"Except they're so banal and half-arsed it hardly seems worth it." I sighed. "I swear to God, I found one that opened '*Bleak House*, the Victorian novel by the Victorian novelist Charles Dickens'... Oh my God, I've wasted three years of my life."

"You haven't wasted them," Nik said consolingly. "You just haven't done any work in them."

I made sad otter noises.

"Seriously, it'll be fine. Worst-case scenario is you get a two-two."

"Worst-case scenario is I fail or get a third."

"And imagine how glamorous that'll be."

"I won't look like a loser?"

"No, you'll look like a misunderstood genius."

Nik's voice was getting even more sinister and whispery. Great, I was essentially making a sick person comfort me. "Maybe you shouldn't be talking. Does it hurt?"

"No, but it's weird as hell. It's like my voice has just disappeared."

I offered a sheepish smile by way of apology for being self-absorbed. "Did you make a dodgy deal with a sea witch? Don't you know, you've gotta kiss de girl."

"I'm worried I'll give de girl a throat infection."

Unscrewing the cap, I took a swig of *wine* straight from the bottle. "There was something seriously wrong with that guy."

"What guy?"

"Prince Eric."

"What's wrong with Prince Eric? He was kind to animals, lived in a palace. Good dimples."

"Yeah, but how can you respect a man who needs a singing lobster to tell him when to make a move?"

Nik gave me a withering look. "Sebastian's a crab."

"How can you remember that? Are you sure you're mostly straight?"

"He was a comedy sidekick with a racist accent. You don't forget that shit unless you're too busy speculating about whether the male lead is any good in bed."

"You're right," I conceded. "That is pretty gay."

I took the opportunity to consume more alcohol. A toast. To myself: *Disney queer failing Oxford.*

"So," asked Nik slyly, "who *would* you go for?"

I made a thoughtful hmmming noise. "It's a hard one."

"Or you're hoping it is."

"You do know"—I regarded him with severity—"that not every observation your token pansexual friend makes is a cock joke, right?"

"I would, if my token pansexual friend made fewer cock jokes." He waved a hand imperiously. "Come on, Arden, who's it going to be?"

Maybe the telethon had left me in a funny mood but I found myself wondering how I'd feel when I looked back on this: another night with my best friend in a dreamy, golden city, talking about the Disney princes I'd like to bang. I wondered if I'd still understand or if I'd think I was ridiculous. Or if I'd feel some sense of loss. "Well," I said, "it's not exactly a great pool, is it?"

"Bunch of hot royals? Jesus, man, what are you looking for?"

"Um, somebody real? Somebody who loves me? Somebody who'll fold me up like a fishing stool and fuck my brains out. Give me that and I'd scorn to change my state with kings."

"From the amount of people who've trooped through here, doesn't seem like you're short of volunteers."

I pulled my knees to my chin and let my gaze drift out the window to the quad below. A typical Oxford night: green grass and ancient stone, ghosts of the gold-washed dark. "Eh, they're all Erics."

"They're taking dating advice from crabs?"

"There are no crabs anywhere near my sex life, thank you very much." He gave a wheezy laugh, and gratified, as I always was to please him, I went on. "Which leaves me with… God…the early princes are kind of nonentities, aren't they? And on the date-rapey side in the case of Phillip. And Aladdin's out, obviously."

Nik raised his brows.

"Not because he's Middle Eastern. Because he's a delinquent. I know I'm not exactly awesome, but I think I can do better than a homeless man."

"You'll have a degree in English. You're going to *be* Aladdin."

"Oh shut up." I ran quickly through the pantheon. It was slightly scary how much Disney I'd watched over the years, some of it fairly recently. "Prince Naveen is cute with his ukulele."

"I thought you didn't like hipsters."

"Good point, well made. Better be Prince Adam, then."

A slight pause. "Sorry, who?"

"From *Beauty and the Beast,*" I mumbled. "Y'know, the Beast."

A more substantial pause. "Is this your way of coming out as a furry?"

"What? No! Fuck you."

"Dream on, gayboy."

"I do, I really do, thinking of your bronzed and manly thews clenching around me in undeniable homosexual ecstasy."

"My…thews are homosexual?" His ears had gone pink.

"By association when they're clenched around me."

"Look." He did have an excellent, firm voice, a little bit football captain, a little bit headmaster. "Can we go back to you fancying animals, please?"

"I don't fancy animals. The Beast is only symbolically bestial."

"I know I'm a scientist and therefore don't understand these complex literary motifs, but it looks pretty literal to me when he's beating up wolves and roaring."

"Okay, so he's protective, passionate, strong—"

"—has a tail."

I gave him a look. "Has clearly suffered but is not less deserving of love for that."

"Yeah, but what kind of prick denies a beggar woman a loaf of bread?"

"What kind of beggar woman rocks up at the front door of a palace? That's like a *Big Issue* seller getting pissy because the queen doesn't carry cash. Also, the Beast's got his own dungeon. I respect a man with all the conveniences."

Nik tried to laugh again, and it came out like a rusty gate in a gale.

I winced for him and eyed my wine guiltily. "Um, can I get you something? You sound grim."

"Sounds worse than it is." He shrugged in this noble *I'm going out for a walk and may be some time* sort of way. "I just feel bad for letting the telethon down."

"We're doing okay. And I spoke to this guy named Caspian Hart, who's apparently super-rich. That could come to something."

Nik's eyes went wide. "Caspian Hart? Seriously?"

I made what I hoped was a modest, *l'il ol' me* gesture.

"You don't know who he is, do you?"

"Of course I do! It said on the sheet. He's like a finance guy or something."

"Arden, he's a big deal and famously unapproachable. He's the second youngest self-made billionaire on the Forbes list. He's been on the cover of *TIME* and everything."

"Well, y'know, so's Donald Trump."

"And," Nik added resignedly, "he's really hot."

Ah. That was more like it. I put down the wine bottle and reached for my laptop.

"I mean, if you're into dicks. Literally and metaphorically."

"He wasn't a dick. A bit...intimidating maybe. But I guess if you're that awesome, you would be." My cheeks were getting warm just remembering the conversation. "He was kind to me, actually."

"You'd have to be a monster not to be. It'd be like kicking a kitten."

"Excuse me, I'm incredibly sexy and— Oh my God." The results of my image search had just popped up.

"You are such a letch."

Peeping at Nik over the top of the screen, I gave him double eyebrows. "Shit. I invited him to the dinner as well. What if I have to talk to him and look at him at the same time?"

"I guess it'll tear a rift in the space-time continuum and we all die."

Okay—I deserved that. I laughed, blushed a bit at my own ridiculousness. "I bet you anything I end up making a complete idiot out of myself."

"People like that are insanely busy. He probably won't even make it."

Yes. That was a good point. And it would save me a lot of embarrassment.

Except I couldn't help feeling disappointed too. I mean, not just because he was gorgeous—I was shallow, but not *that* shallow—but because...Meh, I was probably reading too much into it.

But it would have been nice to meet him.

Hear that soft, unexpectedly shy laugh in person.

"So"—Nik broke into my daydreaming—"are you going to be working or do you want to watch *Luke Cage*?"

I checked the clock on my computer—it was past ten now. Hardly worth starting revision. Although, let's face it, it was that kind of attitude that got me into this mess in the first place. "Is there room under that duvet?"

"Always."

I settled the laptop on the table, fired up Netflix, and snuggled in next to Nik. "You're not contagious, are you?"

"Only if I snog you."

"Hey, it's possible. You might be overcome by base lust and unable to keep your tongue out of me."

He flung an arm around and pulled me closer—he smelled slightly like an ill person, but also cozy and familiar. "Yes. That's definitely a real danger that you're in right now. With Mike Colter right there."

"You mean, you're gay for Mike Colter but not for me?"

"Shhh."

I'd had this ...almost-maybe-actual crush on Nik for basically ever. It could have damaged our relationship, but in my experience, there were two kinds of straight boys in the world: the ones who were terrified that being liked by a gay meant getting bummed the moment they let their guard down and the ones who were comfortable enough to be into it.

Nik was in the second category.

And, honestly, there were probably two kinds of queer boys as well: the ones who had wholesome, healthy relationships with other queers and the ones who preferred to be in love with people they couldn't have because they were slutty commitmentphobes.

I was also in the second category.

A friendmance made in heaven.

CHAPTER 3

Okay, how do I look?" I turned away from the mirror over the sink and struck a pose.

Nik's expression was carefully neutral. "Honestly? Like a kid in his dad's suit."

The post-telethon dinner was black tie and I didn't have the right kit, so I'd borrowed Nik's. Not completely grasping the impact of Nik being six foot four and an athlete. When I was pretty much the opposite of that. "What if I rolled the sleeves up?"

"Don't you fucking dare. That's my best tux."

As I walked across the room, the trousers slipped ominously down my hips. I tightened the rainbow canvas belt I'd hidden under the cummerbund and managed to stave off disaster.

Nik winced. "Do you really want to meet important alumni looking like that?"

"It's not that bad." My hair was having a small rebellion of its own. I'd quiffed six ways to Sunday but the whole thing had fallen sideways like a drunk on Saturday night. But fuck it. Caspian Hart wasn't coming anyway. Not because of a single conversation.

He'd probably forgotten about me the moment he'd put the phone down. And I wasn't going to be...sad or disappointed or messed up about it. Nope. Not even a little bit. The amount of time I'd spent Googling him probably counted as immersion therapy anyway.

He wasn't all that. Okay, he was fairly—well, very—good-looking, but he wasn't...photogenic really. He never smiled. Always the same flat stare, as though he regarded the camera as an enemy, his body caught at a moment of artificial stillness: a tiger about to spring away through the long grass.

"I'm telling you," Nik was saying, "it *is* that bad."

I waved a hand, implying that he could—if he so chose—talk to it, and picked up the bow tie he'd laid out for me. Turning up the collar of Nik's dress shirt and slipping the silk around my neck, I abruptly remembered I had no idea how to tie the thing. The last time I'd had to do this had been matriculation and it hadn't gone well. Maybe because I'd still been drunk from the night before. Or maybe because bow ties were bullshit.

I messed with the ends, crossing them over each other and moving them about randomly, as if this would miraculously make a bow appear under my chin.

Nik sighed. "You don't know how to do that, do you?"

I shook my head.

"Come here."

I went there and Nik stood up, pushing my hands out of the

way. And then, just like that, his confidence seemed to desert him. We'd always been fairly snuggly, but this was different somehow: my eyes turned up to Nik's, him frowning down at me, a piece of black fabric twisted between his fingers, so close to my throat that it felt like a promise or a threat. "Shit," he muttered, "it's hard to do it backwards."

There were about sixty-four million jokes I could have made. Instead I closed my eyes. Tilted my chin to make it easier for him. "I trust you."

He fiddled, the touch almost aggressively impersonal. "Left end lower than right, bring it over, make a loop, up and through…fuck." A knock on the door and Nik jerked away from me, the ungainly knot he had created unraveling instantly. "Um, yeah?" he called out.

Weird Owen stuck his head in, gingerish curls flopping haphazardly. "Message from the Lodge. You've got a visitor."

Nik looked startled. "Me?"

"Nuh-uh"—he pointed at me—"that one."

It couldn't be…could it? "Who?" I asked, like a disingenuous fuckwit.

"Hard somebody? No. Hart. He's waiting for you."

"Oh my God."

Reality hit me. A cartoon anvil dropped from a balcony. *Dong*. Little tweety birds flying round my head. Caspian Hart. Not just a name on a list, a picture on a screen, a voice on the phone. He was here. He had come. To see me. And he was waiting.

Oh fuck.

Oh shit.

Oh fuck shit fuck.

I'd thought "suddenly nerveless fingers" was something that only happened to people in novels but one minute I was holding a fallen-apart bow tie and the next it was on the floor. As I bent to pick it up, I realized my hands were sweating. What a totally fabulous impression I was going to make.

"I…uh…I guess I'd better be going."

"Yeah, man." The way Nik matched my casual tone ruthlessly revealed it as the lie it was. "Might be a good idea."

Deep breath. "Right. Well. I'm going."

I had to squoodge past Weird Owen, who had no sense of personal space and was right in the doorway.

"Hey, Arden?" Nik's voice followed me into the corridor. I turned and he gave me a two-fingered salute. "Be careful."

It was our cheesy…joke, routine, whatever. I couldn't remember when we'd started but it was a thing. The more banal the activity ("I need to go to the loo"), the funnier it got. Right now, even though I wasn't exactly going off to fight aliens or sacrifice my life in service to my country, it was hard not to take it a bit seriously.

Which made no sense because…I was going to meet a guy, we were going to have a polite conversation, he was maybe going to donate some money to St. Sebastian's, and then I was never going to see or think of him again.

That should not have been a big deal.

Although if I kept him waiting much longer, I probably wouldn't meet him at anyway. The man who didn't have time to read letters was unlikely to have time t for disorganized undergraduates. He'd cast an irritated glance at the empty quad and then get back in his chauffeur-driven who-knew-what or his private jet (okay, there probably wasn't room for a private jet in the middle of Oxford) and that would be that. St. Sebastian's would probably slip right to the bottom of the Norrington Table, fall into financial ruin, and eventually be overrun by zombies. All because I couldn't get my act together.

I whooshed to the staircase, holding up my trousers as best I could and still clinging to that damn bow tie, telling myself there'd be time to fix it later.

Down to the first floor, ground floor, out.

It was a typical late spring evening, powder-puff pink and gold, and I sprinted over the flagstones, heading toward the front quad and the Lodge (and, ohgodohgodohgod, Caspian Hart).

My mouth was tangy with copper, as though I could taste my own too-fast beating heart.

The lawns of St. Sebastian's, like pretty much everywhere else in Oxford, were sacrosanct, but I cut across the corner of one anyway because it was a legit emergency.

And that was when I saw him.

Initially with a faint sense of outrage because, instead of black tie, he was dressed in a midnight blue three-piece suit. And also because my immersion therapy hadn't prepared me properly.

Fairly good-looking my arse.

Those Google images had lied. They had actively lied.

The man was beautiful.

So ridiculously fucking beautiful it was hard to get your head round it somehow. He looked like a film star. Not the modern sort—not one of your amiably shaggable Chris Pines or Charlie Hunnams—but a screen idol from a lost age, all perfect symmetry and effortless poise, the remote and overwhelming splendor of a temple to cold and ancient gods.

I hadn't let myself waste a single thought on what would happen if he actually came to the dinner. Of how I might greet him or what I might say. But I was starting to wish I'd planned and practiced. I could have stepped up to him, just as self-assured, holding out my hand for him to shake like that was totally the sort of thing I did. *Mr. Hart,* I would have purred, *a pleasure to meet you.*

Unfortunately, I caught my shin on the KEEP OFF THE GRASS sign and fell over instead. Face-planting—after a few comedic but ultimately useless arm flails—right in front of his polished shoes. Oxfords, of course, not brogues.

Not the worst place I could ever have imagined being. But not just then.

He made a startled noise and then eased himself to his haunches, giving me an up-close-and-personal view of just how top class his tailoring was. It was all I could do not to follow those crisp creases all the way up his thighs to his—

"Are you all right?" he asked.

What I wanted to say was no. I was seriously abso-fucking-lutely not all right. I'd fallen over like the Andrex puppy. In front of a man I desperately, desperately wanted to…not fall over in front of. I lifted my head a little bit.

God, he was so elegant. This vision of exquisite masculinity carved by a bent Pygmalion. Everything about him flawless, from his graceful, long-fingered hands to that stern mouth, its unyielding curve touched by the faintest hint of sensuality. And those gray-blue wolf's eyes, all ice and savagery, watching me.

"Arden?" His voice sounded different in person, somehow *more*. "Arden St. Ives?"

"Nope," I mumbled. "Definitely not. He's someone else. Someone really attractive and totally vertical."

"Come on."

Oh God. He was touching me. Helping me up. And, thankfully, while it wasn't my most agile ascent, Nik's trousers stayed in place. If they hadn't, it would have been the clincher on whether I had to commit suicide pretty much immediately.

But now I didn't know what to do. It had been easier on the phone when his beauty wasn't burning my eyes like magnesium and my capacity to make a fool of myself was somewhat lessened by distance.

He held out a hand. "It's a pleasure to meet you, Arden."

We shook and I was sure I was limp and sweaty and slightly grassy. "That's not fair. I was planning to say that."

"Likewise."

"You what?"

"Likewise. I find it a useful word in such circumstances."

"Oh right." I smiled at him. I couldn't help it. He was just so…so…He looked like he needed to be smiled at. "Likewise, Mr. Hart."

I thought he might smile back but instead his eyes darkened, and then his attention flicked away from me. "Caspian is fine."

"Okay." I followed his gaze, but he didn't seem to be looking anywhere in particular. Just away from me, which wasn't exactly a good sign. "Um, thank you for coming. I didn't think you would."

"I wasn't sure I would have time."

"Yet here you are."

"Yes." Whatever had troubled him before had passed and he was perfectly composed as he met my eyes again. "Here I am."

"Am I…I mean, is it what you were expecting?" *Oh wow, classy, Arden. Not blatant at all.*

But his mouth finally yielded up its smile. And, like his laugh, it was unexpectedly shy, as though he wasn't used to doing it. It disordered the harmonies of his face, but I liked him better that way, a little bit messy, a little bit realer. God, the man was killing me. Actually killing me. "I'm not sorry I came."

"How does it feel to be back?" I asked.

"I'm afraid I'm not given to sentiment."

I peeped up at him from under my lashes. Yep, it was official: I was flirting. "What? No sudden rush of nostalgia for these dreaming spires?"

He shook his head.

"But Oxford's beautiful, isn't it? Like nowhere else."

"Some might say," he said, in the same quietly playful tone I'd heard him use on the phone, "it's rather like Cambridge."

I gasped. "You traitor."

"That assumes loyalty in the first place."

He had me there. "Um, I think I'm supposed to take you to this reception thing? It's in Melmoth."

"And you're going like that?"

It wasn't really an encouraging sentiment but the slide of his eyes down my body made me hot and cold and tingly. "Well, I was going to wear my bespoke Savile Row suit like you but then I remembered I don't have one."

If I'd been hoping to win another smile, I was disappointed because all I got in response was, "Turn around."

It was a phrase that had come my way often enough and I was pretty fond of it. But the way he said it, oh God the way he said it, turned my insides to honey. Not bossy or rough but implacable.

A command.

If he did it in a voice like that—all steel and velvet and the promise of his approval—I would have done anything he told me.

No matter how slutty or degrading.

Actually.

Strike that.

Especially if it was slutty or degrading.

I turned around, trying to shut down the porno in my brain. We were in a public place, and I was fully dressed (in several layers of formal wear as it happened), but it felt vulnerable. Giving this man, this stranger, my back. My trust.

His arm came around me from behind. And the heat of it, the pressure. The tightening muscles of his forearm made me a bit delirious. I leaned back and his body was right there, all hard planes and angular curves for me to nestle into. I tilted my hips, wriggling my arse until I was tucked in against him, pinned and protected at the same time, at once safe and overwhelmed.

I tried to breathe and an excited little moan happened instead.

Caspian tugged me in tighter still. No humiliatingly inappropriate noises from him. But his heart was thudding hard and fast against my spine. He pulled the bow tie out of my hand and straightened my collar. A finger touched me lightly under the chin and I tipped my head back against his shoulder, exposing my throat. That was when I heard him growl. Softly enough I almost missed it, but there it was. This sound of deep, primitive pleasure that shivered all the way down my back and headed off in a few other directions as well.

As he leaned over me, his breath grazed the top of my ear and that insubstantial caress felt so ridiculously intimate it made my knees go weak. Like I was supposed to be on them. At his feet. His other arm came around me as he did whatever you have to do to make a bow tie happen. He didn't fumble at it the way Nik had. His movements were swift and assured. And, just for a moment, I felt a brush of warmth across my pulse point, like a touch that wasn't.

I only noticed he was done when he gave me a little push. Too busy swooning into his neck and shoving my bum into his crotch like the wanton hussy I was. I turned, stumbling a little, discovering too late I was basically jelly, and just about managed not to end up on the ground again.

"Um, thanks." I lifted a hand instinctively, wanting to feel the shape of the knot, but then stopped. I'd only wreck it.

He just nodded, his eyes slipping away from me again. I wished he'd stop doing that. Was my face that boring? But his color was up, his breath a little unsteady. And, y'know, there'd been movement back there. When I'd been doing my thing. So maybe he was just…embarrassed?

"That's some good tying," I heard myself say. "Is it practice or natural talent?"

That got his attention. And, for a throat-clogging second, I thought I'd fucked everything up already. I could just see the headline in the Book of Making You Feel Bad About Yourself: *Rampant Undergraduate Sexually Harasses Famous Alumnus*. But Caspian's mouth softened into that nearly-smile of his. "What if I told you it was a little of both?"

"Then I guess it'd be my lucky night."

He cleared his throat. "Aren't we supposed to be going to a reception?"

We. "Oh yeah. But, honestly, if you'd rather wile away the evening adjusting my clothing, I'm game."

He reached out, fingers stroking lightly over my lapels as he tried to settle the tux less lopsidedly across my shoulders. "I know a lost cause when I see one." He was right, but I must have looked hurt, because he went on with the same uncertain gentleness I remembered from our telephone conversation. "Did you shrink in the wash?"

"Hah! No. I'm naturally pocket-sized. These gladrags aren't mine."

"Who do they belong to? A gorilla?"

"My best friend. I don't have a set of my own. Don't like wearing the stuff."

"Neither do I."

I gazed up at him, so pristine and exquisite, this sleek, shining Lamborghini of a man. In other words: a ride way beyond my budget. "Yes, but you can get away with it."

"It's quite simple, Arden." He stepped past me, gold-edged by the last of the light, the softer hair at his brow and temples gilded into tempting little curlicues. "Don't give people a choice. If you want to change, I'll wait for you."

(*Or you could come up with me…*) "But you just fixed my bow tie." A swift tug from his fingers and there was that problem dealt with. "Ah."

"Go."

"But…what if everybody looks at me funny?"

"Why do you care?"

"Um, because I'm helplessly inculcated into the sartorial kyriarchy?"

He laughed and I smiled back, feeling indulged by his amusement, petted almost. But then he told me, "You have five minutes," in That Voice. The one I wanted to hear telling me to do utterly filthy things, just so that I'd do them. I felt a drift of air, the suggestion of heat, at the small of my back, as though he'd been about to rest his hand there but had changed his mind.

"Seriously?" It came out a squeak. "You'll really wait?"

"Yes. For five minutes."

"Shit."

I ran, ripping off the tuxedo as I went, like I was the Incredible Hulk or something. Apart from the hulky bit, anyway.

Weird Owen was still lodged in our doorway, talking about, oh, who knew what, as I pelted past. Nik made a crack about Clark Kent as my shirt fluttered over my head but I didn't have time to stop.

I knew, in some distant way, this was ridiculous, but I couldn't deny I was enjoying it. Feeling silly and eager and panicky all at the same time. And thudding along with my quickened heartbeat, the need to please.

I had no idea how long I'd taken, so I didn't dare linger over my choices. I just shucked the rest of the formal wear, pulled on my skinniest skinny jeans (the ones that, it had been suggested, made my arse look like a ripe apricot) and my Manic Pixie Dream Boy T-shirt. Then I grabbed my plum velvet jacket from the armchair and sprinted back to Caspian Hart.

CHAPTER 4

He was sitting on the bench beneath the lime tree, one leg crossed languidly over the other in the way that only really tall people seemed able to manage. He was diddling with an iDevice but he looked up as I skidded to a halt and smiled at me. Not his usual polite, half-smile, but a real one, all heat and unhindered pleasure.

I'd given him that.

"So this is you?" His eyes did the full sweep, making me shiver. His unrestrained attention wasn't quite comfortable—I was too worried about coming up short—but it was somehow exciting at the same time. I wanted to be worth looking at. For him.

"Arden St. Ives, reporting for duty, sir." I threw a pretty camp-looking salute. "Did I make it?"

For a moment, I thought it might have been nothing but an empty game, but he glanced down at his screen, checking the time, before he answered. "Yes. Four minutes, sixteen seconds."

"What if I hadn't?"

"That would be telling." He tucked his tech away, not looking at me. "Shall we go?"

I nodded. It wasn't far, just across the quad and under the arch—a journey I took pretty much every day—but it felt different to be walking next to Caspian Hart. Well, it was more of an undignified scurry on my part because he had this effortless, horizon-conquering stride that seemed to make everything his wake. And I was a shortarse.

The college was slumbering quietly through the vacation. He'd shed this world so thoroughly it was hard to imagine he'd ever been here. Ever been uncertain or self-conscious. The way I was right now—aching to blurt out something stupid like *Is this better? Do you like it? Do you like me?*

"You're reading English, aren't you?" he asked.

How safe. A question that enforced distance, rather than created intimacy. "Um, yes."

"How are you finding it?"

"Honestly? I think I've gone off books."

"That seems unfortunate."

I shrugged. "Well, I'm meant to have read nearly everything written in England between, like, 8 AD and 1930, so I'm pretty much covered."

"In the same way you've read *Ulysses*?"

I probably should have been mortified I was busted, but all I could think was… "You remembered."

"I do try to recall the conversations I've had with people, yes."

Even the quelling tone couldn't diminish my happiness. I

grinned. "Well, all right, I can blag nearly anything written in England between 8 AD and 1930. But that's hardly a transferable skill, is it?"

"You'd be surprised. You don't have plans for after graduation?"

"I guess I thought something would…turn up. Aren't you supposed to get invited to be a spy or whatever?"

"Only if you fit the profile."

"Apparently I didn't fit the profile." A flicker of instinctive pique made me scowl. "Hey, why didn't I fit the profile? What's wrong with me?"

"It was probably your aversion to black tie."

"But I'd be an excellent spy. I'd love being menaced by villains."

Caspian put a hand over his mouth, but I could tell he was amused. "I don't think that's an aspect of the role you're supposed to feel so enthusiastic about."

"Well, it's not like I'm going to find out." I scuffed moodily at the gravel path, sending pebbles springing in all directions.

He was silent a moment. And then, "I'm sure, in reality, it's very dull. You probably sit in a dark little room in Westminster, listening to world radio."

Another of his hesitant offerings of comfort. It was getting embarrassing, really, how much I kept making him do that. Part of it was just surprise I could, that he would. My pathetic little insecurities seemed such an unlikely thing for him to care about. I glanced his way, smiling, trying to salvage the situation before he concluded I was utterly hopeless. "Hey, what do you say to an Oxford English graduate?"

"I don't know."

"Can I have fries with that?"

This time he didn't laugh. "Why English, then? If you didn't think it would take you anywhere?"

"Oh God." I fiddled with the fraying sleeve of my jacket. "I was super passionate about it when I was at school."

"And now you're not?"

I shook my head. "It's just how it goes, isn't it? It's not the way you think it's going to be and the stuff you think is important when you're eighteen…kind of isn't anymore."

We stepped beneath the archway. I tried not think how intimate it could be, standing with him in those gold-struck shadows. Surrounded by centuries of conveniently oblivious stone. I sidled a little closer.

Just, y'know, *in case.*

I didn't really believe he was going to be overwhelmed by lust at the sight of me looking vulnerable and available in a gloomy corner, but a boy could dream, right?

"What's important to you now?" he asked.

That was unexpected as well. You wouldn't have thought a man like Caspian Hart would be a good listener, but there was a quietness to him that intensified my tendency to babble. All the same, I wasn't so desperate for his attention that I couldn't see the other side of it: the more I spoke about me, the less I learned about him. I shrugged and muttered evasively about still trying to figure it out before changing the subject. "What made you go for PPE?" Not exactly deft but it did the job.

"I don't know," he said finally. "Oxford carries a certain cache. And PPE was…a subject."

"Wow, see praise comma faint comma damning."

He looked a little abashed. "It seemed most likely to be useful to me."

"No great adolescent passion for the German philosophers, then?"

"I've never been particularly driven by passion."

I leaned against the wall and tilted my head back so I could look at him. I'd thought he was joking, but his face reflected no hint of it. His mouth was very stern, very sexy. "I'm pretty sure you don't get to be the third or fourth richest man in the UK without passion for *something*."

"On the contrary, that's achieved through hard work. Passion is a hindrance to business."

"But you must be pretty driven? Otherwise we'd all be billionaires instead of people with Twitter accounts."

"Perhaps. Though I think I would call that resolve."

"What kind of headline is that? 'Caspian Hart: Mildly Inclined to Succeed.' How are they supposed to write you up in the *Arrow* now?"

"They're not. I don't give interviews to school magazines."

I couldn't quite suppress a giggle at that. *The Book of Making You Feel Bad About Yourself* was meant to be taken very seriously indeed. "And besides," he went on, "attaining success is considerably more than a mild inclination for me."

I realized then how easily he wore his wealth. How naturally power became him. "I can't imagine you growing up on the wrong side of the tracks."

"Everything I have, everything I've done, is mine and mine alone." He didn't sound proud of it, though. Just sad. "But you're right, my family has always been prosperous."

"Is that what it's about for you? Proving something?"

"Perhaps." He turned his head away, offering me only the cold outline of his profile. "But as a point of principle, I don't take anything I don't deserve."

"Caspian—" If I'd had time to think about it, I wouldn't have had the bollocks to say his name, but there it was, between us like an outstretched hand.

"We should go."

He turned abruptly, vanishing up the spiral staircase, and there wasn't much I could do except hurry after him.

The Melmoth Room was named after a nineteenth-century poet. As you'd expect from a St. Sebastian alumnus, he wasn't actually very famous. Mainly, he'd died of syphilis in a Parisian gutter.

It was a nice room, though, in the usual Oxford style: dark red walls, gold ceiling, oak paneling, epic fireplace, random off-limits balcony that everybody snuck onto anyway. A student in the '80s reputedly plummeted to his doom while shagging against the parapet, but that might just have been the sort of thing they put about to stop you trying. There was also a portrait of Melmoth, looking cloudy-haired and limp-wristed, that was supposed to be by Rossetti but probably wasn't.

We were beyond even fashionably late, and I slunk in after Caspian, hoping nobody would notice. Or, at the very least, everybody would be too busy swooning at his incredible gorgeousity to pay attention to the guy standing behind him.

But I needn't have worried. It was already pretty busy in

there. So many people in monochrome that it made my eyes buzz like static. Honestly, my heart sank when I saw the evening I was in for. I'd known anyway, having spent the last three years in Oxford, but the prospect of free food and wine had somehow made me forget how much I didn't enjoy making stilted small talk with strangers who didn't get me. It wasn't that I was particularly shy or introverted. More that my personal taste in parties centered on opportunities for dancing and pulling. And less on standing around discussing citation indexes and the latest policies of the Planning and Resource Allocation Committee.

At least there was champagne. A whole table's worth, the flutes arranged in shining rows. I peeped up at Caspian. "I hope you're going to get me drunk and take advantage."

His eyes held mine for a too-long-not-long-enough moment. As if I was the only person in the room. "I don't think it would reflect very well on either of us if you had to be intoxicated."

"I really don't." I'd been reaching for the booze, but I dropped my hand so fast I nearly punched myself in the leg.

His lips curled upward very slightly, color creeping across his cheekbones. "One glass, perhaps?"

I nodded. He could have said, *How about a live crocodile?* and I'd have nodded.

As Caspian Hart lifted two champagne glasses and passed one to me, it felt a bit like the scene in a black-and-white movie when the hero lights a cigarette for the heroine. Under the brush of his fingers, silvery condensation gathered and ran down the side of the glass. It made me think of sweat and skin and bodies moving together. Of glistening under his hands. Because I was clearly depraved.

I should have probably done a witty little toast thing but I was too flustered. Instead I just took a massive uncouth quaff and winced as the bubbles shot up my nose.

He looked a little shocked. He probably thought I was a burgeoning alcoholic.

"Sorry. I…" I had to stop and sneeze, and it burned, making my eyes water. "Um. Sorry. I'm not that into champagne."

He took a neat little sip from his own glass. "Well, this is a Piper-Heidsieck Rare Vintage from 2002, reputably their best year since 1996."

Oh dear Lord. I was so outclassed. "You know that just from tasting it?"

"It's, ah, written on the bottle behind you."

His tone was very careful, his expression unreadable, but his eyes were full of secret mischief. And my heart just gave this…lurch, even as I laughed. "You shouldn't have told me. I was all impressed."

"I don't find it necessary to lie in order to impress people."

My head was fuzzy with fizz. "You wouldn't need to. You're—"

"Mr. Hart?" It was a teeny-tiny field mouse woman—who I'd have noticed circling if I'd had eyes for anyone, or anything, but Caspian.

But even as I resented it, I was thankful for the interruption. It meant he would never know what I thought he was, which was for the best because it was going to be some overwrought, champagne-bright word like *magnificent* or *glorious*.

"Yes?" He turned away from me.

"I'm Hannah Rowan, the college's Alumni and Development officer. I'm delighted you were able to make it. It's such a pleasure to meet you."

"Likewise."

They shook hands, and the next thing I knew she was shepherding him expertly off. Away from me. To where the important people were.

Inevitable, really.

I tried not to…what? Feel sad? Lost? Faintly jealous? I had no right.

I watched his back, a ripple of navy in a sea of black. I imagined being able to recognize him anywhere from the line of his spine, the set of his shoulders. Like if we were back in that movie, I'd be on some pavement—*sidewalk*—in New York and a man would pause in the gray haze of a crowd. He'd turn, and it would be him, and I'd smile an Audrey Hepburn smile, and the credits would roll.

Yeah right.

I idly picked up the little cardboard doohickey that was supposed to tell you about the champagne. Floral character apparently. Hints of manuka honey and demerara sugar and notes of cigar leaves.

Cigar leaves? I took another gulp. No cigar leaves.

Which was surely a good thing?

I wished Caspian was still with me. I could have shown him, and he would have…well, he wouldn't have laughed, but his mouth, his stern, beautiful mouth, would have promised mirth the way some promised kisses.

This was getting silly—lingering by the drinks like a wallflower, pining after a man who'd taken my absence for granted. I tossed back my drink and defiantly helped myself to a second glass. He had been so sure of me, so sure of being obeyed, I half expected (hoped?) to feel the heat of his body behind me, the pressure of his fingers on mine. *I said have one.*

Except no.

I spotted some of the students I'd got to know during the telethon and insinuated myself into their conversation. Nobody ever talked about anything real or interesting during these sorts of events, but it was important to look part of something. I thought I caught Caspian's voice sometimes, no words, just the tone or the timbre of it, woven through the blur of other people's. It was all I could do to stop my head turning, seeking him. An iron filing jumping to a magnet.

His presence was everywhere. Filling up the room. I could feel the attention of people who didn't even know who he was straining toward him. Sometimes I'd catch their eyes when I was doggedly not looking at him.

Whatever he had, it wasn't charm exactly. He made no effort to engage anyone, but he drew them regardless, like planets to the sun. I didn't know what else to call it but…mastery. That unyielding certainty of power.

It wasn't…*nice*. It was a feral thing, perhaps a cruel one.

But I wanted it anyway. I wanted him. All his ice and strength and darkness.

His rare smiles.

Though he probably didn't think about me at all. Or if he

did, it was likely only as a diversion, a curiosity. Someone it amused him to temporarily indulge.

"Arden St. Ives?"

I cringed. It was the junior dean. Or Bad Cop as she was known. I'd spent most of my first and second years being non-sexily castigated by her for various negligible infractions.

Probably because she suspected I was involved in the *Bog Sheet*, St. Sebastian's most informal student newspaper. Which was fair because I did run the thing. Not one for the CV, really, but it did mean I got to cast her as a deranged Space Nazi in the weekly cartoon. It was pretty accurate.

I pasted a smile on my face. "Uh, hi, Tash."

"Did you not read the invitation properly?" She glowered at me from behind thick, black-framed spectacles. She was in a tuxedo herself, doing the full Dietrich, and I would have normally thought it was cool. But she was Dr. Tash Vijayendran and she ate fun for breakfast and I refused to think anything good about her. "You do know there's a dress code? Why aren't you in black tie?"

I opened my mouth to answer. But I had nothing. What was I supposed to say? *Because Caspian Hart told me not to?*

"Well?"

I felt like a kid who had come to school without his uniform. "Um..."

"Because"—Caspian hadn't even raised his voice but the room fell quiet around him anyway—"he doesn't like it." All that determined not-looking for him and he'd been close enough to hear me speak.

Tash blinked. "Oh. Well. All right, then."

Of course, it wasn't a *real* explanation for what I was wearing. If I'd tried to say something like that...God, my mind flinched from imagining it. Best-case scenario—everyone would have laughed at how fucking ridiculous it was. As if two hundred years of Britishness were just going to roll over for the sake of my comfort. I'd never have been able to get away with it. Not in a million years.

But Caspian could.

And he'd done it for me.

I tried to catch his eye as conversation resumed, but, actually, it didn't matter if he looked at me or not. It was enough that he was *aware* of me. Watching out for me. I liked it. It made me feel sort of...his.

As though he could claim me again without a glance or a word, simply by willing it. Like that G.K. Chesterton thing about the unseen hook and the invisible line.

The rest of the evening went pretty much the way these things always did. We milled around for a while in Melmoth, there was a brief (well, brief in the Oxford sense, meaning under an hour) welcome from the Master, and then we trooped along to hall for a fairly decent three-course meal. With great poise and finesse, I managed to use all the right cutlery and I didn't put my elbow in my bread roll once. But, as the hours trickled past, boredom seeped into me like drizzle.

I was too far away from Caspian to be able to steal secret glances at him or listen to his conversation. And by the time we were herded back to Melmoth for yet more booze and speeches, he was nowhere to be seen.

He'd probably already gone. I should have expected it, but

somehow I hadn't. And I wasn't quite prepared to be disappointed. To be hurt. I wasn't exactly picking out wedding crockery but the least he could have done was say goodbye.

The Alumni and Development officer was going on and on about the St. Sebastian's campaign. And my eyes were stingy with tears because I was sad over the loss of a man who had never been mine anyway.

What an idiot.

I slipped onto the forbidden balcony to wallow in aforementioned idiocy in private.

And there he was.

CHAPTER 5

It was as though he'd been waiting for me all along…except, well, he hadn't.

He was standing by the crenellations, looking out at the city, which was all shadows and spires and streams of golden traffic in the distance. Cliché or not, he looked good by moonlight. Sculpted in silver and steel, a man so coldly perfect he was barely real at all.

Maybe it was some essential contrariness but his very untouchability made me want to…touch. To spark his beauty to life with passion and surrender.

He lifted a hand, bringing a cigarette to his mouth. He was briefly illuminated by a flare of amber and then he tilted his head back, eyes falling closed as he exhaled a sinuous plume of smoke into the darkness.

And God, his face like that. Open in pleasure. The suddenly undeniable sensuality of his parted lips.

I must have been staring at him like a cartoon American cop

at a doughnut because, at that moment, his eyes snapped open and I'd never seen anyone shut down that fast, his expression becoming a mask again: smooth, composed, impenetrable.

I tried to think of something nonawkward to say but instead blurted out, "I didn't know you smoked."

"I allow myself one."

"A day?"

"A month."

I didn't dare tell him that was kind of completely…adorable. "Why?"

"I like smoking. But I believe in controlling one's vices."

"Really?" I strolled across the balcony as casually as I could. Pretending I just wanted to admire the view, rather than be close to him. "Because I believe in letting them run riot."

He gave a soft laugh and passed me the cigarette. "Then indulge yourself for me."

"I thought you'd never ask."

As it happened, I hadn't smoked much tobacco. I'd done a bit of weed, because it was available at student parties. Well, at the dull ones anyway, where you sat around talking about Kant instead of getting laid. But when I was fourteen, my mother had given me a cigarette in order to teach me how deeply uncool smoking was.

And, honestly, it had worked.

It was hard to find things rebellious or subversive when your mum introduced them to you.

But there was no way I was passing up an opportunity to share something with Caspian Hart. To put my lips and fingers where his own had lingered. Perhaps leave the taste of me for him. And I could just imagine us, monochrome in the moonlight, so elegant and sophisticated as we passed the cigarette between us like lovers in the movie I kept inventing. He would be played by Gregory Peck and I would be Lauren Bacall and at some point I'd be terribly willful and he'd be obliged to seize my wrists and kiss me cruelly until I'd learned my lesson.

"Arden?"

"Yes?"

"Do you want this or not?"

Oh God. "Sorry, yes. Thank you."

Our hands brushed as I took the cigarette, that small touch of skin to skin crackling through me, electric-neon, lighting me up. I'd expected to look effortlessly sexy, with my cancerous accessory, but I wasn't sure how to hold it. It was different to a joint, and I felt self-conscious. Like the pretender I was.

And if I didn't act quickly, he was going to notice.

It tingled when I put the filter to my mouth. I could have sworn it was still warm from him, but that was probably wishful thinking.

How hard could this be?

I braced myself and sucked heartily.

Ashy heat rushed into my mouth and burned all the way down my throat. For about 0.124 seconds I fought valiantly not to make an idiot of myself in front of Caspian Hart and then I just died. Coughing, wheezing, smoke pouring out my nose, water streaming from my eyes, the whole deal.

I must have looked really attractive. Same as when I fell on my arse.

I'd dropped the cigarette in the general carnage. I was

vaguely aware of one of his perfectly shined shoes grinding out the embers. And the faint warm pressure of a hand between my shoulder blades, rubbing soothing circles against my jacket.

Then he was offering me a handkerchief. Monogramed, of course. I couldn't breathe very well but I could still see how fucking exquisite he was. Where did he get all that poise? Was he just born gorgeous? Had he never been clumsy or messy or desperate like me?

"You don't smoke, do you?" he asked.

"Not as such." I wiped my face, feeling hot and smeary. "I think I nuked my lungs."

His expression shifted in a way I'd never seen before, his brow creasing faintly with confusion. "Then why did you say yes?"

It was a legit question.

"Because you offered?" Yeah. That made even less sense when I said it aloud than it had in my head. But what was I supposed to tell him? *"I wanted to impress you"*? I stared at the ground because you never knew when it might be obliging enough to swallow you up. Of course that also meant I was stuck staring at the crushed remains of his cigarette. "Sorry I wrecked everything."

His fingers were chill as marble against my chin, the gesture as fleeting as it was unexpected, tender and yet insistent as he turned my face up to his. "You didn't wreck anything, Arden."

"You only have one cigarette a month and it's"—I pointed with melodramatic self-recrimination—"*there*."

"I only smoke one cigarette a month, but I don't carry it

around in state like the Ark of the Covenant. I have the rest of the packet."

The shadows had softened the icy splendor of his eyes, making it easier somehow to see—or imagine—that other side of him. The man who had teased and soothed me over the phone, who seemed so full of power and gentleness and need. "You really carry around a packet of ciggies, knowing you can only have one of them a month?" I asked. "How is that possible? I can't even leave the second bar of a Twix."

"It wouldn't be temptation if it wasn't tempting."

"Yeah, but I've never figured out what you get for resisting it."

"Personal growth," he told me gravely.

And when I giggled—how could I not?—his lips curled slowly into an answering smile. Though all too soon, he was turning away, reaching into his jacket pocket for his cigarettes and a lighter.

It was a swift, graceful ceremony, sensuous in its way, the crackle of paper, the swoosh of the flame, and the deftness of his fingers. I liked watching him. It felt intimate. I imagined all the times he must have done this to have grown practiced at it, developed it into ritual. Standing alone in the dark.

He moved into the space between the…wossnames… uppybits of the crenellations, braced his elbows on the stone, and blew out a wisp of cloudy smoke.

There was just enough room for me to squeeze in next to him, so I did, not quite realizing that *just enough* would bring my leg against his, his hip to mine, our upper arms into a warm L of togetherness.

"That ain't no Marlboro Light," I drawled.

"No, it's a Dunhill. If you're going to sin, you should sin thoroughly and with conviction."

Words to live by. "It's one cigarette. If that's your idea of sin, I have to admit I'm slightly disappointed."

"Oh no." A few flakes of whitish ash drifted away like cherry blossoms in spring. "I have a familiarity with sin that is as profound as it is unglamorous."

He sounded bleak, and I ached for him. Wanted to make him smile again. "Maybe you've been committing the wrong sins."

"All the more reason to resist temptation and restrict myself to cigarettes."

We were quiet a little. But it felt okay. Not scary the way too much silence can be sometimes. There was something relaxing about the steady inhale-pause-exhale of his smoking. He kept his face turned away, so I only caught the scent a little and it wasn't nearly as unpleasant as it had been up close and personal.

Honestly, I was far more interested in *him*. I had no idea what cologne he was wearing, but he smelled good enough to eat. All this cocoa-dark and honey-velvet, sandalwoody deliciousness that made me want to either bury my nose in his armpit or go raid his bathroom cabinet. Except whatever he idly spritzed himself with in the morning was probably worth more than I was.

He let out a soft sigh of peace and pleasure.

And I thought how marvelous it would be to give that to Caspian Hart. And how fucking tragic that he would only trust himself to a paper cylinder of nicotine and tar.

I wouldn't have to be rationed. You could give in to me.

But all I said was, "I don't know how you acquire acquired tastes."

He glanced at me. "What?"

"Well, why bother acquire them when you could just, y'know, cut out the middle man and consume something nice?"

"You mean smoking?"

I nodded.

"I never had to acquire it. I've always liked it."

"So you just woke up one morning and decided to take up an unhealthy habit?"

"I...ah." His fingers tightened on the cigarette, creasing it.

"What's the matter?"

He shook his head. "Arden, I prefer to avoid personal conversation."

"That's not personal; it's just conversation. Personal would be: *Have you ever been in love?* or *What's the thing you'll always regret?*" Oh shit. I shouldn't have had that second glass of champagne. "I just mean...I'm a stranger. I'm not going to tell anybody and even if I did, it wouldn't matter because you'll never see me again. I'm nobody. I'm safe."

For what felt like forever, he didn't answer. Then, very quickly, "I liked having something to do with my hands." I couldn't help looking at them: his pale, perfectly groomed, perfectly controlled hands. Hard to imagine them ever doing something inelegant or being restless. As if he read my thoughts, he went on. "I was...different when I was younger. And I've been smoking since I was fourteen."

"You iconoclast you."

He didn't smile this time. Just crushed out his cigarette against the stone and then put his back to the battlements, the city, the deep, blue-black sky. "I like the way it makes me feel. It eases the tight spaces in my mind. And it's private." He cast me a glance from under the shadow of his lashes. "Usually."

His voice was so soft that it felt more like a caress than a rebuke. I smiled up at him, treasuring these unexpected confidences. This odd moment of being together in some small sense before the world remembered to turn and draw us our separate ways.

"I tried to give up at university, but it didn't happen. I had a philosophy tutor here. Hilary Rupert Baskerville he was called..." He made a sound of quiet amusement, surrendering momentarily to his memories and something that seemed close to affection. "I had the nine a.m. tutorial slot and we used to smoke a cigarette together, leaning out of his window, before he dismantled my essay."

"Wow"—I tried not to sound wistful—"that sounds like proper Oxford Memoirs stuff. I never had any cool tutors. I mean, they're nice, especially Professor Standish. She's like this super-intelligent grandma person. But you get all keyed up to be taught about Life TM by an eccentric genius. And then that's not what it's like."

"I'm not really sure Hilary taught me anything much about philosophy, let alone life. But I do remember the day I told him I had decided to give up smoking." Caspian's voice dropped into a plummy register: "'*Oh but whatever for?*' I told him it was for the sake of my health and he said it was the most appalling hubris he had heard in all his life. '*Why, my dear boy, you could be squished by an automobile tomorrow.*'"

I tried to imagine the scene, and this younger—apparently different—Caspian with his restless fingers. "And you've been smoking ever since?"

"When I choose to, yes."

"Always at the same time every month?" I stepped away from the stone, tucking my hands in my pockets, trying to pretend it was a casual movement. And not a brazen desire to be able to look at him straight on. He was spectacular in profile—he would have been from any angle—but even harder to read.

"Whenever the occasion calls for it."

I was pushing my luck as usual but it was my luck, so I pushed it. "What called for it tonight?"

"I'm sure many smokers reach for a cigarette after wine and a fine meal."

He was giving me this *I totally know what you're doing* look. I gave it right back to him—with extra eyebrow arch—because that was some pretty fucking blatant evasion right there. And I wasn't going to let him think he'd got away with it.

What this meant, in practice, was that we were standing there, staring at each other in this almost-playful-almost-not way. Like eye duelists.

I'd normally have yielded. If past experience was anything to go by, good things happened when you yielded. And, in other, less exciting contexts, it meant you avoided getting into an argument.

But, for some reason, I didn't do that now.

And he… Well, a man like Caspian Hart would never yield. I wouldn't have wanted him to yield. Just give a little. Not as in *up* but as in *gift*. But he *somethinged*. Conceded maybe. "I… just wanted some time to think."

"This is supposed to be the place for it."

"This balcony?" He made a slightly airy gesture with his fingers, like Prospero over his spellbook, and suddenly I could see the ghost of his old self: a young man who had not quite grown into his height, his grace. And all that power inside him, a piece of potassium waiting to ignite.

"Hah. I meant Oxford. Though, honestly, I've spent the last three years doing as little thinking as I possibly can."

"I'm sure you had better things to do with your time."

"I used to believe that. But now I'm wondering if I just fucked around pointlessly." Okay, that was way too much honesty. Saying it aloud made the fear inside me curl up even tighter. "What were you thinking about?"

"Ah." I wasn't sure he was going to answer. The gloom had muted all colors except the city's gold, but I thought he might be blushing. "Embarrassingly, I was thinking about my father."

"How's that embarrassing? Don't you get on?"

He was very still. "No. On the contrary, I admired him very much."

Past tense. And there was my foot. Put right in it. "Oh shit, I'm sorry. I didn't mean to… God. Fuck. Sorry."

"It's quite all right. I was fourteen when he died. I've been alive without him for almost as long as I was alive with him."

I bit my lip to stop something crass and inadequate falling out of my mouth. He'd spoken so lightly, I was sure he was expecting me to respond similarly, but how could I? Not when he didn't even seem to realize he'd kept count. "He must have been young?"

"Forty-two. Which"—again, that gentleness of his, that promise of smiles—"would probably have amused him."

I wanted to cry for him. Or hug him. Or hug him and cry. *You didn't admire him,* I wanted to say. *You loved him.* Maybe he genuinely couldn't recognize it. Or maybe it just hurt too much to say the word. "You must really miss him."

"As a matter of fact, I don't think about him very often."

"He'd be super proud of you, Mr. Hart."

I thought it was a pretty reasonable thing to say. Everyone wanted to do good by their parents—even hopeless little me—and this guy was a billionaire, for God's sake. And, though it probably wasn't the sort of thing your dad would notice, a stunningly put together specimen of manhood into the bargain. The embodiment of a myth: the type of man women were supposed to want, 90 percent of men were supposed to want to be, and the rest of us were supposed to be grateful for being on Team 10 Percent so we could fancy him too.

But he didn't react at all, the silence getting deeper and heavier all around us, while he just stood there, a creature of stone, starlight, and secrets. And then he said, "No, he wouldn't."

It wasn't the words, but the terrible certainty of them.

Completely broke my heart.

It just seemed impossible to me that Caspian Hart could believe something like that. And I needed—with this terrible sense of helplessness, or perhaps what Hilary Rupert Baskerville would call hubris—to make it better.

To remind him who he was: someone magnificent and rare and deserving of all the pride in the world.

I reached out, wanting to comfort him, to bridge the spaces between us—the chasm of our lives—with touch.

"Don't." He caught me by the wrist, fingers as cool and implacable as steel.

I was sure, on his part, it was nothing more than the desire to stop me doing something he didn't want. And while I had *tastes*, I wasn't so consumed by them I couldn't tell the difference between intentional and incidental.

Except...

Maybe because it was him. Maybe because he'd been gentle with me when he didn't have to be. Protected me when he didn't have to do that either. Trusted me with a handful of his secrets.

But when he held me—that suggestion of restraint, of strength greater than mine—it ignited me like fireworks.

And oh God. The sweet shock of skin to skin. My pulse swollen with heat and sudden energy beneath his palm. Needles of awareness running all the way up my arm. My heart pierced by the sharp longing to be controlled, to be taken, to be *his*. Even if only for a little while.

For a moment I was transfixed—perhaps we both were—by that narrow strait of me claimed by him. And then I looked up, and so did he, and his eyes were intent in the darkness, the blue of them bleached by the shadow and the reflection of the moon bright in his pupils. It made him a little wolfish. Hungry and distant. But I wasn't frightened of him. I wanted him. To be close to him. Remembering not his savagery but his hurt.

"Don't," he said again.

Though he didn't let go. Didn't step away. If anything, his fingers tightened.

His breath came harshly through the silence.

It was only when I felt cold stone beneath me that I realized I'd gone to my knees, my hand slipping from his grip. I barely knew how I got there, let alone understood why I'd done it, but it seemed… right somehow. That it would be good for him to have me there. Something I could give that he could accept. Easier, for him, than comfort.

A different sort of understanding.

I gazed up at him. He looked sharp and stern, harshly etched by the moonlight, brows pulled tight in anger or confusion or something he was trying to conceal.

"What are you doing?" Whatever he might have wanted me think, his voice betrayed him. It wasn't quite steady.

And gave me the courage to tell him, "You know what I'm doing, Mr. Hart."

"No, I mean yes—" It was the first time—no, the second time—I'd ever heard him flustered. Maybe there was a bit of the other side of the coin in me because I liked it. I liked it a lot. Not flustering him precisely. But *affecting* him. "Stand up. This isn't right."

Maybe it wasn't. But it sure as hell felt awesome. Peaceful in some strange way and powerful in another. "Fuck right." I drew in a deep breath. Held his eyes. "I want to…" Which was, of course, when I ran out of bravado. How was I supposed to finish that sentence? *Help you? Save you? Take care of you?* I couldn't say any of those things. They'd sound weird and embarrassing and way too much. But I had to finish somehow. I was already at his feet. Already committed to doing something stupid. "Suck your cock," I finished.

And oh fuck. How had I ever thought that might be better?

CHAPTER 6

I cringed, anticipating bemused rejection, but instead his fingers brushed my cheek—the touch as hesitant and as fleeting as his confidences had been. I turned my face into his palm and kissed it, embarrassment drowned in a rush of pleasure.

"We shouldn't," he said. "You don't know what you're doing—"

"Oi." I nipped his thumb. "I think you'll find I do."

He made a shaky sound, a sigh or a laugh or a little bit of both. "You don't know what you're doing to me."

"Then let me. Please."

"Arden, I—"

"Please."

Silence. And I was trembling with urgency. Whatever I'd apparently done to him, I'd managed to wind myself up into a right state. I couldn't remember ever being so aroused on so little.

Except it wasn't little, not really.

It was him, and kneeling for him, and begging him, and knowing he wanted me too. And it was better than any everyday fucking or sucking I'd ever done.

I couldn't tell which of us he shocked more when he gave this—God—this *groan*, this deep, lovely, slightly helpless groan. And his hands moved to undo the button of his trousers. The scrape of the zip sounded so ridiculously loud that I half expected the balcony doors to fly open and the guests to come pouring out in fear of the machine gun.

But, no, it was just him and me and…and this.

Waiting with the cold seeping into my already-aching knees. Watching the faint trembling in his fingers as he pushed down…oh my…I was glad for the semidarkness because otherwise I'd probably have been completely overwhelmed by the sheer classiness of his silk modal boxer briefs. I only got a glimpse, but the way they clung to him—sleek and gorgeous and far too explicit—I would have given anything to be the one peeling them off him. Revealing him. Worshipping him. His flanks beneath my hands, tight with anticipation and flush with heat, the skin ivory smooth.

Although in all honesty, and greedy fantasies aside, what was happening now was almost on the brink of being too much. It was like some weird semi-pornographic fairy tale. A spell I was going to break at any moment when he saw my finery was nothing but ashes and my carriage a pumpkin. Not that this was the sort of thing that happened in the Brothers Grimm. Even taking into account all the *Oh no, real fairy tales are dark, man, dark* bullshit.

And then I saw his cock and the nervous babbling in my brain snapped off as if he'd hit a switch.

Just.

Um.

Wow.

It looked like marble in the moonlight and it was beautiful, sculpted almost, a cock that Rodin would have dreamed up. I'd seen my fair share of knob in my life—I'm sure some would say more than my fair share—but this was cream of the crop. Platonic ideal. Sizeable and proportional and tantalizing with a graceful curve to it. It made my stomach knot with yearning, empty places waking up inside me, aching for him to fill them and take possession of me.

I leaned forward and licked all the way up the underside of the shaft.

He tasted good. Heat and salt and skin. And, at the top like a prize, a glistening drop of pure desire. It zinged on my tongue. For me.

Caspian gasped. Such a rough sound, a little bit grudging, as though he'd tried to keep it trapped in his throat.

I pressed in closer, wanting more—more of his sounds, more of his pleasure, more of everything—and slid my hands up his thighs. The muscles drew tight under my palms. He was so unexpectedly responsive, this cold man, so very full of hidden fires.

But then he seized my wrists again—one in each hand, this time—and pulled me away. At first I thought he intended to stop me (and, of course, I would have stopped) but he just trapped me there, kneeling at his feet with my arms outstretched in this pose of peculiar surrender—a little bit crucified, a little bit "don't shoot me."

I'd been pretty much making a beeline for his cock, but I felt odd without my hands. Exposed. Also—as much as I hated to admit it—I was a trifle lazy in the gamahuching department. Well, maybe not *lazy*, because I was certainly enthusiastic about it, but I usually cheated a bit. The ol' hand round the base technique.

And I know it made me something of a failgay but I was scared of deep throating. Scared in a good way in principle, but in practice...well, it didn't tend to quite work out. There'd be moments of rough hands and breathlessness that would flush me with hectic heat—leaving me feeling helpless, feeling thrillingly used. But then all that promise of something dark and sweet and dirty would be lost in worrying I was about to throw up on some guy's dick. And, just like when I was a teenager, going on fairground rides that scared me to stop my mates calling me a sissy, I'd be left feeling sick and hurt, asking myself, *Why are you doing this? What are you getting out of it? What are you* supposed *to get out of it?*

But then I'd never wanted anyone the way I wanted Caspian Hart.

And I trusted him. As he had trusted me.

I let him keep my hands, fingers curling as I yielded to his grip. And, with less finesse than I might have hoped, I opened my mouth over the head of his cock, pulling it clumsily inside like a stick of Blackpool rock.

Only, y'know, thicker and harder and hotter and oh God. Oh *God*.

Caspian Hart's cock. In me. Well, about half in me. Enough to flood me with the taste of him: salty, masculine, and clean. So exciting, the intimacy of that, along with the heat of palms, pressing into me like shackles. I angled myself, trying to take more of him, feeling him stretch my lips and rub against the interior spaces of my mouth. He wasn't pushing, but it wasn't hard—um, difficult—to imagine what it would be like if...when...he did. How powerless I would be. At his feet, with my hands in his, my body given over to his will and the violence of his passion.

Surrendering to it. And inciting it.

The thought made me fluttery. Sensation and expectation and anticipation knotting into a quiver-inducing tangle. Making me moan in this needy, greedy, cock-muffled way.

His fingers tightened in response. It hurt, but I'd never minded a little pain, if it was done right. And, just now, it was so right, melding with the aches in my knees and my jaw and—frankly—my dick until I was music. Everything I felt, pain and pleasure and lust and submission, conducted by him.

I was starting to wish I'd been less wussy with my other partners. Because I wanted to make him *feel* right back. Come apart because of me and for me. Safe with me.

Maybe if I did a lot of tongue and lip work it would be enough.

I got to it. With gusto.

Whatever my concerns about letting relative strangers block off my airway, I'd always enjoyed giving head. But with him, with Caspian Hart, it was...God. I felt like a *Cosmo* guide to oral sex: worshipping my (well...*a*) man.

With a cock like that, it would have been impossible not to worship. It was practically fashioned for it. And worship I did. In long, deep pulls, my lips locked as tight around him as his hands on me, dragging up and down that spit-slick, velvety flesh. I lapped up the fluid that gathered at the head and tongued at the underside, where I could taste the heat and the pulsing of the veins.

I pulled out every trick I knew to please him. His every bitten-back sound made my heart jump, my pulse fly, my cock drip. And, when I dared, I squinted up through the hazy moonlight so I could watch him. Caspian Hart, head thrown back, every muscle taut, eyes closed, mouth open, sweat gleaming on his brow, a little bit unraveled, a little bit mine.

More gorgeous than ever.

I was starting to hurt for real now—my knees especially—but I would have sucked him until my jaw fell off if he'd wanted. It was just unbelievably good to be able to do this to him. To feel the shudders running through him, hear his ragged breath, his soft groans. To feel exposed and controlled and strong at the same time.

But then he released my wrists and I'd grown so accustomed to him holding them, and to the pull in my shoulders, that it felt like loss. Left me more unbalanced than when he'd first taken them and unexpectedly vulnerable, when surely it should have been the other way around. I nearly reached for him again, but then I remembered how he'd reacted when I'd touched him before. Instead, I pressed my palms to my thighs and kept them there.

It probably looked a bit odd—a supplicant engaged at profane prayer—but he muttered something. I was too dazed, really, to make sense of the words, but I remembered them later. Remembered them, obsessed over them, didn't quite believe them.

What he said, or what I thought he said was, *God you're stunning.*

His fingers curled into my hair, sending a delicious shiver through my skull, into the nape of my neck and down my spine.

"Will you trust me?" he whispered.

Hard to answer with my mouth full, and I would have thought my actions implied pretty heavily that I did, but I stilled, nodded, and made an undignified attempt at a yes.

We must have made a pretty ludicrous tableaux, but the way he was looking at me, his eyes all light and shadow and ferocity, I didn't care.

"Flatten your tongue, stretch out your neck."

An anxious noise leaked from around his cock. But I did what he told me. Of course I did. His soft commands were like fingers inside me: a tender assault on some hidden pleasure center. I could probably have come from them alone.

He was already wet, from him and me, and I was already pliant with yielding. I had expected him to be rough with me, forceful, now that I'd ceded my last threads of control. But he was annihilatingly gentle, his cock gliding into my throat with a kind of smooth inevitability that my body almost didn't resist.

Almost. I still gagged. Still got teary-eyed and snotty. Still got that instinctive "I can't breathe" flood of panic that made you somehow forget you had a functional nose. But he was pulling out before it hurt, before I got really scared, his hands soothing in my hair, as he gave me time to gasp and splutter. When he pushed back in, the panic was still there, but it felt different, hot and bright and almost sweet, far closer to adrenaline than fear.

My cock, which had briefly surrendered to anxiety, perked up like a fox hound hearing the view halloo. Flipping from "I'm not sure about this" to "ready to explode" in about two seconds flat. Especially when Caspian started talking, almost helplessly, telling me in this passion-wrecked voice how good I was, how beautiful and perfect, which weren't the sort of things people usually said to me.

The weirdest thing was that, right then, breathless and wet-eyed, I...believed him. I felt cherished. By his touch. By his words. By the care he took as he claimed me. I would have welcomed harshness too; I would have welcomed anything that brought him pleasure, but it didn't seem like he needed anything except my surrender.

Which I gave too. Waiting at his feet for him to use me however he chose.

And I loved it. Soared on it. Peaceful and free and proud and so fucking horny I would have begged for more if I'd been able to do anything except choke and moan.

"Oh God, Arden, Arden." He sounded shocked almost, and wild. He gripped my hair, sharp pain layering over blunt, all of it feeding into the pleasure until I couldn't tell them apart anymore. Couldn't remember they had ever been different.

All it took was one hard thrust. His cock shoving into me

like it was meant to be there. My name on his lips as he did it. The heat of his climax in my throat.

And I came all over myself, practically untouched but thoroughly taken.

Entirely his.

He pulled out quickly, his fingers snagging in my curls, hurting me for the first time carelessly.

I winced, shocked by how cold I suddenly felt, and how deeply shaken.

God.

I could have been the poster boy for the dangers of the homosexual lifestyle. I'd just let a stranger fuck my face. Come in my mouth. On a balcony. During what was probably an important speech about education and…stuff.

And I'd loved it.

Would go again.

Although the silence was getting to me now. And I would have really liked it if he'd…touched me. Yes, it wasn't exactly a prime cuddling location, but he could have stroked my cheek again. Helped me up. *Kissed me* even.

Instead, he was just staring down at me. Face locked up tight. Eyes as empty as glass. "Arden, I…" He drew in a sharp breath. "Forgive me."

And then he zipped up his trousers and left.

Left me kneeling on the ground in the moonlight.

Without even a glass slipper to show for it.

CHAPTER 7

Needless to say, my ball was over too. I didn't exactly fancy slinking back to the party covered in come. And my throat was in a bad way. I probably sounded like Johnny Cash.

Besides, the best thing about the party—the only fucking reason I was at the party—had just made extensive use of my mouth and gone home.

As I hobbled back to my room, I catalogued my aches (mostly superficial) and sorted through my feelings (probably the same). It wasn't the first time and—assuming I lived the life I fully intended to live—it hopefully wouldn't be the last that I indulged in some no-strings, no-holds-barred entirely casual sex.

It just happened to be the only time I'd been left so raw by it. Physically and emotionally.

On the other hand, it had also been...impossibly hot.

Maybe the best sex I'd ever had.

And, in some strange way, the truest. The closest to what

I ached and dreamed of but didn't entirely know how to get. Which wasn't to say I hadn't messed around, online and off, let the occasional one-night stand be a bit rough with me. Mumbled my "yes, sirs" and tried not to giggle, feeling self-conscious in entirely the wrong sort of way.

It had been different with Caspian.

Somehow I'd trusted him to take from me exactly what I needed to give.

Thankfully Nik was already sleeping, which meant I didn't have to answer any difficult questions. Questions to which the answer would unavoidably be "I sucked off Caspian Hart." Wriggling out of my clothes, I flung my boxers into the laundry basket and dived under the bedcovers. It took a while, but I warmed up eventually, and my brain settled down.

It wasn't like I'd been expecting...well, anything. You don't give a guy you've only just met a blow job and then wait for the proposal.

And, frankly, even the blow job was its own little miracle. Well. Intriguingly above-average miracle. My cock gave a hopeful twitch just remembering. Caspian Hart, the most perfect man I'd ever met, shuddering with passion, clinging to me, and coming apart. And all because of me. I liked to think I was fairly decent in the sack, but I'd never affected anyone the way I did him. Or maybe it was just the change in him. Like watching a stone lion come to life, all fire and claws and thunder.

I put my fingers to my lips. They still felt a little puffy and I traced the edges of my mouth, where he had stretched me wide.

God.

And to think the most I'd hoped for had been a stilted conversation. Sending him off with vaguely positive St. Sebastian's feels for when the next telethon rolled around.

Admittedly, his exit had been more abrupt than I would have liked, but maybe he hadn't known how to handle the postcoitus. In case I got clingy or demanding or something. I wouldn't have. Cuddles were good, breakfast was better, but we were on a balcony at a party and I wasn't exactly the boyfriend type. I'd tried it, a couple of times, and it had been…fine, but if you couldn't be a tart at the age of twenty, what was the point of being young, moderately attractive, and armed with a student card that got you cheap beer?

Besides, what else did I need from him, after an experience like that? I was smiling as I snuggled into my pillow. It had been a good night. An extraordinary night. And I was going to think well of Caspian Hart until the day I died.

***

Nik got me up the next morning to go to breakfast and I was shockingly discreet. Or hungover. In any case, I didn't give him any gossip about Caspian. I only said he was hot but aloof and that we hadn't spoken very much.

Which was basically true.

It was slightly insulting, actually, how quickly Nik accepted it.

I did feel just a little bit guilty about the fact that I hadn't made more attempts to talk to Caspian about, y'know, fundraising, but I'd already spent a week on the phones talking the talk, and the dinner wasn't supposed to be a hard sell. It was meant to get people gently drunk and nurture their nostalgia. I guess I could have at least tried to give him a tour.

Of something other than my mouth.

After I'd put away about a gallon of orange juice and a couple of tons of scrambled eggs, I went casually down to the Lodge to check my pidge.

I didn't really think Caspian would have left me anything. Flowers? A diamond-studded cock ring? A discreet little note saying, *So long, and thanks for all the sex*? But there was something in there. An envelope, heavy cream and posh-looking. Not the usual student mail by any means.

I tried not to get too excited.

Except for the part where I got excited.

Imagining an intriguingly dirty arrangement where I met up with Caspian every now and again. Got flown to exotic locations in his private jet to blow him or provide other necessary, um, body services. And maybe sometimes he'd hold me afterward, or we'd go out to dinner, and he'd smoke a cigarette and tell me the things that he didn't tell anybody else.

Which was when I saw the college crest on the envelope, killing that poor little fantasy before it had a chance to flourish into full-fledged wankbait. Inside, was a neatly typed note inside inviting me to visit the Master at—

Oh shit, I was already late.

I pelted around the quad, through the archways, past the graveyard, and across to Reni, which contained the Master's office and residence. Up another spiral staircase. And then I was being summoned, panting and sweating and really wishing

I'd showered, into the sanctum sanctorum of St. Sebastian's College.

I'd never been in there before, which I strongly believed to be a good thing, and I wasn't exactly in the mood for sightseeing. It was the usual Oxford grandeur, cherrywood and dark leather, big arse desk, behind which the Master sat in state. In one of her typically alarming houndstooth numbers.

Dame Frances Cavendish was her name. Her letters, which were embossed on the door and the official letterhead and found their way onto pretty much every collegiate publication, were DBE, FRCPysch, FRCP, FRCPI, FRCGP, FMedSci. No clue what any of them meant beyond "I am better than you, bitches."

I was fucking terrified of her. Everyone was. She had this scrawny black cat called Pongo (who called their cat Pongo?) with Gollum-like eyes that exactly matched her own. He was rumored to be a demonic manifestation of her will. And he wasn't here now, which, to my mind, confirmed it.

"Ah." She showed her teeth in something that, in a human, might have been a smile. "Mr. St. Ives?"

Oh God. I hated the way she addressed everyone with this strained, borderline sarcastic courtesy. "Oi, Shithead" would, at least, have had the virtue of authenticity.

"Sorry I'm late. I didn't, um—"

"Have a seat."

I had a seat. It was a small seat. Made me feel like a fucking Goomba. "I haven't done anything."

"Oh, but you have, Mr. St. Ives. You've been very busy indeed."

Fuck. She knew about the blow job. Wait. How could she possibly know about the blow job? I stared wretchedly at the rug at my feet, which was emblazoned with the college crest and its (deliciously defaceable) motto *Mens Conscia Recti*. I didn't know what to say.

She rose suddenly. She wasn't a tall woman but, damn, she gave good loom. I just about managed not to cringe visibly. "Would you care for coffee, Mr. St. Ives?"

"N-no thank you."

Dame Frances was known universally as Damn Frances. Apparently there'd been a typo somewhere once—nobody could remember the details anymore—but the appellation had stuck. She stalked past me to the posh cafetiere waiting on one of the sideboards and proceeded to make coffee in a manner I found subtly disturbing.

It smelled good though. Classy.

And that was probably exactly what Persephone thought when she saw that pomegranate.

"Um, Damn...Dame Frances...can I ask what this is about?"

She turned, cup in hand, and did the teeth thing again. "I wanted to thank you for your work for the telethon."

Breathing. I suddenly remembered it was a good idea. "Oh, no problem. Anytime. Can I go now?"

"Of course, Mr. St. Ives. I have no intention of keeping you long." I was halfway to the door for maximum looking like an idiotness when she continued. "You know, you were our most successful fund-raiser. By quite a significant margin."

"Team effort. Probably nothing to do with me at all."

"Oh really?"

I nodded frantically.

"Then perhaps you'd better take a look at this."

I heard the rustle of papers behind me. I couldn't really run out of the room, however much I might have wanted to, so I sloped sheepishly back to the desk and picked up the document the Master had laid out for me. It was numbers. Lots of big numbers. The sort of numbers that made me feel like I was failing GCSE maths all over again. "What's this?"

"It's a full scholarship to be awarded yearly to an exceptional undergraduate experiencing financial hardship."

"Cool."

"We're calling it the Arden St. Ives Scholarship."

"You're what?" As ideas went, it was so far out of left field it wasn't even near the grass anymore. I tried to understand what something like that might mean, but it just slithered out of my brain, unable to connect with anything already in there. *The Arden St. Ives Scholarship?* Holy fuck. "You don't have to do that."

"On the contrary"—her evil cat eyes met mine over the paper—"Mr. Hart was quite insistent."

"Mr.... wait. Caspian? Caspian did this?" That wouldn't fit in my brain either. Why would he... Oh fuck, no. I hadn't asked him for anything. "Why?"

She gave me what, in the heat of the moment, I interpreted as an *I know what you did last supper* look. "You must have made quite an impression on him."

I probably mumbled something.

And she probably said something in return.

And then...oh whatever. Everything had vanished into this blur of awfulness where I felt weird and dirty and guilty and used in a way I just hadn't before.

As if I'd done something *bad*.

And a little bit like everybody knew about it. Or at the very least darkly suspected.

By the time the Master let me go, with congratulations and good wishes and apparently increased hope for my future success, I was trembly and nauseous with pretending to be okay.

It was mainly shock. And newfound shame.

And a kind of hopeless fury that I'd trusted him and, in return, he'd turned something good into something icky.

Is that how he saw me? Someone who'd had sex with him in order to score a big donation?

God, I'd thought he liked me. He'd made me believe I was safe with him. But all the time he'd seen me as disposable. Someone to be used and dismissed and paid off and forgotten.

I sat down on the library steps and put my head in my hands, the gold and green of the quad smearing into the tears I definitely wasn't crying.

Jet-setting fantasies aside, I'd known—I'd known right from the first moment I set eyes on him—that I'd probably never see him again. That we wouldn't kiss or date or talk or do any of the things that most people counted as meaningful. That I wouldn't be telling my grandkids, or probably Nik's grandkids, about that enchanted evening long ago when I let a stranger fuck my throat until I came.

But that hadn't mattered when what we'd done had been special to him in the same odd sort of way it had been special to me. That we'd both trusted and shared and taken and given.

Except now I knew it wasn't like that: I'd been nothing to him all along.

Which was probably why the last thing he'd said had been *Forgive me*.

Barely out of my mouth and he was regretting me. Planning to get rid of me. Ensuring he'd never have to think of me again. Turning what we'd done into transaction.

It wasn't as if I'd never been treated badly before—as the saying went, if you kissed a lot of princes, sooner or later you were bound to sleep with a frog—but it had never been like this. It just wasn't something you thought to protect yourself against.

Not exactly the whole "having the billionaire you just sucked off donate a scary amount of money to your college's endowment" because how in God's name could you prepare for that? But discovering the distance between how you saw something—and saw yourself—and the way someone else did. And feeling cheapened by that distance.

Hurt.

So there I was, struck deep in some unexpected vulnerability, left bleeding by a blow I never saw coming. No pun intended.

It was my own fault. I should have never—

No, wait.

It *wasn't* my fault. I didn't do anything wrong. *He* made it wrong. And *I* didn't deserve to be sitting here feeling like fucking nothing.

And that was when anger made itself my champion. It made

me feel strong instead of weak, righteous instead of used. And, through my drying tears, before I actually tried to take action, it looked a lot like courage.

Which was how I ended up on the Oxford Tube, heading for London. Convinced I was going to be able to stand in front of Caspian Hart, look him in the eye, and tell him with terrifying dignity exactly how not okay his behavior was. Genuinely believing that this was something I could do. That it wouldn't be absurd and embarrassing and futile. That he deserved to feel as bad as I did. And that—most ridiculously of all—I had the power to make him.

CHAPTER 8

I shoved through the front door of Hart & Associates—which didn't go as well as I might have hoped because it was revolving, and I had a hard enough time getting through those things when I was completely compos mentis—and then went plunging across the foyer. Everything was a haze of glass and steel and marble. Beautiful in a way, a godless cathedral, full of echoes and refracted light, but it was also the kind of space designed to make you feel shabby and small.

Which, if you asked me, was an architectural dick move.

I kept catching glimpses of myself in too many gleaming surfaces. Wildly out of place in Hart's Temple of Mammon in scruffy jeans and a T-shirt, and my favorite jacket—the velvet one I'd worn to the dinner, with holes in the elbows and all the nap worn away, my rainbow pride bracelets disappearing under the fraying sleeve. I hadn't even taken the time to engineer my hair so it was multidirectional and ridiculous. Basically, I looked like a rentboy who'd let himself go.

A voice called after me, "Can I help you?"

And I called back, "No," as I jumped into the lift and hit the button. He would be right at the top because the top was the best. I'd seen *Pretty Woman*. I knew how this stuff worked.

The glass bubble shot silently skyward, floor after floor after floor rushing past in streaks of silver, burning at the corners of my eyes like I was about to cry.

But I wasn't.

I totally wasn't.

Because I was angry. Angry and invincible. Not sad. And definitely not scared.

The doors swooshed open *Star Trek* style and the lift disgorged me onto what would have been a landing in a less intimidatingly designed building. It was probably the closest thing to an antechamber I would ever stand in.

And, oh shit, there was another receptionist. A stately blond, built like an underwear model. Calvin Klein, not ASDA George.

"What are you doing here?" he asked.

"I'm looking for Caspian."

"Why do you need to see him?"

It was a fair question. I couldn't think of a single plausible explanation why someone like Caspian Hart would know someone like me. Which was why I ended up blurting out the truth. "Because he's an arsehole."

The receptionist's hand dipped below the edge of the desk, and I'd seen enough movies to know it was the "summoning security" gesture. I probably had about 0.2 seconds before I was dragged out of there by burly men with Tasers.

Fuck, I'd blown this. Ironically enough, considering I'd also blown Caspian.

I wheeled around on an inexplicable instinct—awareness or recognition or some painful entangling of both—and there he was inside a glass-walled conference room: Caspian Hart. Still the most impossibly beautiful man I'd ever seen, as cold and perfect and unreachable as a star.

Except he'd reached for me. And then cast me aside.

Blindly—God, maybe I *was* crying—I ran for the door. Pushed it open. And practically fell over the threshold.

Caspian paused midsentence. And gazed down at me with his hunter's eyes, no expression on his face at all. Just the sight of him made me ache with wanting. With wanting to please, to yield, to warm and gentle him. To relieve such stark loveliness with the messiness of joy.

I'd prepared a speech. On the bus down, I'd rehearsed it over and over again in my head. It had been dignified and devastating, but now I couldn't remember any of it.

All I could remember was Caspian Hart's fingers, tight and desperate in my hair. The careful pattern of his breath breaking. The sound he made, pleasure-wrecked, as he came down my throat in a hot, harsh rush. And how I'd followed helplessly, touched by nothing but his need.

"You...," I said. "You're a...a dick."

It sounded so childishly inadequate. Just like me.

I tried again. "And I'm not your—" *Whore*. Except calling yourself a prostitute in an insulty way seemed a bit rude to the oldest profession. After all, there wasn't anything inherently wrong with exchanging sex for money, as long as you both knew that was what was happening. "Um, non-negotiated sex worker."

It turned out I wasn't angry or invincible at all. Just far too young for a game I hadn't understood we were playing. "What the fuck, Caspian?" I finished helplessly. "Why did you do that to me?"

He blinked. Once.

That was all I got.

Then, "This matter would be better discussed in private."

Wait. What? Private? Oh God. Of course. He'd been talking when I'd burst in, and for some reason, my jumbled brain hadn't quite grasped what that meant.

I turned, limbs heavy and awkward as if I'd suddenly become part robot, and sure enough, there was my audience: five of them, be-suited and exquisitely composed, regarding me with the careful nonreactiveness British people adopt when you've mortified yourself so severely that they're embarrassed on your behalf.

I closed my eyes for a second on the off chance all this would have miraculously gone away when I opened them again. But no. Everything was right where I'd left it. I was in London, in Caspian Hart's office, my heart spattering on the expensive carpet in front of a group of total strangers and the man who'd smooshed it in the first place.

Anger was rubbish. It had deceived me into thinking I was strong and bold and undefeated. And now I wanted to die.

What was I supposed to say? How did you make something like this better? *Non-April Fool!* "Um…sorry. I can see I've interrupted."

Caspian's hand closed over my wrist. It was not a reassuring grip. Under different circumstances I might have liked being held that way, trapped and controlled. But right then, not so much.

I tried to pull free and his fingers tightened, the message undeniable: he wasn't letting me go. He was probably about two seconds from dragging me, struggling, out of the conference room like I was the heroine of a 1950s Hollywood movie. That had also recently been a fantasy of mine, but at the moment, it was such an awful vision that I stopped fighting.

I'd done enough damage for one day. Make that one lifetime. Maybe in sixty years I'd be able to find this funny. *Hey, your granddad once*... No. Just no. Even imagining looking back on this made my stomach fizz with shame.

Caspian's gaze flicked to his colleagues. "We will continue this after lunch."

And then he hauled me out of there.

Past the hot blond guy and into what was probably his office—corporate grandeur and the gray London skyline—where he practically threw me into a chair. My wrist throbbed with the impression of his fingers.

"Um—" I tried again.

"Don't ever do this again. This is my place of business."

And that was when I got it: he was furious with me. Not just *a loser interrupted my meeting* furious but coldly, personally furious. And he was way better at it than I was. He really did look invulnerable as he stalked across the room.

He was dressed in a three-piece suit (so far so city) but he wore it like armor, the hard contours of his body perfectly framed by bespoke tailoring. It wasn't usually a look I went for and it could easily have crossed the line into fussy or old-fashioned, but on him? Maybe it was his height, or the way he held himself—utterly controlled—but he looked ridiculously fucking good. The epitome of modern masculine power. A predator in pinstripes.

And still, in spite of everything, I wanted to be on my knees for him. Unburdening him, my most ungentle knight, until we were nothing but skin and surrender.

He stood with his back to me, etched in cold light, staring out at the horizon. While I just huddled there, shaking. No idea what to do or say.

At last I managed, "Well don't treat me like that again."

"I have already expressed regret for my behavior." He folded his hands behind his back, the set of his shoulders unyielding. "And tried to make amends."

Just when I thought he couldn't hurt me any more. "You regretted fucking me so much you made amends with *millions*?"

"I didn't fuck you. It was oral sex."

"That's semantics. You join your body with someone else's in pursuit of pleasure, that's fucking. And if you pay them afterward, that's prostitution."

His fingers clenched. I remembered them on me. Rough in my hair, soft against my cheek. I imagined touching them now, easing the tension from them.

Idiot.

"You wanted a donation for your college," he murmured. "That was why you contacted me in the first place."

I was going to cry. End of a perfect bloody day. "It wasn't why I sucked you off."

There was a long silence. The phase *sucked you off* belonged here about as well as I did.

"What do you want, Arden?" He sounded weary suddenly. Not angry anymore. Just sad, like me.

And I didn't know how to answer him. All the revenge fantasies I'd let run riot through my head were just that—fantasies. The things I truly wanted were stupid and impossible: *I want it to have meant something to you. I want you to like me, just a little bit.* "I…"

"There's no need to be timid. You've made your point."

"I have?" I wished he'd look at me. It was eerie talking to his back and the wavering ghost of his reflection in the window.

"Why else would you come to my office?" He half turned, showing me the pale edge of his jaw, the line of his nose. "What will you do? Go to the press? The police?"

The plot. I had completely lost the plot. "Uh, what?"

He put a hand to the glass, the bones all ridging up beneath the whitening skin. "Stop playing games with me. Is it money? I'll pay."

"Oh Jesus." Now I got it. "You think I'm blackmailing you?"

It was so…ugly. So beyond anything I would have thought or expected that, for a moment, I was numb. It felt like the moment after you cut yourself on something really sharp and you see the blood on your skin before you feel the pain. And then it hit me, all this bewilderment and shame and anger and hurt, and I burst helplessly into tears.

Through a silvery blur, I saw him turn away from the window. "What are you doing?"

"I'm"—I hiccoughed snottily—"c-crying, you arsehole."

"Then please stop."

"It's not a conscious choice." I scrubbed my sleeve across my face. My eyes were sticky and swollen, the velvet of my jacket making my skin sting. "How can you think these horrible things about me?"

The carpet smothered his footsteps as he crossed to where I was sitting and I tried not to notice how good he looked in motion, silent and effortlessly graceful, some glorious hunting beast. Probably coming to rip me to shreds.

He crouched down in front of me, the fabric of his suit tightening across the sleek muscles of his thighs, outlining them for me in all their strength and elegance. Like the chalk sketch of a murder victim except the deceased was my pride. He was just so beautiful. It was unfair. His eyes held mine in a cool, gray-blue forever. And then he told me, "I don't know you."

I tried to laugh but it clogged in my throat. "You don't know me and *prostitute blackmailer* is where you went straight out of the gate? Is your glass half empty or what?"

"Why else would you come here?"

"God, because"—the truth exploded out of me—"I liked you and…and you made me feel really cheap, okay?"

"I know." He rose to his feet and then he was off again, toward the window. It was weird—compelling, in one way, painful in another—how much stillness there was in him. And how much restlessness at the same time. It made every room feel like a cage. "My behavior…it was inappropriate." He was silent a moment. "It was wrong."

Was that what passed for a sorry in Caspian Hart Land? Except he seemed to be almost-sorry for completely the wrong thing. The one bit of this whole hideously humiliating business I definitely didn't regret. "Wait. Are you talking about the blow job?"

"It's not my usual practice."

Oh shit, no. This was turning into an ever-deepening well of fail. The only thing worse than having enthusiastically gone down on someone who thought he had to pay me after was going down on someone insistently straight. Enshrined forever as some guy's sleazy little secret. A pit stop at Queertown. "You mean you're not gay?"

"No, I'm gay. But I don't know what…happened to me. I shouldn't have lost control like that. I could have hurt you."

"Caspian"—his name slipped out of my mouth before I could stop it, the words of a magic spell, a curse or a blessing—"you *did* hurt me. You hurt me when you tried to buy me off or whatever it was you thought you were doing."

"I was trying to apologize," he snapped.

"You didn't need to apologize. The fact that you thought you did offends me. And, actually," I added, on a roll now, "you know what else offends me? You thinking I can't take a bit of deep throating. I did *excellent* deep throating. I only gagged because you've got a big dick."

His shoulders shifted. I must have been getting good at back reading because I thought maybe I'd embarrassed him. Though probably not in a bad way. I'd never a met a man who didn't like having his bits admired. But I'd noticed this in Caspian before—the oddest touch of something almost like shyness.

That was when something else occurred to me. I mean, while it was pretty grim to have someone think you'd sleep with them on behalf of your college's endowment, how much worse would it be the other way around? If your first assumption when somebody touched you was that it wasn't you they wanted. Maybe it was one of the perils of being way too rich, but he was also way too attractive. Surely people were falling all over themselves to put his cock in their mouth?

I slipped out of the chair and followed him to the window. Rested my hand lightly on his back, feeling the heat and tightness of him through stupidhigh superfine. And he shuddered under my palm like an unbroken stallion.

"You didn't do anything I wasn't up for," I told him.

He sighed. "I am sorry, Arden. I thought the donation would compensate for the way I'd treated you."

"Well you thought wrong. Shoving your dick down my throat is okay. Even shoving your dick down my throat and never speaking to me again is okay. Shoving your dick down my throat, never speaking to me again, *and* starting an 'oops, I'm sorry I shoved my dick down your throat' scholarship in my name is seriously doubleplus unkay."

Now that I was closer, his reflection was clear enough to show me nuances of expression: the slight softening of his lips, the hint of amusement. And I remembered that making him laugh was almost as satisfying as making him come.

"I wasn't expecting anything," I added. "It's pretty fucking miraculous you'd want me at all. It's not every day a boy gets to wrap his mouth round a gorgeous billionaire."

"Arden, Arden."

I adored it when he said my name. My memory was bliss-hazy but I thought he'd whispered it to me that night as well. *Arden, Arden, oh, Arden* the same way some people called out for God.

"Stop."

"I loved being on my knees for you, being breathless for you. I loved everything we did. I didn't want or need anything else. And it makes me really fucking sick to think you might regret me."

He turned abruptly. Nothing between us now, between me and his beauty, his pale gray-blue eyes startling vivid against the dark profusion of his lashes. And oh those lashes, so unexpectedly opulent, the only touch of softness in his face. I thought of him stretched out beneath me, or beside me, lax with satisfaction, my fingertips finding all his secrets. It was, honestly, a little hard to picture. He wasn't a man for quiescence. It was something I had uncomplicatedly liked about him. But, all the same, maybe lust-tamed he would let me.

"I don't regret you. I…I…" His voice had gone hoarse, the words ragged, as if they'd had to tear themselves out of his throat. "I can't stop thinking about you."

"Seriously?" I hadn't meant to come across quite that pathetic or uncertain, but it was the last thing I'd ever have expected him to say.

Caspian Hart couldn't stop thinking about me? Me?

He must have meant it, though, because as I stood there

staring at him blankly, he caught me by the lapels of my jacket and pulled me round so my back hit the window. My heart jumped and I couldn't have told you whether it was excitement or fear. The glass was cold and solid behind me, but it seemed unreal just then, as though nothing held me but him.

"Oh God." A low groan, frayed and frantic. He'd sounded like that with his cock in my mouth. "I can't...I shouldn't...oh God."

"Yes," I whispered. "Yes."

You can. You should.

I reached out to draw him closer but he seized my wrists and pinned them over my head, stretching me out, making me helpless. His knee nudged my legs apart, slid up one thigh, brushed the groove of my groin as he leaned into me. He smelled far too good. Clean, expensive, undeniably aroused: skin and sex and that amazing cologne of his. Sweet and dark, just like him. And, oh, the way he touched me, restrained me, made me wait.

It was perfect. Perfect. Everything I wanted.

Whatever he'd claimed about his usual practices, he certainly knew how to please a boy like me.

I wriggled. Moaned. Let the sheer needy excitement of everything he did to me fill me up like fireflies, buzzing and dancing and shining.

His lips were bare inches from mine. The heat of his breath brushing me in prelude.

I'd never been so sure of anything as I was at that moment. Him and me and the possibility of all the things he could do to me—the things we could do together. Romantic and tender and sexy and wicked. I met his wild eyes. Tried to control my shaky breath enough to beg. But all I managed was his name.

And then he covered my mouth with his.

CHAPTER 9

Truthfully, I'd always been kind of take it or leave it on kissing. I'd enjoyed it, of course, but in the way you enjoy canapés at a posh party. Very nice and everything, artful even, but wouldn't some real food be better? It was hot on the dance floor—kissing, not canapés—tongues grinding like bodies, somebody's fingers tangled in my hair, before we stumbled to their place, or mine, to finish things off. But mainly it was prelude to the good stuff.

Not with Caspian Hart, though.

It was a no-mercy kiss. A brutal claiming, full of teeth and desperate hunger, forcing my surrender to his will and his passion.

I strained toward him, opened to him, as if we were at the end of the journey, not the beginning. More than that, he made me forget there was a journey. There was only his mouth on mine, his hands holding me, his body pinning me. And just like that, everything I'd felt—listening to his voice on the phone, seeing those icy predator eyes of his, talking with him on the balcony, the woody-acrid scent of his cigarette, being on my knees for him—yes, everything I'd felt was real again.

And he kissed me like it was real for him too.

Attraction, symmetry, freedom, trust. Something a little bit magical, even if its bewitchments were on the hard-core side.

When he drew back, I felt taken and tender, mouth-fucked afresh.

His eyes held mine, dazed and wild, gleaming with all the light from the horizon at my back. "Arden, I—"

"Oh no." I just about managed to catch my breath enough to speak. "I've had bad experiences with you and sentences that begin with my name."

"Yes, I—" He had the grace to look faintly uneasy. "I can understand that. I know I've treated you badly. It was never my intent."

I wriggled my hands, enjoying the way his tightened. "Kiss me again and I'll forgive you."

"God," he muttered. "I really need to stop doing this."

But he kissed me anyway. Slowly this time, conquering me by inches, seduction of a kind.

The kind I liked: thorough and deep and merciless.

He tasted of heat and coffee. I hadn't liked nicotine, but if I had maybe it would have been like this. A smoky velvet kiss drawing me softly into danger, into addiction.

He was breathing hard after. A little flushed. A lock of hair had fallen like a wayward comma across one eye. If he hadn't had me so deliciously trapped, I'd have pushed it back for him. "Arden—"

I gave him a look.

He closed his eyes briefly, a frown line crinkling at the top of his nose. Something else I would have loved to touch. Smooth away. "I have to tell you, I don't do relationships."

"Oh, that's fine." I hooked a leg across his hip. "Let's just have sex."

He let me go so abruptly I nearly toppled over. Saving myself only by slithering sideways over the glass like a smooshed insect. "I don't do that either."

My mouth fell open. "You don't have sex?" The words bounced crazily off the walls and the polished floor. I'd accidentally used my interrobang voice.

But he only smiled his distant smile. "I don't have casual sex."

"Why not?"

"Because it sometimes leads me to forget myself."

"Well, we don't have to have casual sex." I rubbed my wrist, my thumb lingering on the spot where his own had pressed. "We can have…smart-casual sex. Or formal sex."

"I thought you didn't like formal."

Oh God. His teasing undid me almost as thoroughly as his savagery. Or perhaps it was knowing he was capable of both.

He'd retreated to his desk. If you could call that curve of edgeless glass a desk. Bare, of course, except for an equally sleek laptop, a phone, and a lamp. And a frighteningly futuristic-looking ergonomic chair: this del Toro monster of steel and black leather. I could imagine him sitting there against the darkening sky. His own little world, his own circle of light, as stark as the rest of his office.

"I would do formal for you," I said.

He glanced away. "I would never want to make you do anything you didn't want."

"You never have." I probably sounded pathetic, but since I'd just chased him to London, interrupted his meeting, and then burst into tears, it was a bit late in the day to be worrying about my dignity. "I don't think you could. I think"—my mouth had gone dry—"if you wanted something, I'd want it too."

"We can't do this." He braced his hips against the desk, hands on either side. It was a nonchalant pose, except for the tight grip of his fingers.

Even I could tell it was slightly mortifying how quickly I jumped on the fact that he went for "can't do this" over "don't want to do this." I wasn't quite enough of a dickhead to call him on it though. "Why not?"

"I've already explained."

"But there's an entire spectrum of behavior between relationship and casual sex."

"I'm sure, but I'm quite a busy man, Arden, and I have neither the time nor the inclination to embark upon something both complicated and inevitably unsuccessful."

And again with the half-empty glass. "How can you say that without even trying?"

He sighed, a finger stroking the crease between his eyes, as though it pained him slightly. "Because I know myself. I know what I'm capable of and I know what my life permits."

"But what's the point of"—I made a not-very-eloquent gesture—"any of this if you can't...uh...have your wicked way with a cute boy you met at Oxford?"

He stepped away from the desk and crossed the room toward me. His shadow engulfed me but I wasn't threatened by it. Up close, like this, with nothing sexual between us, the difference in our heights seemed more than usually ludicrous. He put his hands on my shoulders. I didn't exactly feel infantilized by it—just physically small, which I didn't mind. But I also had a sense he was trying to be fraternal, which I, well, did. People who fucked your mouth didn't have the right to pretend they hadn't.

"I think," he murmured, "you underestimate my wickedness."

And, just like that, my irritation was gone. I grinned up at him. "Oh I really hope I don't."

"You don't know me."

"Then let me."

Yeah. That was deliberate. I was hoping he would remember the last time I'd said that to him. For a moment, he seemed to soften, his touch turning almost into a caress. It wouldn't have taken much—just a hint of pressure—to send me to my knees again. I could have rested my head against his thigh and he could have run his fingers through my hair. I imagined his expression, open and at peace, like when he smoked.

But even as his hands made promises, his eyes were winter days, just ice and emptiness. And then he told me with terrible gentleness, "I'm saying no, Arden."

Um, right.

Well.

Not really much I could say to that. At least, nothing that wouldn't be pleading or sound creepy. There were names for people who didn't take no for an answer, and I had no intention of being one.

Suddenly I wished he wasn't this close. I didn't want the heat of his hands or to see the silver filigree in his irises. But unless I started sliding across the window again, there was nowhere for me to go. "You kissed me."

"I know. I...I'm not devoid of feeling. I'm just usually in better control of myself." He glanced away. Frown back. Mouth to match: another tight line. "I don't know why you...how you do that to me."

I let out a shuddery breath. "So I'm not making it up. It's there for you too? This is *something*."

"It's nothing I want. And I have to get back to my meeting."

It shouldn't have been a surprise. He'd done the same thing on the balcony, after all, just less kindly. But it still made my heart reel: the ease with which he could think one thing—*feel* one thing—and do another. That he could share even a small piece of my pleasure and still turn away.

That it could be *nothing he wanted.*

But then I had no idea what kind of life he lived. Maybe thrilling sexual connections were falling into his lap like summer apples. Or—more likely—gauche twenty-year-olds were a lot easier to find than breathtakingly beautiful billionaires. When I was gone, he would probably phone through to his Calvin Klein secretary and be all "bring me my coffee and unleash the boys." And then twenty-four university students would come bounding in and fight to the death for the privilege of deep throating him. Talk about a new twist on *The Hunger Games*.

I had no idea what my face was doing. My eyes felt big though. And my mouth pouty. But whatever it was, it made him touch my cheek like he had on the balcony. "I'm sorry, Arden. I never wanted or meant to hurt you. On the contrary I…I like you very much. I think you're…delightful."

He'd gone a little pink along the top of his oh-so-defined cheekbones. It would have been adorable if he hadn't been in the process of rejecting me. "Well, thanks. But that's pretty scant consolation. I like you but I *still* don't want you?"

"I don't like the way you make me behave."

"Caspian, your cock didn't suck itself."

"I'm very aware of that." He sighed. "I shouldn't—"

I knocked his hand away, the impulse sudden enough that I only realized what I'd done when the harsh slap of flesh against flesh resounded through the room. "Stop fucking regretting me, okay? You liked it. I know you did. So you might as well just fucking admit it."

"I just did. I said I liked you."

"And you liked what we did. You liked having me on my knees, choking on your—"

"Arden, we're in my *office*."

"Sorry. But it's true."

He made a stifled noise, almost a growl. "Yes, it's true. But that doesn't make it right."

"There's nothing wrong in—"

"Right for me."

And there it was again. That unbreakable wall, built of his own convictions and the things he believed he truly wanted. I didn't have much grace or dignity left—not that I was over-endowed with either at the best of times—but I mustered what was left of it and said "okay" in what I hoped would be a brave voice.

Though it ended up being a small, somewhat pathetic voice.

Eh, in for a penny, in for a pound. I took a deep breath and met his eyes. So much steel and certainty. I couldn't have said why, but it made me oddly sad for him. This man behind glass who had briefly been mine. "Just don't think bad things about me."

He nodded. "I never intended for you to believe that."

"And you need to get my name off that scholarship thing. It's weirding me out."

"I was trying—"

"To say sorry, I know."

"And thank you."

There was a longish silence while I wondered what to make of that. In the end I laughed. "Next time just send flowers."

He smiled, and it was real for a moment or two, gentling his eyes and his fierce symmetry. But all he said was, "I'll arrange for a car to take you back to Oxford."

"It's fine. I bought a day return."

Yet ten minutes later I was sitting in the back of a Maybach being whisked through the streets of London. It was like a very small hotel in there. Hell, it was more comfortable than my actual bed.

And I felt completely dazed. By loss and luxury, and the suddenness of both.

I'd been pretty firm on the whole not needing to be chauffeured sixty miles up the M40, but nobody had listened to me.

Caspian hadn't exactly been aggressive. More sort of implacable. Telling his lovely assistant—Bellerose, apparently—to have a car brought round and handing me into it (yes, he really did that) while I was still protesting I was perfectly capable of getting the bus like a normal person.

It was a ridiculously fucking nice way to travel though. I was sure, if I'd dared to peek, there'd have been a bottle of champagne in the cooler. But instead I just reclined the seat, closed my eyes, and drifted into a half-dream, remembering Caspian's hands on me, his mouth, the consuming urgency of his kisses.

All in all, it could have gone worse.

Yes, I'd embarrassed myself in about six different, unique, and special ways, but he hadn't had me arrested or thrown out of his building. Reported me to college as a dangerous lunatic.

He'd said he liked me.

For reasons that, now I thought about it, seemed hard to understand.

Maybe it had just been a really boring meeting and he was glad to have been interrupted by a crazy student.

Slipping out of the car a little over an hour later and—having no idea of the appropriate etiquette—awkwardly thanking the driver, I thought that would be the end of it.

But when I checked my pidge the next day, I found a scrap of paper telling me I had a parcel to pick up.

It was a bouquet. A simple hand-tie, in crisp, crinkly paper. Not, perhaps, what you'd expect from a billionaire.

Except he'd sent me tulips.

My own private rainbow, so riotously bright on an otherwise gray Tuesday before spring had properly found its feet.

Nobody had ever given me flowers before.

I didn't even own a vase but Nik lent me a tankard and that did the job nicely.

I kept them until all their colors were gone. Until they looked like they were made of paper. Until they started to make my room unpleasantly swampy-smelling.

Until I had no choice but to let them go.

Along with the man who had sent them to me.

CHAPTER 10

Nik had been in the bar the night before his first exam. "If I don't know it now," he'd said, "I'll never know it." I tried to do the same but my nerve broke after one pint of Guinness, and I fled to my room.

I had some vague intention of cramming, but, God, where did I start? I picked up a copy of *The Complete Works of Shakespeare* and then put it down again, feeling jumpy and sick and unable to remember what happened in *Timon of Athens*.

Was it the one with the incest? Or the one with the financial mismanagement in Greece?

Fuckfuckfuckfuck.

I was going to fail Oxford. Which was basically the same as failing life.

And I could have avoided it at any point if I'd just done some work.

At Nik's prompting, I'd gone to the Careers Service a couple of days ago, where I'd read a lot of leaflets that had essentially confirmed I was unqualified for everything. I'd also spoken to a nice lady, who was apparently a careers advisor, but since my opening gambit had been "Hello, I'd like a career, please," she hadn't really been able to do much advising. She suggested I put together some ideas about what I wanted to do and slipped me a *Those That Can Teach!* brochure. We'd talked about things I liked and was good at (clue: not teaching) but all I'd been able to come up with was the *Bog Sheet*. Which had led to a slightly bemused lecture about how journalism was an incredibly difficult field to break into, even with a degree from Oxford, and how I should have been applying for internships last October.

In short: things were not looking good.

I was actually pretty talented at emotional procrastination, but I'd run out of distractions and excuses. And now I was on my own in my room, the night before my first exam, not quite drunk and not quite sober, and absolutely fucking terrified. Tomorrow I would have to put on a suit and a bow tie and my crappy commoner's gown and walk all the way down to the Examination Schools. Stand amidst the marble and gilt. And probably burst into tears the moment someone put a paper in front of me.

Twenty questions, half of which would be random quotes from people I inevitably hadn't read, occasionally appended by a somber "discuss." I'd been feeling brave enough to check out a past paper a few days back.

Big mistake. Huge.

The first question my eye had alighted on had read: "Happy the man whose wish and care / A few paternal acres bound [...]" And that was it.

What did it *mean*?

How the fuck was I supposed to do any of this?

I suddenly couldn't breathe. I scrambled over my bed and threw open the window. It was right on the turn: that moment between evening and night, suspended in a golden haze. The air moved sluggishly. Tasted sticky. I rested my head against the edge of the casement.

Too hot. Too cold. Too fucked.

People were moving to and fro across the quad like incidentals in a T. S. Eliot poem. Friends and lovers scattered under the trees in the fading light.

And I'd never felt so fucking alone.

Rationally I could just about locate a non-panic-saturated part of my brain that believed I would definitely maybe sort of be okay. Yes, the next few weeks weren't going to be very pleasant, and I wasn't likely to do brilliantly, but it probably wasn't going to be a complete disaster either. I was relatively clever, though not half as clever as I'd thought I was before I'd come to Oxford. I'd read quite a lot of books. And I'd been dashing off my essays since my second term, so producing semiplausible drivel on demand was a skill I'd accidentally nurtured.

Maybe I did have a future in journalism.

Oh God. I was doomed.

In a moment of absolute mindless lonely terror, I rang the Samaritans. But hung up again when the man I spoke to sounded terribly disappointed I wasn't suicidal.

Then I made another attempt to do some last-minute revision.

Cried instead.

Got into bed and pulled the duvet over my head.

Got out of bed again. Made sure I had the right clothes for tomorrow. Tested my pens to make sure they…y'know…wrote.

Nearly threw up in the wastepaper basket.

Checked my phone to make sure I'd set an alarm for tomorrow.

Got back into bed.

Thought about calling home but didn't see any reason to worry the shit out of my family.

Lay in the semidark. Heart beating too fast. Tears gathering but not falling. Stuck somewhere.

I was going to be exhausted for my first exam.

My brain already felt like toffee.

Then my phone rang. I scrabbled for it and answered without even checking the caller ID.

"Yeah?"

"Arden, it's—"

I sat up so fast I practically hit my head on the shelf over my bed. "Caspian." God, I'd never expected…why was he…"How did you get this number?"

"I put my considerable resources to the task."

"You can do that?" I snuffled discreetly into sleeve of my T-shirt. Of course, he couldn't see me but I had my pride. "I feel like I'm living in some kind of cyberpunk dystopia ruled by megacorps."

"It's on your Facebook page."

"Oh." He'd looked? And then he'd called me? As if you got to do that after you'd had someone chauffeured out of your life. I knew I should have been furious but I was too messed up right then, and some part of me was desperately, desperately happy to hear his voice again.

Even if he was telling me rather sternly that I had absolutely no sense of online security.

I tried to gather my thoughts. "Well, you grant things power if you try to hide them. Like there's this...kind of public privacy, you know? If something is right there, chances are, nobody'll think it's worth caring about."

"How very twenty-first century of you."

"Hey, it works. Nobody has ever rung me randomly off the Internet before." And then, because I was confused and stressed to buggery and afraid of blurting out something gauche like *What the fuck are you doing?* or *I'm scared* or *Please help me*, I stretched out like a Restoration rake and drawled, "To what do I owe the unexpected pleasure?"

There was a silence. Maybe he'd noticed this was weird and awkward. "I wanted to wish you luck with your exams."

My stomach did an awful flippy thing. Worry and disappointment and generic insecurity. He'd been pretty certain he didn't want me when I was relatively put together. How very, very heartbreakingly, self-esteem destroyingly certain would he be if he could see me now? Wrecked and hopeless and pathetic. "Um, thanks."

Another silence.

"Arden, are you all right?"

"Yes," I said tightly, "I'm fine."

"You don't sound fine."

"And what's it to you how I sound?" Eeesh. Way to come across like a petulant child.

"It matters." His voice dropped into its lower register, the thrilling, growly one, except right now it felt oddly soothing. Tiger balm to my pulled-tight nerves. "Now answer me."

"I'm... I'm really scared."

"What are you scared of?"

"Um, slugs, growing old, all my hair falling out, enclosed spaces, relationships, my *finals* for fuck's sake. And if you tell me everybody feels this way I swear to God I will punch myself in the face."

"I'd rather you didn't punch yourself in the face. But it's very natural to be apprehensive—"

"I'm not apprehensive. I'm fucking terrified and overwhelmed and..." Whatever else I was vanished into a hiccoughy sob.

"Arden, Arden"—God, now gentleness—"you'll be fine."

I knew the right thing to do was nod bravely, stiffen my upper lip, and say something like *Of course*. Apologize for having made an arse out of myself. Let him feel he'd helped with his entirely generic consolation.

But I just didn't feel capable of being gracious or strong or polite. It was some combination of closeness and distance. Residual trust left from when I'd let him push his cock into the deep, vulnerable places of my throat and the sense of not really having much to lose with the relative stranger who had already told me no.

So my mouth just kept babbling truths, panicky, ugly, embarrassing truths. It was almost a relief, the same way vomiting can be sometimes, when you're seriously Bad Drunk. "I won't be fine. I haven't done enough to be fine. And even if

I am fine, I don't know what I'm supposed to do afterward."

"It's not important. When was the last time somebody asked you about your GCSEs or your A-level results?"

"Um, my university did. And presumably my future employer—whoever they may be—will be vaguely interested in how I spent the last three years."

"Yes, most likely. But unless you want to be an academic—"

I made a strangled noise.

"—which it seems you don't, your degree classification will be as relevant to your actual life as the number of A's you got at GCSE."

"You got a first, didn't you." Not really a question.

He cleared his throat. I wondered what he was doing. Where he was. In his office, leaning back in his chair, surrounded by dark glass and a glittering city? "Yes, but how did you know?"

"Because things only don't matter if you've already got them."

"I got a first, because I did nothing else, had nothing else. Do you understand?" He sounded a little strange, and not for the first time, I wished I could see him. Not that he tended to give much away, but at least I'd have more to go on than an unfamiliar note in his voice. "That's all ambition is. A fire that burns in empty places."

"That's an odd thing for a super-successful billionaire to be telling me."

"Not one who has some understanding of your capacity for happiness."

Capacity for happiness? There was something at once alienating and fascinating in getting glimpses of yourself through someone else's eyes. Nobody had ever said that about me before. Or if they had, they'd put it less kindly. *Shallow*, for example, had come my way more than once. *Fickle* too. "I'm not sure that's a very useful characteristic," I mumbled. "Job descriptions aren't like 'the ideal candidate will be a good team player, show good attention to detail, and have a deep capacity for happiness.'"

His soft laugh. "Probably not. But that isn't the only indicator of value. And there's no point worrying about whether you're suited to something until you've decided if *it* suits *you*."

"Except I don't know what I want to do." God, it was depressing, talking to someone who had probably never failed at anything his entire life. I abandoned the insouciant pose he couldn't see anyway and huddled up at the top my bed, knees tucked under my chin. "I always thought I'd be a journalist, I mean a magazine journalist not a reporter for the *Financial Times*. But apparently I was supposed to have sorted this out in October and now I'll have to live in a cardboard box under a bridge. Or go back to Kinlochbervie."

"Sorry, where?"

"Kinlochbervie. Where my family is. It's the last bit of Scotland before you fall into the sea."

"Must be quite a view."

He surprised a giggle out of me. "Yeah, it really is, if you don't mind living without shops or a cinema or mobile phone coverage."

"I wouldn't last ten minutes."

"Well, then you could scenically drown yourself in the Loch."

There was a brief pause, and then he went on. "I didn't realize you were from Scotland. You don't have an accent."

"I'm not Scottish. We moved there when I was eight."

I nearly told him about that long drive. The dreamy caterpillar of the motorway in the dark taking me from one world to another. And that was when I remembered how fucking weird it was that we were having this conversation at all. Why the hell did he care where I came from? But then he'd also managed to calm me down. Somehow made things…normal again. For a little while, anyway. An odd sort of power for the most remarkable man I'd ever met to possess.

"Look," I said quickly, "I get it, but you don't have to do this. Thanks for…thinking of me, or whatever."

"Are you going to be all right?"

"Are you aware that you ask a lot of questions?"

"Yes."

Damn him. I wasn't sure whether I was amused or annoyed. "Well, will you answer one for me?"

A moment of hesitation. "You mean another one?"

"Hah." A pause of my own, preparing for the taste of his name in my mouth. "Caspian, why did you call me? Really?"

I tried to imagine his expression. Stern, most likely, his eyes betraying his secrets. "I…oh I don't know. I don't make sensible decisions as far as you're concerned. I was…I wanted to hear your voice again."

Complicated way of putting it but I wriggled with pleasure anyway. "I missed you too."

Strange to admit it aloud, but I had. A kind of backward

nostalgia—missing a man I barely knew and something that could have been.

He was quiet for so long, I thought he might have hung up on me. I wouldn't have been entirely surprised. It was basically the long-distance equivalent of stuffing me in a car and going back to his meeting.

"Um. Hello?"

"Arden, if you're interested in journalism, I know some—"

"No way. Nepotism is icky."

"If you're concerned about nepotism, you've attended the wrong university."

He had a point. "Yeah, well, that still doesn't mean I want donations for blow jobs or to only have what I have because I knew somebody who knew somebody." He made a noise I couldn't quite interpret. "What are you *fnuh*-ing about?"

"I think you're being naive."

It's my life rose hysterically to my lips, but I held it back. There were no circumstances under which saying that was ever the right thing to do. I'd shouted it at my family once at breakfast—couldn't remember why, something that had seemed world-crushingly important at the age of thirteen—and they'd all burst out laughing. Called me CAPSLOCK!ARDY for weeks. "Maybe. But not thinking exactly like you do isn't necessarily a deficiency in my worldview, y'know."

"Ouch."

That had come out way more insulting than I'd intended. I should have stuck to *It's my life*. "Fuck, sorry."

"No, it's fine. And you're right, of course. It's just"—a very faint sigh, almost if he was embarrassed—"I don't like to think of you being upset or afraid."

I swallowed. Not quite sure what to make of that. My stupid-arse heart uncurling like a cat hopeful for caresses. I knew it would be safest to make a joke (*"Good job you weren't there for the final episode of* London Spy, *then"*) but in the end I just shrugged—even though he couldn't see it—and said as lightly as I could, "That's nice, but it's not your problem."

Another of his hesitations. "No, but if it was. If you were…"

"If I was what?"

"If you were mine."

Now it was my turn to freeze, the distance between us solidifying in the silence. I knew how I should answer: *But I'm not.* And then say my goodbyes, try to sleep, face my exams with some pretense of courage or fortitude.

"What if I was?" Why was I was whispering for no particular reason? I tried to sound confident and flirty instead. "What would you do to me?"

I'd been expecting something sexy back: *Bend you over the nearest piece of furniture and make you scream,* would have done nicely.

"I'd want to make you feel safe," he said. "And I'd make sure you never forget the extraordinary man you are."

CHAPTER 11

It was the last thing I ever could have imagined. Far more shocking than depravity. Far more powerful. I made an embarrassing sound into the phone. A shocked, wanton, needy little moan.

God, to be wanted in that way by Caspian Hart. To be claimed, protected, cherished. So that, for a little while at least, I didn't have to be scared or small or lonely or failing.

I could be his.

Until I could be my own again.

I briefly thought about telling him he'd got it wrong. That I wasn't extraordinary at all. But, honestly, I'd rather he kept his flattering delusions. Even if they made me feel like a con man. Like I was leprechaun gold and he was going to see me clearly at any moment: just a handful of pebbles.

"Can we"—I asked—"c-can we pretend I'm yours?"

He let out a long, not-quite-steady breath and I thought he was going to refuse. I wouldn't have blamed him. I don't think

I could have come across as more stupid or pathetic if I'd been actively trying.

"Um, sorry, you don't ha—"

"Yes."

And just like that I was breathless. Unable to think of a damn thing to say. And, apparently, neither was he. The limitations of the phone had never seemed quite so eerie, even when he'd been nothing but a voice to me. Now that I'd seen him, felt him, tasted him, being only able to hear him felt noticeably less.

"If you're mine," Caspian murmured, "you have to do what I say."

Fuck, I just couldn't read his tone. I went for coquettish. "Oh really? Is that the rules?"

"It's my rules."

"I'm not very good at following rules."

"But you like doing what I tell you."

He had me there. I did like doing what he told me. I liked it a lot. Something stirred beneath my frazzled nerves. *Oh, hello, libido. Guess you're not dead after all.* "It's..." My mouth had gone dry on me. "It's pretty rewarding."

"You'd think differently if you knew me better."

"Why? You have a dungeon you want to show me?"

"I don't have a dungeon." His most severe voice.

"Then you shouldn't tease a boy." He laughed and I relaxed a little. His or not, pretend or not, we were still *us*. Whatever that meant. However fragile and unlikely it seemed. "So... um...is there anything you'd like to tell me to do now?"

"I'd tell you, quite insistently, that you're going to be fine.

Finals aren't as important as you think they are, and even if you came away with nothing, if you decided you couldn't bear to sit a single exam, I'd still think the world of you. And then"—that enthralling tenderness vanished abruptly—"I'd point out that it's very late and tell you to go to bed."

"Oh." I pouted to my empty room. "You're right. That's not very rewarding."

"You might feel differently when you're not exhausted tomorrow."

"I'm trying, but as soon as I close my eyes, my brain starts whirling and I start dreading everything and then I just get overwhelmed."

"But you're with me now. Lie down, Arden. Rest." And there it was. That irresistible mixture of authority and gentleness. Seducing and conquering and soothing me at the same time. "I'm not going to leave you."

Balancing the phone as best I could against my shoulder, I unrumpled my duvet with my feet and wriggled under. I closed my eyes, trying to brace myself for a fresh flood of panic. Sure enough, even with the whisper of his breath over the line, the first image my mind conjured was a finals paper. A jumble of unintelligible word-spiders crawling over white. "This isn't going to work. And you can't stay with me all night."

"I would, if you needed me."

I was warm under the covers, so my shiver was all surprised pleasure. "You shouldn't. I'm really not going to be able to sleep."

"What do you normally do when you feel restless?"

"I…um, get up again, until I don't?" There was no answer.

But I could imagine his expression easily enough. The rebuke in the set of his mouth. The chill of his eyes. "Or maybe read a book? Wank myself into a stupor. The usual stuff."

"Does it help?"

"Depends on the book."

"That's not what I meant."

Ngh. His voice. That note of command, cool and unyielding, like chains wrapping me up tight. "Um, yes. Tends to quiet my brain. If nothing else, it's distracting."

There was a silence. Distorted, as ever, by the medium of our communication, and unreadable.

"Then perhaps you should try that," he offered.

"Are you telling me to?" It was out before I could think better of it.

My toes curled hopefully. Yes, I was still probably going to vomit hysterically over the steps of the Exam Schools and then fail all my papers, but that was tomorrow. Tonight there was phone sex with a billionaire. At least, I thought there might be. Or I'd just hideously embarrassed myself.

Was this a good pause or a bad pause?

If only I could see his face. Maybe he'd been joking? His manner was so controlled, it was hard to tell sometimes. Or maybe he'd meant for me to hang up politely and then proceed with the solitary vice.

"Yes."

Oh phew.

Except shit.

I'd never done this before. And now I felt silly and unsexy and very conscious of the fact I was wearing a pink Superman

T-shirt and a pair of leopard-print boxers. Rather than, say, a silk dressing gown or rouge and a leather collar or whatever else would be exciting for him.

"Um now?" It came out a weird little squeak.

"Unless"—I imagined the sardonic arch of his brows—"you're otherwise engaged?"

"N-no, I'm good."

"Take off your clothes."

I mustered my failing bravado. "How do you know I'm wearing any?"

"Take off your clothes, Arden."

"Yes, Mr. Hart." I meant to sound cheeky, but it didn't come out that way at all. Turned out he'd been wrong when he'd said I liked it when he told me what to do. I *loved* it. It made me feel everything he'd promised. Safe and taken and filthy and free.

I put the phone on my pillow as I dragged off my T-shirt and shimmied out of my pants.

"And no hiding under your duvet."

How had he known? I pushed the covers out of the way. And settled gingerly back on my bed, completely alone, yet feeling more naked than I ever had in my life before. My skin prickled with a kind of wild awareness, heat rushing everywhere, making me shudder and flush and gasp.

"Are you ready?"

I nodded. Before remembering that nodding was stupid. "Um, yes."

"Here are my rules."

"I…I do what you say?"

"You do what I say. You touch yourself only to my direction.

Your body is mine, your pleasure is mine, your hands perform my will, not yours. You don't come until I allow it."

I was already breathless. Already ridiculously aroused, my cock bobbing about like a superfan in a mosh pit.

"Put the phone on speaker and keep it close by."

Fumbling, I did as he said, damp fingers sliding ineptly over the touch screen. "Okay."

"Oh, and, Arden?"

He sounded farther away, a little tinny, and I missed the odd comfort of holding on to the thing that connected us. But probably he had other things he wanted me to hold.

"Yes?"

"Don't keep anything from me. I want it all. Every sound you make."

His voice was rough with need and power, but there was the faintest trace of…I suppose I would have called it uncertainty. Which was when I realized that even if he wasn't arranged starkers on his bed with a raging hard-on, he was—in a way—just as exposed as I was. It was so close to being ridiculous, what we were doing. So impossibly tenuous. But he was trusting me. He was trusting me to listen, to obey, to accept.

To believe.

To let this be as real for me as if he was here in the room.

And I wasn't going to let him down.

"I'm yours, aren't I?" I said. "That means everything."

"Yes. Mine." Something like a groan crackled over the line. "God, Arden, I wish I could see you."

"I…I…um…could tell you if you like? Or…send a picture?"

"You shouldn't do that. These things always get out."

"Yeah, because Random Naked Nobody is totally going to go viral."

"You might be somebody someday. Tell me instead. How you look and how you feel."

I opened my mouth but I had no idea what I was going to say. This was way more awkward than I'd thought it would be when I'd suggested it. "Well, uh, you kind of already know? I'm kind of short and skinny and...squinting down at myself is not the most flattering because all I can see are my ribs, and my cock, and my tattoo, and my rainbow toenails, and my knees look super-knobby."

"Are you hard?"

"Yeah. Like fucking titanium." I stared at my own dick, which was straining so urgently the foreskin had pulled almost all the way back, exposing the head, which looked shiny and vulnerable and glisteny with precome. I blushed in some crazy combination of desire and anticipatory embarrassment. I was going to have to tell him. "And...uh...dripping. I'm really, uh...I really want you."

I was quietly dying, but he practically purred at me: "Well, I'm not ready to touch you yet."

I closed my lips on a sound of frustration but then remembered my promise and let it free. And there I was: alone in my room, horny as fuck, and whimpering into my phone for the pleasure of a man in another city.

"What else?" he asked.

I let my head push against the pillow, exposing my throat to nobody but imagining the heat of his breath, the brush of his fingers, my pulse jumping to meet him. "God, I don't know. I'm just me."

"I wanted to see that day in Oxford. Strip those jeans off you, though they didn't exactly leave much to the imagination."

"Im—" My breath caught, thinking of him thinking of me, all those dark thoughts locked behind his cold eyes. "Imagination is overrated."

"Your nipples are pierced, aren't they?"

"How did you know?"

"I could see through your T-shirt. I think you had a butterfly in one."

My nipples were tingling now, peaking like the attention-seeking little sluts they were. "Yes. Just a rainbow pincher in the other. It's rings tonight, though." Oh God, if he didn't let me touch myself, I was going to die. Combust right there, leaving behind only ashes and quirky body jewelry.

"Put a finger in your mouth."

It was what I'd been waiting for but still the instruction—the fact I was being instructed—startled me. But I did it, of course I did. I actually groaned, even though it was me I was tasting, me pressing past the barrier of my lips and into the damp heat of my mouth.

"Make it wet."

I imagined it was him. Taking all the slick, tender places inside me.

"Touch your nipples. Gently though. Just a brush, a slide. The way I would."

If you'd asked me to rate my nipples by sensitivity, I'd probably have gone fair to moderate. Maybe a bit more since I'd had them pierced. But when I danced my damp finger lightly over the left one, it felt like I'd been hit by lightning. Hit by lightning in a good way, an awesome way, arching my spine and crackling through my skin and dragging this *sound* out of me, needy and frantic. "Fuck. God. Caspian."

He answered with a groan of his own. "I wish I really was touching you."

"You are, oh you are." I clenched my hands in my sheets to stop them acting without his direction. I could feel traces of drying moisture as sharply as if they were grains of sand. A deep, helpless shiver rolled through me. "Please touch me again."

"Yes. Softly though. Tease."

Maybe I should have been more aware of just how fucking weird it was, tormenting myself for a voice on the phone, but self-consciousness was dissolving, leaving only this dazed and desperate arousal. The same desire to please I'd felt kneeling at his feet.

I'd never really paid much attention to my own nipples. Well, who did? My lovers had sometimes. Sort of in the fashion you swing into a motorway service station: very much a waypoint on a journey. But, right then, they were tight and aching, magically transformed beneath the lightest caresses of my own fingers and wired directly to my cock, my arse, all the places I wanted to feel him and be possessed by him.

"OhGodohGod, Caspian, I need more."

"Do you now?" There was something dark in his voice. Maybe I should have feared it, but I wanted it. The promise of exciting and terrible things sending little shocks of fearful pleasure all the way through me. "Pull on the rings."

Whoa, I'd meant more touching. Not—

"Hurt yourself for me."

"Oh no, please…I can't…" Except somehow the need in him, the rawness of it, meant my hands were already there. "Don't make me."

But, of course, I wanted him to make me.

I wanted to be commanded.

"Do it, Arden. Do as I say."

I was whimpering, gasping, and I'd barely done anything. It was the anticipation, more than anything, knowing what I was going to do. What I was going to choose to do. I liked it rough, sometimes, but it was different when it was somebody else. Pain, that was probably closer to shock, disappearing into pleasure almost as soon as it was recognized.

I squeezed my eyes shut and…tugged. Tugged hard. A metal-bright flash of sensation that tasted hot and coppery and forbidden. Made me yelp and groan, not sure whether I wanted to push into it or pull away or whether it held me bespelled and frozen in an all-feeling moment. A spill of dampness across my stomach that I thought meant I'd come, but thankfully turned out to be just a gesture of exuberance on the part of my cock.

"Ah. God. Arden, my Arden. You're so good." Barely audible, Caspian's words rushing to me in an incoherent flood. "So beautiful."

He couldn't see me, of course. But I'd pretty much forgotten.

I *was* beautiful. I was alive. I was fucking fabulous. Tingly and blissed out and softly full of fading hurt.

"You...you want me to do it again?" I asked with perhaps unbecoming eagerness considering I was seeking permission to torture my own nipples.

He laughed at that. Not his usual laugh, but something rich and deep, full of joy and sex and wickedness. "Oh yes please."

A hot dread rose up the moment he said it. Kind of a mind-fuck. Wanting it and not wanting it, feeling terrified and daring all at the same time. I squirmed, fingers trembling, breath catching. "Ohnononononopleaseno." And then I did it.

And it was glorious.

Kaleidoscopic free fall: my skin all full of impossible lights and my eyes full of tears. Thighs pushing wantonly wide. Cock slicking precome as if it was monsoon season down there. I wished he could have seen me, hot and wild and spread for him.

"Nrggh," I said. Not sure if I could bear the awful bliss of it if he told me to do it again.

But he soothed me, murmuring the sweetest nonsense down the phone, telling me how brave I was, how strong, how much he wanted me. It should have been odd, the context, and the contrast, but somehow it seemed all of apiece, his cruelty and his tenderness, his darkness and his light.

"You deserve a reward," he told me.

"I think...I think I'm already getting one."

And then we were both laughing, both shaken, the rhythm of our breaths meeting in ways we couldn't.

He made me touch myself then.

The stubble-rough line of my throat. The sensitive spot beneath my ears. The smooth interior of my forearms. My ribs and sides and flanks, the crease of my groin. The inside of my thighs. The inside of my elbow. The places behind my knees.

Everywhere.

Everywhere but my fucking cock.

My brain was blank and the noises I was making were practically animal and the pleasure felt as pure, as bright as pain, and I wasn't sure if I loved it or feared it. Maybe both.

Then he said, "Beg me, Arden," naked just like me.

And I did that too. I begged for the privilege of touching my own cock because, right then, I belonged to him and he needed it as much as I did. "Oh God. Please. Let me. I need it. Need you."

Maybe it should have been embarrassing. Well, it was, except the embarrassment was muddled up with everything else, so things that I would have expected to feel weird, things I would have expected to feel scary—like being exposed and vulnerable and mindlessly horny—felt powerful instead. And sexy as hell.

"God help me," he murmured, "you're perfect."

I was pretty out of it. Could hardly hear him over the thundering of my heart and the rasp of my breath and the hunger in my skin. Later, I'd remember how sad he sounded when he said it. How broken. But all I did at the time was scrabble against the sheets, hands reaching for nothing, and my head thrown back to bare my neck to my not-there lover. "Please, Caspian, please please, make me—"

"Now."

It was the shortest wank of my entire life. It didn't take much more than a couple of strokes and I came noisily, blissfully, and gratefully in this epic, spine-cracking, toe-curling rush. It was like my whole body was in it, not just what you'd imagine to be the relevant bits: all of me, mastered and consumed by pleasure.

By his will. Without even the brush of his fingers against my skin.

For a few seconds after, I couldn't breathe, couldn't move, couldn't think. Complete mental and physical whiteout.

Incredible. Terrifying.

And then I noticed the silence. Sat up like the kid in *The Exorcist.* "Caspian?"

After a moment, he answered, "I'm still here."

I flopped back onto my pillow. "I thought you'd gone."

"I…no."

"Like a sexual hit-and-run."

Another pause. "Are you all right?"

"There's come in my eyebrow. I think that counts as pretty fucking good, don't you?"

His soft, slightly uncertain laugh. "If you say so."

With one limp, still trembling hand, I pulled the duvet up to my chin. Felt it settle against various sticky places. I should probably have cleaned up, but I was too fucked out and I didn't care. I curled up next to the phone and closed my eyes. Some parts of my brain tried to remind me that I had an exam tomorrow. But the only coherent response I could form was *mmmmmmm*, my mind as languid as a cat in the sun.

Suddenly, I thought of something important and wasn't

sure how to ask it. If it was even okay to ask, despite what we'd just done. "Um, Caspian?"

"Yes?"

"Did you...are you...can I..."

"I'm fine, thank you."

"Yes, but—"

"I'm fine."

Well that was crushing. "It...uh...didn't do anything for you?"

"No, it did," he said with mollifying swiftness. "I just have no intention of becoming a man who masturbates in his office."

"It's nearly midnight. You're still working?" It didn't seem a particularly glamorous image anymore. It seemed a lonely one.

"Not right now, clearly."

I snuggled down. My limbs felt heavy and light at the same time. It was a good, blissy feeling, deep satisfaction and this...pride? Peace? "But you'll think of me later, won't you?"

"Arden."

It was his stern voice but I was too sleepy, too content to heed it. "Don't Arden me. You totally will."

"Yes," he said at last. His own small surrender. "I will."

"And then I'll think of that. It really is the gift that keeps on giving."

He sighed in this put-upon way that—even over the phone—I could tell he didn't mean.

I wish you were here so you could cuddle me.

"I...ah...I'm not very good at cuddling."

Shit. I'd said that aloud? Sex had clearly blown up my brain.

"There's nothing to it. You'd just hold out your arms and I'd find some little nook to—" *Okay, Arden. Stop. Reality check.* "I'm never going to see you again, am I? Again."

"No." It was bewildering the way something you expected and understood could be still be fucking painful. "I can't. What we did tonight was—"

"Amazing."

"You…" His voice wavered and then steadied. "You make me want things I shouldn't want."

Sex? A relationship? "Why shouldn't you want them? Everybody else does."

"I'm not like everybody else."

I yawned. I'd picked a bad moment to try and make a convincing or coherent case for keeping me. "Your tutor was right. You really do have a serious case of hubris."

He laughed at that. Amused but also…not. Sad again. "You need to sleep. I think you can now."

I let the reality of finals rise up from wherever Caspian Hart had banished it. Still scary, for definite, but the raw panic, the frantic, lonely distress: all gone. "Yeah I can," I told him.

"You're going to live a wonderful life." I wasn't quite sure how to answer that, but he went on. "And thank you for tonight. You gave me something very special. I will treasure it always."

And then he hung up.

I was already half unconscious, but I did try to imagine him: his perfect hand on his perfect cock, his mind all full of me. Where would he be? In the shower? In his bed? What did his bed even look like? Probably some kind of handcrafted designer fantasy with a gazillion thread count Egyptian cotton sheets.

Except I couldn't quite picture it. Picture him.

I wanted to. Wanted to imagine him relaxed, debauched, and dreaming of me. But I kept coming back to the balcony. The shadows curling around him as he smoked his solitary cigarette.

My hand was still clutched around my phone as I drifted into the most effortless, welcoming sleep ever.

CHAPTER 12

I probably hadn't failed my exams.

I'd written the required number of essays, and while they weren't likely to be first quality, they weren't *I am a fish* either.

It had been an epically unfun experience—a grim ritual of formal wear and frantic scribbling enacted beneath vaulted ceilings—but I'd survived. And it was a relief to realize I'd never have to do anything like it ever again as long as I lived.

My final final was the worst final. It crawled by. Such a vast room and it was still stifling. Full of identi-kit people in black and white, heads bowed over papers, hands moving in jerky lines. Silence broken only by the occasional rustle. The *scratch-scratch* of nearby pens. A long, deep sigh.

Oh. Wait. That was me.

As I scrawled out a few more desultory sentences.

My concentration wasn't so much flagging as flagged. Post-flagged. Beyond the reach of even the most determined flags.

I shifted in my chair. I was sweating through my shirt. And even my carnation—the red one Nik had given me that morning to mark my last exam—was wilting.

Blah. Fuck it.

I threw down my pen. Watched it roll off the desk and click onto the floor.

Well, I wasn't going to need it again. I was done. So very, very done.

The ornate hands of the equally ornate clock at the far end of the room seemed to be hovering in the vicinity of 12:17.

Thirteen minutes until freedom. I should probably have been trying to make the conclusion of my third essay more, well, concludy. Or, at the very least, be reading over what I'd written in order to polish it up as best I could. But the idea of having to re-experience my own tawdry drivel was enough to make me want to strangle myself with my badly tied bow tie.

12:18.

I wondered if Caspian Hart would call me. He'd said he wouldn't, but he'd said that before.

I could too easily imagine it. His cold voice warming, deepening as he told me, *I just wanted to offer my congratulations.*

I could also imagine lots and lots of ways he could congratulate me.

Although it really wasn't such a brilliant idea to dwell on them in a room containing approximately nine hundred of my peers and a collection of individuals specifically hired to keep an eye on us. In case we were cheating, admittedly, but given that the proctors—Oxford's equivalent of Scotland Yard—were willing to fine you for wearing the wrong socks, sporting a massive (well, moderately proportioned) erection was probably against regulations too.

12:23.

My stomach was legit fluttery. I couldn't tell if it was the anticipation of being done with Oxford or thinking of Caspian.

"Pens down, please."

Oh!

God.

Joy. Relief. Accomplishment. However ill-deserved that last one.

Great waves of raw *feeling* rolling through the room, connecting us for a few brief moments in this one immense, shared experience.

Like the world's quietest, most stationary rave.

What with being an *S*, it took me forever to get out of there. Watching the rest of the room proceed in an orderly fashion to freedom.

I was itching—*aching*—to check my phone. Nik was keeping hold of it since I couldn't bring it with me, but what if Caspian rang while I was still stuck here?

And when had I become so certain that he would?

Finally, I was released, and I made my way through marble corridors, full of yellowing sunlight, and out into the world again. Merton Street was awash with berobed celebrants, the air full of shrieks and laughter, the pop of champagne corks. Glitter glinted riotously amidst the cobbles, such an odd juxtaposition in that ancient, golden place.

I blinked against the glare, feeling disorientated and suddenly less happy than I surely should have been.

And then Nik was pushing his way through the crowd.

"Well done, Arden!" He pulled me into a big, squeezy hug.

I wheezed my thanks into his manly man chest. Mmmm-hmmm.

I'd actually accrued a gratifying crowd: Nik; Weird Owen; Nik's on-again-off-again girlfriend, Sophie; various folks from LGBTQ-Soc; a scattering of other people from various corners of the university. And I was patted and congratulated and cheered and hugged and hugged again and gently glitterified (even though it was against the rules) and someone—Nik, probably—shoved a bottle of cava into my hand and when I tilted my head back to drink, the bubbles poured down my chin and the sky reeled blue and bright forever.

"By the way," I asked, super caj, "did you bring my phone?"

"Of course I did."

It was all I could do not to snatch it. No missed calls. Various texts. None from him.

I took another gulp of cava. This time it tasted like mouthwash.

Except this was supposed to be my day. So I let my friends sweep me off to the tapas place where we had mojitos, and sharing plates, and baklava with yogurt and honey.

(No missed calls. No texts.)

Then to Tesco, where we bought Pimm's and lemonade and more cava. And finally back to St. Seb's, where we found a spot in the graveyard and lazed there in the dappled sunlight through that long, long afternoon.

Idle talk and laughter. Nobody seemed to expect me to be anything other than utterly dazed.

Nik even let me lie with my head in his lap, his fingers stroking absently through my hair.

(No missed calls. No texts.)

I was lightly Hemmingwayed for most of the afternoon and slaughtered at the point we were meant go on to a club.

(No missed calls. No texts.)

We ended up at Oxford's only full-time gay bar. Despite being about 60 percent ethanol by this stage, I felt weirdly…unpartyish.

Like I wanted to go to bed.

Which was probably just…anticlimax or something?

But I did a few shots and went to wriggle about on the dance floor. It helped. Made me feel a bit more…real again, a bit more like me, as though my edges were solid, not wibbly.

It certainly didn't hurt when a guy detached himself from his mates and got all up close and personal with me. It was hard to tell because my vision was blurry and he was saturated in disco rainbows but I thought he was probably hot. Tall, blond, posh. Some kind of athlete if his thighs were anything to go by.

He was not aggressive, precisely, but sure of himself.

I wasn't entirely convinced that was preferable.

There was this particular type of arrogance that Oxford bred: a shiny invincibility, I half envied and half disliked and had been, I suppose, on some level attracted to. It wasn't until I'd met Caspian that I'd understood the difference between internal conviction and external complacency.

These boys—for, yes, they were *boys* really—had never had anything bad happen to them their entire lives. Probably believed it never would. And, probably, they'd be right. There was likely nothing Mummy's money or Daddy's contacts couldn't get them. Or get them out of.

But Caspian (no missed calls, no texts) had earned his confidence.

And this Andy or Rupert or Harry or Marcus was a bloody poor substitute for Caspian.

But he was *here*.

Touching me. Clearly wanting me.

Which surely made Caspian the substitute. The substitute for a real fucking person.

I tried to slither enthusiastically up to my new friend, except I wasn't entirely steady, and I fell into him instead. Did the job though. His hands slid from my hips to my arse and urged me against his crotch, where I obligingly ground for a while.

Couldn't feel much. Just a bumping of bodies. Not even in time to the music. Or each other. An awkward, ill-matchy business.

"Want to go somewhere?" Not exactly a loverlike whisper so much as a bellow in my ear, but it was enough.

"Sure."

He took my elbow and steered me across the dance floor and out a fire door. Into the alley that ran between the club and the sandwich shop next door, where the bins hunched in the gloom like openmouthed toads.

It smelled of stale smoke and refuse.

My stomach promptly tried to eat itself. And it was a wonder I didn't vomit immediately.

I was still fighting the urge when my, uh, date spun me

around and pressed me into the wall, his breath hot against the side of my neck. When he'd said "go somewhere," I thought he'd meant back to his room or mine.

But this was...adventurous, right?

Excitingly sleazy and spontaneous.

The wall was moss-slick under my hands. Like it was sweating.

Ew.

My head reeled to match my stomach. Away from the lights, with the music reduced to a distant thump, I felt tired and dizzy and uncertain. Everything was muted: inside and out. I thought I didn't want to be here, but I couldn't really remember why, and it didn't seem so very important, just a low-grade anxiety, sourceless and sluggish.

"I don't..."

"Oh, come on." He nuzzled into the crook of my shoulder.

I pulled in a shuddery breath and wished I hadn't. Now my mouth was full of the taste of fetid air. "Look, I—"

"Stop playing hard to get, you dirty minx."

It was the kind of shit you could only get away with saying if you were insanely posh. I would probably have enjoyed it under different circumstances, but I wasn't feeling especially minxish. And only dirty in the literal "I'm not sure this is hygienic" sense of being groped in an alley.

God. What was wrong with me? Why was I doing the sexual hokey-cokey when I'd come here looking for, well, not *this* exactly? But something like it.

It was what I wanted. Celebrate the end of my finals with—no pun intended—a bang.

Better than sitting around pining for the man who couldn't decide whether he wanted me or not. The man who made me feel wonderful and awful, sometimes at the same damn time.

And who had made me no promises at all.

It was too late for second thoughts now anyway. I wasn't a cocktease or a quitter. I was Rizzo, not Sandra fucking Dee.

So why did I feel so…so nothing and everything? So empty and like I was about to cry.

The guy shoved up against me, which meant I got even more intimate with the wall. I pushed back. Wanting away. Wanting him off. But it just brought us closer together. The curve of my arse unintentionally greeting his cock.

He made a breathy approving noise: *uh-yah*.

I nearly started struggling, but he was just…really solid. Solid and everywhere. And, more than anything, I didn't want to know how it would feel to be helpless with this stranger. To be forced to confront, in some definite way, that he was bigger than me and stronger than me and I was dependent on his goodwill and cluefulness.

"Stop!" It came out as a wild squeak. Hardly dignified, but at that point, dignity was way down the list of my concerns.

He eased up a little and let me swivel around. I stared blearily into what I should have found a reasonably handsome face: square-jawed and symmetrical, classically English.

"Oh, don't be such a girl." He put his hands on either side of me, once again making me far too aware of him for all the wrong reasons. "Getting me all frisky for nothing."

"Um, sorry…I'm just…" I was in control of this. I had to be. Because I didn't know what it meant if I wasn't. I squirmed a hand between our bodies, fumbling for his cock. "How about you let me…" Fuck, I hadn't meant to say it like that. I didn't want this to be any sort of echo. It had nothing to do with Caspian. It was its own thing. That I would never, ever have to think about again.

"Let you what?" Hard to tell in the gloom but he seemed both lustful and annoyed. It seemed, just then, like an impossibly unpleasant combination.

"Get you off?"

"Well, mind you make it good."

He pawed heavily at my shoulder and I realized, with a fresh bout of nausea, that I probably wasn't going to be able to get away with a hand job. Even a really stellar hand job.

I steeled myself—now was not the time to get all sick and shaky—and slid down the wall.

Which was when…well, I didn't know exactly what happened.

One moment the guy was standing right over me. Then he wasn't. Something—someone—pulled him away. Hauled him round. The dull smack of flesh against flesh. And two cries. Both pained and slightly shocked.

"Ow, my—"

"What the fuck—"

My date was staggering, clutching his face, blood squeezing from between his fingers. And behind him was Caspian Hart, looking stern and shadowy and unbelievably *there*. Cradling his own hand.

I should have been beyond humiliated. I *was* beyond humiliated. But it didn't seem like anything that mattered when I was just so happy to see him.

"He was telling you no," he said in his quietest, iciest, most implacable voice.

"He was *offering*, you deranged bender." Sebastian-Miles-Crispin-Whoever dabbed at his mouth. "Shitting Christ, my tooth. You don't just hit people."

I was almost glad I couldn't see much of Caspian's face because whatever it was doing made the other guy take a hasty step back. "For every rule," he murmured, "there is a necessary exception. I suggest you leave before you induce me to make it a second time."

My ex-date squared his shoulders, his upper-class armor snapping back into place—impressive, in a way, considering he was drooling blood. "You'll be hearing from my family…and my family's lawyer…and probably the police as well."

As threats went, even I could see it was trying to do too much at once. But if I'd been on my own, I would still have been fucking terrified. My family had mice in the basement. His family—whoever they were—had a lawyer.

Caspian just handed over his business card. "I shall await your call."

Tarquin-Robert-Hugo stood there for a second or two longer, radiating dissatisfaction. Then he turned without another word and strode off.

I didn't see where he went.

I didn't care.

I pushed myself upright on shaky legs—thank you, friend

wall—and ran, thoughtless, heedless, frantic, into Caspian's arms.

I wasn't sure what I was expecting. Maybe that he would push me into a puddle as I deserved. But he just held me tight, whispering into my hair, "Oh, Arden, my Arden." And then in quite a different tone, giving me a little shake, "What the hell is wrong with you? How could you be so stupid?"

"I'm sorry," I wailed. "I…I didn't think you were coming."

"Well neither did I. But that's no reason to fuck someone in an alley."

"It was oral sex."

"I think you'll find that's semantics."

I tried to surreptitiously wipe my eyes on my sleeve. "I'm sorry, I'm sorry. Please don't be angry. I didn't want to be with him, not really, but I'd been leading him on all evening and I didn't think he was going to stop and—"

That was when the tears came. Couldn't I have one encounter with Caspian Hart where I didn't cry?

He made an exasperated sound. "Would you…please don't do that."

"S-sorry."

He reached out a hand. Maybe he was trying to comfort me. Or intending to hold me.

If so, it would have been nice.

Unfortunately, my body chose that moment to register its disapproval of that night's particular cocktail: Shitty Times Up Against The Wall With A Twist. Misery, anxiety, shame, and fear, muddled with far too much alcohol and served long.

It felt briefly like I was turning inside out.

And then I was wretchedly sick.

In that intense, interminable, helplessly disgusting drunken way. Sobbing and heaving and shaking with the force of it.

Eventually I became aware that Caspian had an arm around me, keeping me steady against his body. And then he was pushing a soft, cotton handkerchief into my hand. And, oh fuck oh fuck oh fuck, I'd probably just thrown up on his shoes.

I opened my mouth to apologize but that just made my stomach decide that more of my innards wanted to be outards. The second wave was even worse than the first. Painful spasms of mortification and bile, when I was already weak from my previous adventure in Vomitlandia.

And when I was done—done again—I felt like lying down in the street, ideally to die.

Caspian sighed.

It was the most devastating noise I'd ever heard.

And absolutely the last thing I wanted from a man who had once maybe fancied me. Fancied me enough to put bits of himself into bits of me at any rate. You probably didn't feel that way about boys who'd just regurgitated their guts all over you.

I mumbled another sorry. What the fuck else was I going to do?

He sighed *again*. "For God's sake, stop apologizing."

He would probably have stepped away from me—and I wouldn't have blamed him—but the moment he moved, I wobbled pathetically, and he pulled me back to his side. It wasn't a kindly hold. It was protective like Kevlar, which was to say: solid and impersonal. But I was feeling so fragile and hollowed out that it was just what I needed. A certainty of strength.

I turned into him, as though I could hide from everything—him, me, the whole damn universe—in the crook of his arm.

"Come along," he said.

He tugged and I followed, stumbling as the world rocked around me. "Where are we going?"

"I'm taking you to bed."

I was drunk enough for this idea to swing me effortlessly, and almost instantly, from the depths of shame to wild optimism. "I thought you'd never ask."

"Where you will sleep."

"Oh." I peered up at him. Making my eyes as big as they could go.

He cleared his throat. "Alone."

I flopped against his shoulder as he hustled me along. Vaguely aware we were on the street now. All gold and hazy.

"That's your stern voice," I told him. Because it was. "I love your stern voice."

"Arden..."

"Thass your stern voice too. S'all sweet and shudder-making." I moaned with longing, stumbling into him this time, trying to get even closer. "Makes me want to get on my knees for you. Feel your hands on me. Your teeth. Your cock inside me. Want to suffer for you and scream and beg and make you happy—"

"This is my annoyed voice, Arden. Because I am annoyed. It's a wonder you're not in hospital. Or at the police station."

I smiled up at him. Floaty somehow. "But you rescued me."

"I didn't rescue you. I just…happened to be there."

"In *Pretty Woman*, when Richard Gere comes to rescue Julia Roberts, she rescues him right back."

"What in God's name are you talking about?"

I was going to answer, I really was, but everything was spinning away from me. Darkness lapping at the corners of my eyes.

I felt weightless suddenly, and I thought I'd fallen.

But there was no ground. Only sky.

And warmth. Such deep warmth. Covering me. Holding me.

Then—

Nothing.

CHAPTER 13

My first thought on waking up was that I wished I hadn't. Unconsciousness had been suiting me just fine.

Holy God.

Everything hurt. Literally everything. My stomach, my head, my throat. Even my fingernails were throbbing. I tried to open my eyes but my eyelashes had been replaced with needles and the light sliced right into the squishy bits of my face.

I would have groaned but it was absolutely beyond me.

Rolling over, I nudged my head under the pillow, finding some small solace in the darkness there.

Which was when it hit me: this wasn't my bed. This wasn't my room.

I had no fucking clue where I was.

Ahhhhhh.

I spread my arms. Then my legs. Didn't even get close to the edge. The covers felt crisp and light and smooth against my skin, the way only really expensive stuff does. Certainly not like my budget duvet and inevitably unwashed sheets.

Against my *skin*?

Oh fuck. Nakedness.

I was naked.

What had I done?

I eased the pillow off my head. Unlocked my eyes. Tried not to whimper as the light came at me again, brighter and harder this time.

Gradually, though, my vision cleared and I managed to focus on a glass of water standing on the posh table thing next to the bed. It looked like just about the most beautiful thing I'd ever seen. Clear and cool and perfectly pure.

I groped for it, motor functions also somewhat compromised, and took a swallow. It settled a little uncomfortably in my stomach, but it tasted amazing. It tasted of nothing. Of *clean*. In the filth that was my mouth.

And left me feeling at least 20 percent alive.

Then I heard the rustle of a page turning. I had another go at *looking* and the middle distance resolved itself into a hotel suite. Not a room. A suite. A really posh one if the chandeliers were anything to go by. French doors led from the bedroom bit, where the ruin of Arden St. Ives was to be found, to the living area, where Caspian Hart was sitting on a purple damask sofa, reading the *Times*.

Images from last night hit me like shrapnel: being carried in his arms through the foyer of the Randolph Hotel, the press of his body against mine as I blundered through the streets, the alley behind the club, the boy I'd pulled—

God.

All disordered fragments.

And too many gaps.

"So you're awake." Caspian didn't glance up from the paper. He seemed slightly more rumpled than usual without his tie and jacket, the sleeves of his shirt rolled up to show his forearms, all sinewy loveliness, flecked by dark hair. But even a little bit undone he was unassailable. Exquisite. A study in absolute assurance.

"Um." It came out as a croak. "Yeah."

The nakedness thing was rapidly becoming a big deal. Parts of my body I'd never previously considered—my elbows and knees and flanks—were getting prickly and self-conscious. "Look, uh, why are you...I mean...why am I...did we..."

He put down the paper. Turned the impossible blueness of his eyes on me. All ice this morning. "Arden, are you seriously asking if I fucked an inebriated child immediately after extricating him from a situation that would very likely have devolved into rape?"

Well at least he hadn't been put off by the vomiting.

"I'm not a child," I mumbled.

"Then stop acting like one."

"I'm pretty sure that going clubbing and getting drunk are PEGI 18 activities."

"Being immoderate, undisciplined, and incapable of taking care of yourself, however, are not."

I tugged the covers up to my chin. "I can take care of myself. That guy wasn't going to...going to do anything."

"Considering how excised you were when you thought I'd offered your college a donation in exchange for a blow job, I'm somewhat surprised at your willingness to sexually barter yourself in an alley."

"I wasn't bartering." I tugged at my hair, which felt awful and smelled worse. Clubs and smoke and sweat and other people's hands. "I just…I just didn't want him to fuck me."

Caspian sighed. The sound felt familiar somehow. He rose with easy grace and came into the bedroom. There was something weirdly normal, even domestic about it, as if I were his lover and this a morning in our life.

Except none of that was true. This was a hotel room. He was Caspian Hart. And I was naked and ashamed.

He sat down on the edge of the bed. "Didn't anyone ever tell you no means no?"

"I'm not an idiot or a psychopath. I was taught that at school, by my parents, by my own conscience. I would never—"

"I meant you."

I flinched from the way he was looking at me. Sometimes his gentleness was the most terrifying thing of all. "I wasn't saying no."

"Did you want to have sex with him?"

"Well, no, but that's not the point."

"What was the point?"

"I…that way…I wasn't…" I was way too hungover for this. "I was still in control, okay? It was still my choice."

His mouth tightened but it seemed his annoyance wasn't for me. For once. "I could kill that boy."

"I'm okay. He was just…a bit…"

"Violence is not the only form of coercion, and coercion has no place in sex. And you shouldn't do things you don't want to do. Ever."

"I know. It's just..." I picked at the snowy white sheets. "I don't want to be punished for liking sex. It's not my fault the world is fucked up."

Now it was his turn to glance away. "And I don't want you to get hurt."

"No offense, but that's pretty ironic coming from the man who rejected me twice."

"That was...I thought it was for the best."

"And you know something else?" It was hard, after last night, to have much by way of credibility, but I was still the same person who'd been thrilled to suck him off on a balcony. Who'd chased him to London. Who'd hurt myself for his asking and my own pleasure. "Yes, last night wasn't what I wanted. He was wrong and I was messed up and I'm glad nothing happened. But I know what I'm doing and I know what I like and sometimes"—it was even harder saying this shit to a man's profile—"with the right person when it's done in the right way...that can include...I guess...certain types of coercion." *Like your hands on my wrists, your voice on the phone.*

I waited for him to get it. To understand. To admit the connection between us.

Instead he was silent for...well...basically ever. And then, "So you intimated last night."

Not what I was looking, or hoping, for.

And...wait...I did what?

Sorting through last night's memories was like peering into a stranger's sock drawer.

And then: me, him, this bed, with its canopy and pristine sheets. He was trying to get me to drink water, exasperated with my drunkenness, my lack of caution, my lack of self-restraint. And I—oh God—I'd sprawled over his lap, offering myself up eagerly for any punishment he wished to bestow.

He hadn't of course.

My arse clenched in shame.

"Why don't you take a shower?" he asked, dismissal couched as a question. "You'll probably feel better after."

"Okay." Like I was *ever* going to feel good again.

He disappeared into the living area, closing the doors behind him. There was a fluffy hotel dressing gown at the foot of the bed. I couldn't help wondering if he'd worn it as I shambled over and struggled into it. Then shuffled miserably to the bathroom.

It was all shininess in there, hurting my eyes and making my head ache.

I curled up in the bottom of the bath and let the shower pound me. It was so typical that, after three years of student facilities, I wasn't in any mood to appreciate the awesome on offer here. I'd missed really hot water and really clean baths. And hotels were exciting: all those little bottles of luxury shampoo and conditioner and body wash and moisturizer, jewel-bright in the gathering steam.

Right now, I was too depressed to even think about stealing them. I wished I could swirl away down the drain with the rest of the dirty water.

And I couldn't help indulging myself with a mean little fantasy that, maybe one day, somehow, Caspian Hart would be vulnerable, exposed, and I would be the one choosing to be kind.

Except it would never happen. I was the faller-over and the fucker-upper, and he would never, ever be vulnerable to me.

And I owed him. I owed him big-time.

It was the hollowest feeling of all: gratitude to this man—this beautiful, cold, unexpectedly compassionate man—who didn't want me.

I turned off the shower and toweled myself dry. Wrapped myself in the dressing gown again and went back to receive my third...fourth...fifth rejection from Caspian Hart.

He was sitting on the sofa again, his face turned toward the bow window, beyond which I could see the leafy boulevard of St. Giles and the intricate carvings of the Martyrs' Memorial. It was a little odd to be parallel with the top of it. I'd eaten kebab-van chips on the steps often enough.

On the table in front of him was a properly impressive breakfast, complete with little baskets of pastries, racks of perfectly browned toast, those individual pots of jam I'd always found super tempting, and a collection of shiny cloches concealing what was probably full English deliciousness. I could smell bacon and while the spirit was definitely willing, the flesh was slightly dubious.

Caspian's attention flicked from the picture-postcard vista to the decidedly less picture-postcard me.

"Um, hi." I was all covered up, but there was something startlingly intimate about damp hair and bare feet.

Even more so when his eyes lingered on me. "You look different."

Try defenseless. Without my tight jeans and my engineered

hair, my jackets and my jewelry. My armor of queerness and accessibility. "Thanks for last night. I'm really sorry for putting you to all this hassle."

"It was nothing."

"How did you even find me? Were you looking for me?"

"I…yes. You'd posted pictures of your activities on various social media platforms, so you weren't exactly difficult to track. I arrived at the club just as you were leaving with your…with your swain."

"You didn't have to do all this though." I gestured at the room. "I'd have been fine."

He shrugged. "I didn't feel comfortable leaving you alone."

Oh wow. Way to make me feel even more of an unpleasant imposition. "Look, I should, um, go—"

"Sit down, Arden."

The command crackled up my spine. And, for once, I resented it. He didn't get to do that. Not now. "Where are my clothes?"

"I said sit down."

I sat down mutinously. Fuck.

Then he went all quiet on me. There was water on the table, in one of those classy-looking misted bottles, and he leaned forward to pour me a glass. "You should keep drinking. And maybe try to eat something."

"Right." I didn't want to be snapped at again and it was good advice. Only semi-mutinously, I took a sip of water. Wishing he would get on with it. Whatever *it* was.

But, for some reason, he still wasn't saying anything. He was just sitting there, watching me, as unreadable and unreachable as ever.

Except, there was a tightness to his jaw, to his carefully positioned hands. And I wasn't sure, but his foot was... not quite moving, but twitching as if he was trying very hard to keep it still. It was my first true glimpse of the restless boy he'd told me he used to be.

It softened me toward him.

Even if I was still confused and hurt and embarrassed and epically hungover.

"Arden," he began.

"Still here. Sitting as ordered."

"Arden, I want to fuck you."

He wanted to... Gosh. Well. I hadn't been expecting that.

Especially not when I felt—and probably looked—like I'd been shat out by a gastrically distressed camel.

But it was Caspian Hart. Offering me something I could barely even begin to imagine. Would he fuck me like he kissed me? As though I were his world to be conquered? Come undone as he had with his cock down my throat? Passion-flayed, whispering my name like it was the only word he could remember.

"Um, sure, okay." I stood and undid the cord of the dressing grown. "Let's go."

He recoiled a little. "Not now. Not like this."

"Oh." I grinned hopefully at him. "Are you going to take me to dinner first?"

"Please sit down. And be serious. This is a negotiation."

I hadn't been aware of being unserious but I sat down again, not sure I was entirely happy with where this might be going. "Sleeping with me is a negotiation?"

"Well." He crossed one leg over the other, his whole body taut now, a bow bereft of an arrow. "You said yourself there is a spectrum between casual sex and a relationship. I require neither, but I do wish to have sex with you on a short-term, prearranged basis."

Was I dreaming? Or still drunk? He wanted me? He really wanted me? Wait. He wanted me on a...*short-term, prearranged basis*? "Wow, you could turn a boy's head with dirty talk like that."

He gave me a look that probably made him the terror of boardrooms from here to New York: banked ferocity and merciless conviction. But it was so...so *practiced*, I wondered if he was nervous.

Nervous?

No. Caspian Hart would never be nervous.

"You have expressed quite plainly your desire to sleep with me on no less than three occasions. And on at least one of them you were sober. There's very little purpose in dissembling now."

He was right. But also wrong. It wasn't that I was unconvincingly attempting to play hard to get. It was just difficult to get all that excited about negotiation. "I'm sorry, I'm not dissembling. I'm just, you know, swept off my feet here by the passion of your invitation."

"I would not be suggesting it if I did not want this very much." He sounded faintly irritated. As though admitting he wanted me was some kind of concession he'd been obliged to make. And his foot did this jerky little tap that he stopped almost at once.

I tilted my head, instinctively quizzical at all the contradictions here, and then wished I hadn't because it made my dehydrated brain flop around painfully. Was this why he'd come to Oxford? To arrange to have sex with me? Or to actually have sex with me, only to discover I was pissed off my head and about to go down on another bloke? "But you said no before. What changed?"

"Nothing changed. That is"—he hesitated a moment—"what changed was my understanding."

"Um, I'm going to need more than that."

His fingers twisted. Knotted. Turned white at the knuckles. "I've always wanted you. I just overestimated my capacity to resist it... resist you."

"And me throwing up all over myself totally sealed the deal? Because I'm pretty sure some people would have been put off."

"You were worried about that?"

"Well, yeah, just a bit."

He gave me an odd, soft smile and this whimsical "abracadabra" gesture. "It's forgotten."

I found myself smiling. The most painful thing about Caspian Hart wasn't desiring him; it was liking him.

"And while," he went on, "I would prefer you didn't make a habit of inebriation, I found far more to dislike in the way that boy was touching you."

"I wasn't too keen on it myself." Trying my best to make light.

"I hated it."

The fervor in his voice surprised me. I glanced up and discovered him looking particularly wolfish, eyes burning with this possessive, predatory light I—honestly—found wildly exciting. And felt bad about finding wildly exciting. "Um, sorry."

"I hated his hands on you. I hated seeing you on your knees for him."

God. Moral quandary. On the one hand, this was way better than negotiation. On the other, it seemed mean-spirited to feel good about someone else feeling bad. Although maybe if he'd sounded less irritated about being into me, I wouldn't have been stuck hoarding scraps of jealousy. "I wasn't really on my knees. I was more sort of too drunk to stand."

"I've never struck anyone before." Some of the wildness faded from Caspian's expression, leaving him the closest to flustered I'd ever seen him, a flush caressing the arch of his cheekbones. "It was inappropriate."

Surely he wasn't embarrassed?

"Oh no." I slipped from the edge of the chair where I'd been perched and knelt down next to him. Not in a subby way, just in a needing to be close way. I wanted to touch him, but I didn't quite dare. If he'd been a different man, if we hadn't been *negotiating*, I'd have propped my chin playfully on his thigh like a puppy. As it was, I just smiled up at him. "It was heroic. The most heroic thing anyone has ever done for me. It made me feel like a princess."

He laughed, the flush deepening and spreading beautifully. I wondered if he would blush like that when I touched him. Life breathed into marble. "I'm afraid I'm a poor choice of knight. I don't think punching people lies within my skill set."

That was when I noticed the mess of his knuckles. "Oh, Caspian."

He covered one hand with the other. "It's nothing."

"It's not nothing." I reached out and he drew away. "You're hurt."

"Faces seem to be harder than hands. Teeth especially."

"Can I see?"

"It's hardly—"

"Please."

He wouldn't look at me but he let me uncurl his fingers. Rest his palm lightly on mine as I contemplated the damage. Truthfully, it wasn't so bad, except for the fact that he'd earned those wounds for me. He'd cleaned himself up, but there was still some swelling amid the scraped skin and the shadows of burgeoning bruises.

He had such gorgeous hands: elegant and strong and lived in, with pronounced bones and ropey veins, long knotty fingers and well-kept nails. Acquisitive, powerful hands, for taking and claiming. I wanted them on me. In me. I wanted to make them tremble.

But right now, I didn't want him to hurt because of me.

"I've got an idea." I reached behind me to where I'd left my water glass. There were still some pieces of ice in the bottom. I chased them with my fingers until I managed to snag one. Sucked it until it was completely smooth. And then brought it very gently to his knuckles.

He gave a soft hiss.

"Too cold?"

"It's ice, Arden. Ice is cold."

"Maybe if I had something to wrap it in. I think I saw a washcloth in the bathroom."

I was about to stand when his other hand caught me by the wrist. "Don't go."

Ridiculous really because it was only a room away but such was the intensity of the moment that I forgot.

I forgot everything except the pressure of his hand and the urgency of his voice. The stark yearning in his eyes.

Icy water was dripping into my palm, sliding down my arm, my fingers turning numb.

But I didn't care about that either.

Just his mouth, hot on mine, as he leaned over me and kissed my chilled lips. It was an awkward position, unbalancing, but I arched into his touch, letting desire shape me. I loved being unbalanced by him, controlled by him. It was its own power—its own freedom—and it made me feel so good. So good, so safe, and so marvelously claimed.

Next thing I knew he was bending me back, pushing me down onto that plush hotel carpet. He caught my other hand and pulled them both over my head. He seemed to like me that way, pinned, stretched, helpless, *his*.

Well. That made two of us.

Although there was part of me that ached to touch him back. To know what it would be like to tangle my fingers in his hair. Stroke the skin at the nape of his neck. Feel the muscles of his shoulders tighten like wings beneath my palms. I wanted him to have everything. All the pleasure it was in me to give.

His suit was rough against my skin and I expected his kiss to be rough as well.

But he didn't kiss me. Only looked at me with lust-glittery eyes. Then groaned. "Oh God, how do you do this to me?"

CHAPTER 14

It was a reasonable question. And I was buggered if I knew the answer. As far as I could tell, there was nothing about me that would attract—let alone hold—the attention of someone like Caspian Hart.

Capacity for happiness notwithstanding.

And, yes, I did remember every nice thing he'd ever said to me. Squirreling them away like string and marbles in a kid's keepsake box.

"I don't know," I told him. "But I like it."

He frowned, the pained line I so wished to soothe away appearing between his brows. "I don't like it. I don't want to want this. But I can't stop."

Way to bring me back to earth with a bump. "Pro tip. When you're attempting to negotiate a short-term, preapproved sexual encounter with somebody, maybe don't tell them how much you're resenting it?"

He released me and sprang to his feet, leaving me sprawled

and disheveled on the carpet like a virgin sacrifice. Well, except for the virgin bit, obviously. I sat up, hugging my knees and trying to protect what little was left of my modesty while Caspian paced.

He looked irritatingly gorgeous. Those long, lean lines of his and his natural grace, the flow of muscles beneath fabric far too suggestive of the way they might shift and tighten against me when we moved together.

If.

If we ever moved together.

Which was looking unlikely if he continued with the sub-Darcy "in vain I have struggled" crap.

"I'm sorry, Arden." He swept around and gazed at me with a kind of bewildered anguish that was as heartbreaking as it was frustrating. "I don't mean to insult you. I've just never..."

He seemed to run out of steam, so I tried to help out. "You've never fancied someone before?"

"I've never been consumed by it before. Never taken beyond reason. Never allowed it to distract me."

"Sometimes I don't know whether I want to hug you or punch you."

His lips curled into a wry, wary smile. "I wouldn't advocate punching. Clearly there's an art to it."

Goddamn him. The gorgeous impossible contradictory bastard.

Refusing to smile back, though everything in me wanted to, I scrambled to my feet and curled up on the edge of the sofa. "Right. Well. We both want to shag. What are we negotiating here, exactly?"

After a second or two, he sat down next to me. It was probably the most normal moment of togetherness we'd ever had, and at first, I didn't know how to handle it. It said something about your relationship with someone when you were more freaked out by sharing the same piece of furniture than wanking for them down the phone.

"I don't want you to have any false expectations about what I expect from you," he said. "And about what I can give you."

"Really? Because after that opening, I'm expecting a proposal any second now." I gave him my most coquettish, under-the-lashes look. "For the record, I'm planning to say yes."

He pulled away. "This was a mistake."

Fuck. *Fuck.*

"Nononono. It wasn't. Tell me how it would work. Please. I'm listening."

"I'm not precisely experienced in this area myself."

"And what area would that be? The short-term, preapproved sexual-encounter area?"

He was quiet a moment. "Arden, I'm not trying to hurt you or insult you. I want you. I want you very much indeed. But I am simply not accustomed to...to feeling like this." I was about to make some crack about how we experienced emotions sometimes on planet Earth, but he went on gently. "And I'm not going to lie to you. I won't pretend I enjoy being at the mercy of my inclinations. I won't claim I'm not hoping that we can do this and then I will be free of it."

"You mean free of me."

He nodded.

"So let me get this straight. You want to bang me silly until

I'm out of your system and you can get on with your life?"

Another nod.

"Well, while that's very flattering, I'm not entirely sure what's in it for me?"

His fingers curled lightly over my wrist. It was probably the closest he had ever come to a touch that wasn't sexual and I didn't know what it meant. Only that I liked it: the play of his skin against my own. "You get me out of your system too."

I stared stupidly at his hand on mine as if I was expecting a magic show, all rainbow light and sparkles of happiness flowing between us. Hastily looking up, I met his eyes instead. They were cool and composed again, just like he was. "But what if I don't want you out of my system?"

"You should. You will. I won't be good for you."

By accident or design, his thumb was resting against my pulse point, the gathering heat its own caress. I heard myself make a shameless, gaspy noise. "I think that's for me to decide."

"God, Arden." He let out a harsh breath. "Are you always like this?"

"Like what?"

"So responsive."

It was a complicated question. Without going all Xtube about it, I didn't see the point of *not* being responsive. Otherwise where was the fun? Having sex and not responding would be like going on a roller coaster and not screaming. But, no, I didn't usually swoon when somebody touched my arm. "Um, maybe, but it's...it's different with you," I admitted. "Maybe it's a pheromone thing?"

"What?"

"I read in a magazine once that there's something about… how people smell. Like if somebody smells delicious to you, you're probably more than usually sexually compatible." I leaned in a little and inhaled the fading traces of his cologne, that old-worldy mix of wood and spice and cocoa, and the clean, masculine scent of his skin. "And you always smell amazing."

He shuddered, eyes half closing in what could only have been pleasure, the promise of sensuality softening his loveliness like shadow. "Can we please restrict ourselves to the topic at hand?"

"This *is* the topic at hand. What if you get me out of your system before I get you out of mine? What if I'm cyanide and you're arsenic?"

"Then we'd both be dead."

"Yes, but you'd be dead quickly and I'd linger in confused agony. I don't want to linger in confused agony."

His lips twitched. "No, I can understand that. Which is why I believe we should agree on an end date."

"I don't think we've even agreed on a start."

"We haven't agreed on anything," he said sharply, "because you keep interrupting."

I could have pointed out that *he* nearly kissed *me*. But I just apologized meekly—though probably not entirely convincingly—and waited for him to continue.

"Do you have plans now that you've finished your degree?"

"Um, you've met me, right?"

"I assume that's a no. In which case, why don't you stay in London? In one of my apartments."

For a negotiated prearranged wossname, that seemed kind of intense. "You want me to live with you?"

"No, in one of my apartments."

And that wasn't much better. "Like your...your...mistress?"

"No." He sighed. "Like someone who is staying in the apartment of someone he knows."

"But I should pay you rent or something, right?"

"Arden, believe me, you could not afford the rent. I'm simply offering you somewhere to stay so you don't have to worry about accommodation or living expenses while you apply for jobs or internships and decide what you want to do with your life. Something I expect you would find difficult from Kinlochbervie."

I smiled at him helplessly, warmed, charmed, as touched as I had been the first time he recalled some minor detail about my life. "You remembered."

"You knew I would."

I swallowed. What he was offering seemed...I had no idea. How were you supposed to think about something like that? And it wasn't exactly like I could phone a friend. Nik would probably tell me I was nuts for giving the guy the time of day after he'd had me peremptorily chauffeured out of London.

But I liked him and I wanted him. And he'd come for me when I'd needed someone. Needed him. Looked after me when he could have, well, not done that.

"And this is the plan?" I asked. "I live in your place and you...uh...we...uh...and after a set time we stop?"

He nodded. "I'm aware it's probably not...not what is commonly done."

I could have responded with the *you think* he deserved, but he looked so uncertain I didn't have the heart.

"But," he went on, "I'm afraid it's what I can offer. I've tried to make it practically appealing for you. And I'd be very willing to provide additional financial support, although I suspect that would offend you. I assure you, however, it would be compensation for inconvenience rather than compensation for…services."

There were way too many things wrong with this. But, for some reason, what struck me just then was how seriously he was underselling himself. "Look, if I do this, it'll be because of you, not because of what you can do for me."

He glanced away, blushing a little, hand tightening on my wrist. "I believe you. But I…I'm afraid I have some particularities—some limitations, perhaps—upon which I cannot compromise."

"Well." I twisted my fingers back to brush against his. "I'm pretty sure that's what being human is like."

"You know," he said softly, "you could sell this story."

"Oh don't start that again. First off, nobody would believe me. Second off, I'd look like a complete dick."

He brought my hand to his mouth and kissed the inside of my wrist. And while I was busy dying and melting and catching fire and stuff, he murmured, "Truth has no place in journalism. You really don't have any notion how the world works, do you?"

"Your world, where people only have sex in exchange for stuff and constantly think of selling shit to the papers, no." It sounded good in my head, but unfortunately my voice came out all wobbly. Because I could feel the texture of his lips and the warmth of his breath against the very softest places of my skin.

"I considered trying to intimidate you with a nonsensical NDA. But I could never have held you to it."

"I'm not a— Oh God that's..." His tongue. Tracing the vein. "I'm n-not an idiot. You couldn't...like sue me for breach of sexual contract."

"No." His eyes met mine over my captured hand. "I have to trust you."

Desire was a powerful thing on its own terms, but mixed with tenderness it was almost overwhelming. What an extraordinary and unexpected gift: trust from a man who clearly didn't offer it often. "You're safe with me, Caspian. I promise."

He laughed. "I'm not safe. Not even a little bit. But thank you."

There he went again with the doomy pronouncements. But I didn't really mind. It just made me more determined to prove to him that he could have all this with me. Normal, everyday things. Loyalty and happiness and sex. Maybe the loss of them was the price of everything else he had. But what was the point of having so much if it cost you so dearly? "Tell me these non-negotiable conditions."

I was kind of, not braced exactly because it didn't require bracing, but at the very least waiting for him to disclose the shocker that he was more than a little bit kinky.

Which I'd definitely already noticed. What with having two eyes and a clue.

And the memory of sore nipples.

"I'm afraid," he said, "that I must insist upon a certain logistical inequality."

I'd been indulging an exciting little fantasy involving handcuffs, a peacock feather, and one of those jeweled butt plugs I'd seen on the Internet. I stopped. "You what?"

"I'm a very busy man. And my schedule is both restrictive and inflexible. It's not something I can change, and I'm afraid—selfish as it may be—I don't want to be troubled by any disappointment or frustration that may cause you."

"You mean, when you want me, you expect me to be available and you don't want to have to worry about my feelings?"

He had the grace to look embarrassed. "I...yes."

I thought about it. On the surface it sounded pretty unappealing but, then, in most of my attempted relationships, I'd usually been left feeling smothered and impatient by my partner's apparent insistence that I live in their goddamn pocket. So maybe an arrangement like this would suit me better. And, looking at it purely rationally, it made a degree of sense. Maybe when I was a billionaire instead of a graduate, then we could live to my schedule. "Sure."

"Are you quite certain?"

"Yeah, it seems fair. It's not like I'm going to be busy. What's next?" I grinned.

Okay, now *tell me all the terrible, wicked, shocking, wonderful things you want to do with me.*

"I expect our arrangement to be exclusive."

"That's fine. Next?"

To my surprise, he didn't seem entirely pleased by my answer. "At least think a moment, Arden."

"What's there to think about?"

"Do you understand what I'm asking?"

"Yes. You don't want me to fuck around while I'm fucking you, which is no concession at all because, frankly, if I'm going to be fucking you, I can't imagine *wanting* to fuck anyone else."

"And you'll need to take the full battery of sexual health tests."

Okay, that was going a bit too far. "What the hell are you implying? Yes, I've slept around but I'm not Alexander Fleming's petri dish."

"It's nothing personal. I'll be doing the same."

"Or, alternatively, we could not perpetuate the stereotype that—"

"I have no intention of using a condom when I take you, Arden."

Well, that was different. Exciting. And shiver-inducingly intimate in a way I wouldn't have expected. I'd never...well, nobody had ever...it had never come up before.

His voice had turned husky, edging toward that growl I loved inspiring. "You'll be mine, and I will not countenance even a scrap of latex between us."

And oh good God. I was painfully hard, dripping into a hotel dressing gown on promises alone. I didn't trust myself to sound even a little bit not desperately aroused, so I nodded. *Yes. That.*

"Then I believe the matter is settled."

Was it? But what about the...the other stuff? Or did he just assume I'd be up for it? Which, considering I'd spent last night presenting my arse like a clay pigeon for him to take potshots at, was entirely reasonable.

I wondered if I should have been volunteering the fact that, barring a few not entirely successful experiments, my enthusiasm far outstripped my experience in this particular area. But I didn't know what to say or how to ask him: *Sooo, Caspian, are you just into pinning my wrists and roughing me up or will I be crawling on the floor and calling you master?*

"What…um…what about the end date?" Okay, I wussed it.

"I would suggest six months. You'll probably have something else to do at that point anyway."

He probably meant a job.

Well, I could hope.

It'd be nearly Christmas by then, and it seemed like forever and yet, somehow, no time at all. I couldn't even imagine what it might be like or how I'd feel afterward. For a moment, or a lot of moments, I couldn't tell; I just sat there, horny and confused and hopeful and anxious, torn between feeling wanted and feeling *handled*.

But, seriously, what was I going to say? *No, I won't live in your house for free and be your logistically unequal prenegotiated sex partner. No, I'd rather have nothing than six months with you on your terms. No, I don't want to be yours.*

He was very still beside me.

"Okay," I said. "I'm in."

It was probably a really stupid idea.

But then he smiled at me and for this brief, uninhibited second, he looked so happy that I was sure I'd done the right thing.

That everything was worth it for the power to give Caspian Hart just a little bit of joy.

CHAPTER 15

I wasn't quite sure what being the not-quite-live-in lover of a kinky billionaire was supposed to be like. But my imaginings turned out to be way off.

The apartment Caspian had nonchalantly offered me was part of this crazy glass and steel-bladed monolith called One Hyde Park. He sent a car to pick me up from Oxford, which was, y'know, considerate. Except somehow I'd expected him to be there when I arrived, so we could fall on each other in a mutual frenzy of desperate passion and have sex everywhere, in all the ways—up against the wall, knocking stuff off tables, even on the stairs like in the remake of the *Thomas Crown Affair*. I mean, for example.

But it was the middle of the day and Caspian was obviously at work and waiting for me instead was— Oh no. The blond guy from Caspian's office. The one who'd had to call security on me.

He was even more intimidatingly attractive up close: all lips and cheekbones and symmetry, the sort of face you'd expect to see on a billboard for a product that would cost the earth and basically make no difference to your overall attractiveness.

"You must be Arden." He shook my hand before I had a chance to make sure it wasn't sweaty and awful. "Justin Bellerose. I work for Caspian Hart."

"Um. Yes. I remember you."

"Likewise."

I gave a horrified bleat. "You sure you haven't muddled me up with someone else who turned up without an appointment and called your boss an arsehole?"

He didn't laugh. Didn't even look a teensy bit amused. This was going super well. "Caspian asked me to help you settle in. And you'll need a retinal scan."

"What? Why?"

"Security."

It felt a lot like being arrested—well, the way being arrested looked in the movies. I was scanned, coded, fingerprinted, visually identified, practically strip searched, and eventually permitted into the lift with Bellerose, who had waited with this terrible patience through the whole extensive procedure.

He reminded me a little bit of Caspian. Not that they were actually all that similar, unless you counted the fact that they were both scary hot, but I could imagine them having devastatingly efficient conversations together. Even more disconcerting was the realization that Bellerose couldn't have been much older than me, and he was already executive assistant to one of the richest, most powerful men in the UK.

Oh God. I was doomed.

"This way, please."

I trailed after him into the apartment and it was…I mean, holy fuck, it looked like a picture in a magazine. Beautiful in this totally unreal way. Everything was marble and granite and silk and…*designed.* In these somehow extravagantly muted colors, taupe and cream and pearl gray. I was lowering the value of the place just by being there.

"Guest bedroom," murmured Bellerose, pointing languidly, "and bathroom. Guest cloakroom. Master bedroom."

So much…gleaminess. And the sense of space. I think they called it lateral living or something. For people too rich for, like, rooms.

Bellerose peeled my hands off my embarrassingly shabby suitcase, put it down by the bed, and ushered me into the master bathroom, where he showed me how to use the shower. It was this shining marble enclosure where water came at you from everywhere. I wasn't sure how much of it I took in but, honestly, there were probably U2 spy planes less complicated to operate.

Then back out into the…for want of a better term…hall area.

"Kitchen, sitting room, reception room—"

"Sitting room *and* reception room?"

An elegant shrug. "One for sitting, one for receiving—"

As ever when slightly nervous, I regressed to about the age of thirteen and started giggling.

"—guests," Bellerose finished coldly.

"Sorry."

"Dining room, study, shower room, balcony."

"Thank you."

"Finally, this is for you."

This was a phone—the latest model iSomething. I took it instinctively and then wished I hadn't. "I thought only prostitutes, drug dealers, and spies needed two phones."

"There's an app on there that controls the apartment. You can use it as needed or program it in advance, if you want the heating or lights or a particular electronic device to activate or deactivate at a certain time, for example."

"And I couldn't just download it for myself because…?"

Bellerose clearly had a PhD in ignoring people. Well, ignoring me. "The phone," he went on smoothly, "also contains Caspian's contact information in London, New York, Lisbon, Berlin, Tokyo, and Beijing. And you can access one of Caspian's drivers, a range of restaurants and private caterers, masseurs, hairdressers, manicurists, tailors, and similar services, all of whom are at your disposal. The apartment will be maintained daily and the details of the cleaning company are likewise to be found in the address book. In the unlikely event of an emergency, a private security contractor can be summoned by using the relevant application. Or by triggering any of the panic buttons situated around the apartment."

"You do know that I'm not going into witness protection, right?"

"Finally, I am on speed dial one." He gave me a surprisingly sweet and boyish smile—though there was something chilling in it, too. Maybe it was just a little *too* perfect. "Please don't hesitate to call me should you need anything."

I shuffled, feeling overwhelmed and faintly awful. "Um. Thank you. But surely this isn't your job."

"My job is whatever Caspian needs."

Wow. Because that didn't have a ring of "pet assassin" or anything. Or maybe all the talk of panic buttons and private security firms had gone to my head. "I'll try not to bug you."

"Arden." It was the first time he'd used my name to directly address me, but he said it *meanly*, like I was someone else's dog who'd pissed on his carpet and he didn't feel it was his place to rebuke me. "I've been asked to look after you and I will do it to the best of my frankly considerable ability. However, if you make things more difficult than they have to be out of some misplaced bourgeois guilt, I will be quite displeased."

As I opened my mouth to reply, I hoped something appropriate and vaguely sensible would emerge. Except what happened was, "And I won't like you when you're displeased?"

Because weak attempts at humor had served me so well so far.

There was a tense little pause and then Bellerose continued. "Caspian mentioned you would be resistant to this next proposal."

Well, it was nice to know I'd briefly crossed his mind while he was making all these arrangements. And, oh God, I was being a dick. Caspian was letting me stay somewhere frankly incredible and my internal monologue was being super ungrateful about it. Just because I'd imagined—okay, hoped for—something different. "Um, okay?"

He produced a credit card. One of the terrifyingly plain

and discreet ones that you only got by having assets in the unthinkillions.

"Oh hell no," I said.

"He's not suggesting you go on a spree. Well, not unless you want to." His eyes, maybe unintentionally, did that up-and-down thing that people on TV property shows did when they were stuck with a fixer-upper. "But it's for emergencies."

"You mean so that when I'm kidnapped from the fifth floor of an impregnable building and haven't been able to summon a private security task force I can pay my own ransom?"

He sighed, very softly. "Take the card, Arden. Put it your wallet or in the freezer. I don't care. You don't have to use it."

"I don't want his money."

"He's not giving you money. He's giving you access to money in case you need it." Bellerose stepped past me and put the card on the dining table. The neat click of plastic against glass sounded way, way too loud. "And I should have mentioned, the building also contains a range of leisure and entertainment facilities, including a swimming pool, sauna, steam room, gymnasium and exercise studio, and spa. Now, do you have everything you need?"

"I have way more than any reasonable human could ever need."

"Then I can return to the office. Enjoy your stay." He sounded like Caspian again: polite and implacable. I wondered if it had rubbed off on him, same as pets were supposed to get like their owners—oops, that sounded bad—or if he'd always been that way. Maybe it was what had led to him being hired in the first place.

"Um, okay. Thanks."

He gave me a Jeevesy nod, if Jeeves had been infinitely hotter and quite a bit scarier. Then turned and walked away.

This threw me into a mini-panic because, since I technically lived here now, it was my middle-class duty to politely escort him to the door. Except, he was all tall and graceful with long strides like Caspian, which left me scampering after him in a ridiculously futile fashion.

"I guess you think this is pretty weird," I blurted out, just as he was about to leave.

He paused. "What I think has no relevance whatsoever."

And he was right. Apart from, y'know, the bit where I cared what he thought. I couldn't help it—he was close to Caspian; in fact, he was the only person I knew who *was* close to Caspian. So I didn't want him disapproving of me. Or believing I was a leechy gold-digging sponge type person. Or maybe I just wasn't used to having my personal logistics handled by someone else. And it was just about possible Bellerose was part of the whole arrangement in ways I far too pure-minded to contemplate.

Actually I *could* sort of imagine him standing discreetly to one side with the implements. Helping with the knots. Making the occasional suggestion…Okay that was pretty sexy. Apart from the bit where his suggestion would probably be "Why don't you fuck somebody better?"

I took a deep breath. "Look, you were honest with me earlier so…I guess I'll do the same? I really will try not to make your job more difficult but can you maybe be a touch less Mrs. Danvers about stuff?"

"What?"

On reflection, it wasn't the best comparison I could have made. "She's like this—"

"No, I get the reference."

"Oh good. I mean…not good. I mean, sorry."

He stared at me and I could almost feel frost crystalizing on my eyelashes. "I'm not entirely sure what you think is happening here. Caspian asked me to take care of you in accordance with his instructions. Quite why this has resulted in you casting me as a sinister housekeeper with suppressed lesbian desires I can't begin to imagine."

"Um"—I shuffled my feet, appalled at myself—"because I'm an idiot?"

To my surprise, he nearly smiled. "I'm only ever glad for Caspian's happiness. And, for the record, I would never maintain a shrine to his ex."

With that, he was gone. Leaving me alone in One Hyde Park. In an apartment that looked like a scene from a Tom Ford movie. For which I had been hideously miscast.

I unpacked my suitcase—though it took me longer to figure out how the wardrobes worked, since they were cunningly disguised as the wall. And then I laid my laptop ceremonially down on the desk in the study alcove. Where I would definitely be incredibly productive, and not spend all my time staring in blank intimidation at the sparkling temple of Harvey Nichols, which was literally just across the road.

And then I…honestly, I just sat around gingerly for a little while, feeling overwhelmed. I mean, here I was, in London, ready to take on the world. Except, oh God oh God oh God, how did you do that? How did you even start? Even leaving aside the fact that Oxford had left me woefully underprepared for entering into weird nonrelationships with emotionally distant billionaires.

Thankfully, when it came to that, I still had Julia Roberts in my corner. And so I knew exactly how to handle finding myself living in unexpected luxury.

Which was to say I ran into the master bedroom and flung myself across the perfect sheets with a "Wheeee!"

And, oh wow. It was like being cuddled by candyfloss.

A+

Would enter weird nonrelationship with emotionally distant billionaire again.

CHAPTER 16

In a little while, the new phone wuzzed—it was a text from Caspian, letting me know he'd be coming round later that evening. Which provided just enough motivation to make me stop rolling around the heavenly cloud of bed and investigate what else One Hyde Park had to offer.

Bellerose had run down a rather intimidating list of facilities, so I decided to investigate the swimming pool first, since I at least knew what a swimming pool was and what to do with it. Unfortunately, finding the damn was its own adventure. I ended up creeping through endless silent corridors, surrounded by mirrors and aluminum and padded silk—a bit like living in the world's most expensive sanatorium, all the time caught in the unblinking Argos gaze of innumerable security cameras.

When I eventually got there, the pool was pristine, its water still and silver-green. It was beautiful but also slightly eerie—like if I was in the wrong movie and tried to swim here,

I'd get knifed to death by a masked man for my lax sexual morals. But I splashed around for a while and wasn't horribly murdered. Which was nice. Afterward, I went back to the apartment for a shower and some, ahem, personal grooming because I wanted to look my best for Caspian. The prospect of seeing him again was giving me stomach flutters. This sense of mingled hope and anxiety. What if he took one look at me and decided he'd made a terrible mistake? Although, let's be fair, if I managed to be in his presence without either falling over, throwing up, or having a nervous breakdown, I'd be substantially more appealing than on pretty much every other occasion he'd interacted with me.

Comforting.

Or not.

It took him long enough to arrive that I'd passed through various cycles of waiting for him and had somehow lost track of time. Determined to be dazzling, I'd initially slithered into my tightest, sexiest, sparkliest jeans, but since I couldn't sit down in them, I'd had to take them off after an hour. Which meant that, when Caspian did finally turn up at about ten o'clock—in dark blue pinstripes, a white shirt, and a plain blue tie, looking classically austere and so *Business Insider* gorgeous, it made my hands tremble—I was curled up in the sitting area, creepily Google-stalking him for information about the ex Bellerose had mentioned and wearing leopard-print lounge trousers and a pink I'm a Pansexual Elf T-shirt.

Was I ever going to catch a break?

I guiltily slammed the lid closed on my laptop. "Um, hi."

"Hello, Arden. How are you?"

Honestly, I was giddy and dazed and so desperately thrilled to see him that I wanted to jump into his arms. Except I got suddenly self-conscious because...well, I was staying in his apartment, and the reason I was staying in his apartment was to facilitate a prearranged sexual encounter, and I wasn't sure how I was supposed to behave.

"I'm happy to see you," I managed finally.

"Likewise."

OMG. *Likewise?* His cheat word?

I gazed at him, speechless, mortifyingly wounded by a social tic. And then I felt like an idiot because what the fuck was I expecting? He'd made his terms super clear and I'd agreed to them. It was hardly a scenario that was going to involve him romancing my face off.

"Are you settled in?" he asked.

"Um. Yeah. Thank you. It's quite a place."

He glanced around as if his own apartment was totally unfamiliar to him. "When I heard of the development, it seemed like it would be a valuable investment."

"Y'know"—I snapped my fingers—"that's the first thing I thought about it too."

I'd made him laugh and my heart unknotted itself a little. He leaned over me, his hand brushing my cheek. "Do you want to...?"

I did want to. I *really* wanted to. But suddenly I panicked.

I'd given him a blow job on a balcony, crawled drunkenly over him, trying to make him spank me, and got myself off to his commands down the phone. It shouldn't have been a big deal to have sex with him in a bed in a multimillion-pound investment property. But it did.

It felt different. And I didn't know why.

"Um, actually"—I did my best to muster an appealing smile—"I was wondering if we could maybe...talk first."

"Of course. Anything you want."

Well, that was easy. My smile still felt like it had died on my face but I could breathe again.

He unbuttoned his jacket and perched on the arm of the frighteningly designer sofa. I was still a bit overwhelmed by the opulence of the apartment, so it was disconcerting to see someone treat it like it was just another place. But then he possessed his own kind of splendor, sitting there in his perfectly tailored Savile Row suit and his Vacheron Constantin watch, all that poise and beauty and wealth.

It was no more unlikely that I'd be living somewhere like One Hyde Park than I'd be dating someone like Caspian. Yet both were true.

Sort of anyway.

I was just wondering what the fuck I was going to do, having demanded we have a conversation, when he added, "But I don't have very much time tonight," in this tone of polite indifference.

Which threw me straight back into flail mode.

Nothing seemed more likely to inspire the failure of our short-term, prearranged shagging type relationship than not doing any shagging.

"Oh no." My attempt to sound insouciant was mildly diminished by a frantic hand flap. "It's fine. It's cool. We can do...do the other thing."

"I wasn't trying to…that is, I'm perfectly willing to—"

"No, no. We have an agreement. I didn't know you were in a rush." Fuck, I was a sexual drive-through. Did he want fries with me?

"Arden, I…"

Double, triple, quadruple fuck with a cherry on top. I was a sexual drive-through and he was *reluctant*. I shoved my laptop out of the way, bounced off the sofa, and made a run for the bedroom, ripping my T-shirt over my head as I went.

My trousers were a pimpin' puddle on the floor by the time he caught up with me. I shivered, suddenly realizing that while being naked, goose-pimply, and semi-flaccid in front of a man in a three-piece suit was rife with kinky potential, in reality it was just embarrassing.

But we got to it anyway. Him still pretty much dressed, me bent over the bed, staring down at Hyde Park, the green trees, and the silver-gray river.

"Nice view." Fuck, that was me.

And absolutely not the right thing to say when somebody was putting a cock in you.

I'd been resting on my forearms but now I dropped my shoulders to the bed, mainly to muffle my stupid mouth before it offered up any further observations. Something about the soft furnishings maybe.

At any rate, the movement changed the angle, forcing him deeper, the pressure and the pleasure pulling each other along like lovers on a summer's day.

And, in spite of everything, that felt good.

Wow, what was wrong with me? I was nervous and awkward and feeling desperately unsexy but apparently all my body needed was a dick in a hole and a man on my back and it was ready to rumble.

I tried not to be a total whore about it but…nope. I was moaning helplessly as he fucked me into the mattress, his fingers digging into my hips, pinning me in place. The strokes of his cock inside me were unerring: stretching me open and shoving me inevitably toward orgasm.

Close, and closer, but…not…quite…close enough.

I worked a hand under my body, except then he landed a crisp slap right on my arse. It hurt but not really. More this hot sting that sent a sudden sizzle of increased awareness rippling through me and made me arch my spine hopefully in case he felt like doing it again.

Apparently, he didn't.

No matter how enthusiastically I wiggled.

I'd always assumed that pain and pleasure were opposites. Opposites that could get interestingly muddled in the proper context. But the way the bright flash of his palm had cut through the dull, sweet ache of being about to come…it was more like two tastes that went great together. Like cream cheese and marmite. Salt and caramel.

Oh God. I really wanted him to hit me again.

And the thought felt outlandish even inside my own head.

Maybe if we'd been on the phone—that tantalizing mixture of closeness and distance and trust and hope—I'd have dared to ask. But things felt different now. Even more uncertain somehow. And the stakes were a lot higher. I honestly wasn't entirely sure that he wouldn't just call me a painted

Jezebel and leave me there, unspanked and unfucked.

To say nothing of seriously embarrassed.

And that was when I formed the closest thing to a cunning plan I was capable of with another man's dick pounding against my happy place and turning my brain to pre-orgasmic mush. It came down to a second, and even more theatrical, attempt to get at my cock.

This time he seized my hands and pulled them round to the small of my back, holding them there with my wrists forced together and trapped beneath his palm.

"Oh no you don't," he growled. "You come when I let you."

If I'd had breath or focus, I'd have told him that getting all mean and bossy probably wasn't going to be much of a hindrance to me coming. But, instead, I just gasped out, "Now would be nice."

Of course, that made him stop. And I guess I'd known that it would.

He kept my hands where they were, sliding an arm around me from behind and tugging me back against his chest. It felt like falling except there was nowhere to fall and then he drove his cock so deep into me that all I could manage was a hitchy little whimper, caught on the tender edge of pain.

"You're so beautiful when you're suffering." Caspian's breath was hot and unsteady against the side of my neck. "So responsive."

"And you're s-so..."

His fingers skated up my quivering stomach and tugged at the jeweled cherries dangling from the bar through my left nipple, and whatever I had been about to say vanished into tingling, sharp-edged bliss.

"What am I?"

"Cruel," I whispered approvingly.

"I did warn you."

He had. And I'd signed right up for it. I let my head fall back against his shoulder, wishing he was naked like me. Turned out I liked my cruelty as intimate as possible. But, as it was, I was probably just covering his shirt with sweat.

"I could keep you like this." His touch became a caress—a taunting one, traveling across my body, seeking the places where I felt vulnerable and sensitive: my flanks and collarbone, the arch of my ribs, my inner thighs, the pleasure both inseparable from the sense of being controlled and almost a side effect of it. He lingered over the lines of my tattoo. "I could make you wait. Or not let you come at all."

I nearly broke my neck trying to see him. Worth it though. He'd sounded pretty composed, threatening me with erotic torments, but his face betrayed him. He was gorgeously flushed and wild-eyed and sweat-glittery. And his mouth, oh God, that stern, beautiful mouth of his was so…so *soft*. Full of kisses. I would have done anything for that look.

"Yeah," I mumbled, squirming fruitlessly on his cock, "you could."

If you'd have asked me an hour ago, I'd have told you I was pretty sure I wasn't into orgasm denial. I was into the opposite of orgasm denial. All the orgasms. All the time. But now? For him? There was honestly something a little bit appealing about it. As if I was the hero from a myth or fairy tale committed to some impossible task: spin straw into gold, harness the man-eating mares of Diomedes, forgo my own gratification for

Caspian's. To melt the ice around my prince's heart.

I twisted even farther, nuzzling clumsily into the side of his neck. "Are you going to? Leave me all tormented and desperate?"

"You'd do that for me?"

"If...if you wanted it." I gave a shuddery laugh. "And as long as you were very, very merciful afterward."

He didn't reply. But I could feel a strange tension in him.

"I might even, y'know...enjoy it," I offered. "It'd be like being with you even though you weren't there. And you'd be thinking about me, too, wouldn't you? Imagining me yearning and frantic and horny. All for you."

He made a sound—but it was a good sound, a deep, rough groan, albeit reluctantly surrendered. I took it as encouragement.

"I guess you'd be at some meeting or something. But secretly planning all the terrible things you'd do to me later. And I'd be so hot for you, so needy, I wouldn't know whether to beg you to stop or...to not."

Caspian pressed his face against the curve of my shoulder. I caught the edge of his teeth, the thready rhythm of his breath.

I was—it was hard to describe—*gently* in pain, my wrists hot and achy in his hold, my shoulders forced back, my cock actually throbbing with urgency, my body feeling tight and thin and fragile where he entered me. But I was...I was okay. Better than okay. Floaty and light, sensations washing over me like waves over sand. And Caspian's heart was thudding thunderously against my spine, his lips shaping my name with unexpected reverence. Just like on the balcony.

Wow, I'd been worrying for nothing. Because here was the man I'd done this for—intense, complicated, controlling as hell. Who somehow made very ordinary little me feel extraordinarily precious.

We were going to be just fine.

"Though in the best of all possible worlds you wouldn't have to leave," I said. "You'd use me and fuck me and stay with me. Watch me suffer. You like watching me suff—"

His free hand was suddenly tangled in my hair. And I found myself facedown, arse up on the bed, my startled squawk thankfully muffled by the covers. I barely had time to suck in a breath before he was fucking me ferociously, his every thrust striking my prostate like Big Ben sounding orgasm o'clock.

Which should have been a good thing but somehow wasn't...in ways I couldn't quite figure out. It was kind of relentless. Just on the wrong side of rough, as if he wanted to force me to all the pleasure he'd been tempted to withhold. Emotionally I balked, but my body was too far gone. Teased and denied and overstimulated and sore, I came all over the bed in less than a minute. And for some reason it felt like defeat. Hollowing me out. Leaving me breathless and empty and wet.

Caspian finished a moment or two later, with nothing more than a swallowed groan. He pulled out and away as soon as he was done. And I flipped over just in time to catch the last visible traces of his passion: the fading flush, the bitten lip, the lock of hair that had fallen damply over his eyes.

I was sprawled and sticky, bewildered and bruised in unexpected ways, but I still wanted him to stay. So I could smooth his hair and lick the salt and come from his skin. So I could kiss the still quickened breath from his mouth.

So we could be messy together.

"Um," I said.

Caspian gazed down at me, blinking as if he was just waking up—and whatever he'd dreamed hadn't been pleasant. He lifted a hand and then lowered it again. And finally sat down on the edge of the bed. Well. Sort of sat, anyway. In a less elegant man, it would have been a flump. It was secretly a little bit gratifying to have temporarily stripped him of his usual grace. That I could affect him at all still seemed its own private miracle.

We were silent for what seemed a longish time. What a weird fucking tableaux we must have made. Like a painting that would once have ended up on the Toast under the heading "Awkward Postcoital Moments in Western Art History."

"So," I tried again. "How was the prearranged sexual encounter?"

He half turned. He looked tired—and not in the fun shagged out way—and bleak. "You don't have to do any of that."

"The sex? You don't want to sleep with me anymore?" I just about managed to keep my voice seminormal. But inside I was horrified. How had I managed to put him off already?

"No, of course I do. I meant…the rest of it. The other things you said."

For a split second, I had no clue what he was talking about. And then I remembered my lust-dazed litany of filthy offerings, which were suddenly way too much and super embarrassing.

His hand curled around my ankle. "You're everything I want. Just as you are."

It should have been a lovely thing to hear. I mean, it was probably the closest he'd ever got to a romantic sentiment and, if this was a romcom, we'd be about fifteen minutes from kissing in the rain while the credits rolled. But it also felt kind of disconnected from, well, everything. And from me. The boy who'd just enthusiastically incited the pounding of a lifetime. It wouldn't even have crossed my mind that what we'd just done could be incompatible with liking Arden St. Ives: the Whole Package. Just the opposite, in fact. So now I was all nervous again that he didn't want me.

I was about to say something but then his fingers brushed over my hip. "Oh God, what did I do?"

His touch woke a warm ache and I glanced down to discover bruises blossoming on my skin where he'd held in place. They didn't really hurt but, holy hell, did they make me look well used. I loved them.

"And your wrists too," he murmured. "I'm sorry."

"It's fine." I grinned sleepily at him. "They'll give me something to remember you by while you're away doing your billionaire things."

"I'd rather you didn't remember me hurting you."

I matched my fingertips to the marks he'd left. "You know I'm okay with a little pain in a good cause. Especially when the cause is you. I think it's hot...actually. Knowing you lost control because of me."

"That's not a side of myself I'm proud of."

"Oh, Caspian." I sat up and threw my arms around him—not an entirely successful maneuver because he went all tense and stiff and elbowy, so it was a little bit like hugging a piece of modern art. "Well, it's a side of you I'm really into. But even if it wasn't, I'd tell you what you just told me."

"I just told you lots of things." He sounded wary. "Which did you mean?"

"That you're everything I want. Just as you are."

He pulled out of my clumsy embrace and turned. I thought he was going to kiss me, but he just leaned in, his brow resting for a moment against mine. It was a chaste and unexpectedly tender gesture. His eyes closed, the lashes silky soft and vulnerable against his cheeks. "I'm never quite prepared for how sweet you are."

"Sweet?" I repeated, somewhat disappointed. "I don't suppose you mean sexy and dangerous, like a homme fatale?"

"That too." Except he was smiling, which rather diminished the plausibility of his assurances.

Not that I minded. Not at all. I wanted to put my lips against his, to feel the shape of his smile beneath my mouth, and tease it gently open into a kiss.

I went to suit the action to the thought, as Conan Doyle would put have it, but for some reason that made Caspian draw back. His thumb moved idly over the smudges that ringed my wrist. "You don't deserve this, Arden."

I'd never been a big fan of deserving. It always seemed like something other people decided for you. "What about what I want?" I asked. "Don't I deserve that?"

I thought it was a winning argument, but Caspian only glanced at his ridiculously complicated, double-faced watch. "Arden, I have to go."

Not what I'd expected. Even though he'd told me he didn't have much time. "Right now? Like that?"

"Well"—he reached self-consciously for the open collar of his shirt—"I'll change first."

I swallowed. And tried not say anything too stupid. How had I ever convinced myself I was sophisticated enough for this? It was a peril-strewn no-man's-land between casual fuck and boyfriend, and I had no idea what the etiquette was. What it was safe to want and to ask for. What I was supposed to do. What he expected me to give him or take in return. Basically, which relationship fork to use.

"You really can't stay longer?" I asked. And, wow, I sounded pathetic. No wonder he wanted to run.

"I'm afraid I have to be in Tokyo tomorrow." He wouldn't meet my eyes. "But thank you."

The idea of lying there, naked and fucked and watching him leave, was pretty bloody awful. So I peeled myself off the bed and fled into the shower, drowning his footsteps and the click of the door in a torrent of water.

CHAPTER 17

I woke up pretty late the next day and pattered woozily in the direction of the kitchen, noticing only just in time that the place was full of cleaners. I was sure Caspian paid them generously, but nobody needed my unsolicited wang at eleven o'clock in the morning. Diving back into the bedroom, I lurked under the duvet until they were finished. I mean, obviously I could have got dressed and gone about my business, but I didn't want to be in their way. And also the bed—as I'd previously discovered—was ridiculously big and cozy, probably because the mattress was Swedish, cost six figures, and contained a gazillion pocket springs, and the sheets were Egyptian cotton with a thread count higher than my salary would be. When I had a salary.

Wow. How was this my life? Even just for six months.

Eventually the cleaners left. And, respectably trousered—well, semi-respectably as, actually, they were my rainbow unicorn pajama bottoms—I crept over to the kitchen. The fridge, I discovered, was full of…I guess you'd call it gourmet luxuries? Or to put it another way, food that nobody really ate. Caviar and quails eggs and wild strawberries—oh, okay, I'd eat those. My drinking options were Veen Velvet, which I finally figured out was water, and champagne, which I identified instantly because I was just that classy. There was also a coffee machine, but it looked like a torture device, and I was too scared to use it. Clearly, living the high life was going to be tougher than I'd imagined.

And that was when I caught sight of the flowers on the dining table. I wasn't sure I'd ever seen a hundred roses before, but there they were: a splash of wild scarlet in the middle of all that muted, designer extravagance. Caspian had sent a note too: *Thank you for a wonderful evening.*

Well, that was nice. Sort of. I definitely appreciated the thought. Except it seemed more of an *I took you to the opera, where your heartfelt response to the music warmed my cynical cockles* gesture than an *I fucked your arse until we came* type of thing. But then, Caspian was inconceivably wealthy: they did things differently on his planet. I guess I was just lucky he hadn't tried to endow a professorial chair or name a building after me or something. *The Guy I Shagged Memorial Library & Ancient Languages Center*.

Anyway, it probably meant he'd enjoyed what we'd done together. Despite the awkward beginning. And the awkward middle. And the—well, honestly, the whole thing had been awkward. But hot too. And there were places I could still feel him, a deep, warm ache in my skin, like kisses he had left behind. Better than any other gift he could have given me.

I breakfasted on strawberries and tap water, sitting rebelliously on the edge of the gold-veined marble worktops. Then I swam and did some yoga, feeling somewhere between the Real Housewives of Kensington and Will Smith in *I Am Legend.* In the sense of being kind of on my own a bit. Not in the sense of fighting any zombies.

But the truth was, I wasn't used to being alone. My living arrangements in Oxford had been highly prestigious in student terms, and guests had often come by to point and gasp at our genuinely nice sofa, but they'd still amounted to three rooms and a kitchenette I was sharing with another guy.

Plenty of people in our friendship circle had moved to London—either chancing it like me (although most likely without the billionaire backing) or to take up actual positions in investment banks or the civil service or whatever else properly ambitious Oxford graduates did when they finished their degree. But if I wanted to casually socialize with anyone, I'd probably have to *arrange* it. Which wasn't to say I couldn't, but it felt very different to trotting down the corridor with a packet of Hobnobs, hoping someone would put the kettle on.

I knew it was pretty normal. That it was just growing up. That it was just change. But, right then, it seemed more like loss.

Still, there was no point getting all days of wine and roses about it. Speaking of which—roses, that is, not wine—I owed Caspian a thank you. Grabbing my drug dealer phone, I took a photo of the flowers plus my face, whapped a flattering filter over it, and sent it off. A response came back in less than a minute.

I'm glad you liked them. Do you want anything from Japan?

I wasn't quite sure how to answer. Since I was pretty sure someone like Caspian would have been able to get anything from anywhere just by making a phone call or getting someone else to make a phone call, it was incredibly sweet that he would offer to pick up something for me personally. And so I really didn't want to say no. On the other hand, my materialistic desires weren't quite global enough for a challenge like this. On top of which, I didn't actually want to put him to expense or trouble. After a moment or two, I sent: *Some Glico chocolate crush matcha cookie pocky and a photo.*

Of me buying pocky?

I laughed. *Just you.*

Nothing.

Please? I typed shamelessly.

And a second or two later, a Caspian Hart selfie popped into my inbox. He was on a plane—private jet probably, considering how plush it was—and he looked pale and dark-eyed, his tie loose enough to expose the lickable places of his throat.

Did you sleep okay? Oh wow, fussing over him. Very attractive, Arden.

Yes. I just had to get up early.

Suddenly I felt incredibly bad about last night. I'd been so upset about Caspian's leaving, I hadn't paid much attention to his—no innuendo intended—coming. When what really mattered wasn't that he hadn't been able to stay long; it was the fact that he'd made the effort to see me at all. Most people who were about to fly six thousand miles might reasonably have fancied going to bed early with a cup of cocoa.

Not having sex with an ungrateful dickhead.

Can you rest now? I asked.

I could, but I need to stay on London time.

Wow. The man didn't even yield to time zones. But I guess it made sense. Given how much he probably traveled, the alternative was probably permanent jet lag. *I could help you stay awake.*

I need to work. But I think I'd prefer your methods.

I grinned. *How do you know? I didn't say what they were. I might sing a song that'll get on your nerves right in your ear.*

Then I'd gag you.

Yes please.

He didn't text back. But I felt we'd left the conversation in a promising place.

Besides, I was also supposed to be working.

Settling myself in the study, I opened my laptop and stared miserably at the arid desert of accomplishment that was my CV. Did my best to spruce it up. Truthfully, I hadn't been completely idle at Oxford—if anything, my near pathological avoidance of my degree had made me pretty productive in other areas. I'd written for any paper, magazine, and doomed websperiment going. And then there'd been my celebrated stretch as editor of the *Bog Sheet*—indeed, upon such foundations were Pulitzers won.

Ho hum. But at least it meant I had a portfolio. And that

was...that was *something*, right? My social media presence wasn't bad either. Twitter could go bite a rabid baboon, but my Instagram was popular-ish, even with people who didn't know me personally. Basically, I was probably a credible potential candidate.

Apart from the bit where I had nothing to apply for because the career advisor had been right and I should have sorted this out last October and been on an internship right now—or an emerging writers fellowship as they'd had apparently been rebranded on account of indentured servitude being frowned upon nowadays. Of course, there was always next year but that was, well, that was a year away. Which was ages.

I was still going to try because it was probably the best way to get a foot in the door. I mean, probably they wouldn't be all, "That intern, we mean emerging writer, is so cute and makes the best tea, let's spontaneously hire him!" but maybe if I happened to get an interview later they might remember my face in a positive way. In the meantime, though, I was on my own. And probably I needed to apply for things and pitch things and—

Ahhhh! It was scary. Really scary. And seemed incredibly amorphous, much like revising for finals. And look how well that had gone.

It was getting pretty late and I was feeling a bit Lady of Shalotty up in my tower, which made me think I'd earned the right to give up for the day. If nothing else, I was going to need food I could actually eat so a visit to my local supermarket was probably in order. Unfortunately, that turned out to be Harrods, so, err, no. The nearest Tesco was about a mile away but there were two Waitroses and a Marks and Spencer less than five minutes down the road. Clearly this was the supermarket hierarchy of Kensington.

I stocked up on crumpets and Coco Pops—yes, okay, I panic-shopped—and grabbed a bunch of magazines as well, intending to use them for research and inspiration. My writing talents, such as they were, had always tended toward the parodic, which probably meant I had no literary identity of my own but could be useful for speculative freelancing. Once I had a good grasp of the house style, I'd probably be able to put together some appropriate pitches. That I would then have to pitch.

Ahhhh!

Everything I'd heard or read about breaking into journalism suggested you had to be persistent and thick-skinned and initiative-taking. So, now I thought about it, not an ideal career choice for me, since I would really have flourished in an industry that rewarded people who were flaky, sensitive, and lackadaisical.

Except, ever since I'd written my first...article I guess (which had been a searing and witty takedown of the school cafeteria's top ten worst puddings, rapturously received by its audience of nine-year-olds and my mum) I'd just taken it for granted that this was what I was good at. That it was what I was going to do.

But what if I wasn't good at it? What if I had no chance of doing it?

As I was slinking back to One Hyde Park, my non-drug-dealer phone bleeped. It was Nik, wanting to crash with me next week before he flew out to Boston. He was spending the summer at MIT, helping with a research project, the details of which I'd phased out on because science blah blah polymers blah blah nanocomposites.

I honestly felt a bit nervous about letting him stay—he might, entirely fairly, think my living situation was off and Bellerose hadn't said anything about guests. What if Caspian wanted to sex me while Nik was there? But, equally, I didn't want to miss a chance to see my best friend before an ocean got in the way. Even if—with Kik and the rest of the two hundred and nine social media accounts Nik posted gym selfies on—we talked nearly every day anyway.

In any case, I had time to figure it out. An abundance of time, in fact, as I was increasingly coming to realize.

It was quiet in the apartment as I unpacked my shopping and found unobtrusive cupboards for it to lurk in. The sun was setting spectacularly—not in the decorous coral-swirled skies of Oxford, but in great, bloody gashes. The way the light came flooding red-tinged across the polished floor made the whole place look like the dying warren in the animated *Watership Down*. Which, incidentally, is not a movie that should ever be shown to kids. That shit is Stephen King terrifying.

Wandering out onto the balcony, I rested my elbows on the rail and took in the view. Hyde Park was my back garden: this blur of green, with the city glittering behind. I was getting that *I Am Legend* feeling again, although the Legend part was especially ill-fitting. *I Am Minor Folktale.*

Caspian was probably in Tokyo by now, though it must have been three or four in the morning over there. I imagined he was in some glassy hotel gym, running or swimming, or doing whatever he did to get that amazing body, keeping himself awake for a 7:00 a.m. meeting. I wondered if he was missing me a little bit—most likely not because he'd been literally inside me less than a day ago. But did he get lonely? Always working and traveling and…actually, I didn't know what else he did.

In any case, he'd been extremely clear about what he wanted from me. And the compensations were certainly very… compensatory. But I guess I wasn't quite prepared for how it might feel—being someone's prenegotiated short-term sexual encounter. Which was weird because I'd spent nearly all my time at university having one prenegotiated short-term sexual encounter after another. And resenting it—and feeling trapped—when I wasn't.

I guess that made me a big ol' hypocrite.

Or maybe it was because I felt differently about Caspian. Partly, yes, there was a certain amount of dazzlement going on there. After all, he was rich and powerful and beautiful…and apparently into me. He was the human equivalent of an offer from Oxford: difficult to get, impossible to turn down, and guaranteed to make you feel as if you'd only been chosen because of an administrative error.

But the truth was, there was more to it than that. I wasn't just flattered to have earned his attention. I think…I genuinely really liked him. And what drew me most of all was what lay beneath the wealth and the status and the rest of it. The man who laughed quietly, made awkward gestures, and seemed so terribly afraid, sometimes, of hurting me.

He was like a nearly-there Rubik's Cube—this sealed box, all perfect edges and matched-up colors, except for the occasional hopeless misalignment, a lost orange square and a yellow piece stuck in a corner. Though why I thought this made me the right person for him I have no idea.

I'd never solved one of those fuckers in my entire life.

CHAPTER 18

Caspian was back in a couple of days, probably having made, like, $100,000 an hour while I'd flailed around trying to come up with pitches and eating a lot of Coco Pops directly from the packet. It was disconcerting because I'd never lacked for inspiration before. There'd always been something going on at college—news or gossip or drama or simply a fresh target for satire. And even at school, I'd got serious column inches out of stuff like the time Glen Lowrey got a D on his chemistry homework, set it on fire with the Bunsen burner, threw the smoldering pieces in the bin, and then the bin exploded. We went to print with the headline BIN BURNER LOWREY IN NEW ARSON SHOCK. And I'd got detention for gratuitous sensationalism.

The problem was, here at the top of One Hyde Park, there was nothing. Just wealth and quiet and bulletproof glass. I mean, unless I wanted to write about being the…kept man?

temporary fucktoy? of a gay billionaire. Except no. Just no. I would never do that to Caspian. Or, for that matter, to myself.

In any case, I was glad for the promise of distraction when Caspian texted to tell me he was on his way. And, of course, excited to see him. Because yay for prenegotiated short-term encounters. Also I was hoping now we'd got the nervous-making first bonk out of the way he'd feel more comfortable sharing his kinky side with me. Of course, I could have been reading too much into a few rough kisses and the occasional command, but he seemed to get off on being in control. I could still remember the way he'd responded when I'd gone to my knees on the balcony. The raw need in his voice over the phone before my finals. And I was so very up for more of that: his unheld-back self, unleashed for me.

Except there was also how dismayed he'd been, apologizing for the bruises he'd left on my hips. His mouth-fucking hit-'n'-run at St. Sebastian's. Probably he was worried about hurting me or pushing me into something I didn't want, and I guess I could have done a better job of reassuring him I was okay. Admittedly, I only had passing practical experience with BDSM but pornography could be super educational and I'd been seriously hot for everything Caspian had done up till now. Besides, I think I just...liked sex. In all its innumerable, multicolored shades.

The trick, though, was making sure Caspian got that. How did you broach that sort of topic without it being embarrassing or just incredibly presumptuous? I even semi-wussed out on thinking about it properly—settling, instead, for dangling a teeny-tiny pair of decorative handcuffs from one of my nipple shields. Just as a kind of…hint.

Of course I still needed other clothes. At least, probably? That was the thing about waiting for someone to explicitly come over and shag you: there wasn't really a dress code, unless it was nothing but a come-hither look, but I didn't quite have the bollocks—so to speak—to try it. In the end I settled on a fairly generic pair of lounge trousers, because they were comfortable, easy to take off, and didn't make me look completely terrible, and my HUFFLEPUFF FOR THE REST T-shirt, because it was the last clean top I had. Oops.

And then I just had to wait.

Aaaaand wait.

Until, at last, Caspian arrived, having been caught up in traffic. Probably the day would come when I wasn't a puddle on the floor at the sight of him—all icy-eyed and exquisite, in his three-piece suit—but that day wasn't today.

"Hi," I croaked. "Nice trip?"

"Very productive, thank you." He brought his hand out from behind his back and presented me with a box of matcha chocolate Pocky. "I believe this is what you wanted?"

I'd honestly forgotten I'd asked for them. "Oh wow. You found some."

"Mmm. The chairman of the Nakamura Corporation was able to locate a convenience store that had them in a stock."

I suppose I shouldn't have been surprised that Caspian had links to the Nakamura Corporation. Or that he'd apparently asked the chairman about obtaining my favorite Pocky. "You…he…really didn't have to do that."

"He was happy to help."

I couldn't resist. "People always do what you tell them to do?"

"When I'm making them a lot of money? Yes." He gave me a bewildered look. "What are you laughing about?"

I smothered my giggles with difficulty. "Nothing. Sorry. Just...someday you have to watch a movie. I mean, any movie. But *Pretty Woman* would be a good starting point."

"I don't have time for films."

"Maybe"—I peeped up at him hopefully—"we could watch one together?"

"Tonight?"

Shit shit abort abort. "Well, uh, I thought maybe there was something else you might want to do tonight?"

"Now you mention it...I did have a few ideas."

He offered his hand and I took it, letting him draw me off the sofa. It was an unusually romantic gesture for Caspian—and for me actually—and I definitely didn't *intend* to immediately climb him like the monkey bars. But the next thing I knew I was in his arms, my legs wrapped around his waist, and he was carrying me off to the bedroom.

Where he stripped me and sexed me with this kind of ruthless intensity. He touched me in places I didn't think I'd ever been touched. Err, not in a kinky way, just nobody had ever kissed the crease of my elbow before or stroked the knot of my ankle. It was like he was...learning me? No, more than that—like he was *conquering* me inch by inch. Which was the sort of thing I should have been into but it was all so very about me it was on the verge of uncomfortable-making.

And not enjoyably uncomfortable-making. I mean, the attention was nice—being the gaspy, shivery subject of Caspian's unrelenting focus—but I could have done without the detachment.

Or maybe *detachment* wasn't the right word either. It was hard to think in the middle of the sensual onslaught to which he was subjecting me. And probably that I was trying to think at all was a sign of some hitherto undiscussed messed-upness on my part. But I guess I just wanted him to be more involved? I wanted pleasure to be this bottle of strawberry wine we passed between us on a summer day. I wanted it to be sparks in a plasma ball jumping from me to him and back again. And I definitely didn't want to be serviced by a beautiful bonk robot as if I was stuck in *Westworld.*

Which was totally ungrateful of me because there was some amazing stuff going on. My body was having a really happy time—but where was Caspian? Every time I tried to touch him back or participate in any way he'd move my hands or reposition me with infuriating gentleness. I wouldn't have cared if he'd pinned me or overpowered me, come at me rough and cruel and full of threats of torment. Except, instead, he just held back and held back until his control was nothing but distance.

The worst of it was, I think in some terrible way he thought he was taking care of me. That he was showing me something I needed to see. When all he was really doing was denying me what I needed most of all which was... him. And I didn't know *why*. What I'd done to turn him into this careful stranger less than a week after he'd plowed into me like a werewolf in heat just on the promise of hearing me beg.

I thought about stopping him but I didn't know how. *Please don't make tender love to me because, apparently, I'm a weirdo.* And, besides, I wasn't quite that much of a masochist—the man had serious bedroom skills and I wasn't about to turn down a 'gasm, even one bestowed by a sexually talented alien who had briefly taken over Caspian Hart. It was good sex. It was just, having seen his naked desire, I knew it wasn't real.

I came though. Of course I did, with my body alive beneath his hands and his cock deep inside me. And then—when I was too limply postcoital to protest—he flipped me over and finished off in this, well, hurried way. Which was considerate since I got sensitive after but it also made me feel a little bit like a teenager's sock. The best bit was when he got close and his breathing turned ragged and his whole body curved over mine, his teeth grazing the back of my neck. It was so excitingly predatory of him that it almost got me going again.

But at that point we were pretty much done and Caspian was rolling away from me and I was doing my best impression of a well-fucked starfish, flattened on the bed, with my limbs pointing in whatever direction they'd flopped.

After a moment or two, I turned my head to look at him. At least he'd undressed this time—not that I'd been able to appreciate it. Even naked, there was something armored about him, his perfect body as much a shield as his tailored suits. If he ever let me touch him, my fingers would probably slide over him like glass.

How could he be further away lying beside me than when he'd been a voice down the phone?

Come back to me, I wanted to say.

Except that would have been totally ridiculous.

"Um, was that okay?" I blurted out.

Which was so much better.

His eyes snapped open. "Why wouldn't it be?"

"I don't know...I just...oh my God. Can't you just say yes or no like a normal person?"

He opened his mouth. Closed it. And said finally, "I'm not sure how to answer that."

For a moment I couldn't work out how frustrated I was but I ended up laughing instead.

He looked briefly flustered. Then perilously close to amused. "I wasn't trying to be evasive. Context is important. And I'm not sure what you're asking."

That was fair. Especially because I wasn't sure either.

The thing was, I'd have been happy to be as vanilla as cupcakes with Caspian if that was what he wanted. But the problem was I just didn't know anymore. It felt like something had changed between us. Or maybe I'd been imagining shit all along?

"I guess I want to check that I'm...um...that you're happy with me? Was that...what you like?"

There was a silence I couldn't read. Then, "Did I hurt you again?"

"What? No." This was going the opposite of well. And rapidly developing into a conversation I didn't want to have with my arse in the air. I rolled gingerly onto my side, trying to draw courage from the plink of the handcuffs as they swayed on their tiny chain. "It's more about... The thing is, I want to be the very best prenegotiated sexual encounter I can be for you."

"Arden"—somehow he managed to sound both fond and exasperated—"you don't have to worry about that."

"I know I didn't exactly cover myself in glory at Oxford but I can be a devoted student when I'm passionate about my subject."

"Sex?"

"You." I gave him a hopeful, if slightly terrified, grin. "Which is why I was wondering if there was more I could be doing. When you're, y'know, when you're with me."

"What do you mean?"

Nope. It was impossible to talk about this kind of thing casually. But I tried my damnedest. "Oh, just if you had any special preferences or fantasies or anything."

"Nothing in particular." Caspian was better at casual than me. He could build a fucking wall of casual.

But, because I was an idiot, I ran at it anyway. "Well, what sort of things do you think about?"

A very small pause. "Investment strategy, asset allocation, and risk management, mostly."

"No, I mean when you're..." Holy shit. Was I really asking Caspian Hart about his masturbatory habits? Apparently I was. And now I was thinking about them. Imagining him, stretched out and naked, much as he was right now, except taut and abandoned, his hand working his own cock. Gosh. What a vision. I would have given pretty much anything to see it... in the flesh, as it were.

He turned slightly. "When I'm what?"

I wussed out and made a gesture.

"Ah." The hand I had speculated about was resting on his chest. I was a little bit envious of it, to be honest. I would have liked to draw my palm over the smooth skin and elegantly defined muscle—learn the texture of the curling, silky hair for myself. "If you must know, I think about you."

He did? "That's unexpectedly flattering."

"It's the truth."

"So, err"—I wriggled a little closer—"what sort of things do you think about doing with…or to me?"

"We just did them."

"*All* of them?"

"Arden, I—"

"No, it's fine. Sorry. I shouldn't have asked. I guess I just thought it would be hot."

"Did you now?"

The words, and his tone, were super-quelling. I commenced quietly dying inside, waiting for him to go, so I could curl into a shameball.

But instead he rolled on top of me, bracing himself on his forearms and settling his body over mine. The shock of closeness and the shock of, well, shock drew a little gasp from me. He'd touched me plenty when we'd been doing it, but not like this. Not in a way that let me participate. I raised a knee in welcome and he sank into the warm, cuddly space between my thighs.

"Since you're interested in fantasies," he murmured, "why don't you tell me one of yours?"

"Uhhh..." It was only when he'd turned it round on me that I understood how intimate a question it was. How exposing. Dear God, what had I started? My mouth had gone completely dry. My brain completely blank. His eyes holding me in a cold, blue prison.

"Well?" The cruelty in his voice was both sweet and terrifying and shot straight to my cock. I squirmed and tried to turn my head away, as if this could somehow conceal that I was bright red up top and totally hard down below. His hand slid into my hair, pulling me back. "What do *you* think about? In the dark. On your own. When there's nobody to know what you imagine?"

I was blushing even more. I was blushing everywhere. Heat rushing through my body like a river undammed. This was so embarrassing. Except it was an oddly sexy embarrassing—a kissing cousin of desire—because I liked... I liked that he was insisting. It meant I was right. That he *did* want something more from me. And that maybe he'd let me give it.

"Come on, Arden." He leaned down and kissed me lightly. A tease, perhaps, or invitation. Reassurance, too, of a kind. "You're going to tell me."

Of course I was. "Give me a minute," I grumbled. "My fantasy life happens to be rich and complex."

His mouth curled into a rare, soft-edged smile. "I would expect no less."

There was a silence.

Oh shit. It was supposed to be my line.

"I, uh—" My throat had clogged up. I tried to swallow in a

sneaky and subtle fashion and ended up making a Gollumish gulping noise.

Maybe I couldn't do this after all…

I gazed up at Caspian. It was a little bit magical to have him so close to me. I could see the silver fractals in his eyes. Feel the lightest ripple of the breath from his mouth. And I realized how much I cared about pleasing him. Far more than I cared about being embarrassed.

"I think about being…um…menaced." There. I'd said it. And it didn't feel bad at all. In fact, it suddenly seemed a bit ridiculous to have been worried. These were just my fantasies. Nothing to be ashamed of. And there was nothing humiliating about sharing them. Just revealing.

And I didn't mind revealing myself to Caspian Hart.

Because, in a way, he had revealed himself too. In wanting to know things about me at least as much as I'd wanted to know them about him.

"Menaced how?" he asked after a moment.

"I…Well. Like James Bond."

"Spies again?" There was laughter lurking in his voice.

And I remembered sharing Oxford's golden shadows with him, the brush of his fingers. He'd been an impossible stranger then. Now he was a possible one.

I fake-pouted. "I'm not repetitive. I'm *thematic*."

"Is he really all that menaced?"

"Are you kidding me?" I couldn't move very much, so I attempted to challenge his skepticism by wrapping my legs around him and squeezing. "Fleming was a massive pervert. Bond is the most menaced man in popular culture."

He moved a little restlessly, his arms tightening until the sinews stood out like carvings. "If you insist. I can't remember the last time I thought about Bond."

"You haven't seen the Daniel Craig films?"

He shook his head. Which sent my imagination springing back to Movie Night With Caspian Hart. Him and me and a bowl of homemade popcorn. And Daniel Craig emerging from the sea in his very tight trunks. Glory be to God for dappled things.

Except the man barely had time to fuck me. And it seemed to be an either/or.

"You might like them," I offered, all impressively noncommittal. "He's superhot when he's suffering."

Caspian pulled back abruptly. Liberty had never felt so cold. "You have some odd ideas about what I find appealing."

I nearly got sassy and retorted, *Well, you won't talk to me about it*. But he looked ... absurdly dignified, kneeling naked and affronted between my legs, and trying—for whatever reason—to pretend that he hadn't just pinned me to the bed and coaxed my mortifying sexual fantasies out of me like a cat letting a mouse scamper between its claws. So, all I said was, "I just think it's cool that a guy who's like this massive symbol of masculine pride and strength is actually a raging masochist who spends quite a lot of his time naked, vulnerable, and overpowered."

He was quiet for a moment, watching me. The intensity of it was shiver-inducing. But I had no idea what he was thinking. About me or about anything. Probably he was just going to tell me he had to leave. To my surprise, he trailed a finger along the outside of my leg, scraping lightly with the nail. "That is, indeed, quite interesting. But I believe I asked for a sexual fantasy, not your dissertation."

"Maybe it's both." My blush was back. I was so obvious. But I'd been pretty chuffed with the dissertation: "I Just Wanna Feel: Masculinity and Masochism in the Works of Ian Fleming and Chuck Palahniuk." Of course, it was Oxford, which meant it would probably wind up in the marking pile of someone who would give it a third for not being about Chaucer.

"Is that really what you do?" Caspian asked. "Imagine you're Bond?"

"More that I'm *like* Bond. I'm still basically me, except for being a spy. And I get captured a lot."

"That would make you a very ineffective secret agent."

His teasing was sunlight and firelight and all the bright, warm things between. "It's wankbait. Not a work experience placement."

"I apologize. What happens after you get captured?"

I squirmed as if I'd fallen into one of my very own fantasies and was undergoing a rigorous interrogation at the hands of a committed sadist. "Well, my nemesis—"

"You have a nemesis?" His mouth had gone all amused and kissable. "This seems very intricate, Arden. However do you find time to come?"

"That's what *in media res* is for. I jump straight to the bit where I'm sweaty, naked, and in chains, being threatened with naughty things."

"And you enjoy that?"

My cock twitched excitedly, slutty little minx that it was,

giving me away. "Um, yeah. I mean... there's a massive, massive difference between fantasy and reality. I wouldn't *really* want to be tortured by the KGB. But being tied up and sexily menaced by someone I liked could be pretty fun, don't you think?"

"I think," he murmured, "the boundaries of fantasy are less permeable than people realize."

"Um? What?"

"I just meant, it probably seems glamorous and edgy and exciting in your head. But in reality, you would most likely feel frightened and degraded. It's an ugly thing—the will to hurt someone you love."

So much for flirty pillow talk. I shuddered, suddenly cold, despite the heat of his body. Turned out, there were conversations I didn't want to have either.

"It can be," I said finally. "But not all hurt is abuse."

"Pain is pain, whoever inflicts it."

"That's... just not true. Context matters. And so do people." I closed my eyes—discovering abruptly that talking about sex acts got even more revealing when you tried to articulate the feelings behind them. "The thing with my imaginary nemesis is that... I'm special to him."

"You don't have to earn someone's care with suffering."

"Oh my God, no." This was turning into the conversational equivalent of the way we'd just had sex: a hideous combination of mutual goodwill and incomprehension. "The kink is there because I think it's hot. And the rest is because... it's a never-ending movie that's all about me. It's got exotic locations, a supporting cast, lashings of sex and violence, and a love interest who's part villain, part hero, wholly infatuated. I know this is going to make no sense to you, but for someone like me? It's fun not to feel ordinary sometimes."

I'd said too much. I'd said way too much.

He was quiet for ages. Long enough for my insides to curdle.

And then, in the sharpest tone he'd ever used with me: "Arden, I find your persistent conviction that you're ordinary extremely irritating."

I stared at him, jolted out of self-consciousness about my masturbatory habits. Somehow I'd annoyed him. And it was *terrifying*. Like when he was aroused—the same ferocity, but none of the heat or the thrill. He was giving me frostbite in my heart.

"I'm sorry?" I tried.

"Then stop doing it."

I nodded frantically. "I will, I will. Um, stop doing what?"

"Telling this lie to yourself and others."

"Which lie?" My brain was so mushed I could barely remember what we were talking about. "That I'm kind of ordinary? That's not a lie. It's—"

His hand came down over my mouth. "What did I just say?"

"Mh mhm mgfh mh," I explained, "mgfhmh mgfhm mhhm mh mh mhm mgh." Which had started life as *I can't tell you, because your hand is in the way.*

He stared down at me, anger fading, ice thawing. And then, very slowly, let me go. "Enough of this nonsense."

I dazedly touched my lips, where I could still feel the pressure of his palm. I wasn't exactly scared of him, just oddly shaken. And convinced I'd accidentally perpetrated an enormous fraud. I mean, it was super nice that he seemed to feel there was something remarkable about me but what was going to happen when he discovered there wasn't?

"The thing is," I said quietly, "I've been to Oxford. I'm sleeping with you. I know what extraordinary looks like. And I'm just me."

One of Caspian's brows lifted into a devastating arch. "Are you truly telling a man who made his first million at twenty-one and his first billion at twenty-five that you are better qualified than he to judge what is extraordinary?"

"Yeah but...*millions*. Some of my coats don't even have buttons."

"You're not listening to me." Unexpectedly, he smiled, a swift, lovely thing, as unhesitating as a rapier thrust. "That, in itself, takes a courage few possess."

It wasn't courage so much as utter overwhelm, but I thought it was probably best to keep my mouth shut.

His breath fell softly against my lips like its own, ephemeral kiss. "You're always yourself no matter where you are or who you're with. You're generous and passionate and honorable. You make me laugh. And, though many would believe me the last person on earth to need it, you've always been kind to me."

Oh. My. God.

The wanking-related blushes were nothing compared to the hellish inferno currently raging on my face. My head was Jackson Pollock whirly, and for a moment or two, I thought I might cry. But I just about managed to control myself.

Gave an unconvincing bleaty laugh instead.

"I guess you're right," I said, "I am pretty awesome."

He leaned in and took my face between his hands. His fingers were cool and light, his touch so cautiously tender that I had another struggle with my tear ducts. "You are," he told me.

I gave him the world's soupiest smile. He didn't return it—Caspian Hart probably couldn't look soupy if he tried—but for a moment his eyes were summer day gentle. And I thought maybe it didn't matter if he was right or wrong or defrauded deranged to think all these bizarrely wonderful things about me. Only that he did.

I thought he might kiss me, but he didn't, disentangling himself instead. "I have to…that is…I should leave."

And, this time, I knew it wasn't rejection. I gave him my best smile—"Of course you do. Those billions aren't going to make themselves"—and let him go.

For a long time after he was gone, I lay there in a happy stupor, in the bed that was still warm from both of us and smelled very faintly of his cologne and his pleasure. The main thought running through my head was: *He likes me. He really likes me.*

It was late enough that falling asleep didn't feel like a total cop-out. Even though technically I could have got up and done useful things, or at least made myself some toast. But I just snuggled down and slipped contentedly into unconsciousness.

Had an absolutely amazing dream.

I was chained up in a dungeon—a proper one, not some sort of BDSM playroom—arms over my head in rusty shackles. Someone was hurting me, the details of it all hazy because it was a dream, until I was running with sweat and blood. And so hard I could have drilled through the stone walls. And then they were inside me. Buried deep enough to burn. One hand at my throat.

And it was Caspian.

Telling me I was generous and passionate and honorable as he took me and hurt me and left me breathless.

Though, of course, I woke up alone.

To another bouquet of fucking roses.

CHAPTER 19

Caspian was elusive after that. Busy, I guess? At any rate, it turned out guests weren't a problem, as long as I gave Bellerose enough notice to clear it with security and update Caspian's diary so he knew I wasn't available.

I was actually super excited to see Nik. And I think he was happy to see me—although it was slightly overshadowed by his reaction to the apartment.

"Holy fuckballs," he said, his bag slipping off his shoulder and thumping onto the floor. "When you said to meet you at Hyde Park, I assumed you were just using it as a landmark and we'd be off to some scuzzy bedsit you were renting in Peckham."

"Yeah, I'm just crashing here while my crack den is being repainted."

Nik turned dazedly, his eyes skidding over glass and silk and marble, much as mine had done when I'd first arrived. As, to be fair, they still did because I wasn't sure how you ever got used to a place like this. "Seriously, Arden. How can you afford it?"

It was an entirely reasonable question. "I'm housesitting, I guess? For a friend?"

"What friend? Mohamed Al-Fayed?"

"Um"—crunch time—"Caspian Hart."

I was being gaped at. I shuffled my feet.

"Do you want to maybe not stand in the hall?" I asked. "There's a sitting area. And a receiving area."

"Sure. Why the hell not. Receive me."

I didn't, in the end, receive him. The sitting area was cozier—cozier, that is, by the standards of the apartment. Meaning it looked basically like a magazine except the pearl-gray sofa was only *very large* as opposed to *inconceivably vast*. You could have fit all my friends and family into the receiving area with room to spare. Here they would have had to squish up.

"Let me get this straight." Nik sank onto a chair. "Your... friend... Caspian Hart. Is letting you stay in his home?"

I curled up in the corner bit of the sofa. Sofas with corner bits were the best sofas and this one, being an elegant U-shape, had *two*. "It's not his home. It's just one of his houses. He was very clear about that."

"Right. But he's just letting you stay here?"

"Only for six months."

"It's not the duration that's confusing me here."

"Is it really so weird that Caspian Hart would offer his multimillion-pound luxury— Okay, yes, it's weird. The truth is, I'm sleeping with him."

"You're dating Caspian Hart?"

"No, just sleeping with him." Squirm. "And while that's happening, this is where I'm living." Squirm. "I know it's a bit prostitutey."

He stared at me. "Are you kidding me? I think it's awesome. Look at this stuff."

"Isn't it neat?" I mustered a limp smile.

"Oh come on. You don't feel bad, do you?"

"Sometimes. A little bit. I mean"—awkward gesture—"this place is just…and I'm not really…"

"Not really what?"

"Worth it." Eep. That sounded bad. "I mean," I added hastily, "in a literal exchange of goods and services way."

"You're not fungible, Ardy."

"Damn right I'm not. I'm very hygienic."

He laughed. "Boom tish. I just meant, it's all proportional. He's a multibillionaire who keeps this place around as his spare…I don't know what. This is nothing to him. And you're something."

I blinked. He actually had a point. Caspian wanted me. Within certain limitations, admittedly, but he wanted me. And it wasn't like I'd be any less interested in being with him if the apartment was no longer on offer. Cards on the table, I was secretly hoping he'd still be into me when it wasn't.

"Besides"—Nik was once again gazing at the magnificence—"I think I'd sleep with him if he let me stay here. And I'm straight."

"I think that makes you heteroflexible at the very least."

He grinned. "No, just mercenary."

"What about the time—"

Before I could remind him about the enthusiastically received hand job delivered by yours truly, he'd bounced off the sofa. "Can I get the guided tour?"

"Um, sure."

It didn't take very long because everything was laid out to look as impressive as possible, which meant most of the rooms flowed together. But Nik gasped and cooed and squeeed over everything, turned on all the devices, opened all the cupboards, poked and prodded and peered, and rolled around on the guest bed like an excited golden retriever. And, for the first time since I'd moved in, I felt…not at home exactly, but unambiguously happy to be there. It was that naughty holiday feeling you got from staying at a posh hotel, knowing you could flump around in the branded dressing gowns and use the fancy shampoo in the tiny bottles.

"This is the best." Nik waved his arms and legs in the air. "I wish I hadn't got onto this research project now. I could have stayed here, leeching off you."

"No, you couldn't. Caspian is going to want to, y'know…bone down on me at some point." Soon, I hoped.

"You could put a sock on the door."

"Go fuck your own billionaire."

Grinning, Nik sat up and gave me what he probably thought was a coy glance. "Well, at least show me a good time tonight."

I'd always been nervy of taking advantage of Caspian's generosity. Which, in practice, meant living on Coco Pops and pretending not to exist. Honestly, if there'd been a cupboard under the stairs, I'd probably have moved into it. But he'd given me access to a lot of really cool stuff and Nik didn't seem to think there was anything wrong with what I was doing so...maybe...just this once?

"Come on, then," I said, holding out my hand. "Let's live the high life."

I took him down to the pool, which was way less murdery when I wasn't on my own. And afterward we tried out the sauna, where I got to enjoy the sight of a largely naked and incredibly glisteny Nik. Unfortunately, I think I probably just looked pink and fainty—so I removed joint sauna taking off the list of sexy things I could daydream about doing with Caspian.

I'd never quite been able to wrap my head around the fact that the building had its own spa—but it really did, and they welcomed us lavishly enough that it made me self-conscious. Nik seemed pretty happy, though, as he was whisked off to do this special gentleman treatment thing called a power lift facial that wouldn't threaten his masculinity. Since I gave no fucks about my masculinity, I had a rose-themed series of massages that left me limp and fragrant from toes to scalp.

"Wow." Back at the flat, Nik had raided the fridge, poured a glass of the water I hadn't dared drink, and draped himself over the sofa I usually perched on. "I can't imagine being able to do this every day."

"I don't," I protested. "Mainly I spend my time failing to be a journalist."

Nik gave me a look. "I think you have to actually *do* something to fail at it."

"You mean I'm failing at failure?"

"You've hardly been here five seconds."

"Yeah, I know." I heaved out a tragic sigh. "But I was supposed to have applied for internships and I didn't, so now I'll have to approach people and pitch stuff and waaaah!"

"Hey," he started dramatically, "I've got an idea. Why don't you approach people and pitch stuff?"

I pouted.

"What? You know you're a good writer."

"Maybe at university. But this is the real world now. The stakes are different."

"Not really. It's the same pool of people if you think about it."

Huh. "I guess."

"Then maybe...write something?"

I opened my mouth—

"And don't whimper about it."

"But I'm so cute when I'm whimpering."

"Save it for your billionaire."

I whimpered anyway. "I don't know what to write about."

"Yeah, you're right." Nik gazed around the flat. "Nothing to write about here."

"I can't...OMG. That would be a total violation of Caspian's trust."

"I'm not suggesting you give us a blow-by-blow of your relationship. But isn't this lifestyle magazine gold dust?"

"Regular reader of those, are you?"

"I went to school with half the people who show up in *Milieu* these days so"—he blushed—"yeah. Of course I am."

Oh my God, too adorbs. I just *had* to tease him. "And

how else would you know what handbag Kate Middleton is carrying."

"Hey, hey." Nik got, if possible, even pinker. "They do this watch and sports car pullout, which is amazing."

More famous still was *The List*, which was a rundown of the UK's top hundred most eligible single people. I could vaguely remember a time when it had been bachelors only but yay for social equality. Last year Caspian Hart had been number seven, sandwiched between Prince Harry and Phoebe Collings-James. Not that I'd looked it up or anything. Ahem.

"It would be completely amazing to work for *Milieu*," I said dreamily.

"Then get scribbling." Nik had obviously reached his limit for talking about my feelings—which, to be fair, was higher than you'd expect for someone whose preferred emotional outlet was running really fast or lifting heavy things. "Is there anything to eat around here?"

"Coco Pops? Or I could make toast."

"Seriously? People who live in places like this dine on breakfast cereal?"

"Well, no. There's private chefs and restaurants I could call, I guess. Or there's...what's it called...in-residence catering from the hotel next door."

"Isn't that one of Heston Blumenthal's places?" Nik gave me starving puppy eyes.

I winced, very aware I was being a rubbish host. Bellerose had explicitly told me I had access to, well, basically anything I could imagine wanting. But running up a massive bill felt seedy as all hell. "Let me check, okay?"

I left Nik devouring the menu on my laptop and went into the hall to phone Bellerose. He picked up on the second ring.

"Yes?"

"Um." Was I ever going to manage to talk to Caspian's assistant, either in person or at a distance, without feeling gauche and stupid? Our survey said: no. "You know how I've got my friend Nik staying?"

"Yes."

"Well, is it okay if we order dinner from the hotel restaurant?"

There was a sharp little silence.

"Yes, Arden. It is okay if you order dinner from the hotel restaurant. If you're very good, you can even stay up till eleven."

Great. Now I wanted to curl up and die. "This is your way of telling me I shouldn't be bothering you, isn't it?"

He hung up.

Ow. Ow. Ow.

Nik was still glued to the screen when I slunk back. "Ardy, this menu is totally whack."

"Order the whole damn thing if you like."

"Don't tempt me." He glanced up. "Are you okay?"

"Yeah, I'm fine."

He held out an arm and I snuck in gratefully beside him. Tried to distract myself with the familiar warmth of his body. And the menu, which was, indeed, whack. "I don't think I know what *any* of this is."

"We could roll a dice."

"Nerd."

"Or pick for each other."

Sensing a prime opportunity to troll my beloved friend, I perked up and went for it. "Let's do that. You're having Rice & Flesh to start."

His eager little face went through several variations of perturbation, distress, and apprehension. "Well, fine. You can have the Savory Porridge. Which is frog legs, garlic, parsley, and fennel. Mmmmmmm. Sounds delicious."

I'm pretty sure my own little face turned gray. "Yay," I said weakly. "I love fennel."

Sadly the mains and desserts offered a lot less opportunity for mischief, though we did our best. I tormented Nik by ordering him a dish just called Braised Celery, which made him get me the most expensive beef thing on the menu—bone in rib, apparently—on the expectation he could share it with me when the braised celery turned out to be a bust. Because, as Nik put it, *fucking celery, man.* For pudding, we went with Sambocade, which was apparently a kind of goat milk cheesecake, and an apple tart, the description of which contained absolutely no references to apples.

While I phoned through the order, Nik opened a bottle of champagne. He'd chosen one of the less-extravagant-looking bottles—just dark green glass, foil that seemed to hover somewhere between gold and silver, and an austere label reading CHAMPAGNE KRUG CLOS DU MESNIL 1988—so hopefully it wasn't too expensive.

All that time I'd spent thinking champagne was meh? Turned out I was wrong. Very very wrong.

"This," said Nik, "is like... if there was a unicorn made out of vanilla and sparkles, and it was running through a field of primroses on a spring morning to meet its best unicorn friend for honey cakes…like…if that was champagne."

I nodded. "Or like…if you had a pear, right, that had lived a life of absolute virtue and had reached a higher state of pear…and if that pear was nestled into the bosom of a nymph, with flowers in her hair, bathing in a crystalline spring in the Elysium fields."

"Yeah. Just like that."

"It's…it's really good, isn't it?"

"Yeah."

We contemplated this for a while.

"You don't think," I asked, "it was special or anything, do you?"

"Nah—1988 isn't that old."

"It's older than me."

"Yeah, but you're not mature. Or champagne."

I pressed a hand to my heart. "If I was, I'd like to be this champagne."

"If you were, I would drink you."

"I'd probably let you."

Sometime between opening the bottle and finishing the bottle and embarking on another one, we had decided to lie on the rug to better appreciate the beauty of the universe.

Which was when dinner arrived. It was super *super* weird to be served in your home like it was a restaurant, except it was hard to imagine One Hyde Park being anyone's home really, and we were tipsy, which helped with the embarrassment factor.

The food went by in a blur of faint weirdness. They'd brought us this complementary starter, which was an orange and some burned toast, except the orange was actually pate and Nik exploded it with a knife when he tried to slice into it like you would a piece of fruit. The Rice & Flesh turned out to be saffron risotto with cow bits on top—although it was delicious—and my savory porridge was the worst thing in the world. Probably it tasted okay once you got over the fact that it was bright green and the frog legs croquettes had the bones sticking up like they were flipping you off.

I got my revenge with the mains, though, since the braised celery was still, y'know, braised celery, despite being covered in cheese. Whereas I was presented with most of a dead animal in this amazing sweet-sticky-smoky sauce and crispy, thick-cut chips like you get in gastro pubs. Although, if those were my terms of reference, probably I didn't have much of a future as a food critic.

By the time we got to dessert, we were basically dead of indulgence. The caramelized apple tart turned out to be literally a caramelized apple on a pastry base, with ice cream on the side. So that was sort of hilarious. As was the fact that Nik cut into it super carefully, having obviously been scarred for life by the disguised orange experience.

What was left of the evening found us in a pile on the sofa, under a duvet dragged from the guest room, watching *Supergirl* on the enormous wall-mounted TV. Nik idled his fingers in my hair and it was like being at Oxford—except university had been this closed system, made up of habits and proximity and inevitability. Now we were in the world. And the world was kind of…ours.

Full of possibility.

Or I was just full of champagne.

"What's he like?" Nik asked.

"Hmm?"

"Caspian Hart."

"Oh." Tricky one, that. "Complex."

"Wow, you've really developed this keen insight into him, haven't you?"

I *gnang*ed his shoulder. "I'm not sure what to say. He's rich, powerful, and insanely hot. He lives in a different world from me."

"Yeah, but do you like him?"

I wondered how to explain.

"The fact that you're taking so long to say yes isn't a great sign, Ardy."

"Oh my God, of course I like him. I just…I'm not sure I *know* him."

"Well, you only met him a few months ago."

"I get that but"—I chewed my lip thoughtfully—"it feels…deeper somehow. Like maybe he doesn't want me to."

Nik was quiet for a moment or two. "This reminds me of the time you broke up with that guy because he didn't like *Labyrinth*."

"Yes, because what sort of monster doesn't like *Labyrinth*?"

"Um…maybe this isn't about *Labyrinth*. Just saying."

I peeped at him over the top of the duvet. "You mean—dum dum duhhh—it's about me."

"You do have a way of getting out of relationships."

"But," I pointed out, all logical-like, "I'm not in a relationship with Caspian."

"And yet you're still looking for the thing that's wrong with it."

Wow. He'd got me there.

"Wow," I said, "you got me there."

He pulled me in closer and attacked my hair until it was all fluffy and annoying. "I'm really going to miss you."

"I love you too."

I snuggled down even farther. Vaguely turned my attention to *Supergirl*—who was saving the world with her compassion and sincerity, and some hard-core punching. Mainly, though, I was thinking about what Nik had said and if it was true. I mean, yes, it was. Kind of.

Or maybe it was a totally different problem this time. Because, for once in my life, I didn't want out of a relationship: I wanted *in* one. But that meant finding my way—probably through dangers untold and hardships unnumbered—past the man Caspian kept trying to be, the one who sent me flowers by rote and touched me by rote and didn't seem to see me when he looked at me, to the one who had whispered to me down the phone, laughed with me, listened to me, comforted and believed in me. The man who had come for me at Oxford when I most needed him to be there.

And whose harsh kisses stripped bare his needs to me as surely as I bared mine to him.

CHAPTER 20

The next day, I called a car to take Nik to the airport—just about managing not to ask Bellerose's permission this time—and since I wasn't exactly overendowed with things to do, went along with him.

Which was a daft move because saying goodbye at the airport turned out to be awful. It felt all *final*. And I got clingy as hell, trailing around the concourse with Nik, holding his hand like a kid at the supermarket. But then he wasn't exactly shaking me off either.

We parted at the last possible moment with a pathetic amount of hugging. I was crying openly and Nik was snuffling manfully.

"I'm going to come back and visit all the time," he said. "I really need another one of those facials."

I nodded. "You'll need it. America is bad for the complexion."

"And we can still Kik and buddy watch stuff."

"Yep yep."

"And you can obsessively like all my Instagram posts."

"I only care about the ones where you're shirtless. Fuck this cappuccino foam art bullshit."

"I made a little cat."

"But were you shirtless?"

He laughed, then checked the time on his phone. "Shit, I'd better go."

I wiped my eyes and put on my best brave face. "Travel safely."

And that was…it. I guess that was the thing about goodbyes: they were always smaller than you expected.

The flat seemed even quieter and emptier without Nik. And the worst of it was the cleaners had hit hard. The duvet was back on the bed—actually it was probably a fresh duvet, the other having been whisked off to be scoured of all traces of humanity—the leftovers were gone, and the champagne glasses were back in the cupboard. It was like Nik had never been here at all.

And there was still no Caspian. Not surprising, honestly, because he'd warned me he was very busy. Probably he wasn't even in the country.

I located a branch of WHSmith and popped out to buy a copy of *Milieu*. Spent the rest of the day trying to be witty and gay on the subject of…of…well, that was kind of the kicker. Molten shell treatments? Finnish premium spring water? I tried, I really tried, but it didn't go well. I was too full of sads. And, in the end, I broke and rang Bellerose.

"Yes, Arden?"

I opened my mouth and nothing came out.

"Yes, Arden?"

"Is Caspian away?"

"No, he's at a meeting of the CBI. Why?"

"Oh. No reason. I just. Um. Thankyouverymuchsorrygood-bye."

Well. That had...been a thing that happened. What was still more excruciating, though, was the text I got from Caspian a few hours later. He said he'd be coming round that evening, and I couldn't tell whether it was nothing more than a coincidence or if Bellerose had told him.

Mr. Hart—oh wait, he called him Caspian. *Caspian, the annoyance you installed in your Kensington apartment wants your attention.*

Or, y'know, maybe now was not a reasonable time to descend into a whimpering pit of paranoia. Because it was very possible he genuinely wanted to see me. And the fact that he hadn't given any indication of doing so for nearly a week could have meant absolutely anything.

Not necessarily that he was bored of me already.

Urgh my brain. It was like I had this insecurity pendulum: I'd just about convince myself everything was okay and then it would swing back even harder and hit me right in the face.

I managed not to be visibly freaking out when Caspian finally arrived. I'd spent the intervening time profitably at any rate. Okay, that was a lie. I'd showered and painted my toenails blue and silver and tended my...uh...whatever the male equivalent to the ladygarden was. The boylawn?

Nothing major—just a delicate trim to frame the general

area and the personal eviction of a few non-brunette hairs. It was the St. Ives family curse: brownish on top, reddish below. At least, I assumed it was genetic. I hadn't *asked* my mum about her curtains or anything. But her head hair matched mine. And what that meant for me was the occasional bright ginger pube, waving wildly from amongst its more socially acceptable fellows like a Miley Cyrus fan at a Taylor Swift concert.

Anyway, Caspian arrived, looking blah blah gorgeous, because did he ever not, his intimate hair probably perfectly groomed beneath his pinstripes. He was carrying a bottle of something. Dark green glass, silver-gold label. Uh-oh.

He held it aloft, his lips curving into what—on a less austere face—might have passed for a teasing smile. "I understand you've developed a taste for this?"

"Well, we drank a couple of bottles the other… Wait a minute, how do you know that?"

"The app monitors the contents of the fridge."

"That's incredibly creepy."

"It's for restocking, Arden. Not spying."

"Tell that to the milk."

He laughed and went to replace the champagne. And, after a moment, I trailed worriedly after him.

"It was okay, wasn't it? For us to drink it, I mean."

"Of course. You might, however, want to go a little easy in the future."

Ouch. Although considering my postfinals performance, it was no wonder he'd concluded I was a burgeoning alcoholic. "I know you probably won't believe this, but I'm not really a big drinker. I'm not going to drain your cellars dry or anything."

"That's not what I meant. It's just this happens to be somewhat of a rare vintage."

"Somewhat?" My heart curled up like a dead slug. "You don't mean somewhat at all, do you? You mean...extremely or remarkably or exceptionally."

He didn't have to say anything.

I windmilled my arms. "Oh my God. Oh my God. Why was it just in your fridge? That's like a totally irresponsible way to store expensive wine and shit. Even I know that and I know nothing about expensive wine and shit. What the fuck were you thinking?"

"I'm sorry, Arden."

"Don't laugh. This isn't funny."

Caspian closed his eyes. Brought up a hand and pressed his knuckles to his mouth.

"I said don't laugh!"

He laughed.

A great undignified spluttering thing and if I hadn't been so angry-appalled I'd have been *delighted*. Because to see Caspian anything less than absolutely controlled was a victory.

"How could you let me do this?" I wailed. "I've never even heard of clos du mes...mes...whatever it was. Although I guess that should have clued me in to not drinking it."

He drew in a rough, unsteady breath. And, within seconds, was almost his usual self again. "I don't care that you drank it. Since I'm neither a collector nor an auctioneer, that's what wine is for."

"Not wine like that. It was just in your fridge." I was repeating myself like a traumatized crime scene witness. "Why would you have something like that sitting in your fridge?"

"To impress the people I usually have staying here."

"That's...a little bit wanky."

"I work in financial services." His mouth softened with a faint, fleeting trace of mischief. "I know a lot of wankers."

We were silent for a bit, hovering awkwardly in the kitchen. Now the initial shock had worn off, I was beginning to calm down.

"I don't want this to happen again," I said finally. "I get you're amused. But I feel really bad about it."

"You didn't enjoy yourselves?"

"Well, of course we did. It was the most amazing champagne I've ever tasted. But I can't in all honesty say I derived sufficient pleasure for the likely cost."

"My little puritan." His fingers traced the line of my jaw before gently turning my face up to receive an unexpected kiss. "No pleasure is worth the cost. Some things are beyond price."

Unfortunately, I'd gone weak-kneed and wobbly and wasn't really up for a discussion of the transience of material wealth and the transcendental nature of the superficial. Because mouths and hands and bodies and—"Nrgble."

"I want you to be happy, Arden. You know, you can have whatever you want."

I made a sort of lunging nuzzle into his palm. This was sweet of him. And confusing. But not quite what I needed to hear. Basically it was emotional umami. And I didn't know how to answer. Except then I blurted out, "But I don't want things. I want you."

Caspian froze. It was like lights going out. Security doors coming down. Then he leaned in and kissed me again, and it was all teeth, all savagery. He spun me round, driving me back against the fridge, his mouth still on mine, one hand trapping my wrists and the other sliding down to rest against my throat. It was a pretty threatening way to be pinned, with my pulse beating under his palm and the heat of him surrounding me.

So, obviously, I was super into it.

He finally broke the kiss, leaving me breathless and dizzy and full of the taste of him. Pressed in even closer, his eyes a flare of ice blue—sun glare across glaciers—and his lips a little red from mine. "No, you don't."

"How do you know? Don't you trust me?"

His thumb circled a shivery spot below my ear. "It's me I don't trust."

"What do you mean?" Swoony with sex feels, I swayed into his touch. Maybe I should have been more concerned about the whole hand-around-my-neck thing but…I wasn't. It was intimate—intimately scary—and I liked it.

"Oh, Arden. I want so much I shouldn't." Abruptly he let me go, but it was only to gather me close for a moment, his breath shaky against my skin. "But most of all I want to be good for you. Please, let me be good."

He didn't often let me get my hands on him. I took major advantage and wrapped him up tight tight tight. "You are. You're amazing. And I want to be amazing for you too."

"I can't seem to control myself very well around you."

"Why do you have to?" I threaded my fingers through his

hair. And this time it was me, gently urging him to lift his head. To look at me. "Unless you're trying to tell me you're going to eat me with some fava beans and a nice Chianti?"

He gave me a startled look. The man paid so little heed to popular culture he might as well have been an inadvertent time traveler: one of Georgette Heyer's exquisitely sophisticated Corinthians adrift in the twenty-first century without his matched grays and his gentleman's personal gentleman. (Though, let's face it, the whip was transferable.) Once, it might have made me laugh, but now it was just another weird gulf between us. Another way we couldn't communicate or understand each other.

"I mean," I explained hastily, "unless you're trying to tell me you're a serial killer or something."

"I'm not a serial killer. But you should still be wary of me. I'm just...I'm not good at caring for people. I try. But it becomes such a twisted thing."

This was starting to scare me. Not because I expected him to chop me up and put me in the freezer, but because he sounded so completely fucking desolate. "I don't believe this for a second. You've been extraordinarily nice. And, frankly, ridiculously generous."

"You deserve nothing less."

"Call me easily pleased, but that seems a pretty decent level of caring to me."

He made a soft, frustrated noise. "You don't understand. Yes, I care for you. Yes, I want to make you happy. Yes, I would lay the whole damn world at your feet if you would let me. But I also want to hurt you. I want you on your knees. I want you in chains. I want to have you crying and screaming and begging for me."

"Would," I squeaked, "would I get a safeword?"

He tore out of my arms and slammed his hand hard enough against a cabinet to make me jump. "Arden, this isn't a fantasy or a game."

"You think I don't know that?" I tried not to get shouty. But it happened anyway. "You're the one who acts like it's a game. Like you can keep me in a pretty box and only ever show me this…I don't know…perfect benefactor you've decided I need."

"I'm trying to protect you."

"I can protect myself."

"Which I suppose is why," he snapped, "when I found you in Oxford, you were about to be raped in an alley."

Well, he did say he wanted me crying. Mission accomplished.

Fucking bastard.

They were the worst tears though: the kind that happened when somebody made you feel so utterly small, your body couldn't cope with the immensity of your emotions anymore. And then they burst out of you in this rush of humiliation, fury, and salt.

I couldn't even think of a fucking retort.

Nothing that would properly communicate my shock and betrayal. He'd used a moment of vulnerability against me when I was already vulnerable.

When I was making myself vulnerable *for him*.

Because I thought…oh who knew what I thought.

I walked away. And as I passed the dining area table, the roses threw back their heads and laughed at me with red mouths.

I picked up the vase, turned back to Caspian—who, of course, was as calm as fucking ever—and very deliberately let it slip between my hands.

The smash was epic. Glass and water and bloody petals.

For about 0.3 seconds, I felt better.

Then I felt worse.

And still Caspian didn't respond. Just watched me with those high windows eyes of his: deep blue air, nothing, nowhere, and endless.

Fleeing into the bedroom, I locked the door and dived into bed. It was childish as fuck but I didn't know what else to do since Nik had been right about me. I didn't stick around in relationships long enough to reach the god-awful row stage. What happened now? Did I have to go back out there? Was Caspian supposed to apologize? Was *I* supposed to apologize?

Because that was never happening.

Weeping helplessly, I stuffed my head under the pillow so Caspian wouldn't be able to hear. Was that how he saw me? One—admittedly fucked up—misjudgment and I couldn't be trusted to know my own mind? That I was nothing more than a victim waiting to happen? Was that what people thought about Mum?

Movement in the hallway outside.

I went still as a rabbit, not sure what I wanted. Part of me wanted him to push his way in and apologize. Hold me and comfort me. Tell me he didn't mean it. The rest of me would have bitten him if he'd come within range.

But, no. He was just leaving. His footsteps receded. Another door closed.

Taking advantage of having the place to myself, I let go and cried in earnest, with abandon. I really wanted to phone Nik but he was forty thousand feet in the air, somewhere between London and Massachusetts. Actually, he'd probably landed but Sobbing!Arden wasn't exactly the welcome to Boston call he needed.

What was I supposed to do? I couldn't exactly stay here after that. Whatever Caspian believed, I had some pride. Or maybe it was nothing but a misunderstanding and he would...fix it.

Except he'd just gone. But, then, so had I.

And I'd also broken a vase.

But he'd—

Arrgh. My head had gone all ouroboros. And I wasn't quite sure where right and wrong began or ended anymore.

Just that I was angry and sad and confused and fucked up.

So, what with one thing and another, I wasn't exactly paying much attention to time passing. But it was probably an hour or two later when I heard someone come in. And, even though I'd been lying there, swearing myself blue in the face that I was going to be *a stone* whatever Caspian did or said, and probably leave in the morning anyway, the possibility that he'd come back made my stupid little heart do the fandango.

Hurling myself out of the room, I crashed straight into one of the cleaners. Apparently he'd been called in to deal with a broken vase.

Which...y'know.

Of course he had.

CHAPTER 21

I woke up miserable and slightly shocked I'd been able to sleep at all, with all the crying and raging and soul-searching I'd been doing. But unconsciousness and a small amount of distance had calmed me down.

Yes, Caspian had been, to put it bluntly, a dickhead. But we'd been having a very intense conversation and he'd probably felt exposed and pounced on, and—in any case—I shouldn't have reacted by trashing the place like I was Keith Moon. And while part of me really didn't want to be dependent on Caspian's generosity in the middle of a fight, it seemed a bit off to throw up my hands and run away immediately.

Not that I didn't want to. Right now, I would have preferred to be pretty much anywhere than One Hyde Park, including with my family up in Kinlochbervie. But, even putting aside my lack of relationship experience, it seemed pretty fucking obvious that being in the same country was likely a major factor in resolving romantic conflict.

And, hopefully, waking up somewhere across the city—actually, he'd probably already woken up and been at work for sixty-seven hours—Caspian was reaching the same conclusion. The drug dealer phone was almost out of juice because I hadn't bothered to charge it last night, but a quick check revealed no messages. My thumb hovered over sending one myself, but in the end I didn't.

He'd started the argument. He could start the peace negotiations.

Although, by three o'clock, I was starting to think that maybe he wouldn't—and we'd be locked in unending, unacknowledged conflict, like he was Russia and I was Berwick-upon-Tweed. Or, more likely, he would simply send Bellerose to evict me and that would be the end of everything.

The rest of the afternoon dribbled away. Still no word from Caspian.

Several messages from Nik though—and a picture of him shirtless, about to drink a cappuccino, which stopped the day from being 100 percent abysmal, and got it down to a mere 94 percent utter shite.

I had no idea what Caspian was thinking. But maybe he had no idea what I was thinking either. If I'd secretly entertained fantasies of groveling apologies and kissing at the airport while random strangers applauded, the cleaner had put paid to them. Honestly, at this point, I would have settled for a text.

When none came in by bedtime, I'd circled back to the get-the-hell-out-of-Dodge plan. Possibly I was being petty and who contacted who wasn't important...but no matter how reasonable I tried to force myself to be, it still *felt* important.

I mean, what was I doing here? What did he want from me—if he wouldn't trust me, wouldn't believe me, wouldn't fucking pick up the phone and call me?

Miserably, I began packing my stuff. It took longer than I expected because it turned out I'd been colonizing. And, while One Hyde Park still intimidated the shit out me, I'd managed to accrue a fair few good memories. That evening with Nik. Eating the Pocky Caspian had bought me. Caspian's hands on me, when he'd lost control and touched me like I was real. The times I'd made him laugh. The times he'd listened to me.

Gah.

No more crying, Arden.

I crawled into bed and set an alarm for nasty-early—it was going to take the best part of a day to get back home, unless I flew, which wasn't exactly in my budget, given my income of nothing-a-month. But it was better than hanging around here, waiting for Caspian to decide whether he still wanted me or not. Once again, I didn't expect to sleep much but I must have dropped off because I was woken up again a few hours later by…

Sounds in the apartment?

My first, hopeful thought was that Caspian had finally come to talk to me. At 4:00 a.m.

Oh shit. There was no way it was him.

Which meant there was someone else here. The cleaners? Surely not at this hour. Was it a burglary? A home invasion? The revolution? Was I about to be executed as a presumed minor dictator or Russian oligarch?

I spasmed into a sitting position. Fuck fuck fuck. I'd left my mobile in the study and the drug dealer phone in the sitting area, so I couldn't even ring someone. The police or the front desk or the private security company Bellerose had mentioned.

Probably my best option involved diving under the bed and waiting until the thieves...invaders...assassins...zombies had gone but if the noises they were making were anything to go by, it didn't seem as if they were leaving anytime soon.

Also, once I started paying proper attention, they weren't particularly aggressive noises. More...laughy-talky-drinky noises.

Right.

Nothing for it.

I was going to have to go out there.

I took a deep breath, de-cocooned myself, and glanced around for something I could use as a weapon. Unfortunately, the closest thing to hand was my Lelo Billy and that probably wasn't going to do the job. Unless I intended to scare them off with my liberated approach to self-pleasure.

There were various designer knickknacks elegantly positioned here and there about the bedroom—not actual *possessions*, such as ordinary humans owned, so much as things that looked good and matched the décor—but I wasn't sure if I'd feel any safer wielding a...was it a vase? Or a candleholder?

Well. Okay then.

I slipped into the corridor and headed for the receiving room.

Where I found a bunch of strangers making themselves very at home. Sprawled over the sofas I still hesitated to touch.

Splashing champagne over the exquisitely simple, clotted cream rug I feared to put my feet on. Prepping lines on the pristine glass of the scary designer coffee table.

I felt like Bilbo Baggins if the dwarves had come to Play 'n' Party.

"Um," I said, taking control of the situation.

Silence fell.

A slight figure—a mere shadow against the floor-to-ceiling windows—turned, bottle and cigarette balanced in the same hand with effortless expertise. Regarded me for a long moment, before asking in this husky, lazy voice: "Who the fuck are you?"

"I'm…I'm Arden. Caspian said I could stay here."

Her eyes were the oddest shade, not quite blue, not quite green, cold and contrary and…oddly familiar. I wished I was wearing slightly more than a pair of boxers. "Why would he do that?"

"We…he…" What the hell was I supposed to say? I couldn't imagine Caspian being particularly happy if I disclosed our probably already defunct whatever-it-was to random people who had somehow got into his building. "We're friends, I guess."

"My brother doesn't have friends."

Oh. *Oh*. "Sorry, he didn't tell me he had a sister."

"Google me." She lifted the bottle with a clanking of bracelets and took a swig, bubbles running down her arm and splashing onto the floor.

I tried not to wring my hands in dismay. It wasn't my rug or my champagne, but after Rosegate, I really didn't want to be responsible for any further damage. "You know Caspian's not here, right?"

"Right." She threw herself down on the sofa, slamming a motorcycle-booted foot onto the table, where one of her friends was still faffing about with his drugs. "Fuck. I want some music."

I wondered if I would ever have made the connection if she hadn't told me. I could trace some similarities to Caspian, maybe, in her coloring and the cast of her features, but it was probably confirmation bias. She was nothing like her brother at all. My age, possibly a year or two younger, as careless as he was controlled. Striking, though, with her smoky eyes and her long, coltish legs in their torn fishnets. Her look seemed to be pissed off and messed up, as if she'd rolled out of bed and into her clothes.

"Then what are you doing here?" I asked a little plaintively.

The problem with pseudo-housesitting was not really knowing what the boundaries were. How far to make yourself at home. Was it my responsibility to make sure people I didn't know didn't cut coke on Caspian's furniture? Was I supposed to be welcoming his sister or throwing her out?

"Needed somewhere to crash."

"Um. Okay. So I'll just go back to bed then?"

"Stay if you like. This is—" And she reeled off a list of names I wasn't in any state to remember.

I gave the group a halfhearted wave. Thankfully, they were mostly unconscious, distracted, or making out in that desultory postparty way.

"I'm Ellery, by the way."

"Nice to meet you." And, with a desperate attempt to be a good host: "Do you need anything?"

"Never. I like your tattoo."

I looked down in this idiotic way. As if I'd forgotten it was there. "Thanks."

She pulled her legs up and swung herself over the back of the sofa. It was a move that took a certain amount of confidence—or fucklessness—to attempt, especially in a very tiny tank dress. Though mainly I was worried about the marks her boots were leaving on the cream and gold cushions.

When she was close enough, she traced the letters that were visible over the low-hanging waist of my boxers. "What's it say?"

"Let your life lightly dance on the edges of Time."

"I like these too." Her fingers came up to tug my nipple rings.

She was about my height. I was so used to looking up at people that it was a bit disorientating to have someone else's eyes be inescapable. Hers had an almost hypnotic quality. Or maybe I was just searching for Caspian. I very gently removed her hands. "Thanks."

"I didn't think my brother fucked younger men."

That was information I absolutely did not need. "I'm definitely going to bed now."

She shrugged. "'Kay."

Needless to say, sleeping was well and truly borked now. A combination of noise from outside—some of which was definitely fucking—and general anxiety. About Caspian. About Ellery. About going home. About what the hell I was doing with my life.

My alarm went off a couple of hours later and I felt so completely rotten that I decided to give myself an extra five minutes in bed. And then woke up again at midday. I pulled on clothes, just in case I still had guests, but while the main reception room showed rather brutal signs of its previous occupation—broken glasses, empty bottles, champagne rings, traces of cocaine on the coffee table, and something that looked like a used condom curled up on the floor like a smooshed slug—it was definitely empty now. Glancing round, somewhat despairingly, I felt like the hapless host in an American teen comedy after the mandatory party-gone-wrong scene.

Probably I was a spoiled brat for even thinking it but: where were the cleaners? Urgh. There was nothing for it except to get to work myself.

Which was how Caspian found me. On my hands and knees on that amazingly soft and beautiful rug, trying to blot up the worst of the stains with warm water and washing up liquid.

"Arden." His voice, utterly unexpected right then, made me flinch like he'd struck me. "What are you doing?"

I sat up with a yelp. "I...uh...there was...I didn't mean..."

"Why haven't you called the cleaning company?"

"Oh. I...I didn't think of that."

I pushed the hair out of my eyes with the inside of my wrist, feeling sweaty and sticky and as messed up as the room. All the more so with Caspian standing over me, looking flawless and majestic and sleek in a black suit of the sort of terrifying simplicity you only got when a garment cost more than, say, a car. Against such austerity, his eyes were devastatingly blue, and for a moment I couldn't quite believe this stunning, ice sculpture of a man had been inside me.

Had once gasped and moaned for me.

Tangled his hands helplessly in my hair.

Made me feel special.

I could, however, definitely believe I hadn't existed for him the past couple of days.

"Call them," he told me. In his non-fun ordering-me-about voice.

"Oh, well, I don't really want to bother—"

"It's their job. It's what they're there for." He stepped past me, shoes clicking on the marble floor. "Now where's Eleanor?"

"Who?"

"Don't cover for her."

"I'm not. I don't—" But I was protesting to his back.

"Eleanor." He wasn't quite shouting but he definitely sounded...exasperated. "I know you're here."

"Yeah, I'm here." Ellery came into the room, still in last night's clothes, with the same skillfully mussed hair and smudged eyes. "If I didn't want you to find me, your own house would be a dumb place to hide."

"You missed your appointment."

She shrugged. "I'm bored of counseling."

"Then you should cancel, rather than simply failing to turn up. You're not a child."

"So don't talk to me like I am."

Well this was awkward. I didn't want to be in the middle of it, but I also didn't know how to leave without drawing attention to myself. *Don't mind me, guys, just squeezing past your familial dysfunctionality.*

"Eleanor—"

"It's Ellery."

Caspian's back was rigid. And even though he'd been a total dick to me and apparently not even thought about apologizing, I imagined being able to touch him. Ease him. "We haven't heard from you since yesterday morning. Mother was worried."

"That's her problem."

Wow. It was *Alien* versus *Predator* over there.

"I'll let her know where you are," Caspian was saying, "and that you're all right. And I've had your session rescheduled for this afternoon."

"I told you, I'm done with that."

"No, you said you were bored. That's not the same thing. You should go."

Ellery's jewelry jingled as her hands flew up and then down again, disappearing behind her back. Caspian probably didn't even notice but I did: that hint of restlessness, uncertainty, a crack in her sullen defiance. "Well, I can't."

"You will go to counseling, Eleanor, if I have to drag you there by the hair."

I shivered. He sounded like he meant it. Implacable and without warmth. I'd seen that in him before, even felt it a little when he'd turned on me the other night, but it had never been like this. With me, it had always been banked, tempered by care and the promise of heat in his eyes. For his sister, there was only a blank chill.

I would have been a distraught pile on the floor, but Ellery just rolled her eyes. "Like I'd let you anywhere near my hair. And, anyway, what part of *I can't* aren't you getting?"

"The part where I give a damn."

It hung there for a moment like an icicle and then Ellery shrugged. "Tough. Because I'm going out with... with *him*."

Me?

"You're what?" I wasn't sure if I'd spoken or Caspian. Maybe it was both of us.

"Yeah. We're going shopping."

I glanced nervously between them. Caspian was very still and very pale. And probably very angry.

Despite being an only child and growing up in town with a population of about four hundred, I wasn't an idiot. I could see what was going on here and I wasn't mad keen on being a nonconsensual participant in a sibling power game.

I stared at Caspian desperately. If he'd looked at me, given any sign of remembering I was there—of remembering I wasn't just a less effective alternative to a cleaning company—I wouldn't have agreed.

But he gave me nothing. As usual.

"Yeah, sure," I said.

And *that* got his attention. Not in a good way. But before he had a chance to respond, Ellery had pulled me out of the room.

CHAPTER 22

Nobody was chasing us, but we ran anyway. It gave me a tingly, Ferris Bueller feeling to flee the swaggering modernity and aggressive wealth of One Hyde Park for the crumbly Victorian grandeur of Kensington.

We stopped for breath near Hyde Park Corner. Ellery slumped onto the steps of something pillared, porticoed and flag-flying, and I discovered I'd left the apartment without a coat or my wallet or either of my phones. Thank God the place was above mere human *keys*; otherwise I might have been homeless. Which would have been infinitely preferable to turning up at Caspian's office again in order to tell him I'd locked myself out of the apartment after running away with his sister.

"Well... thanks or whatever." Ellery hugged her knees to her chest, walling herself off with her own body. "But you don't have to stay."

"What, and go back to a pissed off Caspian? I don't think so."

After a moment, I sat next to her and she rested her cheek on her folded forearms, watching me. Her eyes reminded me of the marbles I used to covet as a kid, glassy with a sharp twist of color at the center.

"Are you really with him?" she asked.

"I have no idea. It's complicated."

"You should be careful. You seem sweet and he's fucked up."

This didn't seem like something I should be talking about with Caspian's sister. I mean, yes, he'd been a dick to me. But that didn't mean I got to be a dick back.

I gave Ellery what I hoped was a suitably ironic look. "Right, because you're such a bastion of normality."

"I only hurt myself."

I wasn't sure how to begin to answer that.

But then she stood, shaking out her dress, and asked, "You really want to do stuff with me?"

"Why not?"

"He won't like it."

"He won't care."

She smiled, a thin half-moon of a smile, one side of her mouth pulling up a little farther than the other. "Come on, then."

She held out her hand and I took it. Leather bands and chunky bracelets clung to her wrists, making them look thinner than ever, and her nails were bitten right down, painted with chipped black polish. She was too cold, too frail.

But, hey, at least someone in the Hart family was okay being touched by me.

Ellery took me to Harrods, which I still hadn't got round

to visiting, even though it was just over the road from where I lived. It was kind of dizzying in there. A Victorian wonderland of gilt and excess. The sort of place where you could buy tiaras for three hundred grand and chocolates for twenty quid each. It reminded me of a museum more than a department store, with its myriad rooms and echoing antechambers. The statuary. The Egyptian escalator.

Crazy shit. Beautiful and grotesque in equal measure.

A shop designed by Kubla bloody Khan.

We had oysters. At an oyster and champagne bar. Because, apparently, that was a thing.

Oysters were something else I'd never done. Never seen the point, since they looked like snot and—apparently—tasted of girls. Not that I had any objections to the second.

It turned out to be a lie anyway. They tasted purely, almost overwhelmingly, of the sea. Clean and rich and a little metallic.

I liked to think I was a pro at the swallowing thing—plenty of practice and all that—though I couldn't help notice Ellery chewed. I didn't know if she was trying to psych me out or if I was doing it wrong. Shifty glances at the people around me revealed a mixture of techniques and I felt this sharp and sudden pang that I wasn't here with Caspian.

It would have been so romantic—sexy too—to share something like this with him. He probably knew exactly how to eat oysters. I imagined the curve of his palm beneath the whorled silver-gray shell as he held it to my lips. The slight roughness as I opened for him. Then the flood of flavor across my tongue like the rush of the waves to the shore.

God. I was being a terrible guest. About three melancholy thoughts from weeping into my Krug Grande Cuvée—which was a champagne I definitely recognized as expensive this time.

Somewhere around the third glass of it, I plucked up the courage to ask, "Why Ellery?"

"I didn't like Eleanor." She licked a trail of lemon juice from the heel of her palm.

Once again, I didn't know what to say. I wondered if it was natural talent or an ability she nurtured. If she enjoyed capriciously dead-ending conversations or if it was just about control. Like maybe that was something else that ran in the fucking family.

"Hey, I"—she looked up suddenly, catching at me with her too-bright eyes—"forgot your name."

I half wished I had the balls to take someone for oysters without having a clue who they were. And then to admit it right to their face without a trace of shame. "Arden. After the forest."

"The forest?"

"The Shakespeare version, not the real one."

There was a silence.

Then, with flat disbelief: "Your parents named you after a forest?"

"Well, it's a magical forest. A place of transformation and self-discovery where boys are girls and girls are boys and love is love."

"You like it?"

"I've never been."

"Your name."

"Oh." I'd never really thought about it before. "Yeah, I guess so. Mum chose it. It was kind of a promise."

"What promise?"

I wriggled. Not exactly uncomfortable but very aware we were on the outskirts of Personalville: population me. "To keep me safe."

"People break promises."

"Not my mum."

We were quiet again.

I was trying to decide if I was unsettled or simply drunk, and if I minded being either, when she picked up the last oyster and said, "Going to prick your finger on a spinning wheel someday?"

"Oh no. Um. It was. Well. My dad. He wasn't a great person."

"You don't like him?"

"I don't know him." Could hardly remember him. Which was slightly crazy, since I'd spent the first eight years of my life in his house. But all I had were these memories of fear. His too-tall shadow staggering upon the wall. Like he was the fucking Balrog. "But he drank. And he...he wouldn't let Mum leave."

"How'd you get away?"

"We ran. All the way to Scotland to stay with Hazel. She was this friend of Mum's from school. She's married as well and stuff but...I guess they're all together now?"

"You guess? You don't know?"

"Well, no, they are. It's just some people find it pretty strange."

Ellery shrugged as if the very concept of being surprised was beneath her. "You want to get out of here?"

"Okay."

Well, what was the alternative? *No, I'd rather sit here confiding fragile, complicated stuff about my life and history to a total stranger*?

Except I wasn't exactly telling her secrets.

Secrets implied shame and I wasn't ashamed. My mum lived for years in secrecy and shame with a man who promised her everything and took her apart piece by piece until he thought she was nothing but dust.

And she was still more than he could ever be.

The best and bravest person I knew.

By "get out of here" it turned out Ellery meant "take cocaine in the disabled toilet." She yanked me in with her and tried to share, but I politely declined. I felt bad enough about abusing the facilities that I couldn't really bring myself to break the law in them as well.

At least she wasn't pushy about it.

Just terrifyingly efficient as she sandwiched the stuff between a couple of twenties and ground it to a pale powder with a Coutts bank card that matched the one Caspian had given me.

Afterward we went shopping.

I wasn't even high but London blurred into an endless carousel of boutiques and "conceptual retail spaces" you apparently needed an appointment to be allowed into. They were the kind of places where there'd be just a shoe in a glass cabinet in the middle of a vast white room. Where the whole buying-a-thing aspect of the experience was refined and rarified to such a ludicrous extent that I had absolutely no idea how you actually, y'know, bought a thing.

We ended up in this deeply weird place—the Late Night Something or Other Cafe—located on the ground floor of this scruffy concrete block in a bit of London so wildly ugly it had to be wildly trendy. It was one of the appointment-only gigs and it was all rather too Dali for me. I certainly couldn't remember having felt the lack of orange-lit wooden tunnels in the other shops I'd visited over the course of my life.

In a tiny wooden room, filled with triangular shelves full of books I wouldn't want to buy, Ellery asked, "Did you ever see your dad again?"

I'd thought we were done with this, so I wasn't ready and I winced. "Um, no. I don't even know if he's still alive."

She picked up a copy of Derek Jarman's *A Finger in the Fishes Mouth* and flicked through it without much interest. "I don't remember my dad either."

"You must have been really young when he—" God, how were you supposed to say it? Passed on? Passed away? Departed?

"Died. Yeah. I was six or seven." She picked absently at the mirrored cover of the book. "I have these images but they don't mean anything. And Caspian won't talk about him."

God. He'd talked to me. That night on the balcony. Not much but…

Would it be breaking his trust if I told Ellery?

She was staring at the ground, one arm crossed over her body, fingers digging absently into her own skin. "It's like he doesn't want me to remember. Like he wants to keep him all to himself."

Oh, what the hell. Maybe it would do some good.

"Maybe it's because...um, he told me once that he didn't think his father would be proud of him."

Her gaze snapped up. "He was right."

My mouth fell open so hard my jaw practically clanged off the ground. Not the response I'd been expecting.

We left soon after. Ellery didn't seem into staying anywhere for very long.

It was slipping into evening, the light softening and the shadows lengthening, and I was pretty much boutiqued out. Besides, I had shit of my own to deal with.

"Listen," I said, "I should probably—"

She caught for my hand again. "Want to go somewhere else?"

"More shopping?"

"No. Somewhere better."

Not really, no. Except I made the mistake of meeting her eyes, and she looked almost...almost like she cared. "Well, um, okay."

She turned away sharply, but not before I caught the faintest hint of a smile on her lips.

We took a cab to Canary Wharf—the fancy rejuvenated bit, where all around us the glass towers reflected the gray-gleaming river and the darkening sky. Ellery tugged me across the road to a construction site: about twenty floors' worth of a building, open like a mouth around a giant red crane.

It was touch and go but, yes, it was probably better than another boutique.

"What is it?" I asked.

"Don't know, don't care."

She nudged open a weakness in the barrier and ducked under it. And—after a hasty glance round in case anybody noticed what we were doing—I scrambled after her.

"Is this...I mean...this isn't legal, right?"

She put a finger to her lips and nodded to a security cabin on the other side of the site.

I stifled a whimper. This was even worse than misappropriating the disabled toilets.

Trying to be as stealthy as possible, which wasn't exactly a skill I'd ever cultivated on account of not being a fucking delinquent, I followed Ellery into the shell of the main structure. It was odd, to say the least. I was used to thinking of buildings as these solid and permanent things, but there was something both naked and fragile about seeing the interior of one exposed like that. Metal frames, dusty concrete, and skeletal scaffolds separated by thin plastic sheets that thumped upon the breeze like a heart.

I circled slowly, surprised by the unexpected...well... *beauty* was the wrong word. It wasn't really beautiful. But it was kind of magical seeing something you wouldn't normally see. The grayness of it washed to dirty gold by the last of the day's sunlight.

Ellery beckoned me to the staircase.

Somewhat nervous about the partially-open-no-banister aspect of it, I climbed. It got us to maybe the sixth floor, the noise of the street vanishing into the sounds of the building itself. Private music: the creak of wood and metal, the rush of the wind through the still-open spaces.

After that, we took to the scaffolding.

Which was when I also realized just how high up we were. And that normally people on building sites had safety equipment.

"Um, Ellery?"

"Yes?"

"What happens if we fall?"

She twisted on the bars with practiced ease, the wind catching at the hem of her skirt and ruffling it up to show the pink bows at the top of her fishnet hold-ups. "We'll probably die."

"I don't want to die."

"Must be nice."

"Seriously. Maybe we should go down again?"

"Just don't fall."

"Oh, why didn't I think of that?"

She laughed, harsh and a little rusty, the sound of it swallowed up by the empty air, lost to the sky. Then she spun around and began climbing again.

I peeked between the bars.

Bad idea. Terrible idea. Terrible, terrible, idea.

Through the crisscrossing metal I could see the dark smudges of pedestrians and cars, the streets turned into ribbons, the buildings into toys.

Sweat burst across my palms and between my fingers, and I tightened my grip on the scaffolding before I was chasing pavements in a terrifyingly literal fashion. For a moment or two, I just clung there with my eyes closed. Going up and going down both seemed equally unpleasant just then...so I sucked in a breath of startlingly cold air and pulled myself onto the next bar.

Climbing was hard work once the novelty wore off. And even the fear got boring after a while. All I could hear was the clunk of Ellery's boots and the wheezing of my own breath.

If I survived, I'd probably have to do something about my general fitness. Yoga just wasn't cutting it.

Finally—somehow—I made it to the top. Hot, sweaty, on the verge of a heart attack, but triumphant.

Ellery was sitting on the edge of the roof. Feet dangling over the abyss.

On slightly noodly legs, I went to join her. Eased myself down very, very carefully. And stared out at the city. A chaos of light, green and gold and white and pink. Glittering reflections thrown haphazard across the Thames. The London Eye cast like a hula hoop against the horizon.

"That's…it's…" I raised a hand to brush the water from my stinging eyes. "It's beautiful."

"It's okay." She deployed what I was coming to think of as her trademark shrug. "Sometimes I climb the crane."

"Let's not do that," I said firmly.

She nodded.

I didn't know how long we sat there. Long enough for the chill to set in deep and the dark to settle. But I liked it. I really liked it. It was peaceful. A city of eight million inhabitants reduced to distant noise.

There was something about Ellery that communicated the very strong impression that touching her without explicit invitation would be akin to sticking your hand into the lion enclosure at London Zoo. But I nudged my shoulder lightly against hers. "Thanks for bringing me here. It's amazing."

I didn't think she even heard me. She was staring at her lap and plucking restlessly at her bracelets. "I did it wrong."

"Did what wrong?"

"I did it the wrong way. Look." She held out her wrist, pushing aside one of the leather bands to show me a pale slash of a scar. "You're supposed to do it diagonally from here to here. But I didn't know. So I did it wrong."

"I guess you wouldn't think to Google first."

She gave me a faint twist of a smile. "Yeah. But nobody believes me."

I didn't know if was the right thing to say, but I said it anyway. "I believe you."

"Really?"

I ran the very tip of my finger over the rough, raised skin. And, to my surprise, she didn't flinch or pull away. "Really."

She turned her gaze back to the city, her hand still and quiet under mine.

I was touched and scared at the same time. It felt good to be someone she trusted. But, all the same, she clearly wasn't in...well, a happy place. I wasn't sure she'd have wanted to be, but that didn't mean it was right to encourage her.

Except.

Was I encouraging her? Had she brought me up here so she could jump off a building? What was I supposed to tell Caspian? He obviously didn't like his sister very much, but I didn't think he would appreciate it if she killed herself after an afternoon in my company.

Fuck.

Now I had to do something.

"Would you try again?" Ouch. Awkward. "I mean," I rushed on, "now that you know…um…you know how." Nope, even more awkward.

"I think about it."

That wasn't the answer I'd been hoping for. "Ah."

"But I'm too scared."

"That's probably…for the best. Your mind's way of telling you something."

She gave me one of her most scathing looks. "I'm scared in case I fuck it up a second time."

"Right."

Oh help. I didn't want to just sit there in the silence and have her cheerfully conclude I was on board with the suicide plan. But how did you talk about something like this without sounding clueless or patronizing or falling back on the platitudes I knew she'd despise?

"Why did you do it the first time?" I asked finally.

"Wanted to."

"And nothing's changed since then? Nothing might change in the future?"

"Things change. But it never makes a difference."

Great.

But that was when I thought of something. "Hey, have you heard of Dorothy Parker?"

She shook her head.

"Look her up sometime. She wrote this poem…"

Which was how I ended up reciting "Résumé" for Caspian

Hart's sister on the top of a half-finished luxury apartment block in Canary Wharf.

Ellery was silent for a long time after I'd finished, the heels of her boots drumming against the concrete edge of the roof. Then she said, "So I might as well live?"

I tried to mimic her shrug. "Might as well."

And for the second time that day, she laughed her rough and throaty laugh and I felt…okay. I felt I'd done okay.

Her phone buzzed and she wriggled it out of… somewhere…with a carelessness that nobody sitting on the edge of a building should exhibit. The briefest glance at the screen and then, "Okay. Time to go."

I had no idea how late it was. Maybe ten? Maybe midnight.

"Go where?" I must have been getting old because bed was seeming like a really good idea right now.

Her eyes glittered like the city. "You'll see."

CHAPTER 23

We took a cab to Euston Station and then made our way down a rather gloomy stretch of road. I couldn't help glancing around nervously—it seemed like the London you might see on an episode of *Crime Watch*—but we weren't mugged or murdered.

So…yay.

We came to a corner marked by this derelict Victorian building, its turrets and balconies and crumbling grandeur more than a little bit out of place on the Hampstead Road. A plaque on the wall, between the boarded windows, proclaimed the place LONDON TEMPERANCE HOSPITAL, ERECTED BY VOLUNTARY CONTRIBUTIONS IN HUMBLE DEPENDENCE UPON THE BLESSING OF GOD, FOR THE TREATMENT OF MEDICAL AND SURGICAL CASES WITHOUT THE USE OF ALCOHOL.

Good grief. From what I knew of Victorian medicine, practicing it on the sober was practically an abuse of human rights.

"Arden." Ellery gestured impatiently at me from the other side of yet another barrier. "Come on."

I slipped under it and into an overgrown car park leading to what looked like a garden...oh wait, no, a graveyard behind the hospital.

The abandoned hospital.

The abandoned Gothic hospital.

With its own graveyard.

That we were visiting in the middle of the night.

Holy shit, we were going to die.

"I'm not sure—"

"I said come on."

Ellery pulled herself over the fence in a flurry of fishnets and boy shorts and, after a moment, I followed. Nearly impaling a bollock along the way and landing heavily on what was probably a dead person. A very-long-time-dead person six feet under the ground, but still.

London Temperance Hospital cast spiky shadows across the ground, the hazy moonlight making the edges of the broken windows glint like teeth.

Tl;dr: I wasn't happy.

But then, there hadn't exactly been opportunity for this kind of thing up in Kinlochbervie. There were plenty of deserted crofters cottages and moors over which ghosts could potentially roam wailing, but it was forty miles just to get to school. Inviting a friend round for tea and a spot of breaking and entering simply wasn't practical. Assuming you had friends, which queer English kids generally weren't over-endowed in. So I told myself this was an opportunity to experience a part of growing up hitherto denied to me and that I should embrace it—the fact I'd done pretty well without it thus far notwithstanding.

We climbed an iron fire escape to an open window and dropped down into a long corridor, all white walls and wood paneling, monochrome in the dusty moonlight. The place smelled of disuse and mold as we headed toward a staircase, which had been severely water damaged. I could hear a faint, warm thrum in the distance. Something that sounded—of all things—like a bassline. And increasing sharply in volume as we made our way through the debris-strewn corridors. I peered into the occasional side room as we passed them but they were empty and characterless. Nothing like the grand and Gothic exterior.

Should have been a relief, right?

Except somewhere between my concerns about being arrested by the police or killed by angry, Victorian ghosts, I'd become curious.

Also I could definitely hear music now. Loud, very loud music. Delirious and electric. And a genre I wasn't cool enough to properly identify. Trance or techno or…God, maybe it was dubstep? Oh help. I was out of my depth.

We turned a corner and…yep. I was at a rave. An actual flashing lights, packed bodies, arms and glow sticks, OMG you're all on MDMA rave.

In a gutted derelict hospital.

Ellery turned to me and smiled, the light breaking across her face in neon rainbows.

I leaned in and yelled, "Can't you just go clubbing like a normal person?"

"I prefer this."

She closed her eyes and lifted her arms, the music slipping over her like silk, her body softening, shaping itself to the rhythms. She looked relaxed—happy even—in a way I would never have expected.

The crowd broke open and swallowed her whole.

I stumbled after her, panicking. If I lost her here, I'd never find her again. And I had no money, no phone, and only the barest idea of where I was.

Everything was heat, dark, light, noise.

Overwhelming.

"Here." Ellery pressed something into my hand.

Thankfully I was sufficiently sweaty that I didn't immediately drop it in surprise. Or fumble as I attempted to see what it was.

I shouldn't have needed to look: it was a small, chalky pill.

Probably not a good idea.

But there was something about the insistent tug of the music that made me want to dance…really dance. Be consumed by dancing. Claimed by it. Lose myself in the shadowy figures that surrounded us. Find a sense of connection that had nothing to do with words or touch or any of the usual, civilized mechanisms for human interaction.

I just wanted to be part of something.

And, for a little while, purely physical.

In my body, not my head.

So I did it. I took the pill. Popped it, technically.

Waited.

"Um. I don't feel any different."

Ellery just laughed, pushed a bottle of water into my hand—where the fuck had she got it from?—and kept dancing.

Maybe I was a new breed of super-evolved, drug-resistant human.

Maybe one of the people around us would turn out to be an undercover agent and he'd kidnap me and take me to some secret facility where they'd want to perform all kinds of horrible tests on me.

And maybe Caspian would—

No. No.

Dancing. Not thinking.

And definitely no daydreaming about Caspian.

Who would not be carrying me out of an MI6 research laboratory as it exploded.

Anyway, I didn't really need drugs to dance. Three years of gay-attracting club nights in Oxford had seen to that.

It wasn't quite what was I used to—a distinct lack of Kylie among other things—but I tried to feel out the music. Let my body respond and my heart be free.

Ellery looked already lost. Swaying, twisting, turning, her hands in her hair, on her neck, on her hips. Her face vulnerable in joy, just like her brother.

There was something contagious about it.

It started in small rushes: just these little darts of pleasure, tingling through my whole body. And slowly the spaces between them faded away until I just felt good. So good.

And I think she understood it too because then we were dancing together. We were dancing together and dancing with everyone. All these people touching without touching.

Except for the ones that were.

Sometimes I was dancing, sometimes I was hugging, sometimes I was being hugged.

And it was all good. So good. The heat and closeness of bodies stripped of the threat or promise of sex.

I was also vaguely aware I was On Drugs.

Blatantly high.

But it didn't feel like anything bad.

It was gentle. Tender. Drawing me closer to the music, to the dancers, to Ellery who had her arms around me, her body nestled against mine, her lips against my neck.

We were so with each other right then.

I loved her very much.

Wanted to hold her forever. Like this. Nothing but this. It was perfect. Beautiful.

The music was our heart. The light our blood.

We were shining. We were turquoise and emerald and purple and amethyst and electric blue.

Jewels inside us.

Sparking where we touched.

This was what Tagore wanted. This was how we should be.

Everything was so very clear. Not like the blurry happiness of alcohol or the fuzzy warmth of weed.

And I understood her. Ellery. I understood Ellery. All her sadness and fear and the splintered beauty inside her.

And the best thing was I didn't have to tell her. Didn't have to explain.

Because I knew she knew.

And I knew she got me too.

And all we had to do was dance. Dance and be together and feel the music. Feel the joy with our hearts wide open.

It went away again, of course.

But it was a gentle comedown.

The world was still so soft, so lovely, as Ellery helped me into a cab. Kissing my cheek before she closed the door.

It was a pearly pale morning. The sky almost iridescent. A swirl of cloud cover and the rising sun.

I watched the streets with wonder. Finished a bottle of water. I was exhausted in a distant physical way, but I wasn't tired. An odd distinction, but it absolutely made sense right then. What I really wanted to do was have a long, hot shower and just feel the water against my skin.

It was going to be amazing.

The taxi deposited me at One Hyde Park, which didn't look quite as intimidating as I remembered. I got security cleared and then wandered into the elevator—enjoyed the iris scan and the swift, silent whoosh of the ascent.

Pulling off my T-shirt—gosh, even air was nice, stirring a faint, residual memory of pleasure—I let myself into the apartment.

And discovered Caspian Hart waiting for me in the receiving area.

No jacket. No tie. Otherwise impeccable.

The room itself had been meticulously restored. Even the carpet I'd forlornly attempted to clean that morning.

And oh my word. He'd been here all night?

"Arden." He rose. Smoothed the creases from that stark,

black suit. Regarded me so coldly it gave me the shivers. "I'm glad to see you're safe."

That wasn't exactly what I'd been expecting. But then I hadn't expected him to be here at all. "Why wouldn't I be?"

"Because I have no idea where you went and you weren't answering your phone."

Maybe I should have been touched by the concern. But right now it was pretty seriously misplaced. "You didn't seem to care too much about that yesterday."

"That's not relevant."

"It's pretty fucking relevant to me."

His face got all tight and still—a look I remembered from when he'd been talking to Ellery. "While you live under my roof, you will carry your phone, stay in contact, and use the driver I have assigned to you."

Wow, I'd say he sounded like my mum, except my mum wasn't a total dick. "You have no right to talk to me like that. I agreed to live here, and sleep with you, and fit my schedule to yours. But that doesn't make me your fucking property."

"I'm trying to look after you."

"What? You mean in case I get myself raped in an alley again?"

There was a long, horrible silence. It made me wish I had another vase to drop.

"I shouldn't have said that," Caspian said finally. "And I'm sorry."

"Wow. That is the worst fucking apology I've ever waited nearly forty-eight hours to receive. F minus. See me after class."

He gazed at me steadily. And then said, very quietly, "I told you I wasn't very good at caring for people." A pause. "You keep saying you want me, Arden. Well, this is who I am."

"No." I came at him like a very small but determined tornado. "This is bullshit."

We tangled up into this angry…hug thing? And ended up in the chair where he'd been sitting before, with me straddling him, my hands on his shoulders. It was probably the closest I'd ever been to him—including the times we'd fucked. His eyes were wide and shocked and wary, like a wild animal about to bolt. Or, y'know, rip my throat out.

"I'm really grateful you showed up that night," I said. "But that doesn't mean you get to use it against me. Ever."

"I wasn't—"

"Yeah, you were. You think I can't tell the difference between what happened in Oxford and what I want with you?"

"What…" I felt the shudder run through him "What if I can't?"

I shrugged. "I guess you'll have to trust me then."

"I'm not—"

"Good at trusting people?"

At last. The faintest of smiles. Poor ghostly thing. And suddenly I didn't feel quite so messed up anymore. He was good at putting the world at a distance. But once you got past that, he did look wrecked. I guess having his non-boyfriend disappear with his not-completely-stable sister had hit him pretty hard.

"Can you try?" I asked. "For me? Just a little bit?"

I went to smooth the hair back from his brow, but he caught

my hand and brought it briefly to his lips instead. "I don't know."

"Please?" I leaned in and kissed his mouth through the prison of our entwined fingers.

"What do you want me to do?" He gave this broken-sounding laugh. "*Trust me* is a very nonspecific and difficult-to-measure goal."

Ack. Either I was really bad at being angry or Caspian Hart was secretly adorable. "I'll be sure to prepare a Prezi. But you could start by maybe...spending the day with me?"

"I can't. The situation with Eleanor put me behind schedule and I have too much to do."

"What about tonight then? Can you come tonight?"

"I...I'll try."

"I'm not scared of you, Caspian." I pressed my free hand against his chest—felt the thud of his heart and the way he trembled to my touch. Such heat and longing in him sometimes. If only I could convince him to give them to me. To surrender, just a little, so I could too. "What you said before...I mean, the hot kinky stuff about screaming and begging, not the scary tyrannical stuff about always having my phone and using the designated driver..."

He blushed. "I can't force you to do those things, but I hope you'll think about them. It's not unreasonable for me to want to know where you are and that you're well."

"Maybe not, but it makes me feel like you're one step away from fitting me with one of those GPS tracking collars you can get for your pet."

"I rather like the sound of that."

His mouth pressed hot and hard against my throat. And I glooped all over him like a badly made Baked Alaska. "S-save it for the bedroom."

"I rather hope at that point I'd be well aware of your location."

"No, but you might want to make sure I can't get away. And besides"—I tilted my head for him, baring vulnerable places for his teeth and tongue—"from what you keep telling me I'm going to be in grave danger."

"You can hardly expect me to rescue you from myself."

I pulled away and slipped off his lap. "Of course I do. Why bother with a hero and a villain when you can have both at once? As a businessman, you've got to admit it's efficient."

"I can see you've thought this through."

"You'll really come tonight?"

A terrifying pause.

"Would seven work?" He seemed almost…shy about it suddenly. It was unexpectedly endearing.

I grinned the biggest grin in the entire world. "It's a date."

CHAPTER 24

As soon as Caspian was gone, I actually *eeeeee*-ed and did a little dance. That had gone better than I could ever have imagined.

And tonight...oh my God. My brain went a little haywire with potential scenarios. Most of them sexy as hell. But, honestly, if he just wanted to have dinner and an early night, as long as it was with me, I didn't care.

Once I'd calmed down, I went to shower. It wasn't as exciting as I'd thought it might be when I was completely high, but it was still nice to wash the night from my skin. Also the water drops were noticeably pretty—the way the light defined them in silver filigree—and they did feel unusually good.

Afterward I felt I probably ought to rest, so I went to bed.

Except I couldn't sleep.

It wasn't the bad not-sleeping, like when you're restless or anxious. I was just...awake. As if I hadn't been up for a day and a night but had, instead, arisen in buttery sunlight to a chorus of bluebirds.

Well. I decided I might as well get up and be useful.

Enjoy my day. The anticipation of Caspian later.

First thing, though, was to arrange dinner. I ran down Caspian's lists of contacts, found someone who did sushi, and bunglingly arranged for "whatever was best" (which the man on the phone called *omakase*) to be sent round later. I wasn't entirely sure why I'd gone for sushi other than that it seemed light and sophisticated and the type of thing that could, theoretically, be eaten from someone else's fingers in a titillating fashion.

Then I pulled on my luckiest pants, grabbed the copy of *Milieu* I'd picked up the other day, and settled down at my laptop.

I could do this. I could totally do this.

A couple of hours later, I was the proud father of eight hundred words on my Ellery-mediated introduction to the underground clubbing scene. I'd called it "Dance Where No One Is Watching" and I thought it was…quite good? Maybe?

I wasn't ready to loft it into the void just yet, so I emailed it to Nik instead, along with a !!!-heavy accounting of last night's adventures. Within seconds, the reply came back: *omg we know did you lose your phone?*

My phone? Shit. It was still in the sitting room.

I found it with a bare blip of battery left and what looked like a "you made a racist joke, then took a long haul flight" number of notifications.

Turned out I was all over Instagram. Because

@i_hate_ellery had something like 253k followers and had tagged @ardybaby a lot. As had a bunch of other people because apparently @ardybaby got around. Thankfully, I looked pretty adorable in an off-my-face kind of way.

I also had a long chain of Kik messages from Nik, charting a journey of bewilderment from "how's it going?" to "REMEMBER TO DRINK LOTS OF WATER BEFORE YOU GO TO BED" via various pit stops at "are you okay?" "are you dead?" "wow, you're having a night" and "who's that girl?"

That girl, according to her feed, was currently sitting at the top of a rusty metal staircase that curled up the concrete, copper-pipe-strewn husk of a condemned building. In one hand she was holding a martini, in the other a sign that read IF U DON'T KNOW UR NOT INVITED.

Another text from Nik: *you're internet famous.*

Only a little bit, I sent back modestly.

Though I had accumulated rather a lot of new followers. Despite my last post being my toenails when I'd done them up like ladybirds.

Oh well. At least nobody would be under any illusions about what they were getting.

What are you up to? I asked Nik. And received an impenetrable response about biomimetic materials.

What about you?

I didn't say *Waiting around for a billionaire to rock up and fuck me hard and nasty*. But I was tempted.

Speaking of, I probably just had time for a nap and a self-delicious-making session before Caspian arrived.

The sushi showed up just before seven. All iced and packed up and completely exquisite. I hovered around like a 1950s housewife as an endless parade of brightly colored morsels were arranged on the dining room table. Enough to feed the five thousand some exceptionally extravagant fish.

They did try to tell me what everything was but the words whizzed by so fast—unagi, hamachi, amaebi, ikura, masago—that none of it really went in. Which left me to preside over a feast I had no clue about.

But hopefully it wouldn't matter.

What would matter would be that I'd tried. And that we'd be sharing something.

I did nibble on a...pale, rice-balanced filament thingy while I was waiting. And, oh my God, it was delicious. Intense, but also weirdly delicate. Boom and then gone. Like a mouth orgasm.

I'd been to a Yo! Sushi in Oxford, where the food galloped past you on conveyor belts, the plates color-coded by price. I'd only ever dared try the green and blue dishes for fear of racking up an enormous fish bill, which meant I probably hadn't got the best from my visit. But this was so totally not like that it was almost incomprehensible. The sheer difference wealth could make to the way you experienced something, even if that experience was commonly accessible, was frankly crazytown.

It took reserves of self-discipline I didn't know I possessed to hold back a nomming frenzy. Some date it would be if Caspian turned up and I was all like "I made you some sushi but I eated it."

I checked the time. Seven fifteen.

Caspian would be here any minute. Should have been here already. Maybe he'd got caught up at work? Or in traffic? There had to be some things even billionaires couldn't control.

Maybe one last…wossname…while I waited?

Ngh. So good.

Okay. Right. Enough of that.

I sat down at a safe distance from the food and in sight of the door. Looking forward to the moment that Caspian Hart would walk through it.

And come to me.

Seven thirty.

Huh.

Well, it was London.

And he was a super-busy man.

I went to find my phone, just in case there were any messages.

Nope.

Hmm.

What if he'd said half seven? Or eight? Or tomorrow?

No, he'd said seven.

Could sushi get cold? Or warm? Or whatever.

Go off, it could definitely go off.

Great. After begging him to spend the night with me I was going to poison him with raw fish.

Maybe I should text him. Except that would look insanely clingy.

He was barely late.

Well, under an hour late. That probably counted as barely late for someone like him.

And if dinner was a bust, I'd just have to make sure dessert—i.e., me—was substantially satisfying.

Wow, seductively waiting for someone was boring.

I hit the study to retrieve my copy of *Milieu*, figuring paper still had the edge on machines when it came to being joyfully thrown aside as your lover arrived. Read an article about whether smoking jackets would ever be sexy again.

If nothing else, it inspired to me to reconsider my setup. It was fairly decadent, I thought. But there was always room for more.

Putting *Milieu* down, I opened the apartment app and cranked the heat right up. Then I took off all my clothes and arranged myself in what I hoped was an alluring fashion. One leg resting very carefully on the edge of the table, hands behind my head, my body all stretched out and slender. Best I could manage since I wasn't exactly the gym bunny type and it…well, it showed. But I could be sexy in my own way, right?

Honestly, I felt pretty sexy sometimes. At least, when I was having sex and somebody was pounding into me, all sweat and skin and soul-deep groans.

Perched on a chair with my bum sticking and my bits dangling? Not so much.

Eight fifteen.

My eye fell on the tie and jacket he'd left that morning.

What if I…uh…accessorized? It would be one way of demonstrating I was absolutely and enthusiastically on board with the things he was into.

I approached the tie casually. As if I was underconfidently cruising it.

It was beautiful, like just about everything Caspian owned. Charvet from the label on the underside. A power tie. Dark gold silk with paler gold diagonal stripes. Gorgeous. This splash of bold color, such a contrast to his sober suit.

A moment or two and then I picked it up. Stroked it with my fingers. It was smooth and strong, gathering warmth against my skin like a living thing. Making me ache to be touched. For hands to pin me, hold me, and claim me.

I wouldn't have worn the thing. Not in a million years. At least not in the conventional way. But I twined it experimentally round my wrist and, yep, it definitely looked good there. Felt good, too, sending this shiver of excitement through me, raising goose bumps all the way up my arms.

Which made me freshly aware of the awkward vulnerability of nakedness without context. I probably looked like a plucked chicken.

Hardly appealing.

But maybe he'd like the…exposure? My visible need to be wrapped up in something warm and protective. Like his body.

I sat back down, stole another piece of sushi, and set about tying my hands together. Weirdly enough, it wasn't that difficult. Just required some supple wrist action, which I'd clearly honed over years of wanking. In a couple of minutes, I was secured and pulling the knots tight with my teeth.

Now all I needed was Caspian to show up and rescue me.

Or, for preference, take advantage of me.

While I was helpless and at his mercy. Utterly unable to resist whatever depravities he wished to indulge.

Oh poor me.

Tremble. Gasp.

God, I was getting hard just thinking about it.

Sushi and a boner. What more could a man want?

CHAPTER 25

It was nearly ten o'clock.

And I was still sitting there, naked and alone, surrounded by melting ice and ruined sushi.

I'd tried calling—my wrists were bound but I still had my fingers and, for emergencies, my nose—but I'd gone straight to voice mail.

What if something had happened to him? How would I find out? It would be on the news, right? *Billionaire Killed in Horrific Car Crash While Driving too Fast to Undisclosed Rendezvous. Sexual Distraction Suspected.* Oh God.

Also, what was I going to do about my…predicament? I was pretty sure Bellerose wasn't available for assisting with ill-advised acts of self-bondage.

I wriggled my hands back and forth and discovered I'd done a really good job of immobilizing myself. The more I tugged, the more my knots held. Which would have been great if I was making a rope ladder or escaping from prison down my bedsheets. But, right now, it was seriously non-ideal.

I'd have to wait for Caspian.

Who was very unlikely to actually be dead.

He…

He just wasn't coming, was he? After everything I'd said this morning. After I'd fucking *begged*. And not in a hot, sexy, exciting way.

In a pathetic, awful, humiliating way.

And Caspian was what? Laughing at me? Bored of me?

But how could he have said everything that he'd said and done everything that he'd done…gone out of his way to be kind to me so many times…and leave me like this?

With nothing.

No word. No apology. Nothing.

I laid my head on the table. With an exaggerated gentleness meant to combat the desire to bash my stupid brains out.

Fuck. Fuck everything. And most of all fuck me. For being an idiot. As usual. What was I thinking? Sushi. Nakedness. Kinky accessories. Had I really let myself believe that he was going to turn up and gleefully ravish me? That, based on a handful of words, he would tear down all his walls, abandon everything that held him back, and just offer up his heart for me to cherish?

Of course he wouldn't.

Not when it was infinitely easier to make a fool of me instead.

I sighed and sat up again, accidentally knocking *Milieu* onto the floor. Bugger.

Despite my best efforts, picking it up with my toes just wasn't happening—it made me feel slightly bitter about all those movies where people escaped from jail cells or handcuffs or whatever by manipulating keys around with their feet.

Nothing for it but to slither out of my chair, get on my knees, and use my teeth. Which was embarrassing in a totally not into this way. Thank God nobody could see me. Although, if past history was anything to go by, this was exactly the moment Caspian would turn up.

But no.

Not even being facedown, arse up, and completely naked was enough to summon him tonight.

And that was when I saw him.

In photographic form. Staring at me from the "Beau Monde" section of *Milieu*: that stilled tiger look of his, elegant, powerful, and exquisitely dangerous, captured only for a moment.

And he was with someone. An unsullied angel of a man, a little taller and a little older than Caspian, copper-blond and heart-crushingly handsome.

Impossible to ignore the way they stood together. An easy familiarity of bodies. Not the awkward affection of two male friends—the "I'm not gay" elbow nudge or shoulder pat—but the way you moved when you already knew how to fit. When intimacy had sanded away all the rough edges of touching.

The picture was one of several comprising a double spread on the Royal Brampton & Harefield Hospital's fund-raiser.

The caption read: *Caspian Hart and Nathaniel Priest*.

That was all.

Five words to make me dust.

I suddenly really very urgently wanted to be not naked and not tied up. My whole body felt weird, like a spider had crawled on me and then scuttled away into some dark corner, leaving me violated and twitchy. I pulled frantically at the tie, sweat gathering, sharp-edged somehow, under my arms and at the back of my neck.

I'd once got stuck on a balcony, halfway up a building, wearing only a towel because of a complicated series of misadventures involving a one-night stand, an ill-timed shower, a lecture someone else was late for, and a locked door. It had bagged me a mention in Oxford's longest running gossip column—how was that for classy—and it had been funny. Even to me. I mean, I wasn't so fragile in the self-esteem department I couldn't be ridiculous.

But this.

This was just embarrassing and awful and…and—

And I was going to be sick.

I ran for the kitchen, since it was closest, and spluttered into the sink. But there was nothing to bring up. Just a burn at the back of my throat and in my eyes. Unshed tears and unrelieved nausea and the sound of my own sobbing breaths echoing against too much fucking marble.

When I was calm…calmer…I reviewed the situation.

Tried to think what MacGyver might do had he taken off all his clothes and tied himself up in a strange apartment with no hope of rescue.

And came up blank.

MacGyver would never have got himself into this mess in

the first place. Talk about being your own worst enemy.

In the end, I sidled up to the knife block—which was probably hand-carved sapient pearwood or something—and very, very carefully manipulated a knife from it with my fingertips. Then I lowered myself equally carefully to the floor, trying to put as much distance between my body parts and the path of the blade as possible. Because dropping a knife that looked more like a katana on my foot or decapitating my own genitals with it would have been the cherry on my shit sundae of an evening.

Despite being what A&E visits were made of, it was surprisingly easy to slice through a tie with a carving knife. I got the edge of the blade under the fabric—pointing away from my big, long, blood-filled artery—and applied what pressure I could.

And then I was free.

Caspian's tie reduced to ribbons and knots on the kitchen floor.

The first thing I did was put some clothes on. It was amazing how much worse things seemed when bits of you were flopping in the breeze. I checked my second phone and this time—oh *this* time—there was a message. I guess I'd missed its initial arrival because I'd been too busy trying to unself-bondage myself with the kitchenware.

I moved my thumb over the little envelope. This better be good. Better than good. It had better be fucking spectacular.

But all it said was, *Working late.*

I stared at it like it was the enigma code.

I was so done.

Pulling out my phone, I booked a last-minute ticket on the Sleeper. Unfortunately, I'd already missed the one that would get me all the way to Inverness, but Edinburgh was better than nothing.

And possessed the major advantage of not being here.

Which was absolutely what I needed.

I finished packing, which took less than five minutes, left the magazine, the second phone, and the remains of Caspian's tie on the table with the spoiled and spoiling sushi, and left.

* * *

I was on the train a good twenty minutes before it pulled out of Euston. There'd been a few berths still available but they were expensive and, while they were a nice idea in principle, I'd always found them a little claustrophobic. The seats were fairly comfortable—about as comfortable as first class on a nonsleeper—so I took off my shoes and curled up under my coat.

Rested my head against the window.

Watched the darkness and the light slipping past.

It was seven hours to Edinburgh. I must have slept for some of it. The important thing was that I didn't cry.

We were over the border when the sun rose. Misty gold and rumpled sky and Scotland's indecorous beauty. So different from England's neat patchwork.

Knife-twist in my battered heart: this longing for home.

We arrived pretty much on time, and even though you were allowed half an hour to collect yourself, I grabbed my bag and dashed across the platform in order to catch the 7:44 to Inverness. Four hours later, I was on another train, this time bound for Lairg, and then a bus to Kinlochbervie.

I was travel-numbed, rattled, and weary.

But hey. It kept my mind off things.

Off—

Nononono. Don't even think his name.

I sent a text to Hazel, letting her know I was coming. It was easier that way round because Mum had these spidey senses when it came to my mood and would probably have worried.

The bus finally arrived at the harbor and I limped out. Stared across the rough gray water toward the rough gray hills. The light was already fading. Seeping away in shades of silver.

Fuck. I'd been traveling for nearly eighteen hours. My body was one big ache. I should probably have asked Hazel to come get me in the car, but it was only a half hour walk.

We didn't actually live in Kinlochbervie itself. We lived out in the wilds, near Oldshoremore Beg, in this converted crofter's cottage called Oran na Mara. That meant Song of the Sea, which was a poetic way of saying wet and stormy. But as I'd promised Caspian, there was a great view.

I was trudging along the single track, wrapped in the deep silence of far-flung places, when I met Hazel coming the other way.

"Just thought you might want some company, love." She threw an arm over my shoulders and pulled me in for a quick squeeze. Duration of squeeze was no marker of affection. She was the type of the person who did everything quickly: this rapid-fire woman, all flying hair and hands. "How's things?"

"Fine."

I wasn't sure if I was glad to see her or not. Well, obviously I was. She was my mother's girlfriend and I loved her. But I'd also been counting on having the next twenty minutes or so to plan my story. I had to come up with something between the truth and a massive, massive lie, since the truth included dispatches about my sex life from the frontline of adulthood no parent wanted to hear. Except I was a crappy liar at the best of times. And, honestly, right now, when even smiling seemed slightly beyond the scope of my physical and emotional energy, I wasn't sure how convincing my happy face would be. Pathetic. I was pathetic

Pathetic pathetic pathetic.

Hazel reached for one of my bags and I knew better than to fight her for it. "You came six hundred and sixty miles because you're fine?"

"Oh...just...boyfriend trouble."

"I didn't know you had a boyfriend."

"Yeah"—I tried to force my mouth into the semblance of a grin—"that's the trouble."

"Nice dodge."

"Thanks."

"Funny, but meaningless. Eight out of ten."

"What can I say? It's a gift."

We walked along in silence. The horizon gleamed where the land became sea, the view as familiar to me as my own skin, worn in by day after day of living. I tried to imagine Caspian here, wind-ruffled, his eyes soaking up all the shades of the sky.

Oh what the hell was wrong with me?

This was the unfun masochism.

And I should have guessed that Hazel wouldn't let things go. "I thought you were settled in London."

"Well, I'm unsettled."

"Does that mean you're back for a while? Or is this just a visit?"

"I don't know. I thought I might stay, if that's okay?" I'd meant for that last part to sound considerate and mature, but instead it came out with a prickly sullenness that reminded me of Ellery. Shit. I was regressing to teenager.

She sighed. "Well, it's a bit inconvenient, Arden. I've already begun converting your bedroom into a sex pad. There's a giant swing where your bed used to be.

"Har har."

"Of course you can stay, dingbat. This is your home."

I took another run at a smile. "Thanks."

"Though I can't really see you as a fisherman."

"Oh, but"—I wagged a finger—"he has made me a fisher of men."

She tsked. "You and your *Father Brown*."

I nodded, blinking away an unexpected rush of tears, suddenly desperately glad to be home, where affection and understanding were so very *certain*. For as long as I could remember, our household had been locked into this protracted war over our favorite fictional detectives. Hazel's husband, Rabbie, was Switzerland, the neutral party just like always, Hazel was a massive Holmes buff, and Mum and me... we loved *Father Brown*.

I could remember her reading to me when we still lived with Dad, her voice in the dark, whispering these stories of good and evil, hope and compassion. Holmes, with all his cold brilliance, just couldn't live up.

Hazel poked me in the arm, sending my thoughts scattering afresh. "Come on, Ardy. Tell me what's wrong."

"Oh…oh, there was just this guy. I guess I liked him more than he liked me." Argh. The words had just…happened somehow. So much for being stoic and noble and locking my pain away like a brave little mushroom.

"Then clearly he's a very stupid boy."

"He isn't, though." I sighed. "He's amazing. Like nobody I've ever met before."

"What does he have? Two cocks?"

I felt myself turning red. "Hazel!"

"I just wanted to know what's special about him."

"Everything. He's totally out of my league, just ridiculously smart and successful and beautiful."

"Sounds like a bore."

"No, he's…he's…" God, how did you explain Caspian Hart? "It's like there's all that and so much more, you know? Or I thought there was." My eyes were stinging again. "He kept showing me…I kept seeing these *glimpses*. Behind the perfection. Of this…ordinary man, who was kind and funny and sexy and lonely and needed me and—"

And, shitshitshitfuckshit, I burst into tears.

I heard the thud of my bags as they hit the ground and then I was in Hazel's arms. And, for some reason, that just made me cry even more.

"I'm getting snot on your shoulder," I warned her in a damp, muffled sort of way.

"I think I'll cope."

Eventually I calmed down. Wiped my eyes and my nose.

Let Hazel gather up my things and lead me off the path to the top of this little rise where we sat down.

I took a deep breath. It was cold enough that the air felt almost sharp inside my lungs. Pure. Like I was the first person ever to breathe it.

Hugging my knees, I let the horizon fill my eyes. The rock-stippled grass rolled away into sand dunes. And then came the golden sweep of Oldshoremore Beach and beyond it the impossibly blue sea, the turquoise waves turning silver-tipped, like something from a Caribbean dream. Except, y'know, way up in the north of Scotland where sun was something that happened to other people.

Hazel nudged my shoulder. "Better?"

"Yeah. Sorry. I just feel like an idiot."

"Isn't that what being twenty is all about?"

"Being an idiot?"

"No." She grinned, looking all impish and twinkly. "I meant, falling for unsuitable people. Breaking hearts and having your heart broken. Living the stories that are worth telling."

It all sounded very nice in principle.

Except.

I sighed. "It wasn't like that. It was messed up in this totally uncool way. I got caught up in this mirage of who I thought he was. And I kept stumbling after it, believing in it, like a complete dongle, and letting him hurt me over and over and over again."

I felt her turn tense at my side. "Hurt you how?"

"Oh God, no," I said hastily. "Not like that. He just made feel bad. I mean, sometimes he made me feel wonderful. And the rest of the time…completely worthless." But, then, I would be to a man like that. Why had I ever believed otherwise? Why had he made me? And then burned me down.

"He did what?" She didn't sound very much mollified.

Shit. The last thing I wanted was Hazel on a hate-tear. But how was I supposed to tell her what had happened, when I still didn't fully understand it myself? Except for the rejection bit. That had come through loud and clear. "It was my own fault, really. I put myself in that position in the first place."

"Nobody puts themself in a position to be badly treated. That's all on him."

"I don't know." I picked idly at the grass. "Maybe there's something about me that made him do it."

Hazel gave me a sharp look. "What is this? National Daft Day?"

"I just meant…like…after Mum—"

"Arden! Stop right there, before I find a bucket of cold water and dump it over your head."

"Yes, but—"

"But no. How can you even think that?"

I never had before, and I didn't entirely know where it had come from now. Like pulling your sofa away from the wall and finding a squashed slug under there. "I'm tired," I mumbled. "Fucked in the head."

She was quiet a long time. And then, "I met your father, Ardy. At the wedding."

My stomach did the wet-fish flip-flop it always did when he was mentioned: a physical manifestation of emotional nausea. I nearly asked her to stop, but I didn't. I had so few perspectives on him. Just my own fear-distorted memories and the emptiness in Mum's eyes.

"He didn't have horns or goat feet, you know," Hazel was saying. "He was charming. Had a way about him that made you feel like the center of the universe when he was focused on you. And he seemed devoted to Iris, absolutely devoted. It was like something out of a fairy tale."

Yeah. If the fairy tale was Bluebeard. "But why Mum? Why did he choose her?"

"Not because of something she did, or was, that's for damn certain, you stupid boy."

I blinked back fresh tears. Hideously ashamed of myself. "You won't tell her what I said, will you?"

"Never."

"I didn't mean it."

"I know you didn't." Her voice softened. "And I know it's a hard thing to live with. The past is a dark place for you and your mum."

I nodded miserably. I really didn't want to risk saying anything in case it turned out to be awful again. Some nasty secret embedded in the underbelly of my insecurity unearthed by Caspian Hart's carelessness and my own naivety.

Hazel leaned into my shoulder again, her hair tickling my cheek. "She would never have got away without you, love. You saved each other."

I watched the beach. The endless wash of the waves and the

gleam of the sky on the wet sand. "Okay," I said at last.

"And the fact is, there's a world of difference between a psychopath and a dickhead."

That surprised a laugh out of me. Infinitely easier to think of Caspian Hart, not as some unreachable angel or a demon who had sadistically toyed with my heart, but simply as a bit of a cock.

"Come on." Hazel clambered to her feet. "There's crumpets at home."

Oh, that sounded perfect. Mum made her own and they weren't like the ones you could get in the shops: fluffier and yeastier, served toasty-warm, with the butter melting deeply into the cracks. "Yes. Yesyesyes."

We gathered up my things and headed for Oran na Mara. Its crooked white chimney was just visible between the hills, a beckoning finger, calling us in from the cold.

CHAPTER 26

Welp, I was miserable.

It was hard work, getting over Caspian Hart. But at least being at home gave me time and space to do it. Endless amounts of both. I slept a lot, read every Georgette Heyer in the house in mad, weepy binges, and wandered the hills and shore in a fashion that would surely have made my Byronic locks and long black coat billow in the wind.

If I'd had Byronic locks and a long black coat.

Hazel must have said something to Mum and Rabbie because they didn't bug me. Just let me come and go as I pleased. Talk when I felt like it.

The days moved very slowly.

It must have been a week later, I was sitting in the garden, on this swing Rabbie had strung from our gnarly old oak tree. It was the best spot because you could see all the way down to the sea. And if you went high enough and fast enough, it felt like you could drown in the sky. I'd probably spent hours out here when I was growing up, chasing clouds and daydreaming. Waiting for my prince to come.

Swinging was probably a pretty banal pleasure to most people, but I'd discovered it never got old, the rush of joy as I kicked off just as bright and clean as it had ever been. And thankfully it was a really good swing—well-made and sturdy, with a broad wooden seat suspended on well-tended chains—so there was absolutely no danger of pulling a *What Katy Did*.

I was just getting into the…hah…swing of things, enjoying the ruffle of the wind through my hair and the whoosh of the descent when the back door opened.

And there was Caspian Hart.

Coming toward me down the overgrown garden path.

I damn near fell off the swing. Managing, instead, to jerk myself to a bone-juddering halt, hands wrapped tight around the suspension chains.

For a moment, I half believed I'd hallucinated him, but even my wildest fantasies couldn't have done him justice. I'd never seen or thought to imagine him out of a suit before, yet here he was, slightly wind-tousled, in dark wash jeans, a cashmere V-neck, and a charcoal gray peacoat, its collar turned up to stylishly frame his infuriating gorgeousness.

Power dressing set him like a diamond. Turned his loveliness into this dazzling thing: hard and cold and beautiful and beyond you. This was better. It didn't precisely soften him—nothing could—but there was something undeniably sensuous in the way the fabric clung to him. Oh those long, lean thighs of his. The gentle slope of his pectorals. The suggestive contours of his abdomen. I'd always known he had a body dreamed up by horny angels. But having it showcased for me made my palms ache to touch him, stroke him, warm and worship him.

And the fucknuckle had treated me like shit.

"What are you doing here?" I was a little bit proud that I sounded pissed off. Instead of incoherent with lust or just...confused.

I couldn't tell if it was the cold, but he was a little flushed. Just this edge of pink along his cheekbones to entice the sweep of a thumb. If the thumb wasn't *fucking furious* that is. "I missed you."

Rage ripped me through me, so hard and fast I thought it was going to burst out of my chest like something from the *Alien* movies. Next thing I knew I was off the swing, right in his face and yelling at him. "You mean you missed having an available body at your beck and call."

I think he'd got used to me being hopeful and conciliatory and therefore wasn't expecting me to suddenly acquire a spine and start beating him about the head with it. His eyes widened. And, the worst of it was, some part of me couldn't help appreciating how very bright they were just then. As if all their blues were finally free. He opened his mouth, presumably to respond, but I was in such a state that I actually plowed straight on before he got the chance.

"I tried to give you what you needed. To understand who you were. And heaven forfend I be logistically inconvenient." I had to pause a moment to breathe. Stop my voice shaking with the weight of everything I was finally saying. "But all the time...all the time I was thinking about you and desperate for you and begging for scraps of you...there was someone else."

I felt hot and undignified and undone. But Caspian didn't react. Just stood there, calm and cool, a perfect English gentleman before the firing squad of my feels. "I have no idea what you're talking about," he said at last.

"I saw you." I blinked rapidly. There would be no crying. None. "In *Milieu*. You were at a-a hospital thing. A fund-raiser. With another man."

His face didn't change.

"Tall? Blond? Looked good on your arm and in tuxedo?" *Unlike me.*

At last. A flash of recognition. "Oh, you mean Nathaniel. We broke up a long time ago."

"But apparently you still swan off to benefit events with him."

"On the contrary, he simply happened to be there."

Okay...maybe I'd jumped to a conclusion or two, and Nathaniel wasn't a major part of Caspian's life anymore. But, in some ways, that only made it worse.

"Then why didn't you come?" I cried. "I bought you sushi for God's sake. I mean, well, I guess technically you bought the sushi for yourself since I sure as hell couldn't afford it. But I acquired the sushi. And I waited and waited. And you didn't come."

Instead of answering me like a normal person, he stepped back and turned away. Stood for a while staring out toward the sea.

While I fumed helplessly.

And then, so softly I barely heard him. "You ask too much of me, Arden."

If this had been a movie, I'd have come at him, flying, flailing, trying to strike him and scratch him and make him hurt. Except obviously I couldn't do that in real life because it would be, well, it'd be abuse.

Instead, I just kept shouting. Words flying about like wasps.

"Oh my God, I ask fuck all of you. I do exactly what you say exactly when you want. And I know so little about your life outside the bits of it you spend with your dick in my arse that I wasn't even sure if you were dating some other guy."

He flinched and I was glad for that too. He deserved to flinch. He deserved to flinch lots. Motherfucker.

"You just had to come to dinner. Or not. You could have said no. That's what I don't get. Why build my hopes up if you knew you were going to smoosh them? Was it a game to you? Or did it turn you on? Making me wait for you and ache for you and rip my heart to shreds for you?"

That was as far as I got.

He was on me with all the ferocity of a storm breaking, a hand covering my mouth, his arm curving round me pulling me tight against him. And, fuck me for a blazing idiot, my body wanted to be there. Powerless against his strength. Silenced by his touch.

I tried to bite him. But he must have had lots of experience in gagging and restraining people because my teeth just glanced off his palm. I think if he'd fought me, I'd have struggled. Except he just held me. An embrace with the threat of violence. Or an assault with the threat of tenderness. I couldn't tell anymore.

I was breathing heavily behind his hand. My eyes were heavy with treacly tears I desperately wanted to shed and desperately wanted not to. I hoped I was glaring at him. But mainly, in that moment, what I felt was...relieved. Safely contained. Released from the burden of expressing my fury, my pain and confusion.

He leaned in—God, he was so tall sometimes, always having to accommodate me, to align himself with me—his lips sweeping the arch of my cheek, all the way to my ear. "I'm sorry. I never meant to hurt you like this. But you need to stop pretending too."

His fingers loosened just enough for me to be able to mumble, "Pretending what?"

"It's never just dinner. It's never just sex. You always want more."

"I just want you."

He gave a strange, sad laugh. "You say that so easily. As if it's so small a thing."

"What do you mean?" My anger was already fading, exposing instead the complex strata of longing and sadness that lay beneath it. "I don't understand."

I was sufficiently overwhelmed that even when he moved his hand I didn't pull away. Just stood there quietly, while he kissed my cheeks, my eyes, the tip of my nose. "I know you don't, but I think we could have something good together. If you could just accept its—*my*—limitations."

"We already tried it your way, and you made me feel like shit."

"It wasn't exactly straightforward for me, either. Being constantly aware of letting you down."

I stared at him, shocked and a little bit horrified. He always seemed so controlled and unreachable that I hadn't really imagined the possibility of, well, affecting him at all. "You won't let me down, as long as you try."

"You have no idea what you're asking."

And here we were: going round this mulberry bush again. "Stop treating me like I don't understand my own desires. Or like I can't handle yours." I dragged myself out of his arms with a frustrated noise. "And why are we talking about this? What are you even doing here?"

"I would have thought that was obvious. Come back to London with me."

Honestly, if he'd told me I'd won a scholarship to a school for boy wizards, I would have been less astonished. For a moment or two my brain just wouldn't work. Blanked out by absurdity. "What? No. Not in a million, gazillion, tatrillion years."

There was a long silence.

"Do you hate me so much?" he asked. And, God, for a moment the pale fractals in his eyes looked like broken glass.

"Of course I don't. I would never have agreed in the first place if I hated you."

"Then perhaps we should reconsider our arrangement rather than simply dissolving it."

"Oh, Caspian, the whole thing is fucked up. Can't you see that?"

He'd gone horribly pale. "I had no idea you were that unhappy."

"I wasn't. I mean, not all the time. I mean, it was complicated." I sighed. It was like being trapped in one of those Choose Your Own Adventure books, but every path led to hurt. "It's not that I wasn't grateful for all the lovely things you gave me, and all the ways you tried to take care of me, but I was always the supplicant, y'know?"

"I didn't ask that of you."

A great wave of an achy interior tiredness rolled over me. I wanted to be in his arms again. And I wanted him to go away and never come back. All at the same time. "I know, but it was inevitable. I lived in your apartment and I kept your schedule and everything happened on your terms."

"You're right," he said at last. "I can see how such an inherent power imbalance could have made you uncomfortable. What if I gave you the apartment?"

"You…you can't just give me an apartment."

"Why not? It would mean you were no longer dependent on me."

"Right, because owning somewhere I could literally never afford wouldn't make me feel weirdly obligated at all."

"You wouldn't have to. I bought it as an investment property. I would simply see it as investment in you."

I was…oh my God, fuck knows. Pretty sure my brain was about to start melting out of my ears. I stumbled away from him and collapsed onto the swing. "I don't want it. I'm not even sure I like it."

"Then we can find somewhere—"

"Nonono, stop it." I hid my face in my hands. "How can you like me enough to spend millions on me but not enough to have dinner with me? Don't you understand why that does nasty things to my sense of self-worth? Why it makes me wonder if you want me at all?"

His hands closed around my wrists and I slowly looked up again. He was crouched in front of me, as calm again, but for the tightness of his lips and the furrow between his brows. And when he spoke, there was a note in his voice I wasn't sure I'd heard before—something that almost could have been desperation. "I've wanted you since you were nothing but an imagined smile and a voice on a phone. And I want you still."

"How am I supposed to believe that?"

"Perhaps you're looking in the wrong places? I came to Oxford for you, didn't I? I came here. I'll beg if that's what you need."

"You know what I need."

He gazed up at me and I could have cried over how completely fucking miserable he looked. "But that's a phantasm. If you would abandon these ridiculous, romantic notions, we could have something real. Something attainable and sustainable."

"That sounds like a renewable energy source, not a relationship."

"Do you like me, Arden? Do you like the time we spend together? Do you like the way I touch you? Do you like the things I can give to you and do for you?"

"Yes, but—"

"Then why can't that be enough for you?" His voice had gone rough with urgency. "If you would let me, I would do everything within my power to make you happy."

"Except be honest with me about who you are."

"I would ruin you. And I…I could not bear it."

He still had my hands but my fingers curled with my restirring temper. "You can't know that."

"I've seen it happen. I bring nothing but pain to the people I love."

"You mean…Nathaniel?" You didn't exactly have to be Sherlock Holmes to deduce that.

"And you've met Eleanor. My own sister despises me."

"You did, um, say you were going to drag her to therapy by her hair."

A touch of telltale color had risen to his cheeks. "That was not well done of me, I admit. But she thinks too little of me to be coaxed, so threats are all I have left. And Machiavelli does say it's better to be feared than loved, if one cannot be both."

"Yeah, I think he was talking about medieval Italian politics. Not sibling relations." Fuck. We'd gone way off track. "And anyway," I went on quickly, "I'm not Ellery. Or Nathaniel."

"But I'm the same. I've done what I've done. Made the choices I've made. And my nature is…what it is."

I broke free of his hold. Reached out, took his face in my hands. He shuddered, but then stilled. It was like leashing a wild thing. Or cradling a butterfly on my palm. "I told you in London. I'm not scared of who you are or what you've done. I want you, and that means all of you. And if it also happens to involve some pretty kinky sex"—I managed a grin, though it was frail and slightly crooked—"then that's okay with me."

"You shouldn't have to—"

"There's no *have to* about it. For God's sake, Caspian. Can't you see I'm desperate for you to let go and dominate the fuck out of me? I like it rough. I like it filthy. And, most of all, I like it with you. When it *is* you. Not just the paper-thin façade of the man you think I want you to be."

"It's not that simple."

"Isn't it? It's just sex. And I'm a fully consenting grown-up. No matter how rubbish I am at the grown-up part."

"Those impulses in me aren't…that is, they don't come from a good place."

"Well, neither do mushrooms, but they're delicious in garlic."

Caspian made a sound that could have been a laugh. "I have no idea what you're trying to say."

"Just that maybe it doesn't matter where your desires come from? Only that they're there and I…um…I welcome them."

"But I don't like what they make me."

"Who says they have to make you anything? What you're into can sometimes just be what you're into."

"I…I…" He closed his eyes. "I don't want to make you hate me. I don't want to lose the bright look on your face when you see me. Your smiles. Being able to make you laugh. The way you come with such fearless joy."

I wasn't prepared for him to be sweet in quite such a vivid way.

"The way you blush flamingo pink."

"Oh my God, stop it." But I was laughing. "What about the way I fall over and vomit on you?"

"Endlessly charming."

His teasing was a twist on the blade of a knife I'd forgotten was sticking right the fuck into me. And I was suddenly bleeding with fresh longing.

"What's the matter?"

"N-nothing."

He drew back, but it was only to stand and pull me from the swing and into the crook of his arm. He didn't usually hold me like this, so there was a brief moment when he almost felt like a stranger. But his cologne swept over me like homecoming and I melted. Snuggled. Pressed my cheek into the soft, body-warmed cashmere of his jumper. And then burst into tears.

"What did I do?" he asked, sounding kind of stricken.

I made a grotesque gurgling noise. And finally managed, "I just missed you. I missed you way too much."

"I missed you too. Enough to chase you to the ends of the earth, my Arden."

"Only on a technicality."

"It still counts and I'm taking it."

I sort of laughed and sort of sobbed. "You're not going to lose me unless you push me away. Can't you trust, just a little bit, that I like you?"

"It's hard to believe."

"Why? Haven't you seen yourself?"

"Yes, and you're everything I'm not."

"You mean a short-arsed nobody?"

"I mean…happy and good and free." He tucked his free hand beneath my chin and turned my face up to his. The pale Scottish light had made him a study in contrasts: dark hair, pale skin, those amazing eyes of his, as cold and deep and changeable as the waves of Oldshoremore Beach. I thought he was going to kiss me—I would have been okay with it if he had—but, instead, he simply held my gaze and murmured, "Come back to London with me."

I wanted to. And I was terrified. And I was sure cuddling me was cheating. Because it was unraveling every sensible thought in my head and replacing them with sparkly rainbows and cartoon hearts. "I don't know…I mean…I…oh God. I want to…but I'm scared and I don't know."

"Please."

It was a single word. But it hit my heart like a nuke. *Kaboom.*

I'd always thought that begging—outside the safe context of the bedroom, anyway—would be embarrassing. But when Caspian did it for me? Put all his power and pride aside for the sake of my messed up, vulnerable heart? He didn't seem weak at all. In fact, I couldn't quite imagine the strength that allowed such rare and unbowed humility.

I swallowed, my mouth coppery with the residue of weeping. "It can't be like it was."

"I know what you need from me. You've made that very clear. But, Arden…"

"Yes?"

"Don't expect me too much too soon. This goes against every instinct I possess and I'm going to…stumble."

"All I've ever asked is that you try."

"And I will. For you. If you can learn to be just a little patient."

Oh God, I wanted to believe him. More than anything in the world. Except… "These are both pretty nonspecific and difficult-to-measure goals," I whispered.

"Yes, well…." His mouth curled up a little—that suggestion of whimsy I loved so much. "My efforts at a quantitatively optimized approach to risk management in human relations did not meet with your approval."

"You'll really try it my way?"

"You've already left me once. What do I have to lose?"

I curled my fingers into his jumper. "Can I have some time to think?"

"Of course. You know where to find me and how to contact me."

"Or"—I peeped up at him—"you could stay here? Just for a day or two."

"Is that what you want?"

It seemed, suddenly, an outrageous request to make of a man like Caspian Hart: forget your insanely demanding job and the multibillions for which you're responsible and just chill out in Scotland while I faff about with my feelings. "I know you don't have much time—"

"My time is Bellerose's problem. I'll stay."

"Wow, he's going to extra hate me."

"He's not what's important to me right now." His hold on me tightened and I nuzzled into…well, I guess it was his armpit, which shouldn't have been especially sexy or romantic, but it was delicious in there. This warm, Caspian-scented space for me to be in.

"You might have to meet my family."

"I already have, very briefly. I don't think your mother was entirely impressed with me."

"Who? Mum?" I couldn't picture it. "Are you sure?"

"Well, unless you have a small, glaring woman with purple hair who lives in your house with your father but isn't your mother."

Oh. "Um, actually that's Rabbie and Hazel. And we live in their house."

"You and your mother?"

"Yep. Hazel is Mum's girlfriend. And Rabbie is Hazel's husband. And my dad is...somewhere else."

"You know," he said after a moment or two, "I'm beginning to realize how much I still have to learn about you."

I gave an unconvincing, bleaty laugh. "Who me? No. Never. Open book."

"Trust goes both ways, Arden."

I couldn't think of a good answer to that. Probably because there wasn't one on account of him being, y'know, 100 percent right.

Both what he said.

And the fact that it was terrifying.

And for some reason, Caspian Hart was willing to do this for me.

I gazed up at him, blinking away tears, and tried to smile. "Next time, I'll stick to pokey."

CHAPTER 27

Introducing Caspian Hart to my family went pretty much the way I thought it would: which was to say, it was weird as hell, but everyone was super-committed to pretending it wasn't.

Especially considering I had to skirt around our actual relationship. And he probably wasn't what they were expecting from Ardy's First Proper Boyfriend. He was charming, though. Attentive and courteous. Perfect gentleman caller material. Not shy, exactly, because there was too much assurance in him for that, but careful. Like he'd come to pick me up for prom and was concerned his intentions might not be deemed honorable.

And if my folks knew he was a wildly famous and important type person, they were too polite to make a big deal out of it. Rabbie did ask Caspian what he did and he replied mildly that he was in financial management. And it was only when I spotted a copy of *TIME*—which just happened to have Caspian right on the front, fierce and unassailable, all folded arms and moon-cold, predator eyes—that it became obvious we were being teased.

Caspian probably found the whole business excruciating.

But it made me as melty as caramel.

He made a valiant attempt to extricate himself in order to find a hotel but was met by a triple-reinforced wall of "oh no, we wouldn't hear of it." Because, obviously, putting the billionaire up in our tiny cottage would be much more comfortable for him.

I guess it was just lucky Hazel didn't insist he help with the dinner. But, instead, Rabbie roped him into a game of chess. He'd tried to teach me when I was growing up, but no two ways about it, I sucked. Given I could barely decide what socks I was going to wear in the morning, it was probably fair to say strategic thinking was never really going to feature in my skill set.

We tried to warn Caspian off because Rabbie was a master and had a tough time finding people to play with, but Caspian seemed to take the role of dutiful guest very seriously indeed and soon they were settled over a board. The room filled up with a thoughtful quiet, broken only occasionally by the clack and shift of the wooden pieces.

For a little while, I stood at Caspian's shoulder, hoping I could be the chess equivalent of the woman in a red dress who blows on the dice in every casino movie I'd ever seen. But I had no idea what was happening and he didn't seem to need me to blow, uh, anything right then. Honestly, he looked the closest to peaceful I thought I'd ever seen him—the silk-sharp edge of his remorseless focus directed toward something that seemed to genuinely make him happy.

Another of his secrets, surrendered to me.

Eventually I left them to it and made myself useful by setting the table. Although mainly that was a smoke screen for swiping *TIME*. I was fully intending to read the article but it was full of words like *financial transaction processing* and *asset management*. So I let myself get distracted by the pictures instead. Caspian looked amazing in charcoal gray—all stern and sexy. And a pull quote formed a silver ribbon at the top of the page: *"I have never been satisfied with success. I consider no endeavor complete until I have not merely succeeded in it, but mastered it utterly."*

Oh my.

I was pretty excited at the thought of being mastered utterly too.

Which really wasn't what I needed to be daydreaming about right before a family meal.

The interview with Taylor Swift on the next page provided a calming influence. And, while I was wading through a paragraph about how she was totally, honestly done with boys, Mum came in and handed me an envelope.

"What's this?" I asked.

She gestured toward the game. Mum was even quieter than usual around strangers, but it was okay. We could read each other effortlessly. "Caspian brought it?" I grinned. "Wow, what an inefficient way of delivering it."

He glanced up. "Ah, but not all forms of communication take efficiency as their primary goal."

I giggled. And everyone looked at us like we'd gone mad.

The letter turned out to be an invitation—a very posh invitation, in fact, to Ellery's birthday, which was a ball themed around The Masque of the Red Death. It was printed on glossy black card and embossed in gold, a stylized carnival mask, suggested by a few bloodred lines, hovering somewhat ominously over "Miss Eleanor Isobel Antonia Hart requests the pleasure." It was Ellery and not at all Ellery at the same time. And it was definitely the classiest, most intimidating invitation I'd ever received. It put Damn Frances to shame.

"Someone die?" asked Rabbie.

Caspian waved a hand dismissively. "My sister is turning twenty. She didn't want a party, my mother insisted, and invitations that would better suit a funeral represent a compromise."

Mum ran a finger over the shining tail of the *M*. "Compromises are usually just a solution nobody wants."

"That's how it works in my family. We sit down and come to a civilized agreement we all hate." Caspian spoke lightly enough, almost as if he intended a joke, but I thought I caught a trace of bitterness.

It made me want to kiss him. Fill him with sweetness instead.

But I wasn't quite ready to attempt that level of PDA in front of my parental-type units. Which left me hovering over his chair again in what I hoped was a comforting fashion. "How's it going? Who's winning?"

Rabbie laid his king down with a neat click. "He will. In three moves."

"Wow. Really?"

"Aye." I wasn't sure how Rabbie was going to take this. Chess was kind of his thing and people generally didn't like having their thing taken away from them. "Best game I've had for a long time."

"Thank you." The tone was mild, but Caspian looked a little flushed. Pleased.

"But"—Rabbie glanced at me—"you could've warned me, Arden."

"Hey, I didn't know he'd turn out to be a chess genius."

Though I probably should have guessed. What *couldn't* Caspian Hart do?

"I'm not," he put in hastily. "I haven't played for years."

"If you're trying to make me feel better, you're doing a terrible job of it." Caspian winced visibly and Rabbie took pity on him. "Eh, I'm pulling your leg. But where'd you learn to play like that?"

A moment of silence before Caspian answered, but—to my surprise—he did answer. "My father taught me. And after he died I made something of a study of it." His long fingers curled idly around a rook. "I appreciated the opportunity to play again."

Something I would in no way be able to offer him.

"Rabbie tried to teach me—" I began apologetically.

But he cut me off before I could finish. "Our Ardy has other talents."

"Yes." To my surprise, Caspian slipped an arm about my waist. "He does. And he has many."

Eep. Scuff. OMG. Thankfully, I was spared having to respond to this sudden attack of compliments because Hazel shouted through to tell us food was ready.

We always had seafood chowder on Fridays, and it was always served directly from the Crockpot on the stove. Caspian looked so genuinely confused by this behavior that I ladled him out a bowl, making sure he got plenty of mussels and prawns, because they were the best bits. We ate it with Hazel's homemade sourdough, all smooshed around our tiny kitchen table.

I really hadn't thought through this "bring your billionaire-not-quite-boyfriend home" plan. I'd been so focused on getting to know Caspian it had never occurred to me to wonder about what might happen when he got to know me. The ordinariness of my life. Caspian was not only accustomed to wealth but had also been born to it, and here we were eating help-yourself-soup from mismatched bowls. What if he was hating this? Or scorning us?

"This is absolutely delicious," he said. "Thank you."

And then I could breathe again, a relief-tipped happy wave rolling all the way through me.

Of course the comment led to a lecture from Rabbie about Kinlochbervie fishing, followed by a disquisition about sourdough from Hazel, both of which I'd heard on many other occasions. But right then, it was good to hear them.

It was just good to be there.

Food and my folks and familiar love.

And Caspian.

Who was both nothing like I'd thought he would be and yet still, somehow, everything I wanted. Stern and sweet and rough and gentle, invincible and vulnerable, wickedly sexy and unexpectedly kind. A man who missed his father, didn't understand his sister, resented his own desires, and, occasionally, made me the center of his goddamn universe. And I knew myself well enough to recognize that I was well and truly fished. All it would take was a twitch upon the line and I'd be arse-over-elbows in love with him.

Once we'd taken the edge off our hunger, conversation flowed pretty naturally. I noticed early on that Caspian was doing his thing again, asking lots of questions, discovering where someone's passions lay and letting them talk. But he'd already been way more forthcoming than he had to be—all that stuff about chess and his family—so I left him to it.

And simply enjoyed the way he had of making people feel listened to and important. Watched my mum blush and glow as she haltingly told him about the bakery where she worked. Listened to Rabbie's deep, generous laugh and Hazel's wicked interjections.

And it was...perfect.

Just like the chowder. Which was rich and creamy and tasted of home. And I ate three bowls.

Afterward we normally bickered over who did the washing up, as fairness dictated it couldn't be the person who cooked or the person who did it last time, but I was feeling gracious enough to volunteer.

And, to my surprise, Caspian joined me in the kitchen.

I flapped the tea towel at him in mock horror. "No way, get out. You're a guest. Guests don't help with the cleaning."

"This one does." He caught the end of the fabric and tugged, reeling me in until I was flush against him and I could feel the taut strength of his thighs, the heat of his groin. My lips parted on a "kiss me" gasp and he smiled tigerishly down at me. "You wash, I'll dry."

It startled a laugh out of me. "Tease."

"My sweet, sweet Arden," he said in this deliciously husky way, "you have no idea."

I stared at him in sudden wonder. It seemed both bewildering and amazing that he was here with me. In my family home. In Kinlochbervie. About to help me with the washing up.

"What's the matter?" he asked, his head tilting curiously, whimsically even, like I'd suddenly become a puzzle to be solved.

"I'm just so glad you're here with me. Are you sure you don't want to run a mile?"

"Why would I want to do that?"

"I don't know." How to explain something I barely understood myself? "I think it's just me being funny. You're not always who I expect you to be."

Oh shit, that sounded bad.

"In a good way," I added.

He smiled his rarest, most unreadable smile. "When I'm with you, I'm not always who I expect to be either. And I like it."

I leaned into him and went up on tiptoes—one foot flicking back Disney-style—in order to present my mouth to him in what I hoped was the most tempting, pleading fashion possible.

I would probably have got my kiss, too, if Hazel hadn't

called out, "I can hear canoodling, but no dishes."

Caspian caught me by the belt loops before I could leap away guiltily. I was going to apologize—my folks were hard core about their piss taking—but he was laughing. He bent his head and nudged his nose to mine, a gesture so ludicrously innocent that I was utterly unprepared for its intimacy. I made a little yipping noise, shocked by the deep, fire-in-winter pleasure of such simple affection.

Aaaand I had washing up to do.

I got to it, trying not to dwell on how weird it was that Caspian Hart was helping me. At least, he helped after a while. When I was filling up the bowl and doing the first few items, he stood with his arms wrapped around me and his chin on my shoulder. He was all crazy-soft cashmere and that amazing cologne, and I could look up and see us reflected in the kitchen window. He was basically just a smudge of pale skin and dark hair, but we looked...yeah...we looked good together.

We fit.

Something I only really finally believed in this most unlikely situation.

He let me go after a bit. Got on with the drying. He wielded the tea towel with far more efficiency than I ever did and stacked everything up neatly when he was done. It was almost comical, in a way, the sheer *care* he could give even something utterly banal. Also kind of impressive. And so not like me it was borderline embarrassing. I always left things drippy and higgledy-piggledy.

Oh God, I was getting all starry and fuzzy over his dish-drying technique. This was getting chronic. But I could honestly have gone all night, up to my elbows in bubbles, hip to hip with Caspian in our dinky kitchen, quiet but for the occasional clatter of crockery…just being together.

He was way too efficient for that though. Ten minutes and we were back in the front room, staring into the expectant grins of my family who were sitting round the table, waiting for us.

"Oh no," I said. "Absolutely not."

"Oh yes." Rabbie's grin was the biggest of all. "It's Friday night. You know the rules."

Caspian glanced warily from face to face to face. "What's going on?"

"Friday night is game night." I gave a mortified little wriggle. "But you really, really don't have to—"

"He shared our bread but would reject our games?" Rabbie had a great line in mock, explosive outrage. At least, I hoped it was mock.

I gave him a look. "Steady on, Rob Roy."

"He d-doesn't have to do anything he doesn't want to." That was Mum. And I was so proud of them both: her for speaking and him for making her comfortable enough to do it.

"Well, of course he doesn't. It's just—"

Hazel grinned at Caspian "—we'll think less of him."

"I'm fine to play games," he said quietly.

"Caspian." I made an excruciated noise. "They're just being…themselves. You don't have to do this."

He might have blushed a little. "I'd like to."

They broke him in gently, at least. I wouldn't have put it past Rabbie to pull down Twilight Imperium or something, but we kicked things off with Ex Libris, which I'd bought for Mum a couple of birthdays back. It was more of a party game, really, but it worked like a literary version of Call My Bluff, and had become one of her favorite games. Maybe because she was scarily good at it.

I was pretty interested to see what Caspian would do or if I'd be able to identify his answers. At first, not so much, but once we'd stumbled over a couple of plausibly obscure openings, and they'd turned out to be him, I reckoned I had him sussed. He liked to write things that had nothing to do with the characters or plot summary at all—trying to lure people in with calculated unpredictability. He smirked at me across the table, knowing I was onto him. It felt wickedly good, somehow, like sharing a secret.

Mum still won though—just like always—and I managed to come in a respectable second, mainly by figuring out what other people were likely to do rather than being particularly creative on my own account.

After that, we moved on to Carcassonne, which was this tile-placing strategy game that I theoretically enjoyed but never, ever did well at. I tended to get distracted by building things and making them look pretty, when the point of the game was to score points. But if I thought I'd played poorly before, it was nothing to playing with Caspian.

The man was completely brutal.

I'd never seen anything like it.

It wasn't just the terrifying efficiency with which he built up his own resources; it was the precise way he fucked everyone else over, claiming cities and roads and cloisters and hemming us into corners. It wasn't even particularly vicious, just hideously effective.

We were done in under an hour. It wasn't even worth calculating the score.

"Holy fuck." Rabbie let out a long breath.

"Forgive me." Caspian looked up with the bewildered air of someone emerging from the red mist. "I think I've just been antisocially competitive."

I gave a splutter of laughter. "That's like Genghis Khan apologizing for being antisocially expansionist."

"Oh God." He actually put a hand to his brow, hiding his eyes beneath its shadow.

Hazel whacked me in the arm. "Ardy. Leave him alone."

I'd intended to tease but it seemed like I'd made him feel genuinely self-conscious. "I'm so sorry," he said. "I hope I haven't ruined games night?"

"Hell no." Rabbie was hastily boxing up the Carcassonne demon. "That was...well it was something. All I can say is, I hope I never get on the wrong side of you."

Caspian made an abashed sound.

I didn't actually want him to be embarrassed but, God, it was adorable. It made me want to crawl all over him and curl up tight around him. My poor beautiful man, too aggressive for his own good, a monster at the mercy of his own savagery.

The Carcassonne killer.

"Arden," he growled, "are you laughing at me?"

"Who me? Never." I bit my lip unconvincingly and hoped for later retribution.

"You know," Hazel said, "we should harness Caspian's

power for good and play something cooperative."

We settled on Forbidden Desert—a surprisingly hard-core game for eight-year-olds about repairing a dirigible before dying of thirst or getting buried in sand. Humiliatingly, we tended to get our arses handed to us a lot when we played.

But not with Caspian.

Hazel had been totally right: it was awesome when he was on your side. A little bit intense, since he clearly had absolutely no intention of losing and would coolly rattle off the probabilities of particular cards showing up at particular times. Which felt…not like cheating exactly, but it made you very aware that you were playing a game. Engaging in a battle of mechanics. Rather than, say, escaping a desert in a dirigible.

On the other hand, we won. A scarily close run thing, but we did.

And I heaved out a massive sigh of shocked relief and cheered along with everyone else. Because there was no denying winning was fun and we'd probably never have managed without Caspian.

Rabbie said he was a very brilliant, very frightening man.

And I agreed with him. Though I also found it sexy as hell.

It was getting pretty late by the time we'd put away Forbidden Desert, which led to an intense succession of negotiations around sleeping arrangements. Caspian volunteered to take the sofa but was immediately overruled and my room was out because I only had a single bed. In the end, they packed us off to the third bedroom, which was sort of Mum's room, and sort of Mum and Hazel's room, and sometimes the guest room.

So not weird at all.

Cringe.

"Just remember it's a small cottage," Hazel warned us. "Don't debauch each other too loudly."

Double cringe.

"And make sure Caspian has a towel and a toothbrush," Rabbie added.

Just...kill me now.

CHAPTER 28

By the time I'd dealt with everything and shown him how to find the bathroom, *alone with Caspian* felt incredibly significant somehow. Almost too much.

I'd always loved Mum's room. It'd been storage space when we first arrived but she'd done it up. It was right at the back of the house in—for lack of the correct architectural term—the pointy bit. The bed was tucked under the eaves and Mum had strung up a bunch of fairy lights so it felt like lying under a canopy of electric stars. It was my favorite place to read, tucked under this handmade quilt and propped up on these jewel-colored throw pillows, the sea whispering to me just on the edge of hearing.

It had seemed pretty magical at the time but with Caspian standing there—hunching a little to avoid banging his head on the ceiling and looking as if he'd been airbrushed in from an issue of *GQ*—it seemed more kind of...shabby. Quaint, if you were feeling generous.

And then he pulled his jumper over his head and I stopping worrying about the furnishings.

"God," I mumbled, "you're beautiful."

Because he really was. And he'd previously given me so little opportunity to look at him. He wasn't built, but he was what you might call nicely defined. Elegance and strength and this refined masculinity. Made me want to lick down the groove between his abs and press my mouth to the hollows behind his collarbones. Trace the long veins in his arms with the tip of my tongue. And I couldn't tell if he was exquisitely manscaped or if nature had just somehow imbued him with the most attractive configuration of body hair imaginable: a sleekly delicious treasure trail, like a beckoning finger to his crotch, and a silky scattering across his pectorals, from which his nipples peaked rosily and—to my eager eyes—somewhat coquettishly.

He shifted—embarrassed, maybe. Or perhaps fearing for his life beneath my ravenous stare. "Come on, Arden. I haven't shared a bed with anyone for a long time but I'm moderately certain it involves being *in* the bed."

"Um, yeah. Right."

It was such a small room that it only took him about a step and a half to close the distance between us. He caught my T-shirt and slowly peeled it off me. There was an interesting moment in the middle when I was blind and entangled and helpless...and then I was shiveringly half naked.

Just me, pale and scrawny. Nothing he hadn't seen before but it felt different. Like my skin was thinner.

He flicked the delicate, stainless steel feather hanging from my CBR and smiled. "You're very decorative. It always drives me a little wild, wondering what's under your clothes."

"You really think about that?" I was impressed by how casual I managed to sound. Even though my nipples were all "hello, boys" and my cock about a touch from going the same way.

"Oh yes. I sit in my office, thinking about your body jewelry, and the billions just slip away."

It was enough to banish some of my awkward at least. I laughed and wriggled out of the rest of my clothes. Pulled back the quilt and crept into bed, tucking my knees up to my chin while I waited for him. "Did you have the worst evening?" I asked anxiously.

"I had a lovely evening."

Oh God, he was taking off his jeans. Not that the phrase "taking off" did anything even approaching justice to the austere poetry of Caspian Hart getting naked. Well, almost naked. And I was glad for another opportunity to appreciate his taste in boxer briefs. They were just as good as I remembered. Clinging to all the places where I quite fancied clinging myself.

He sat down on the edge of the bed.

Don't stare at his cock... don't stare at his cock.

His legs were good too. I could imagine them doing all sorts of lewd things. Spreading, clinging, dragging me to him—

And now I was hard. Good going, Arden.

Thankfully, Caspian didn't seem to notice my, err, struggles. "Well," he said briskly, "how are we doing this?"

I flapped the corner of the quilt invitingly. "I know you

said it had been a while, but, well, enter bed, commence snuggling?"

"Truthfully..." He was staring distractedly at a patch of wallpaper. We hadn't been able to afford enough to actually do the room, so Mum had made a collage of samples, which looked less rubbish than you might imagine. "I'm a light and rather restless sleeper. I'm afraid I'll make you uncomfortable."

At this rate, we'd still be discussing sleeping arrangements come morning. "Um, we could go top to toe?"

He gave me this odd, grateful smile and got in opposite me. It was less uncozy than I thought it would be. I could feel his body heat against my skin and I could stare creepily at him, which was definitely a bonus.

He quirked a brow. "I can hear the sea."

"It's nice, isn't it? You can see it too." I gestured vaguely at the little arched window beside us. "And in the mornings you can watch the sunrise. Assuming you're up in time, which I'm generally not."

A yawn came out of nowhere, as if my point needed illustrating, and I cuddled down into the covers. Turned my face to the window so I could watch the ripples of shadow that were the distant waves.

Sleep danced at the edges of my brain but wouldn't come any closer. Not with Caspian temptingly near.

I rolled onto my back again and wriggled my toes against the edge of his knee. "I feel like we're having a sleepover or something. We should play spin the bottle or Truth or Da—"

The end of that sentence vanished into a hastily swallowed

gasp as Caspian's hand closed around my foot, strong and warm, the skin of his palm very smooth. He pressed his thumbs into an exquisitely tender spot beneath my toes and my spine arched like a crochet hoop.

"Hazel said no debauching," I squeaked.

"No, she said any debauching should be transacted quietly." He followed the curve of my foot, squeezing away tension I didn't even know was there, making me groan with helpless pleasure. And then, when I was all languid, my foot his willing slave, he brushed his fingertip down the arch so lightly that it induced a full-blown, full-body shiver attack.

I made a noise like "Nngh."

"Are you ticklish, Arden?" God, he sounded so...so *wicked* when he said it.

I writhed ridiculously, unable to stay still but not wanting to pull away. "No. Yes. Okay, yes, I'm ticklish. Wah!"

His thumbnail scraped against my sole and it was awful and lovely at the same time. Sensation like a tequila shot, pure and bright and cold, somewhere between pleasure and pain. It made me want to squirm and surrender and fight it and ride it all at the same time. And I had to clap a hand over my mouth to stifle whatever unraveled sound was going to spill right out of me.

"Do you want me to stop?"

"No." I threw back my head, the brush of air across my exposed throat as tantalizing as his fingers against my toes.

But he stopped anyway. Which was, well, epically non-ideal.

"What's wrong?" I asked, trying not to whine.

"Nothing. Just..." He'd gone gratifyingly growly. "The things I want to do to you."

Well, now I was wide awake. "Like what?"

"Tie you to my bed and—"

"How?" I hadn't meant to interrupt but the idea was sufficiently enticing that greed got the better of me.

He laughed—the sound so free, his nails still dancing torturously across the tenderest places of my feet.

I could barely breathe for feeling. The exquisite paradox of being indulged and maddened. "I need details!"

"In an X. Every part of you exposed and at my mercy."

I swallowed an eager whimper. I could imagine it so well I could practically feel it. The warm pressure of whatever cuffs or ties he wanted to use on me. The way his gaze would strip me deeper still. How gloriously helpless I would be for him. God, oh God. Now I was indulged and maddened and as hard as advanced calculus. "And then"—the words were sticking to my dry mouth—"you'll tickle me?"

He nodded, glancing away. Embarrassed maybe? As much revealed as I was.

Except I would never leave him alone in desire. "Please do that. I'd love it."

He nodded again. And just when I thought I'd lost him, he murmured, "I'll have Bellerose add it to my schedule."

"That's not funny."

Laughing, I kicked out playfully with my foot, which made him laugh, too, and drag me down the bed. We tussled as quietly as we could, muffling giggles in each other's skin, until we were just embracing, tangled up together. Caspian's hands swept up my spine, bringing heat and a hint of possession. And I gasped, shamelessly eager to be touched and claimed. Full of this unexpected gratitude. I hadn't realized just how empty he'd left me. How much I'd ached for roughness and for tenderness and for him.

"Arden," he whispered. "My Arden."

He brushed the back of my neck. I didn't even know I was sensitive there but I half thought I could feel the whorls in his fingertips. Sensation spilled over my skin like a river breaking its banks, pretty much dissolving me into squirms and whimpers.

"Please, oh please."

I hardly knew what I was begging for. But Caspian did, sitting up and gathering me into his lap, before covering my mouth with his.

Such a good kiss: hot and velvety and very thorough. The need was an inferno inside me but—for once—I didn't snatch at pleasure. I let him give it to me. Let it slip inside me with the press and slide of his tongue. A slick, subtle invasion that I welcomed.

I tried to keep my eyes open. A slightly creepy habit, for sure, but I wanted to see him and all his wolfish intensity dissolving into mutual bliss. It didn't work out. His tongue curled against mine and my eyes closed of their own accord, sweeping me into a warm, dark intimacy.

He didn't take control from me. I gave it to him. Abandoning myself to his tongue deep inside me and his lips against mine. This gentle dominion. Flayed with the softest of caresses. It was so frightening and wonderful and perfect that I moaned. A muffled, undignified, needy sound.

He drew back, breathing harshly, his mouth still shining from my kisses. "God, Arden. The way you *yield*."

In the haziness of his eyes I caught the echo of my own unraveling. And...yeah...I was dazedly proud of it. Whatever Caspian Hart did to me, I could do to him right back, and he wasn't hiding from it anymore.

He ran the pad of his thumb over my lips and I parted for him instinctively. I was definitely game for some sexy digit-sucking action, impatient for the taste of skin, but he didn't press inside. Just stroked me gently for a second or two, riding the crest of my gasp.

I stared at him, aroused and trembling and suddenly full of unquiet questions I wasn't sure how to articulate. And then I just blurted them out anyway. Because that was how I rolled. "Why do you never let me touch you?"

His body tensed against mine. But he did answer me. And so simply it was kind of devastating. "I don't like being touched."

"You...what. Not ever?" A thousand horrible possibilities flashed through my head. "Did someone...did they hurt you?"

A small, unreadable pause.

"No," he said. "Nobody hurt me."

"But how can you not like being touched?" It was probably my favorite thing in the universe. And not just the sexy side of it: being stroked and snuggled and petted and fussed. All of that good stuff.

"I prefer to be in control of what I feel."

"I wouldn't make you feel anything bad."

"That's not what matters to me." He settled us back against the pillows, but he kept an arm around me, which I was glad about. "Besides, you know my tastes run exclusively to dominant."

"Yes, but that doesn't have to be about who does what. It's about how it's done."

He let out a faint sigh. "I need to know what my body experiences is mine, which is easier to manage when I take my pleasure. And I realize this probably sounds a little strange to you."

"Actually, it sounds horrible."

"It's just the way I am."

I lay there for a moment or two, feeling both cuddled and twitchy, which was weird. "Does this mean you're never going to let me…do anything?"

"Define anything."

"Hold you. Kiss you. Stroke you. Fuck you."

"If, by the latter, you mean penetrate me, then no. I don't enjoy it." While he didn't recoil in horror, fling me aside, and vanish into the night, never to darken Kinlochbervie again…he did look out the window in a manner that suggested he really wanted to. "As for the rest, didn't you spend at least an hour this afternoon assuring me of the compatibilities of our natures?"

"We are compatible. But just because I'm largely indifferent on the matter of who puts what where and well up for submitting to you doesn't mean I don't want to *participate*."

"I love the way you respond. Isn't that participating?"

"Yes, but"—I could feel my mouth doing sulky, pouty things—"being with you and not being able to touch you is like working in a sweetshop and not being allowed to eat any sweets."

"I've never worked in retail, but I'm moderately certain that you're not supposed to consume the merchandise."

I went to *gnang* him like I would have done with Nik...but stopped myself just in time. "You know what I mean. How do I spoil and cherish and adore you?"

"Flowers?" he suggested.

It was only the thought of my peacefully sleeping family that prevented me from screaming. "Oh my God, if you send me roses ever again, I will...make you eat them."

His eyes widened. "I send you roses? And you don't like them?"

"Every time we fuck. Don't you remember?"

"I..." He hesitated.

"I have a feeling I'm not going to like this.

"You said to thank with you flowers so I had Bellerose set up a standing order with a florist."

"Let me get this straight. You arranged to have your assistant send me post-buggery roses. As a token of gratitude."

"I didn't know they'd be roses."

"That doesn't help." I pulled away. Curled up sulkily at the end of the bed. "Is that what happened with the tulips?"

"No. I chose those. They were so bright, they reminded me of you."

I took a deep, steadying breath. "Okay. Pro tip: Don't send me flowers for sleeping with you because...well...that's one of those the-gift-is-in-the-giving situations. My reward for sleeping with you is getting to sleep with you. And if you do, for any other reason, want to send me flowers again, choose them your goddamn self."

"I understand. I'm sorry." He did look genuinely abashed. "I can see now it was perhaps... a little odd. But I really did enjoy our time together."

"Good. Me too. Mostly. So you can see why not getting to touch you ever is a bit of a downer for me?"

He didn't say anything for a long time.

Then all warily: "This is one of the ways my trying is supposed to manifest, isn't it?"

"I'm not sure. Maybe? I mean, I wouldn't want to make you do something you hated. That would be fucked up. But"—I pulled on my honesty socks—"at the same time, I don't know if I'd cope being all Keep Off the Caspian."

We were quiet again. And it was honestly pretty miserable. I desperately wanted for this not to be a big deal... but I'd agreed to things I wasn't sure about the last time. And see how well that had worked out.

"You let me suck you off in Oxford," I pointed out.

"More accurately I fucked your face."

"That doesn't alter the fact that my mouth was *all over* your dick. And a little bit on your balls."

He hid a laugh behind his hand. "The point is, I felt in control."

"You can always be in control." I crawled back up the bed and knelt beside him.

"Arden..."

"My hands are yours." I held them out, palms up, like a supplicant. "Tell me how to touch you."

"I...I don't know."

A week ago, I would have assumed he was pushing me away but now that I knew to look for it, I caught the flash of panic in his eyes. "What about kissing, then. Can I kiss you?"

"All right. Just don't put your weight on me, or I'll hurt you."

"I won't." I leaned in and brushed our closed mouths together. "How was that?"

"Fine."

"What about here?" I nuzzled up his jaw to the tender space beneath his ear, not quite kissing him, just stroking my lips over his skin.

I heard his breath catch in the suddenly thunderous silence. Sat back meekly on my heels.

"Do that again," he whispered.

His pulse was fluttery under my mouth. His stubble rough. And his cologne had mostly faded so he smelled of Kinlochbervie: salt and heather and sky. I followed the line of his neck down to his shoulder and then the ridge of his collarbone to the base of his throat, imagining myself Theseus and his body, with all its secrets, my labyrinth.

One of his hands came up and tangled in my hair.

I froze. Glanced up. "No?"

"Just..." Wow, that fine, flawless skin of his could really hold a blush. "Talk to me. Keep me with you."

"You can tell me to stop at any time."

"I know."

I took a moment simply to look at him. Sprawled out over the rumpled quilt, he was gemstone dappled by the fairy lights, an emperor in an ever-shifting kaleidoscope of ruby and emerald and topaz and sapphire. His breathing was a little too fast for pure arousal but the way it made all his muscles tighten was honestly…sexy as hell. As was the fact that he was definitely and undeniably hard. His desire felt *mine* in a way it never quite had before. "You're so gorgeous," I told him.

"I asked you to talk to me. Not flatter me."

As he watched, I pressed my hand flat to his stomach and slid it upward over the impressive topography of his torso. "I'm not flattering. I'm *admiring*. I mean…you do know how you look, right? You have noticed."

"I take care of my body. And I'm aware I meet several of the criteria for conventional attractiveness."

"Yes, but"—I traced a teasing boustrophedon between his abdominals—"you feel beautiful, too, don't you?"

He blinked. "Does anyone?"

"I do. I mean, not after I've eaten so much curry I look like a cartoon frog. Or when I'm waxing my arsehole. But when you're kissing me or touching me or telling me—um, unless you're lying I guess."

He reached out and pulled me in for a kiss, and I just managed to catch myself on my elbows before I crashed down on top of him. "I've never lied to you. You're perfect."

"You're insane."

I felt him laugh before I heard it—such a sweet, strange intimacy. "Beauty is more than flesh and bone."

"If you tell me it comes from within, I'm sleeping on the sofa."

"That will not be necessary. But I think who you are matters as much as how you look. And you, my Arden, are full of light. Is it any wonder I want you?"

Oh God. Another twitch upon the line. And there I was, as besotted as I'd ever been. Caspian Hart's most willing subject recalled to my place at his feet. Exactly where he needed me. "I'm so yours."

We kissed again, a slow deep tangling of tongues and breath, and this time I didn't know who initiated it. Only that it didn't matter.

"I know," said Caspian, when we broke apart, "this is an entirely reprehensible time to ask but—"

"Yes. The answer's yes I'll come back to London with you."

He murmured something shaky and unintelligible. And for once I didn't press, didn't push. He'd given me so much—more than, even in my wildest fantasies, I would have had the bollocks to imagine—and I'd promised him just a little patience.

I could do that. I could definitely do that.

I wriggled carefully into the space at his side and he drew me in closer still, his lips seeking my skin, almost as if he couldn't quite stop touching me. Couldn't quite believe I was really there.

Well. That made two of us.

My heart was overturned like a kid's dressing up box—satin and velveteen and strings of beads, all the thrown-together treasure of cast-off adulthood spun into dreams beyond counting. In the morning, I'd have to gather them up again. Put away my pirates and princesses and lions and faeries.

But for now I could lie in Caspian's arms and listen to the papery rustle of the wind through the oak tree and the *shush-shush* of the distant waves and believe that everything was beautiful.

And anything possible.

Don't miss the next installment of
Arden and Caspian's story,
coming Fall 2017!

See the next page for a preview.

CHAPTER 1

So I had this totally crazy dream. I dreamed I met a billionaire called Caspian Hart and he kind of liked me. Well, he liked me enough to put me up in a ludicrously expensive London flat, but not enough to trust me, talk to me, or spend any time with me. A sufficiently self-esteem-tanking level of liking that I ended up running back to my family's place in Scotland. But, also, a sufficiently *something* level of liking that he wound up following me. And telling me a bunch of things, which made me realize that not only did my level-of-liking scale need serious recalibration, but I liked him enough to give it another go.

Except, oh wait, that wasn't a dream.

It had really happened.

And there was Caspian himself, tucked into the corner where the bed met the window, watching the distant sea. He was pale in the cool, blue-tinted morning and a little tousled—that one wayward lock of his fallen free again. The smile he gave me, as I emerged from the duvet, was slightly shy as if he wasn't sure how to greet me.

"Good morning." I stretched with abandon, spine arching, toes uncurling. "Did you sleep okay?"

"I'm fine. I saw the sunrise."

"Really?" It was a little hard to imagine. Or maybe not? He was probably the only person I knew who would have the patience to do something like that: watching and waiting as the light cracked wide the night. Kind of lonely, though. With me snuggled and oblivious right there beside him. "Um, maybe you should have woken me? Or…I don't know. I might have been grumpy."

"I didn't want to wake you. You looked, frankly, terribly cute."

I looked what now? I wrinkled my nose, unimpressed. "Cute in a way that makes you want to do bad things to me?"

"Oh yes."

He crooked a finger and—after a second of *omg, will I taste of mornings*-based hesitation—I dived under the duvet, surfacing again between his knees. He wrapped his arms around me, hauled me up and kissed me—not roughly exactly, but without mercy. Prizing my mouth open like the lid of a treasure box and taking possession. These simple caresses were infinitely preferable to whatever Ellery had given me that time in London. No feverish ecstasies, but a deep, heavy, and all-consuming bliss. A spell to turn me to butter.

He was smooth and silken against me—his hair surprisingly soft, though I could also feel the wicked tightening of his nipples and the hot pressure of his cock. He smelled of warmth, if that was a thing that was possible. A cozy, sleep-clinging scent of skin with only the faintest trace of sweetness from his cologne. This unexpected nakedness that was just him.

He made a low sound at the back of his throat—almost a growl—and flipped me. I went gladly, though the bed made a god-awful telltale creaking as I landed on my back amid the pillows and rucked-up sheets. I wasn't even sure Caspian noticed, let alone cared, as he came down on top of me.

I'd been kissed and delightfully manhandled enough by him that I had a pretty good notion of what he might like. So I stretched my hands over my head. Giving him my surrender—the safety and the dark thrill of it.

His eyes glinted. Turned stormy.

And he reached up, dragging a finger from my wrist to my shoulder, making me very aware of that line of pulled-tight skin, all exposed and unprotected and held that way by nothing but the desire to please him.

Though, admittedly, there were limits to my good behavior.

As he settled between my thighs I couldn't help arching my spine and tilting my hips, making very, very explicit all the places of my body I was up for yielding.

"God, Arden." I was pretty suspicious of the phrase "ground out" when I saw it in books, but it seemed to apply to Caspian's words right then. Especially when you also took into account what he was doing on top of me. "You're such a…"

"Wanton?" I offered, tightening my calves around him.

"Tease."

Tease. My cock gave an eager throb.

I loved this kind of talk, but it was tricky. There were lines in my head even I didn't properly know how to navigate. And I'd found that asking people to call me names tended not to go so well.

It seemed to make them either act weird or get nasty.

Neither of which I was into.

But *tease*...that was lovely. Made my toes curl with the naughty delight of being *bad*.

And Caspian said it just right too. In this sexy-angry way.

As if being a tease was something wicked, not something wrong.

I was already swooning slightly—because of that, and also because his cock was pressed right against the warm, tingly space beneath my balls. But then he twisted a hand in my hair, yanking my head back, and my overthrow was complete.

The breath shuddered in my throat.

The fear was animal, instinctive, and so very sweet.

He leaned down even further and licked a long wet stripe up my trembly, stubble-speckled Adam's apple.

I made a sound.

I guess you could have called it a whimper.

His teeth found the tender places under my jaw. Playful little nips that didn't really hurt so much as *spark*.

And then he pressed his open mouth to the side of my neck and—

Oh oh oh.

Something at once familiar and surprising about that damp suction and the blunt edge of his teeth: pleasure with a hot heart of pain.

It was sufficiently sanity-consuming that I forgot myself,

moaning shamelessly as I curled my palm around the back of his neck, holding him to me. That strange and glorious push-pull of *yes-no-doitharder*.

My skin was as fiery-achy as my cock by the time he drew back.

He stared down at me, mouth red and eyes wild. "What the hell am I doing?"

"Um." I touched my fingers gently to the throbbing circle he had left on my neck. "Giving me a hickey, I think."

He winced. "I'm so sorry. I'm not some brutish adolescent. I don't know what came over me."

It *was* a little bit ridiculous.

Caspian Hart—billionaire, sophisticate, chess grandmaster—and me with what was probably a glowing red-purple bruise. The proud teenage symbol for "getting some," Which, embarrassingly enough, I'd kind of missed out on when I was an actual teenager, on account of being basically the only gay in the village. And English to boot.

I'd made up for it at university—although now that I thought about it, while I'd occasionally been bitten (with varying degrees of conviction), I'd never received an actual, 100 percent genuine, bona fide hickey.

Turned out, I was oddly glad it was Caspian.

And I liked—more than liked—that he wanted to *mark* me.

Unfortunately, he was looking a little bit traumatized about it.

"No, no," I said quickly. "It was lovely." I twisted my head helpfully. "Do it again."

He laughed, and kissed the bite so that it lit up like a flare and made me gasp. "I think I might have been wrong when I called you a tease."

"I'm not a tease?" I just about managed not to pout, but I couldn't keep the disappointment from my voice.

"I think perhaps"—he'd gone all husky again—"you're worse."

I brightened. "Coquette?"

He didn't answer, just tongued at the wildly sensitive spot beneath my ear.

"Uhh." I swallowed. "Minx?"

He shook his head.

"T-tart?" It was getting increasingly difficult to think of, well, anything. But every suggestion sent a pulse of whiskey-rough arousal through me.

"Worse," he whispered.

And, God help me, it felt like a caress. Like a compliment.

I tried to breathe and realized I was already panting. "Um…"

His eyes had that *all the better to eat you with, my dear* gleam as they found mine. And pinned me as surely as his body. "What are you, Arden?"

I wanted to say it so badly. Have him brand me with it like a badge of honor and sexual freedom.

But I was sort of…scared and squirmy at the same time. In case it wasn't true. Or it would be different outside the safety of my head.

"Arden." There was a low note of warning in his voice this time. It sounded so deliciously dangerous that I nearly came.

And then—just like that—whatever was holding me back wasn't there anymore.

Broken or yielded or simply vanished.

"I'm a slut," I gasped out. "Am I a slut?"

He slid a possessive hand up the naked underside of my thigh. "Yes. Yes, you are. A very depraved, wayward little imp of a slut."

"Oh God." I squirmed frantically. "W-what happens to...slutty little imps?"

"What do you think happens to slutty little imps?"

My tongue flicked across my lips and, wow, they were dry. Almost as if every spare ounce of fluid I possessed had already leaked out my cock. "Do they...do they get punished?"

Which was when he rolled away. Taking all his heat and strength and the promise of erotic cruelty.

Before I could panic or complain, he covered his face with his hands and gave a deeply gorgeous groan. "Get dressed, Arden. I need to get you to London. I need to get you to London right now."

Gah. He had to go and remind me that we weren't living in some kind of magic sex wonderland.

My sudden silence must have been pretty expressive because Caspian looked up again. "Have you changed your mind?" he asked softly.

Last night I'd agreed to go back with him. Live in his apartment and resume our...thing. Only hopefully with more care and openness on both sides. I wasn't regretting the decision exactly, but returning to London didn't just mean returning to Caspian. It meant having to think about my life and my career and my future. Everything that scared the crap out of me.

I shook my head.

"Then what's the matter?"

I stared at my toes. The polish needed touching up. Also, maybe Sally Bowles green hadn't been the best color choice—I looked a little gangrenous down there. "I don't know. I think maybe I'm failing London."

"How could you possibly be failing London?"

"Same way I failed Oxford."

"You have no idea whether you failed Oxford." He curled a comforting hand over my knee. "Your results haven't even been released yet. And, when they are, you'll get a two-one, just like everyone else."

He was probably right. You had to work super hard to get out of Oxford with anything less than a 2:2—probably because it made everyone involved look bad. But that sort of led to a situation in which a lower pass was practically an admission of failure anyway. "Even if I do get a two-one, I won't deserve it."

"It's hardly an assessment of your moral character, Arden."

"I just mean…I got offered this incredible opportunity. And I *squandered* it."

Caspian sighed. I thought he was about to tell me to grow up and stop whining but, instead, he tucked an arm around me. And I was more than happy to take advantage of the opportunity to tangle my feet with his and snuggle in close. "Oxford is just a university," he murmured. "And there are many things besides the academic to learn at university."

"What, like how to go six weeks without doing any laundry?"

"Like what sort of man you wish to become."

"I'm not sure I even figured *that* out."

"Yes. You have." He angled my face to his and kissed the tip of my nose.

The playful gesture was a strange contrast to the sincerity of the words. But I treasured both. Believed in both. Mustered a slightly wavery grin. "Well, I must be doing something right since you like me. But, when it comes to everything else, I don't have a clue."

"You told me you were interested in journalism."

"I am. Except all I've done so far is write a few articles."

"Have you been able to place them?"

A couple of emails had come in during my Kinlochbervie heartbreak exile, except I hadn't really been in any state to appreciate them. "Yes. I mean, mainly online and stuff."

"That's wonderful." Oh God, he sounded all proud of me. "And seems to directly contradict your assertion that you don't know what you're doing."

"I just feel like I'm fucking up another amazing opportunity. You take care of everything and what do I have to show for myself? A satirical review of expensive mineral water brands."

"It's a perfectly reasonable start."

"But I had weeks. I could have learned Mandarin or written The Great American Novel."

"Do you want to learn Mandarin or write The Great American novel?"

"Um, not really."

That made him laugh, his breath ruffling my hair. I guess I was being a bit ridiculous.

"I wrote something I thought might work for *Milieu*," I admitted. "But I haven't dared submit it yet."

"Why not?"

"Well..." I squirmed.

He poked me. Caspian Hart actually poked me.

Which I would have found hilarious if I hadn't been in the middle of a major moop attack. "What if they say no? I'll be crushed. Devastated. Destroyed. Annihal—"

"I think I get the picture." He was silent for a moment or two. Probably contemplating the fact that, after everything he'd just said about discovering who you wanted to be at university, who I'd turned out to be was a loser. "Journalism isn't an industry I'm particularly familiar with, but I do know there are many aphorisms on the subject of trying."

"I *am* trying."

His eyes—too sharp, too beautiful—caught mine. "But are you trying to succeed, or are you trying to fail on your own terms?"

"Um, why would I be trying to fail?"

"Because that way you will not have to feel vulnerable. You will not have to admit what you want. And you will never have to confront your own limitations."

Wow. Way to flay a boy.

"I'm sorry," he said softly. "That was probably too…much."

It wasn't too much. It was too right.

And, suddenly, Caspian's arms were less comforting and

more kind of twitch-making. I pulled out of them and away. Tucked my knees under my chin. And sat there in a sullen huddle. "No, it's, y'know, fine. It's just a bit weird to be getting this speech about facing up to failure from someone who's never failed at anything ever."

"Of course I fail." Caspian sat up, too, bracing himself against a pillow. Somehow, he still managed to look elegant. Whereas my body always liked to be as small as possible—as if it had some kind of moral objection to being attractive. "And it's natural to fear it. But I try not to let it prevent me from pursuing what I truly desire. I'm here, aren't I?"

"But you didn't really think I'd say no, did you?"

He reached for my hand and interlaced his fingers with mine until we were palm-to-palm, like Romeo and Juliet. "As it happens, I did. And it would have been excruciating. But I would have found it infinitely worse to lose you through inaction. Or by convincing myself I didn't care."

I still couldn't quite wrap my head around the emotional risk Caspian had taken for me. And I couldn't help wondering how it would have gone if the situation had been reversed—probably I'd have hidden under the nearest duvet and emerged only to scavenge for food in ruined supermarkets after the fall of civilization.

Urgh. It was pretty shaming, really. I gazed at our gently touching hands. "I...I'll try to do the same. I mean, if you ever need me. To come for you."

He laughed, not exactly in a mean way, but I hadn't been joking. On the other hand, I guess it probably sounded like I was to him. Given he was, well, him and I was, well, me...I couldn't quite imagine in what topsy-turvy looking-glass world he would need me to play rescuer. Getting into stupid scrapes was my gift.

"And"—I took a deep breath—"I'll send my article to *Milieu*. If they don't want me…they don't want me."

"There will always be another dream. Always another opportunity."

"I thought you were only supposed to have one dream."

"That's a sinister lie perpetrated by Hollywood. You can have as many dreams as you dare imagine."

I pulled a dubious face. "If you say so. I'm still trying to figure out what happens when…if…*Milieu* say no."

"You find something else. Whatever quickens your magnificent heart. And success will follow."

"You really believe that?"

He gave me a smile so full of warmth and pride that, right then, I could have turned tides. Pulled the stars from the sky. "I do."

"Does, um, multinational banking and financial services quicken your magnificent heart?"

"I'm not you, Arden."

He sounded sort of quelling and sad. And both were walls, in their way. I gave his cold fingers a little squeeze. "It doesn't mean you have any less of a right to happiness than I do."

"You make me happy."

I wasn't sure if that was romantic or a lot of responsibility. Maybe both.

"Um," I said, "as much as I'd like to lie around in bed with you forever…we might have to move if we want to get back to

London. It's hours, and trains are really ropy at the weekend."

"Then it's fortunate I have a plane waiting at Inverness."

"You have a—" *Of course he did.* "Oh wow. But we've still got to get to Inverness."

"I hired a car."

"You can drive?" I blurted out.

He gave me a reproving look, softened by the hint of amusement in his eyes. "And I can tie my own shoelaces, too."

Being whisked to London in a billionaire's private jet made such a ludicrous contrast to my miserable, lonely—to say nothing of lengthy—journey up. But I guess that was life with Caspian Hart. And life without him.

"And," I couldn't help asking, "you definitely want to go today?"

He went a little pink. "I want to do things to you that I would feel deeply uncomfortable enacting beneath your parents' roof."

"Sure that wouldn't just make it kinkier?"

"Absolutely not."

I laughed and went to dress.

A Note from the Author

St. Sebastian's Hall, Oxford, is entirely fictional and, therefore, not open for visitors. The London Temperance Hospital genuinely exists and really does look incredible. The interior, however, like so much in life, doesn't live up to the façade. And it's mostly flooded anyway, so I wouldn't recommend trying to hold any parties there. In the interests of international understanding, I should explain (for non-British readers) that "candyfloss" is what we peculiar islanders call cotton candy.

About the Author

Alexis Hall was born in the early 1980s and still thinks the twenty-first century is the future. To this day, he feels cheated that he lived through a fin de siècle but inexplicably failed to drink a single glass of absinthe, dance with a single courtesan, or stay in a single garret.

He did the Oxbridge thing sometime in the 2000s and failed to learn anything of substance. He has had many jobs, including ice cream maker, fortune-teller, lab technician, and professional gambler. He was fired from most of them.

He can neither cook nor sing, but he can handle a seventeenth-century smallsword, punts from the proper end, and knows how to hot-wire a car.

He lives in southeast England, with no cats and no children, and fully intends to keep it that way.

To learn more, visit:
quicunquevult.com
Twitter: @quicunquevult
Facebook.com/quicunquevult

www.ingramcontent.com/pod-product-compliance
Ingram Content Group UK Ltd.
Pitfield, Milton Keynes, MK11 3LW, UK
UKHW022300280225
455674UK00001B/116

9 781455 571321